THE UNKIND WORD,

AND

OTHER STORIES.

BY

THE AUTHOR OF

"JOHN HALIFAX, GENTLEMAN," &c., &c.

NEW YORK:

HARPER & BROTHERS, PUBLISHERS,

FRANKLIN SQUARE.

1870.

I Inscribe

THIS COLLECTION OF PAPERS

—SOME ORIGINAL, SOME REPRINTS—

TO MY FRIEND AND PUBLISHER FOR THIRTEEN YEARS,

HENRY BLACKETT.

THE UNKIND WORD.

CHAPTER I.

THERE was—nay there is, for it doubtless exists still—in a certain nook of the Western Highlands of Scotland, a cottage—of which, as of the celebrated cottage over which the "smoke so gracefully curled," it might truly be said—

> "That, oh, if there's peace to be found in the world,
> A heart that is humble might hope for it here."

Very "humble," certainly, the heart should be—for the cottage was humble enough. It consisted only of two rooms; with a byre adjoining: unto which byre the original owners periodically migrated, somewhat to the inconvenience of the cow: while the house itself was let to any summer lodgers who might prefer the primitive and picturesque to the elegant and convenient.

Most picturesque it was: this solitary dwelling, nestling under a perpendicular rock, in the curve of a small bay, with a glorious sea-view in front, and, behind, a magnificent glen, presided over by two lofty ranges of granite hills. These hills from dawn to sunset—nay, all night long, for they never looked grander than by starlight—were continually changing their aspect and color; their forms remaining permanently outlined, through shine or storm, white mist or purple shadow—giving a sense of eternal endurance and majestic calm.

Besides this large beauty of the mountains, there was an infinite perfection of lesser beauty on every hand. Nowhere could be found such heathery moorlands; such verdant bogs, rich in lovely and rare bog-plants; such a pleasant shore, where from curious conglomerate rocks you might peer down a dozen feet, through crystal depths of brine, into the brilliant sea-gardens, waving with under-water vegetation, wonderful to behold. On land, too, all about these rocks, which were strewn everywhere, or left standing upright in great boulders—were nooks that would almost make you believe in fairies' bowers; so that you would never feel surprised to see a wee green man perk up his head from among the delicate mosses and ferns, to ask you what business you had in his especial dominion.

Thus, outside, the cottage possessed every attraction that heart or eye could desire. Inside, perhaps, the less that is said of it the better. Except that it had two merits—rare, alas! in this region: it was undoubtedly clean; and it had windows which were actually made to open! Thanks to these advantages, within its narrow limits had for the last month been stowed away, in the miraculous manner in which people do contrive to stow themselves away in Highland solitudes, a family of six persons; two brothers, three sisters, and a cousin; living that wild, free, Robinson-Crusoe sort of life which is so delicious to the young. For they were all young—the brothers and the cousin being under twenty, the three sisters a little older. Five of these young people were Wyvills—Agnes, Emma, Jane, Maurice, and Richard—motherless children of a grim, poor, proud Yorkshire squire; the sixth was Jessie Raeburn, orphan heiress of the old uncle of them all, a Glasgow merchant. It was through her that the young Wyvills her cousins had been persuaded to spend their holidays in the North,—taking for a month this cheap, out-of-the way cottage, and keeping house for themselves,—for no servant was possible.

Very simple were all their domestic arrangements. The four girls appropriated the one double-bedded room; the other apartment—which, like the cobbler's stall, "served them for kitchen, and parlor, and all"—being made to serve a third purpose as well: for at night, by means of that mysterious arrangement, common enough in Scotland, "a concealed bed," it ingeniously accommodated the boys. They, daily rising with the September dawn, always rushed out at once to their glorious morning bath on the near sea-shore, leaving the kitchen free. When they came home, as hungry as hunters, it was to find it all "redd up," as the Scotch cousin expressed it (and could do it, too, though she was a rich Glasgow young lady), the kettle singing on the rude iron bars which did duty for a grate,—just enough to keep the peat and wood from spluttering out on the earthen floor,—and the breakfast laid out on the one table. A very homely meal it was, consisting merely of a great bowl of porridge, and two jugs of sweet milk and butter-milk. If the boys desired fish, they had to catch it for themselves in the little crook where the mountain burn met the sea; and oh! what splendid sea-trout they sometimes brought home, and what a grand frying there was in the big frying-pan, which, with the three-legged pot and one saucepan, formed their only culinary apparatus. Yet even with these the girls had, during the month, become very tolerable cooks, and maids-of-all-work besides. To be sure, some disasters had at first occurred—such as when Agnes, coming home one day a little in advance of the rest, to prepare what is technically and most truthfully called a "hungry tea," unfortunately filled the kettle, and afterwards the teapot, out of a can, not of fresh, but of *sea*-water! And once, when the "half-sheep," which she was accustomed to order weekly, had (with its corresponding half of course) betaken itself to the mountains, declining to be killed, and also, owing to storms or piscatory ill-luck and incapacity, all the fish, both in sea and burn, unanimously refused to come to the boys' hooks, there was absolute famine in the house. For two days the family had to breakfast, dine, and sup, upon oatmeal porridge: at which they had first laughed, then grumbled, and then taken to quarrelling, as they not seldom did. "And as all brothers and sisters do," they told the little quiet cousin,—who, quite alone in the world, with no one either to love her or to vex her, could not understand this quarrelling at all.

But in spite of such small troubles, they had been very happy together; and now that their holiday was nearly over—it being then Sunday night, and Wednesday would be the first of October and their month's end—they all felt a little sad. They sat over their tea-table in the early closing twilight, without any of the skirmishes which, either in jest or earnest, were always rising up among these strong, rough, Yorkshire natures—warm to love and quick to hate—or, at least, to wrangle, in a way that to little Jessie seemed as if it must spring from, or result in, undying hatred, till she found out that they always made the quarrel up again, or, without any making up, went on in five minutes just as cheerfully as if it had never happened.

"You are the very queerest family!" she would say sometimes. "I suppose it is your English demonstrativeness, which seems to me so odd. You speak out whatever comes into your minds—good or bad—kind or unkind. If any one were to say to me half the things that you say to one another every day of your lives, I should break my heart about it for weeks after: and if I were so irritated as to speak to any body else in that way, it would imply that I had lost all love and respect for them, and I should just go away and leave them, and never be friends with them any more."

"Should you? Then you'd be a little goose!" Agnes would answer. "We all like one another well enough, and we speak to one another no sharper than father always speaks to us. We are used to that sort of thing, and don't heed it. It might have been different had mother been alive."

So Jessie often thought, but did not like to say. She knew very slightly her late aunt's husband, except that she had seen him once or twice: and had long noticed that her uncle, Mr. Raeburn, with whom she resided at Glasgow, always looked "dour" when he mentioned Mr. Wyvill of Wyvill Court. And in her fond little heart—which her solitary life had made prematurely wise—she made great allowances for this rugged family, which had brought itself up much as it chose; with no softening influence of parental love, no restraining hand of parental guidance. And she loved them all—hardly making any difference: at least, none that she then knew. And they all loved her—nor, even in their worst and roughest humors, did they ever ill-use her or say to her the ill-natured things that they often said to one another. As she sat on the settle in front of the fire—so small in face and figure that she almost seemed a child, and so grave and quiet that she might have been a little old woman—she contrasted strongly with the handsome young Wyvills, all large-made, well-featured, hearty-voiced: full of health and spirit and life. No wonder that to her—reserved, rather dreamy, delicate in health, and passive in nature—those wild Yorkshire cousins brought exactly the elements in which her dull, easy, rich, shut-up existence was deficient, and that she had been very happy this month—happier, she often thought, than she had been ever since she was born.

So she told Agnes, and, a little less frankly, told Maurice also, as, after the tea-things had been washed up by the girls, and the fire piled up by the boys, they took their usual evening walk—past the old kirk, and along the burn-side, where the fringing birk-trees were turning yellow, and the rowan-berries a coral red; up the steep hill-road which led to the nearest point of communication with the civilized world,—a fishing village, where, twice a week in summer, and once in winter, a steamer stopped to take passengers and herrings to Glasgow.

"I don't think I'll go up to Glasgow to-morrow," said Maurice, suddenly interrupting the line of procession, which now, as in all their walks had latterly happened, was just two and two and two—Maurice and Jessie, Dick and Agnes, Emma and Jane. "Dick, you could get the money at the bank just as well as I could: and bring it back in time for us to pay our rent on the 1st. You shall go; though I am the eldest, I don't see why I should always be the hard-worked man of business of the family. It would be 'awfully' nice, as you say, Jessie, to get two more days on the hills before I go back to college."

"And why shouldn't I get the benefit of those two days as much as you?" said Richard, sulkily;—he was more given to sulks, and Maurice to quick, short angers. "You'll not make me go up to Glasgow for you, my lad. I'll be shot if I do."

"Hush, don't quarrel, it's Sunday," said Jessie, using the first argument which came to hand, though her heart misgave her that it was a feeble one, seeing there was no reason why people should be less good on week-days than on Sundays. But the Sunday evening silence had more influence than her speech, even over these young lads. Hardly any creature above the nature of a boor could fail to be impressed, consciously or unconsciously, by such a lovely, heavenly night, the like of which is now and then seen in the Highlands just before "coarse" weather sets in a combination of all the beauty of all the seasons—warm and mild as summer, clear as autumn, solemn and soundless as winter.

Jessie Raeburn, who is a middle-aged woman now, could still describe it, vividly as if it were yesterday,—that lonely hill-road, the sunset fading rosily over the sea on the right hand, and the full moon, with a star above her, climbing in a flood of brightness above the black mountains on the left—the two mountain ranges, with the desolate glen lying between them, from which, through the utter silence, rose up the faint far-off ripple of the burn, like the voice of a soul alive in the midst of death. And she remembers,—or whether or not she does, all the rest do,—all save one (and perhaps he does too, in some strange way, belonging to the mysteries which are unfathomable in this world)—how her voice suddenly and involuntarily went up like an arrow of sound through the pellucid air; in a hymn tune, of course. It was that tune called "French," which in Scotch churches is usually sung, as Jessie sang it now, to the 121st Psalm:—

"I to the hills will lift mine eyes,
From whence doth come mine aid.
My safety cometh from the Lord,
Who heaven and earth hath made.
Thy foot he'll not let slide, nor will
He slumber that thee keeps;
Behold, he that keeps Israel,
He slumbers not, nor sleeps.

"The Lord thee keeps, the Lord thy shade
At thy right hand doth stay;
The moon by night thee shall not smite,
Nor yet the sun by day.
The Lord shall keep thy soul; He shall
Preserve thee from all ill.
Henceforth thy going out and in,
God keep forever will."

The psalm ended, they all stood motionless; awed by the unearthly beauty of the scene, and by the involuntary solemnity which creeps over any six persons who have spent a very happy time together, and are now on the eve of parting—with the consciousness which common experience teaches, that it is at least doubtful how, when, and where the whole six may meet—or if they may ever meet together again.

"We shall soon be going home now," observed Richard in a dolorous voice.

"I almost wish we were never going home any more," said his brother.

"Oh, Maurice!" cried Agnes, reprovingly.

At least not to such a dreary home as ours. But some time,"—and the lad, who had hold of cousin Jessie's hand, looked up towards the moonlit mountain-tops with a new expression of manly will and manly hope dawning in his handsome boyish face—"Some time, perhaps, I will make for myself a real happy home."

Just at that moment they were all startled by one of those sudden meteors common enough on Scottish autumn nights. It blazed out from beside the moon, quivered over the mountain peak below, and then vanished into blackness just over a pass which the boys had often talked of trying—fancying it would prove a short cut to the fishing village—shorter, perhaps, than this winding road across the wilderness of moorland, rock, and bog.

"By George, how plain that bit of the hill showed! I'll have a try at climbing it to-morrow."

"You won't, Maurice, my lad," Dick answered angrily. "You'll be far enough off by this time to-morrow."

"We'll see," Maurice said, angrily, too. But either he was too happy or too sad to wish to quarrel: or something else evidently engrossed him, for he walked home without saying a word more. Not even to Jessie.

Presently they all gathered round the kitchen table for their supper; their last meal together, for whichever of the brothers went up to Glasgow to-morrow, he would have to rise before daylight, and cross the country by the mountain road to catch the steamer, returning only just in time on Wednesday to pay the rent, and escort the family to the point where the weekly boat would touch next day. Thus, to-night was the real close of this Arcadian life; they would return to the comforts and discomforts of civilization: and though all the party tried to be exceedingly jolly—nay, Agnes actually brought out the whisky bottle, and unexceptionable toddy made by Maurice was distributed fairly round, even to the silent and sullen Dick—still there was a cloud over them; a cloud long remembered and spoken of with awe.

"Well, boys, do settle the matter: which of you is to go?" said Agnes.

"Richard," cried Maurice.

"Maurice," cried Richard.

"I'll make you do it."

"I'll be hanged if you will."

And from words they might have gone still farther—even to blows, for their hearts seemed hot within them: had not Jessie laid her little hand on the elder brother's arm.

"Don't quarrel,—not this night at least, when we have been so happy. Oh, please, don't."

"Let go of him, Jessie!" cried Dick fiercely. "He's a selfish, domineering, ill-natured brute."

"Am I?" said Maurice between his teeth, when he caught sight of Jessie's imploring face. "Hold your tongue, lad. You and I will settle our affairs by-and-by, after the girls have gone to bed. Good-night now."

They said good-night all round obediently; even Agnes, the house-mother and ordinary ruler of the family: for something in Maurice quite startled them: so unusual was his tone of command, as well as self-command.

"I wonder what has come over the boy?" she said, when the four girls had shut themselves in their bed-room. "How well he kept his temper! Did he not, Jessie? And he usually loses it so soon."

Jessie said nothing.

Shortly afterwards there came a little tap at the door.

"I want to speak to one of you girls for a moment."

"Which of us?"

"Cousin Jessie will do."

And Jessie, who had not begun to undress, but had sat meditatively on her bed, went out, right outside the door into the starlight night, which was the only available place for conversation with Maurice.

"I want to ask you your opinion, Jessie: and your advice, for I know it will be right, and I'll do whatever you tell me. Ought I to give in to Richard, or not?"

"About going to Glasgow to-morrow?"

"Yes."

"I don't know," said Jessie, sorely perplexed at being thus elevated into a sort of Mentor, and, more painful still, a judge between the two brothers. "You are the elder, and have a right to get your own way. But, still—nay, Maurice," she added, suddenly, "I'm not a bit wiser or better than you: don't ask me to decide, for I really can not."

"Then I will," said Maurice, and he looked down tenderly into the gentle face. "I won't vex him, for I'm a great deal happier than he, Jessie. I'll go to Glasgow myself."

And with a thrill at her heart, half of pleasure and pride in Maurice's goodness, and half of pain, Jessie said, "Yes, go."

"Then good-night, for we'll likely never have another night here again."

"Good-night, Maurice. You are very, very good."

"Thank you."

They stood together, these two, girl and boy, little more than children, in the still night under the stars, with the murmur of the sea close below, and the great silent mountains beyond. They hardly understood either one another or their own selves, and yet somehow they did, or one of them learned the secret afterwards.

"Oh Jessie, give me a kiss! Just one!" Maurice breathed rather than spoke.

Either she gave it, or he took it—she hardly knew which—but they kissed one another with a long silent kiss, as Jessie Raeburn has remembered and will remember all her life long.

"Maurice—good, dear Maurice," she sighed lovingly to herself, as she curled round on her hard but peaceful and happy pillow, "how could Richard say to him one unkind word?"

CHAPTER II.

Jessie lay awake for a long time, but no ominous sound of quarrelling came through the thin wall. She concluded the boys had made it up in the easy way that all squabbles were made up among the young Wyvills, namely, by the mere cessation of strife; contrition or forgiveness being things neither given nor expected in this not over-sensitive or sentimental family. She went to sleep at last with a quiet heart—in which the deep feeling waking into existence was only just enough conscious of itself to diffuse a sense of vague happiness throughout her whole being—the happiness of which there is but one kind, which, come it early or late, comes to any human being but once in a lifetime.

When the girls rose, they found the boys already away; nor did either Maurice or Richard return to breakfast, which caused some surprise.

"They can't both have gone to Glasgow. It would be very ill-natured of them; for I want help in ever so many ways. I wonder how they settled the quarrel last night?"

"Maurice told me he meant to go," said Jessie, briefly.

"That's all right; and most likely Dick has walked with him across the hill, and will be back to dinner."

So, after a reasonable time they cleared away breakfast, and fell to their packing cheerily, with all the small jests indulged in under such circumstances by four lively and lightsome girls, who enjoy being busy, and busy all together. In the activity of their work they had quite got over the slight shadow of regret at parting, and were planning new meetings and new pleasures with the hopefulness and elasticity of youth. Afterwards, they looked back upon that morning, when they were all so active and gay, so preternaturally full of laughter and fun, with a kind of shiver, which for years made them pause in the midst of any mirth, as if they heard through it all the soundless footsteps of approaching Fate.

Their gayety was only checked, not suppressed, by the arrival of Richard, in not the best of humors. Poor fellow, this time he had some cause, for he had slipped into a rocky crevice, bruised his shoulder, and scarified his knee.

"It's lucky I didn't hurt myself worse," said he, "for some of those places are confoundedly deep, and so overgrown with heather that one never sees them till one puts one's foot into them. They are regular crevasses, I think, and they are just in that particular bit of the hill-side where we have so often intended to go. I've been, girls. I played old Maurice a nice trick, and slipped off before daybreak. So he would be obliged to go to Glasgow. Is he gone?"

"I suppose so, more shame to you, Dick," said Agnes.

"He meant to go in any case; he made up his mind last night," Jessie added.

"Did he? Now that was jolly of him," said Dick cordially. "But he might as well have told me so."

"Didn't he say any thing last night?"

"Not a word, for I shammed to be asleep. And this morning I left him really asleep, as sound as a church. Well, it was jolly of Maurice, and I'll do him a good turn some day for it."

So Dick quite recovered his spirits, and in spite of his bruises made himself both useful and agreeable all that day and the next; even though the coarse weather, of which that heavenly Sunday was the warning, had fairly set in, and the family were shut up between their two rough apartments, unable even to cross the threshold for blast and storm. Such storm as is only seen in these mountains, where the rain not falls but drives, in absolute sheets of water; and the wind grows into a perfect whirlwind; and the burn rises and roars along in a foaming torrent, thick and brown; and the sea becomes a mass of "white horses;" and dashes itself along the once-quiet beach and weedy rocks in a mad mass of waves and spray. It was a slight forewarning of what winter must be here; and it made the young people feel a little reconciled to the idea of going home.

"Only fancy being out on the mountains on a night like last night;" for the storm began about dusk on Monday. "I am glad Maurice started so early for the boat, and that you were back early, too, Dick. Fancy, if you had been out till now!"

"Pooh, Agnes! I'd have stood it well enough. The shepherds do. And I'm glad I 'did' that pass, after all; only it's nonsense supposing it's a nearer way to the coast —it's ever so much farther. Nothing so deceiving as miles of heather and bog. A horrid place. Ugh! but my shoulder is sore yet."

He occupied a good deal of the girls' time in waiting upon and nursing him, and apparently rather liked their doing it, especially Jessie, who was very sorry for him and very kind to him, as she would have been to any human creature.

The wild weather lasted all Tuesday, but on Wednesday morning it cleared up into that wonderful brightness of calm which succeeds these equinoctial storms. The packing was finished in great glee, and all preparations made for departure, as soon as Maurice should come with the cart that was to convey themselves and their luggage to the little inn where they had agreed to sleep, in order to be ready for the early boat next morning.

The girls prepared a hasty dinner out of the last of their

provisions—had a final "crack" with their landlady, Mrs. McDiarmid, who was expecting her "man" home from a week's absence at the fishing—and then they all kept sauntering about rather restlessly, watching along the white line of road for the black speck which ought to be Maurice. They all felt, and said, that they would be quite glad to see him again: in his absence they had found out how pleasant and useful Maurice had been all this month, and how, with his bright cheery face and unfailing good-nature, he was, even though he had his little hot tempers occasionally, a more important element in the family circle than any one had imagined. Agnes owned, with a sigh, that she was half sorry he was going to Cambridge—the father having at last consented to this step.

"Perhaps it is all the better for him; but we shall miss him very much at home."

"Not a bit of it; you've me," said Richard sharply. "And it's he that's the lucky fellow to get away from home, with father so cross, and you girls always bothering."

"Oh, Dick!" cried Jessie; and then, "Oh, Agnes!" as Agnes returned her brother some sharp answer, in the family fashion. After which little outburst the horizon cleared up; but Jessie would have liked it better had it never clouded, especially just at the leaving of this sweet place, where they had enjoyed themselves so much. She said little, but kept looking wistfully and lovingly along the mountain road for that small speck in the distance, which, as tourists were getting rare now, was almost sure to be Maurice; but he never came. No,—though the afternoon melted into evening, the sun set goldenly in the sea, and the moon rose over the hill-top, in the same spot, and almost as bright and beautiful as on Sunday night—Maurice never came.

"The steamer could not have put in yesterday; it often happens so in stormy weather," Jessie said at last, speaking oracularly, as being the most familiar with these parts, and trying to hide a tremor of disappointment that was perceptible in her voice.

"But how shall we find out whether or no?" Agnes answered. "And it will be very provoking if it was so, for we shall have to wait for Maurice another day or more; and it is too late for Dick to start off and inquire."

"Dick won't do it, neither," emphatically declared that young gentleman. "You must just unpack, and stop here another night. Who cares? I don't."

"But about Maurice," suggested Jessie, meekly. "There, look! somebody is coming down the road." And they all ran forward eagerly.

But it was only Diarmid McDiarmid, otherwise Diarmid Beg, a small man, with hardly an idea beyond fishing-nets and whisky. By the latter he was considerably overcome just then; and it was with difficulty they could make him understand what they meant to inquire—namely, whether the boat had stopped at all yesterday, and if either then or on any other day he had seen Maurice.

"Maybe I did, but I'm no sure. Eh! my heid's no guid at messages. But bide a wee, leddies." And, with a sudden lucky gleam of recollection, he pulled out of his pouch a scrap of paper, on which was written, in Maurice's own bold scrawl, "*I'm off, and I'll be back on Wednesday.*"

"He met you, then? He gave you that note?"

"He just did," affirmed Diarmid Beg, but when or where, his memory failed: or drunkenness had stupefied his faculties, so that from him no further information could be by any means elicited.

There was, therefore, no help for it but to conclude that Maurice had gone to Glasgow on Monday, but that the return boat had not stopped at the fishing village; so that he had been, as not seldom happens in the Highlands to unlucky autumn or winter passengers, conveyed against his will to some farther port, whence he would have to get back how and when he could.

"Very provoking!" Agnes exclaimed; and they all agreed that, on the whole, civilization had its advantages. But they determined to make the best of things, and spent a not very doleful evening, or morning either,—when, sleep having brought Diarmid Beg a little more to "himsel," they called him into the kitchen, and again questioned him. He now declared that the scrap of paper—which, after being passed eagerly round, was left lying about, till Jessie took it up and put it in her pocket—had been given him by Maurice, whom he had met, somewhere on the hill-side, hurrying to catch the boat.

"And did he catch it?"

"Maybe he did, and maybe he didn't," said the cautious

Highlander. But afterwards, being hard pressed, and seeing, with the mingled cunning and kindliness of his race, how very anxiously the information was desired, giving vent to the universal Celtic imagination, he told a long and consecutive story of how, just before the steamer stopped, there passed him a gentleman who he felt sure was the young master, for he called out to him, "unco ceevil," as Master Maurice always was, "Eh, Diarmid Beg, and hoo are ye the day?"

Which story, resting on no foundation at all, or on the slender foundation of two probabilities, perhaps facts, so twisted together as to compose one absolute lie, was eagerly received by the Wyvills: and afterwards repeated and believed with that intensity of belief with which people seize on one only possible clue in the midst of a sea of doubt and misery.

On this fortunate lie, therefore, the family rested, tolerably at ease, for two days more: when, getting no letter and no message, they decided, in general council, that their wisest plan was to take the Saturday boat up to Glasgow. Something must have happened—perhaps their father was ill, and Maurice had been summoned direct home; still, they complained bitterly, he might have contrived to send them some line or word, instead of leaving them in this forlorn condition. It was thoughtless—like all boys.

"Oh! don't blame him, Agnes. Not now!" pleaded Jessie.

"Well, I won't," replied the elder sister, who perhaps felt a relief in being cross. Yet it was strange, and seemed stranger still afterwards, how little real anxiety they experienced at first, and how wonderfully they kept up their spirits—these five young people, to whom life had always been so easy, that they scarcely understood what fear or sorrow meant. And a few physical inconveniences, natural under their forced stay—such as tea without sugar, and no meat to be got for love or money—kept their minds in a state of wholesome irritability and self-compassion, which took away the sense of real dread.

Only the first shadow of apprehension came over them on Friday; when, having explained their position to Mrs. McDiarmid, and given Uncle Raeburn's name as security for the unpaid rent, they counted out all their money, and found it barely enough to carry them to their uncle's door at Glasgow.

"It's very hard, and Maurice knew exactly what a state he was leaving us in. It wasn't like him to forget us so," said Agnes, almost crying. "I hope nothing has gone wrong with him—that he is not ill."

And when, in a somewhat dreary procession, they quitted, with scarce a farewell glance, the pretty cottage, and filed away—some walking, some riding in the cart—along the mountain road, Richard confided to Jessie that he rather feared Maurice was ill,—had perhaps caught a fever—for he shivered several times, and tossed about for a good while, after he came to bed on Sunday night.

"And yet you never spoke to him?"

The boy hung his head.

"And the last thing you said to him was an unkind word!"

"I'll never say another!" cried Dick, in a passionate burst of compunction. And poor Jessie's sore heart melted to see what deep, honest, brotherly love lay beneath the rough and quarrelsome exterior. "Never again, I promise you, Jessie!" But, alas! why had he said it at all?

And so they passed on, a very silent little party, along the familiar road, and lost sight, forever, of the cottage where they had been so happy: the pleasant bay, the singing burn; and, at last, of the sharply outlined mountains, which kept eternal watch, in shower and sunshine, summer and winter, over the desolate glen.

CHAPTER III.

When, on a fearfully wet and foggy night—the sort of night which, dreary anywhere, is unutterably dreary in Glasgow—the five forlorn travellers reached Jessie's home in Blythswood Square, they found that Mr. Raeburn had been five days absent on business in London—and, strange to say, that Maurice Wyvill had never made his appearance at all!

And he never appeared again. Nothing was heard

either of or from him. After that first hour of unspeakable dread, ensued days and weeks of slow suspense and dull misery; lessened and relieved by accidental gleams of hope, for human nature can only endure a certain amount of pain, either temporarily throwing it off, or sinking under it entirely. For a while the excitement kept them up somehow; the perpetual uncertainty, the inquiries started in all directions, with no lack of ingenuity—or money either, for Uncle Raeburn furnished the latter to an unlimited extent, as close-fisted Scotchmen, when once touched, will often do. And there was the sympathy of friends, nay, even of common acquaintances, roused into friendship by the pitifulness of the story, which circulated far and wide, as such a mysterious and melancholy history was sure to do, bringing to light a number of other stories, which people always hear of when something similar happens to themselves. Common the fact is not, thank Heaven! in our civilized community, where "murder will out" however closely hid, and where any strange accident evokes universal publicity,—yet many cases have happened, of individuals suddenly vanishing from the midst of friends and neighbors, with no likely reason for their disappearance, no clue to their possible fate; slipping out of the whirl of ordinary life as completely as if the earth had opened her mouth and swallowed them up—to be never heard of more.

Any who have undergone such an agony, will acknowledge that to weep over the saddest death-bed, to sit beside the most untimely grave,—to be smitten as by a thunderbolt with the tidings, mercifully made certain and sure, of some beloved one passing from the measurable distance of a foreign land into the immeasurable, yet, perchance, scarcely further distance of the land unseen,—is actual happiness, compared to the calamity which befell the Wyvills and Raeburns—including Mr. Wyvill and Mr. Raeburn, the two brothers-in-law, no longer at variance now.

The blow fell heavy upon each and all, but heaviest upon those who were expected to feel it least—Jessie and Richard. The former took it quietly at first—indeed throughout; Jessie was always quiet. But the color faded, slowly and entirely, out of her pretty soft cheek; her small figure grew thin and spare: she seemed within a few months—

nay, a few weeks—to wither up into a little old maid, who might have been any age between twenty and forty. And so she remained—and remains still.

As for poor Dick, after the first excitement was over, when weeks, months, slipped by, and still Maurice was never heard of, he sank into the depression of utter repentance—say rather remorse, which is repentance with no hope of atonement. The last "unkind word," which there was no unsaying now, and which perhaps had goaded Maurice on to that Glasgow journey in which, by some unknown means or other, he met his end, rested on the poor boy's memory with a morbid weight. He harped upon it continually; nothing ever seemed to take it out of his mind: he seemed to feel almost as if he, and none bnt he, had caused the death of his brother.

As a matter of course, Richard took the place of eldest and only son. There was now no rivalry possible either at home or abroad, no jealousy of Maurice's handsomer face or pleasanter manner,—the inexpressible charm which made him, as is sure to be the case, more loved, because more lovable. All these things were forever passed away, and Richard would have given worlds to have had his vexations back again in all their bitterness, if he could but have had Maurice also back once more.

It is good sometimes to be absent—better still, perhaps, to be dead—as regards our own imperfectness, and our equally imperfect friends. How they rise up and praise us for virtues we never possessed, and benignly pardon us for sins we never committed! How tender over our memories grow those who, living, worried our lives out, and might do the same again if we were alive to-morrow! Ay, in spite of the poet's touching verse—more touching than true, perhaps—

> "I think, in the lives of most women and men,
> There's a time when all would grow smooth and even,
> If only the dead could find out when
> To return and be forgiven."

But whether he were dead or not, there was no need to forgive poor Maurice. In his short life of twenty years he had done little harm, and in the shock of his mysterious and terrible fate, any trifling faults he had were totally obscured and obliterated. He who, had he not been so suddenly and awfully snatched from among them, might have kept his place as an ordinarily good elder brother—full of failings, doubtless, but well-liked, on the whole—was now exalted into a family idol. The sisters, who used to snub and scold him—the selfish father, who had neglected, almost ignored him—the brother, who had quarrelled with him, almost daily, and yet could never get on without him—now mourned for Maurice with an anguish unrestrained, and worshipped him with a passionate love, the wilder and sadder that it came too late.

There never seemed to enter the family mind—what crossed strangers' minds, and mouths too, not seldom; only, with the curious tenderness that any deep tragedy awakens in even the worldliest half of " the world," nobody ever hinted it to the Wyvills themselves—that the lad might have been himself to blame in his disappearance. That, having fallen under some sudden temptation, he might have committed some ill deed, which made him dread to meet his father's face: or, with the mingled thoughtlessness and selfishness of his age, might have taken a fit of boyish adventure, and shipped himself off somewhere, to America or Australia—just for fun.

Of his being murdered there seemed far less probability, seeing he had little or no money about him. He had never appeared at the Glasgow Bank at all; and it was very unlikely any murder could have been committed, undiscovered, in that city, whither, with a fatal persistency, his family were convinced he had gone. They were the more settled in this belief by the additional evidence of the stoker of the Glasgow boat, who being hard pressed with money and whisky remembered having that day noticed a young gentleman—fair-haired and pleasant-spoken—who came and looked down into the engine-room; as, with an agony of fond recollection, they knew Maurice, who had a turn for machinery, was particularly fond of doing.

So, amidst all their searching, they never searched, or only very superficially, the mountains round the cottage, or the spot on the hill-road where Diarmid Beg said he had encountered the lad—of which encounter the fisherman now spoke very charily, believing it to be the youth's fetch and " no himself ava." And when, in the midst of winter—which fell very early that year—the tidings came, slowly, as tidings always do come to these remote Highland regions, that the poor young Englishman had never been seen more, Diarmid and his neighbors, slow to take in new ideas, and equally slow to put them together, merely shook their heads with, "Eh, but it's awfu'!"—"The bonnie lad!" but made no inquiries of any kind.

So, in a few weeks more, the mountains wrapped themselves in their grand familiar winter snows, and the storms swept over the little lone cottage on the shore, where the family of the Wyvills had spent that merry month of September. And at last, when hope was dying, almost dead in their hearts—though the girls still resolutely refused to put on mourning—they left Scotland, and went home together to Wyvill Court—without Maurice.

The strange story of the poor lost lad was talked over all that winter at Glasgow dinner-parties; and Jessie Raeburn was pointed at in church or in the street—she never went anywhere else—as, "Yon's his cousin—his sweetheart some say."

But whether she was or was not Maurice's "sweetheart," Jessie never betrayed, and nobody knew. She lived her ordinary life, faithfully doing its duties: attending to her uncle, and keeping his large splendid house in order, neither sinking into bodily illness nor mental depression. Only people noticed—the few people whose society she mixed in—that the hall-bell never rang—the parlor-door never opened—the handful of post-letters never arrived—without Jessie Raeburn's turning with a sudden start and a tremble of expectation—as if even yet, though weeks grew into months, and months into years, she had not given up all hope, but was patiently waiting on for him who never came.

CHAPTER IV.

Wyvill Court lay on the western side of one of the most beautiful of the beautiful Yorkshire dales. It was a comparatively small estate, and the mansion was likewise small; built of the gray stone of the district, plain and old-fashioned within and without. For the Wyvills had been one of those ancient impoverished Roman Catholic families which are still found, here and there, in the wilds of the north country; poor and proud; clinging tenaciously to their ancestral faith, until the last owner, in giving up Catholicism, had sunk into that pitiful moral and mental condition only too common in the beginning of the present century, satirically called Nothingarianism.

But he was dead now, the grim, eccentric, selfish old man, who had broken his wife's heart, and never won, nor attempted to win, in the smallest degree, the hearts of his children. Yet, strange as it may appear, he was unable to recover the blow to his pride,—it could hardly be his affections,—given by the disappearance or death, whichever people chose to call it, of his eldest son.

For Maurice Wyvill never came home. From that fatal 30th of September, when he was seen, as stated by Diarmid McDiarmid, hurrying to meet the Glasgow boat, no light had been thrown upon his mysterious fate. He was searched for everywhere: advertised for, periodically, in England, Scotland, and even the colonies: rewards large enough to have tempted any man, not his actual murderer, were offered for any information regarding him, living or dead; but all in vain.

When, after a lapse of four years, the father died, many difficulties arose. Wyvill Court was strictly entailed, and until clear evidence could be obtained of the death of the eldest son, the younger could inherit nothing. It was only by some ingenious legal arrangements, made to suit the emergencies of this novel and most painful case, and in the hope that Maurice, should he ever reappear, would act with the generosity which had been his characteristic when a boy, that Richard was installed temporary master at Wyvill Court, and lived there with his three sisters upon the small income that was available. For Mr. Wyvill, like many other selfish men, had complicated all troubles by dying intestate, and the girls were wholly dependent upon the heir. So poor Dick, heir and yet not heir, cramped on all hands by innumerable perplexities, could only live on sufferance at his ancestral home, unable to take legal possession of it himself, and, worst of all, unable to adorn it, as his forefathers had always been eager to do, with a wife. For early marriages had long been the hereditary blessing, as the last late marriage had been the misfortune, of the Wyvill family.

Whether Richard wanted to marry or not, he never informed any body. Since his brother's loss, his natural reserve had increased to an almost morbid extent. He attempted no profession: perhaps he had the sense to feel he was not clever enough to succeed therein, and trade was impossible to a Wyvill. So both during his father's lifetime and afterwards, he "hung about" at home, shooting, fishing, or dabbling in agriculture, to which, if he had any bias at all, his taste inclined; he was a born country gentleman.

Almost his only absences from home were periodical visits, at long intervals, to Glasgow; but he never asked his sisters to accompany him, and was as uncommunicative about his uncle and cousin, with whom he was supposed to stay, as he was about most other things. He was not a pleasant young man, and there seemed some curious twist in his nature, growing more perceptible every year, which made his sisters, while they respected him sincerely, find it difficult to love him. At least, with that warmth of love which they had felt, or now believed they had, towards his elder brother.

A chapter since I said, and not untruly, that it is good sometimes to be absent—better still to be dead. That is, for the absent and the dead: but also, in a mysterious secondary sense, for the survivors. Many a man's death earns for him far more love, and exercises a far wider influence for good, than his life might have done. Ever since Maurice's—death they still refused to call it, but his departure, the memory of him, and the anguish of his loss, had brought into his family a warmer, kindlier, softer atmosphere: more patience, more forbearance; more clinging together, as if they felt the slenderness of the links that bound them to one another, and walked always in the solemn shadow of that death which overhangs all mortal life; though, alas! we are so prone to forget it; so prone to live as though we were never to die.

The girls had been good girls to their old father until his death: they had nothing to reproach themselves with on that score: and when Jessie Raeburn had to follow their example, and devote herself exclusively and engrossingly to her old uncle, they did not reproach her, even though it prevented what, in the absence of all intimate female friends, they would very well have liked—visits to her at Glasgow, or her visits to them at Wyvill Court. There was scarcely an obvious reason for the fact—yet a fact it was,—that ever since that Highland journey with its terrible ending, Jessie and her cousins (excepting Richard) had never once met:—and now little Jessie was Miss Raeburn of Blythswood Square and Woodhouselea; heiress to Uncle Raeburn's uncounted wealth, which, by some crotchet which no one either blamed or much wondered at, he had bequeathed to her, and her alone.

Her cousins, though they might have been a little disappointed, since they stood in exactly the same relationship to him, legally speaking, as herself, behaved very well. The Wyvill pride accepted its position, and was too proud to feel or to express envy, or to shrink from Jessie because she was rich and independent. They, poor girls, had scarcely wherewithal to clothe themselves, or to keep up any thing like the decent dignity expected from the Miss Wyvills of Wyvill Court; still less, to suppose that any one in their own rank of life would marry them—though Emma and Jane were both handsome girls; but young men of the present day have sometimes an eye to money, even in primitive Yorkshire dales.

At last, a poor young parson came, who loved Emma, poor as she also was: and then the high spirit of Richard Wyvill, ay, and of Agnes too—the unselfish and motherly Agnes—writhed under new vexations. No settlements could be made; for who was to make them? So closely was the estate tied up—waiting the possible reappearance of the heir (or his heirs; for who knew but that some son of Maurice's might one day make claim to the property?)—that it was with difficulty enough money could be got at to ensure a decent marriage outfit to the daughter of the Wyvills of Wyvill Court. Emma could hardly have been married at all, had not Jessie Raeburn stepped forward and claimed her cousinly right liberally to portion the bride; doing it so sweetly, so delicately, that even Richard had not the heart to stand in the way. Possibly his own heart felt how cruel the position was, and responded to the earnest manner in which Jessie put the matter in her letter, which enclosed a check for several hundreds, addressed to Emma, in an envelope containing merely the well-known lines from Burns:—

"Oh why should Fate sic pleasure have
Life's dearest bands untwining?
Or why sae sweet a flower as Love
Depend on Fortune's shining?"

And so Emma's marriage was made possible and easy, and it was on the occasion of it, to witness the happiness she had caused, that, after long years, Jessie revisited Wyvill Court.

Spring was creeping greenly over the bleak Yorkshire dale, and, in spite of the wild equinoctial winds, primroses were peeping out round the roots of the old oaks, and forget-me-nots blossoming in hundreds by the river,—the bright, daring, rapid river, whose course could be tracked along the dale for miles and miles,—when Jessie came, a woman of seven-and-twenty, to the house where she had last been as a mere child, patronized by the girls, and domineered over by the two boys. And with that uncomfortableness of expectation with which people who know themselves changed, and expect equal change in others, prepare for a meeting long delayed, desiring it, and yet wishing it well over—did Agnes, Emma, and Jane Wyvill stand watching for the carriage in which their brother was bringing Jessie Raeburn to the old familiar place. It was visible at last, crawling up the steep road; and then a little figure, all in black, alighted, and toiled, Richard following though not assisting her, up the weary half mile: but still the sisters were too nervous to run forward, or do any thing but quietly wait for Jessie's approach.

"I wonder if she is altered?"

"Dick says, not much," observed Emma. "Dick likes her very much, I am sure; he always did. So did dear Maurice."

"Ah! yes, and she was very fond of Maurice."

"I wonder," remarked Emma again, with an acuteness doubtless born of her own happy lot, "whether Richard would like to marry Jessie. It has struck me so sometimes. And it would not be a bad thing either."

"Don't speak of it," said Agnes angrily,—Agnes, in whom the sore circumstances of the family had sharpened and exaggerated a strong inbred pride. "What, she with all her money, and he with not a penny! He could not do it. If you ever hint at such folly, I shall wish we had never invited her here."

"I shouldn't call it folly, if he loved her, and she loved him," cried Emma, spurred on to honest warmth by the thought of her own faithful and honest lover. "But, anyhow, I'll hold my tongue."

And then the traveller came close in sight, and the three ran out to meet her,—the same Jessie who had kept house with them in that merry Highland cottage — wandered with them over mountain and moor—shared with them in that terrible home-coming, and in the weeks of agonized search for him who was never found: Jessie, so little changed that at sight of her face the old time came over them like a flood, and they all wept together—those three almost middle-aged women, as if they had been girls still, and all had happened but yesterday.

However, such emotion could not be very lasting: and after a few hours they put aside the unalterable past, and settled down into their present selves. Soon, pleasant daily interests seemed to obliterate those so painful to dwell on. Emma was married—gayly, grandly: and after that, for a week or two longer, Jessie staid on; — she seeming happy with them, and they trying their best to make agreeable to her the old-fashioned dreariness of Wyvill Court. Still, for some things it was a trying visit. When friends or kindred have been parted for seven years —moving meanwhile in totally different spheres, and engrossed with totally distinct interests—a division wider than either years or distance could effect, often comes between them. In vain the cousins rambled together through the Wyvill woods: gathered primroses and hyacinths, and tried to fancy themselves girls again—it would not do. Life's onward footstep has no returning. A new life may come—far higher than the past—richer, fuller, more heart-sufficing: but the old life comes never again.

It was almost a relief when—rather suddenly at last—Jessie said she must go home, and went: parting from the girls very affectionately: but still making no plans for another meeting—at least not immediately. When she was gone, Richard, who had throughout her whole visit kept himself rather uncomfortably aloof from her and his sisters, sank into more than his usual reserve and taciturnity.

One marriage often results in more; and before the summer ended the young parson's best man—an Oxford tutor, who had been very agreeable at the wedding—came back and courted the pretty bridesmaid Jane. Again cousin Jessie insisted on making her wealth common property, and portioning the other sister—" exactly as Maurice would have done if he were here." So she expressed it in her letter, and repeated afterwards when she came to Wyvill Court. But her visit this time was brief, embracing only the marriage-day and the day after. She said her "engagements" prevented her longer stay. And after the first day, Agnes ceased to urge it. With all her sweetness, there was about Miss Raeburn a degree of firmness, ill-natured people might say independence, of character, which made it perfectly clear that she had, in small things and great, the power of making up her own mind, and keeping to it. Besides, Agnes sometimes stealthily watched her brother Richard; his hard, set face; his nervous, restless manner—and without any further pressing, she let Jessie Raeburn go.

It was the night after she was gone—the first night the brother and sister had ever spent together, they two alone—that Agnes first ventured, tremblingly, upon a subject which had caused her anxious thought for a long while. She did so with much hesitation—being a good deal afraid of it, and of Richard; but any thing was better than suspense. Besides, lately, with her sharpened experience, she had felt so certain of one thing—nay, of two things, cruelly conflicting with one another, and neutralizing any possibility of a happy future, or of matters going on much longer in the way they stood now—that she felt it her absolute duty, to try and speak out plainly to her brother, so as to discover his real mind.

"Jessie will have about reached Glasgow by this time."

"Yes," said Richard, without looking up from his book.

"She seems extremely well and cheerful; and how young she looked in her bridesmaid's dress—almost pretty. Didn't you think so?"

"Yes," reiterated the young man; and vouchsafed no more conversation.

"Richard," said Agnes, repressing a wild spasm at her heart, "I have been thinking—I hope your marriage will be the next in the family. If you could find some nice pretty girl, in your own position; neither too rich nor too poor—(though I would rather she were poor than rich: it would be dreadful if any body were to say a Wyvill married for money)—I should be glad, extremely glad to give up my place here, and see the family name kept up, the family happiness complete."

Agnes faltered—stopped; her heart was full. Richard replied not a word.

"I think it is time you married, Richard; I do really. Hitherto I know you could not afford it; but now there is only me to support, and I shall cost you very little; I can live anywhere. I would almost rather work and maintain myself: it would be dreadful to me to think I was hindering my brother from marrying. And if you did marry, you would be perfectly safe, even if Maurice came back. And oh! Dick, I would so like you to be happy."

She went over to him and put her arms around his neck, and then all poor Richard's reserve broke down.

He told his sister—to her unutterable pain, grief, almost indignation—ay, even though she had guessed it before, but it looked so much blacker when condensed by his own confession from a cloudy conjecture into an absolute fact—that the only woman in the world who could make him happy was Jessie Raeburn.

"I have been fond of her all my life, and yet I couldn't ask her. Her horrible money!—five thousand a year I think it is. Agnes, I couldn't, you know."

"It is well you did not," said Agnes, sharply and sternly; "for she would never have married you. I am quite sure of that."

"Why not?" cried Dick, who was the sort of man that contradiction always rouses into resistance.

"I don't know—do not look at me so, for indeed I don't; and yet I feel quite sure of it. You will never get her."

"I'll try!" said Richard hoarsely; and began marching up and down the long, low, dark, oak-panelled room, in stronger emotion than Agnes had ever seen in him since the day of his brother's loss. Upon my life and soul I'll try!"

And nothing would persuade him otherwise. Agnes talked till near midnight—first persuasively, then contemptously, then angrily—for her pride was up that any Wyvill, any brother of hers, should ask and be refused, as she felt certain would be the case; but Richard was utterly unmoved. He was determined to start for Glasgow the next morning.

"And if you do, you are a fool—a mean-spirited, mercenary fool."

Richard's eyes blazed. "And, Agnes, do you know

what you are? A selfish, mischief-making woman. I *will* go! though you and I should never see one another's face again."

With that word he left her, and returned not, though Agnes sat waiting a whole hour, and then crept up to her bedroom in an agony of tears.

"Oh, Maurice, Maurice!" she sobbed; and the bright, frank, boyish face of her lost brother came back through the clouds of many years fresh upon her tenacious memory, contrasting with the face of the brother who remained, in the hardness of unwontedly hard manhood. "If Maurice were only here!"—He might have been: and nearer to her than she knew.

Shortly, a light knock came to her door, and Richard stood there, with all his fury gone, changed and softened to a degree that seemed almost miraculous, as if some spiritual influence had come about him to make him tender and good.

"Agnes, I thought I would come to say good-night to you. There are only us two left now; don't let us quarrel. I must go to Glasgow to-morrow—and know my fate one way or another. But don't send me away in anger; don't let us part as I once parted from poor Maurice—with an unkind word."

"Oh, Richard! I didn't mean it. Forgive me." And she hung upon his shoulder as she had never done before in all her days. "Do just as you like, and may God prosper and bless you."

CHAPTER V.

Miss Raeburn was sitting alone in the very handsome drawing-room of her very handsome house in Blythswood Square. It was dark, and the fire-light danced on her black velvet dress—she almost always wore black: ill-natured people said, because it made her look so "interesting." But these remarks were always made behind her back; and people well knew she would not have cared one straw, or altered either her mind or her costume one whit, even had she heard them. She had that self-possessed dignity which is indifferent to public opinion, especially on trivial and personal matters, where indeed public opinion has no right to interfere at all. She went on her way calmly: accustomed from her teens to be sole mistress in her uncle's house, where she had now quietly become independent mistress of her own.

Young as she was, she had settled at once into the busy responsible life of a woman of property, who had evidently no intention of changing her condition by marriage. To the natural influence of wealth she added a personal influence very considerable, though exercised in a sweet and womanly way. All Glasgow knew her name well;—in charity, in society, in every good and generous work, Miss Raeburn was always sought for, and always easy to find. And it would be idle to say she did not enjoy her position;—she did. A lonely woman must fill her heart and her time with something: Jessie accepted the lot which Providence had assigned to her, and made the best of it, bravely and cheerfully. It had its pleasures. She loved her independence, her power of doing good unquestioned and uncontrolled. Without being in the least ungentle or unlovely, she was already, in a degree, "old-maidish"—that is, she had sufficient strength of character to stand alone. Though barely eight-and-twenty, it never seemed to enter into her own head or that of any other that she needed either protection or guidance. She lived alone, and visited alone, without any one's thinking the fact remarkable. She was just Miss Raeburn, of Blythswood Square and Woodhouselea; and the idea of her ever becoming Mrs. Anybody seemed most improbable.

She was waiting for her carriage to be announced, reading by a small lamp the daily newspaper; until, her eye being caught by the date of it, she laid it down abruptly, and remained with her head sunk between her hands, gazing mournfully into the fire. No wonder, for this day was an anniversary: the first of October: seven years since that first of October when she and her cousins had stood watching for Maurice along the mountain-road, and he never came.

"Seven years." She repeated the words, and then bent down, clasping her hands and stooping her head upon them; low down, as people are prone to do when some heavy wave of misery or sharp recollection breaks over them. "Oh, my darling, my darling!"

Not a word more, nor a sob. Years had smoothed down and softened all things, except the love which was absolute, sole, and undying. Some women have had such loves, quenched so far as earthly fulfillment goes, in earliest girlhood: yet surviving in another form to the very close of life—consecrated by death, or confirmed by total separation into a bond which, in the absence of any other, becomes as strong almost as marriage, being in truth the real marriage of the soul.

It might have been a great mistake—many wise, good, and loving persons may consider it so—that any woman should thus waste her life upon a mere dream: which, if she could have ended it, were far best ended and forgotten. Yet people are but as they are made: and Jessie could no more have resigned her worshipped ideal of what Maurice was, and what he might have become, to sink to the reality of any of the excellent Glasgow gentlemen whom she was in the habit of meeting; could no more have exchanged that first and last love-kiss—young, passionate, mutual love—for the touch of any mortal lips, than a maid betrothed with all her heart to one man could ever put another man's ring on her finger, or pass as a bride into another man's home. It was not merely unnatural: it was impossible.

Yet no one could call Jessie Raeburn an unhappy or disappointed woman. Hers was no unrequited, misplaced, or unworthy attachment: from first to last it had been wholly sacred and wholly her own. Not one pang of bitterness, or remorse, or humiliation had mingled with its sorrow. Hardly like a regret, though full of the tenderest, most passionate remembrance, were the words, "My darling, my darling!" And then the momentary outburst passed: she sat, quietly and meditatively, waiting for the hour when she had to fulfill her evening engagement. For she did fulfill it—even on this anniversary-night. She kept her anniversaries to herself alone. She did not shut herself out of the world, but moved therein—playing her part well—yet letting the world peer neither smilingly nor pityingly into her inner life, which was, and ever had been, exclusively her own.

When the door opened, Miss Raeburn rose, gathering her rich Indian shawl round her, and moving in her usual composed graceful way across the floor, thinking it was the announcement of her carriage. But it was a visitor, so unexpected that she quite started at the sight of him—pale, travel-stained, and agitated Richard Wyvill.

He fixed his eyes upon the little figure before him—the velvet gown, the dainty lace, the glittering diamonds; it had been uncle Raeburn's delight to load his niece with diamonds. And Richard said, in his roughest manner, "Don't let me intrude. You were going out to dinner?"

"I was, but—oh cousin!" And a sudden agony of expectation, not dulled after even all these expectant years, thrilled through her. "Something has happened? What news do you bring?"

"I bring no news at all—nothing better nor worse than myself," said he, bitterly. "And, if you like, I will go away directly."

"No, no, I could not think of such a thing," she replied, with her hand upon the bell. But on second thoughts she went and gave her orders herself, thus allowing Richard time to recover from his ill mood, and giving a brief minute of solitude to herself. For, with a strange recurrence to the ever-abiding thought which under-ran all her life, she had fancied, oh, wild hope! that Richard's sudden appearance might be caused by tidings of Maurice. No, no! Again, for the thousandth time, the vain hope faded, and she said to herself: "It is the will of God."

Ay, it was. Never in our own way, but in His own way, does the Master grant us our heart's desire: and yet still we must "rest in the Lord."

In a few minutes Jessie came back to the drawing-room, cheerful and bright, the white gloves and the shawl removed, though the diamonds still glittered on her neck and in her hair.

"Well, Richard, I don't get a cousin to visit me every day, and so I have sent an apology to the dinner-party; and you and I shall dine together at home in peace and quietness."

"Thank you. It is very good of you," said Richard, his irritability soothed in spite of himself by her frank familiar air, though it caused his heart to sink within him. What if that sweet familiarity boded affection only—the affection which shuts out love? What if his sister should prove right after all?

Still a kind of dogged determination impelled the young

man to remain and carry out his intention: to face the worst; which could not be worse than much he had already suffered. But it was hours before he could find courage to say a word beyond the common-place family talk, the habit of the cousins through so many years. Jessie at last brought her fate upon herself by the sudden and very natural question—

"And now, Richard, tell me why you came so unexpectedly to Glasgow?"

The moment she had said this, she felt her mistake; felt that the crisis, which, with a generous woman's delicate ingenuity, she had contrived to stave off so long, had arrived. She could no longer save either her lover or herself from the half-dozen desperate words, which, alas! would break the pleasant bond of a lifetime. For after this, poor Richard never could be her friend and cousin any more.

The pang of rejected love is nothing new. Most women have had to inflict it, and most men to suffer it, at least once in their lives. It does to neither any incurable harm—that is, when the misfortune is simply a fatality. Only when a woman has willfully led a man on to love her, and denied him—or when he has swamped his honest dignity of honorable manhood in the ungovernable anguish of balked desire—need there be any irremediable bitterness in such a trial. But in either of these cases both will surely reap their own punishment—a very sore one: and they deserve it.

Before Richard had half got out his words, he read his doom in Jessie's eyes. Yet they were very tender eyes—less compassionate than mutely entreating forgiveness, as if she herself must surely have done something wrong. But there was no doubt in them—none of that wavering uncertainty which in this, as in all other things, has destroyed so many a soul. She was perfectly sure of her own mind. She liked him, but she did not love him; and she made him plainly see it, as she had done from the very first. He acknowledged that himself. So, almost before they quite knew what had been said, or answered, the whole thing was over—entirely over and done.

Richard Wyvill was not a pleasant fellow—neither attractive in society, nor very lovable in family life; but he was an honest fellow for all that. Deep at the core of his rough Yorkshire nature lay a keen sense of honor, a sound stability and faithfulness, which every one belonging to him was forced to appreciate. Jessie did, to the full. And now that his bitter secret was out, the young man, in spite of all his disappointment, felt unconsciously relieved. Though Jessie had refused his love, she had not wounded his pride. He saw that he was not degraded in her eyes; nay, more, that with a tenderness second only to the tenderness of love returned, did she regard the faithful attachment which had followed her, unspoken, for so many years.

As to the money question, Richard's soreness on this head was forever healed. He felt instinctively that Jessie rejected him simply and solely because she did not love him; that, had she loved him, she would have thrown her paltry thousands at his feet, saying, "These are nothing,—less than nothing,—but I myself am worth a little, I think; take *me*."

So, strange as it may appear, though he had just staked and lost what he then thought to be the one happiness of his life, the young man was not altogether miserable; for he still could respect both himself and the woman who had refused him. He neither dashed his hand to his brow and fled, nor fell on his knees in frantic entreaty, nor stamped about in anger, nor did any of the foolish things that young fellows are supposed to do under similar circumstances; he kept his place, like an honest man who has given the best thing a man can give—his heart's love; which, though not accepted, had been neither mocked, nor trifled with, nor despised.

He was just considering whether he ought not now to depart, when a servant entered the drawing-room with a message. A man—"a Hielander—a wee bit camsteary-looking mannie"—was wishing a word with the mistress.

"At this hour? What can he want?" said Miss Raeburn, surprised.

"Shall I go down and see?" asked Richard, perhaps a little glad to resume some shadow of the former familiar cousinly ways.

"Thank you," Jessie answered, glad too.

"He says he'll no speak to ony body but the mistress," interposed the old butler, who looked rather strange and perplexed.

"Then show him up here. My cousin and I will see him together."

The man entered, and hung at the drawing-room door, staring about him with bleary eyes; and when Richard asked him his name, he answered, somewhat hesitatingly, that he was "Diarmid McDiarmid—Diarmid Beg, ye ken."

"Indeed I don't," Richard was answering sharply, when he saw Jessie spring forward.

"The man—you remember—whom Maurice met, who was the last person that saw Maurice."

"Ay, my leddy—just mysel'. And it's aboot him I come—the puir laddie. Ye'll no hae heard ony thing?"

Richard glanced at Jessie, who stood listening with lips apart, and hands locked together, white, and rigid as stone. At once, by a sort of revelation, he knew why she had never loved him.

For an instant his human nature recoiled in inexpressible bitterness; then the nobler half of the man conquered. To find his rival in his brother—his own dearly-beloved and passionately regretted brother—it was a heavy blow: but he would bear it. Ay, even though Maurice came back and won her.

"What about my brother—is he alive?"

"Truly I can na weel say," replied the Highlander, "but, I fear me, na. Do ye no ken this, sir?"

And Diarmid unfolded from out his plaid, slowly, like a fearsome thing that he was half afraid to handle, something—it was not easy at first to detect what, so covered was it with mildew, and damp, and moss. But on closer inspection the cousins recognized it as being a strong tin case, fastening with a spring, which Maurice had had made to contain his botanical or entomological specimens: he was very fond of collecting both. Outside, on a silver plate, he had had engraved—and it was legible still—his name and address:—"Maurice Wyvill, Wyvill Court, Yorkshire."

"Where did you find that? Tell us quickly!" cried Richard.

And then McDiarmid explained—not quickly, but they understood him somehow—that a few days since he had been belated on the mountains, in a spot that was seldom traversed—not once in several years, being very dangerous on account of the numerous holes, fissures in the rocks, narrow chasms so overhung with heather that a man might easily step upon it, and be plunged in a moment to the depths below. He, Diarmid, had done this—only, with the Providence which they say guards drunkards and young children, he had managed to crawl out, bruised and hurt, but still alive.

"It was just the Lord's mercy that I was na kilt, like mony a better man; for at the bottom I found this, ye ken"—and he pointed to the tin case.

"Any thing else?" asked Richard, in a low, awe-struck voice.

"Banes. Just a wheen banes."

* * * * * * *

So the mystery was cleared up at last; and they knew that in this world they would never see Maurice more.

Jessie and Richard clasped hands and looked at one another, wistfully and long. Then both—the man as well as the woman—lifted up their voices and wept.

After a little while Richard sent Diarmid away down stairs, made Jessie sit down, and, kneeling beside her, opened, in the way they both well remembered, the concealed spring. Inside the case, and from its substantial workmanship most wonderfully preserved, was a little book, which must have been placed there—Maurice must have placed it himself, in the interval between his fall and his dissolution,—as the slender and only chance he had of ever conveying information of who he was, or how he died. For, it proved to be a psalm-book of Jessie's, which Jessie well remembered his carrying from church for her that Sunday, and never giving her back. One of the mouldy leaves was still turned down at the 121st Psalm:

"I to the hills will lift mine eyes."

He had remembered them, then, in his last hour, and left this token for them, in the only way he could think of. He, unto whom had come no "aid;" whom "He that keeps Israel" had *not* kept, but who, in the awful mystery of Omnipotent will, had been suffered to perish here alone—the handsome, happy, loving, and beloved lad—to be found, after an interval of seven years, as "a wheen banes."

Jessie sat dumb, mechanically repeating to herself the words of the psalm, which seemed at first such a ghastly mockery. But slowly, with that agony of belief which forces itself upon the heart, not the reason, at an hour like this, when all the anchors of faith seem torn up, and the soul is ready to drift out blindly upon a Godless sea, there came into her an almost miraculous comfort—the same which her Maurice might also have had, dying forlorn and alone on the mountain side.

And the more she dwelt upon it, the clearer this comfort grew. If during the few minutes or hours—thank God, they could not have been many!—that elapsed before consciousness left him, Maurice had put the book inside the case, which might preserve it for years, he must, even in his last moments, have had strength and composure enough to remember them all at home—Jessie especially—and thus send them, as it were, a loving message ere he died. And so he had died in a manner not unworthy of their Maurice. Humanly viewed, it was a death so terrible that they dared not suffer their imaginations to dwell upon it, but passed at once to the thought of Maurice in heaven, with his sufferings ended, his new life begun. Still, man's impotence is God's omnipotence. It might have been—and indeed appeared most likely, from the position in which the remains were found—that the end had come so peacefully that death felt to him no more than falling asleep, with the Everlasting Arms underneath him, and his head pillowed on the bosom of Everlasting Love.

* * * * * * *

Maurice's bones were laid, by common family consent, in a spot not far from the place where they were discovered—the little mountain grave-yard, where, during that merry month of September, they had all often leaped the low wall, and sat among the long grass, or read the inscriptions on the ancient stones. There, soon afterwards, another stone was erected by Jessie Raeburn—she asked permission to do it, and Richard allowed her—on which was recorded, in the simple Scotch fashion of kirkyard memorials, Maurice's name, age, and how he died. Nothing more, except the words—incomprehensible addition to many readers, yet full of peace to her who many a time afterwards sat and read it there, with the grand mountains looking on her, and the sea calm and blue, and the heavens shining overhead—"Psalm 121."

When all this was done, Richard went back to his sisters, and they put on quiet mourning for a season. Then, quietly still, without any obtrusiveness either of regret or congratulation, Richard Wyvill, Esq., of Wyvill Court, took lawful possession of his ancestral home.

* * * * * * *

I know it would be more pathetic, more in accordance with the feelings of young and poetic readers, if I were to state that Richard Wyvill never married, but remained all his days faithful to his first disappointed love. But such fidelity is rare in man, and well that it is so. By-and-by, when all hope of Jessie was at an end, Richard found a pretty, merry Yorkshire lass, who loved him—partly because he was so opposite to herself—loved him, and married him, and made him happy; so happy, that he could receive his cousin Jessie as Aunt Jessie in his household, for weeks together, without the slightest pain. And it is thought that some day his second son, Maurice Raeburn Wyvill, will inherit all the thousands that Jessie has to leave, and be in truth her adopted child. His parents can well spare him, for Wyvill Court is full of children, brought up rather differently from what the last generation were,—with more of gentleness, less of impatience and rough disputing—in an atmosphere of sweetness and sunshine which, radiating from the elders, flows down to the younger ones, and makes of them, whatever else they may be, a family of love. For, thinking of Maurice, whose story is told from child to child till it becomes like one of the saintly chronicles of old—thinking of poor Uncle Maurice, how could they ever say to one another an unkind word?

A CHILD'S LIFE.

SIXTY YEARS AGO.

LATELY, taking a leisurely stroll through one of the quaint old streets of Bristol city, Temple Street I believe it was, I came upon an ancient book-shop. Can any body resist the fascination of an old book-shop? I own I can not. Many a valuable minute have I wasted in peering into those forlorn relics of gone-by literature, which lean imploringly against the window-panes, title-page and frontispiece outspread to invite public gaze—that remorseless public which has long since forgotten both. I stopped now. I happened to be writing a book myself, which, perhaps, made me more tender-hearted. I paused to consider whether it too—my *magnum opus*—might not one day swell these pathetic ranks. Ah, my brethren! defunct authors! in a few years more, the same epitaph will be written over us and you—your books and ours—*abierunt ad majores.*

Being in this frame of mind, it was not surprising that one of the books in the window should especially catch my eye. Its title ran thus: "A Father's Memoirs of his Child. By Benj. Heath Malkin, Esquire, M.A., F.A.S." And below was a motto from Sir Philip Sidney's "Astrophel:"

> "Great loss to all that ever did him see:
> Great loss to all—but greatest loss to me."

Its publishers were the immemorial "Longman, Hurst, Rees, and Orme," and the date was 1806. The frontispiece was a miniature of a sweet childish face, and round it a fanciful design of the said child bidding adieu to a kneeling mother, and sailing away upward clasping an angel's hand. The drawing and engraving were good enough to attract me even before I noticed at the foot,

"*W. Blake, inv.—R. H. Cromek, sc.*" Then it became at once a book to be bought.

Few now care much for Cromek the engraver, though he was famous in his day; but most people have heard of William Blake,—"Pictor ignotus," as he is called in a late biography: the painter unknown in his life, and unrecorded in his death, for even his grave, somewhere in Old St. Pancras churchyard, had no stone put over it, and can not now be recognized. Happy, half-mad, loving and lovable genius!—whom Flaxman calls his "gentle visionary Blake,"—his long life of nearly fourscore years has flitted by as shadowy-like as one of his own visions. His works —chiefly etchings and engravings—are found only in the collections of connoisseurs. So great is their eccentricity, so incomprehensible their meaning, that the general public could never be brought to appreciate them. Yet in poor Blake's misty soul shone assuredly a fragment of the "spark divine." His Book of Job, and many of his little poems, stand out, in that age of endless shams and gigantic affectations, fresh as dew, and grand as Nature herself.

Every thing of Blake's is rare enough to be valuable: I entered the shop, and came out of it triumphantly with the book under my arm. It was a "tall," thin volume, roughly got up, with large type and larger margins,—a book to horrify the elegant bibliopolists of to-day, and "make each particular hair to stand on end" of every head of the still-existing firm whose name it bears, at thought of their house having sent forth, even sixty years ago, such an unsightly volume.

My great interest in it was solely for the frontispiece; but on glancing at the letter-press it seemed curious enough to be worth reading and preserving. Not reprinting: nobody in our terse modern era would get through one page of those long-winded, Latinized, Johnsonian sentences; but, reproduced as extracts, I thought it might amuse, perhaps instruct, a later generation. So I went carefully through this history of a little life that had barely lasted seven years, and had ended sixty years ago.

The "father"—he must long since have departed to his rest. He was apparently a somewhat pompous, learned gentleman—doubtless an object of awe to both wife and children—yet loved by them, and loving them too in his way, with a well-regulated and decorous tenderness. He must have been well esteemed, likewise, by a select circle of intellectual friends, among whom we incidentally find he numbered Blake, Banks the sculptor, Clive and Lister the surgeons; and the friend to whom, in forty-eight voluminous pages, he dedicates the book, "Thomas Johnes, of Hafod, Esq., M.P., Lord Lieutenant of the County of Cardigan;" who, we learn, was a gentleman of good estate, and the author of a translation of Froissart. It was in visiting at Hafod that the bereaved parent, resident at Hackney, conceived the idea of writing this memoir, partly for love, and partly for money "to make some little additions to the library of the young survivors, or to their other means of instruction, beyond what else it might be thought expedient for a moderate fortune to supply." He adds, with good-feeling that might well be imitated nowadays: "The trick of converting confidential correspondence, private history, or domestic events, to marketable purposes, has been practised of late years with little remorse, and in open defiance of all prejudice on the side of decency. Yet to drag the privacy of a wife or child into daylight, and expose to an inquisitive world scenes which were never meant to meet the public eye, may be entered in the day-book of the literary trade among its meanest arts."

Its lengthy dedication ended, Mr. Malkin commences his memoir thus:—

> "Infinite pains have been taken by the learned in decyphering the human mind. The dawn of infancy—the meridian of manhood—the sunset of advanced age, have respectively afforded suitable topics of ingenious or profound speculation. Yet the researches of the theorist, without an appeal to practice and experience, avail but little to direct our projects or to console our disappointments."

Stop! After this specimen I am sure the reader will thank me for henceforward re-translating the Malkin English into our modern tongue.

But the child—the little fellow whose bonny face has for sixty years been only dust—let us refer to him; his father does so, chiefly as a peg whereon to hang innumerable dissertations, not very interesting.

Thomas Williams Malkin was born on Oct. 30th, 1795. We are not told who his mother was, or any thing about her, except what comes out incidentally in the account of her treatment of her son, and his great love for her; but this inclines us to believe that she was a very superior woman.

Thomas is reported to have been, as an infant, "acute, active, robust."

"Yet he was by no means forward in speaking. It was not till he was full two years old that he began to talk, but he was familiar with the alphabet almost half a year sooner. He not only knew the letters when given to him as toys on sets of counters, but as expressed in books, to which, from seeing them constantly about him, he directed his notice at a very early period. Before he could articulate, when a letter was named, he immediately pointed to it with his finger."

But my plain English must tell the story a little faster than Mr. Malkin does.

It seems little Thomas taught himself spelling after a sort of phonetic system of his own; and, before he was three, had, still of his own accord, learnt to write, first in printed and then in writing characters. On his third birthday he executed in pencil his first letter to his mother.

"As it now lies before me," says the father, "I find the forms of the letters to be accurate and well-shaped, though their sizes are disproportionate, and the lines, though few, extremely uneven. At the bottom he has written the Arabian numerals in succession up to twenty. There is nothing in this letter to call for its insertion; but I have received another from a lady, which he wrote to her only two months afterwards. This is also in pencil, written much better, and sufficiently straight."

Here it is:

"MY DEAR MISS,—Thomas has been reading Tit for Tat in the Evenings at Home: and Thomas laughed at 'The fellow tried, and tried, and tried.' I wish you would come and see Tom. T. W. M.

"December, 1798."

Two more:

"MY DEAR COUSIN S. M.,—I thank you for your letter. I have read it often enough. My love to you. Maps are for setting up. Papa was so good as to bring Tom maps. Benjamin hasn't lived long enough in the world to know his letters. When he is big like Tom, then mamma will buy him a box of letters. He will then run and say, Is this A?

T. W. MALKIN.

"April 4, 1799."

"MY DEAR COUSIN S. M.,—I have a new map. Thomas can put it together, and when mamma takes some countries out, Tom can tell what they all are. I think you are very beautiful. I wish you would come and teach Tom to read Greek. Benjamin has got some more double teeth coming. Tom gives him all his playthings, and makes him very happy.

T. W. MALKIN.

"June 18, 1799."

These letters do not require the lengthy paternal criticism which follows them. Parents who have hoarded up such—the more tenderly because no after letters from the youth or the man were ever written—will feel how interesting they are; and how evidently a child's letters—undictated and uncorrected.

At this age, three and a half, Thomas could read "any English book; likewise the Greek alphabet, and most Greek words not exceeding four syllables."

Unfortunate child! In spite of Mr. Malkin's disavowals, we suspect the already too precocious brain had been overstimulated, so that the little body, "robust" as it was, would have small chance. Far better, a thousand times, to have thrown English and Greek books together on the back of the fire, and helped, encouraged, nay, even forced, the child to be only a child—that in Nature's slow but sure development he might become successively a boy and a man, which he never was to become in this world.

His education—self-education the father continually repeats it was—rapidly advances. Let him describe it himself in one of his pretty birthday letters,—ah, how few!—written yearly to his mother:—

"MY DEAREST MOTHER,—I was four years old yesterday. I have got several new books: Mrs. Trimmer's English Description; Mental Improvement, by Mrs. Priscilla Wakefield; and a Latin Grammar, and English prints. I think I have got a great many besides the old ones that I had before. Every day I lay up all my maps and chronological tables. My maps and tables are all dissected. I know you love me very much when I am a good boy, and I hope I always shall be a good boy. Benjamin knows all his letters, except one or two, and I hope he will know how to read soon. Papa is going to teach me Latin on Friday. That will be to-morrow. T. W. MALKIN.

"October 31, 1799."

"*Papa is going to teach me Latin.*" Luckless, innocent admission: contradicting all Mr. Malkin's statements of having left his boy's mind solely to self-development. But perhaps he really thought he had.

Another letter comes between two birthdays, its date being January, 1800; following it is the birthday letter of the same year.

"MY DEAR MOTHER,—In the illustrious heads that I have seen, there was Catherine Howard, not Catherine Parr, (and these were all queens of King Henry VIII.,) and Lady Jane Seymour, Catherine of Arragon, and Elizabeth Plantagenet. But she was queen of Henry VII. and daughter of Edward IV. I saw Oliver Cromwell too, and William Shakspeare, and Sir Isaac Newton. He was a very good man. In the third volume of my Evenings at Home, I read about him being led to some of his discoveries by seeing an apple fall from a tree. And that was very pretty...... I never was drunk, nor I shouldn't like to be in that shocking way a bit. To be about to be; I hardly know whether that is any sense or not...... As I know I am a good boy, I believe I shall be better still......"

"Hackney, Oct. 30, 1800, is the year at this time.

"MY DEAR CHARLOTTE,—I shall give you a reason why I wrote Charlotte instead of mother to you, and the reason is because I thought it would be prettier. I also think that I shall be very glad when I am six years old. I am five now, and to-morrow I shall begin to go on for six. In my walk to-day I saw some persons clipping a tree: and I saw a man killing a poor pig, which you told me that one might well squeak if a man was to kill it. I also think that I shall learn a great great deal of Latin from my Latin Dictionary. I shall now, when I do my exercise, do it out of my Latin Dictionary, and I shall have my Exempla Minora to look out some words in it. And I shall have my Latin Grammar to turn to when I want it. Also, I think my pocket-book is a very nice thing especially: for in it there is a tweasers, bodkin, scissors, and knife to cut with; pencil to write memorandums with upon the asses' skin; and there is a clasp to it on the outside to open and shut the pocket-book with...... Dearest mother, as you are not well, I will do what you like me to do; to make you better, mother, I shall read to you to-day, and to-day do some exercise. After I have looked a little in my Latin Dictionary, which I use in my exercise, I find the words that I want to find in it. I do not find the great dictionary too unwieldy for me; but I think I can manage it very well. I think I will not tell you any Latin words. At Lea-bridge I have so very fine a view of Essex! The months of the year are (he here repeats them). Civilized nations, in January, they in general agree to begin reckoning the new year from the first of that month. Water is, when frozen, expanded; that is, takes up more room than before. Ice is lighter than water, and swims upon it. I am quite sure never to spoil the garden, that the mower has been making tidy again. My Latin Dictionary is so very useful to me, so is my stool. The trees now are rotten. I have seen two trees that were rotten all at the top: one was a willow-tree; but I do not know what tree the other was. The Calendar of Nature is very useful to me, and I think it was very good in Mr. Aiken and Mrs. Barbauld to write these employing books for little boys instead of grown people. The index of the English Exercise-book does not apply to those I am in, but the dictionary. T. W. MALKIN."

Poor little fellow! how plainly one can see him, perched on his stool, "lugging" wearily about with him the great Latin Dictionary, running occasionally into the new-mown garden, but "quite sure" not to spoil it; full of interest in all sorts of knowledge and of natural facts; acute to observe, and accurate to detail. A very good boy, somewhat conceited perhaps, as clever children often are; and with his tongue too full of those "employing" (*sic*) books, which he is always poring over; but still a loving little fellow, and especially loving towards his "dearest mother."

The next letter given is dated Oct. 10th, 1800. In it a good deal of "priggishness"—I can find no better word—seems already cropping out.

"In my Mental Improvement I have read that the wood of the beech-tree is useful to the turners for dishes, trays, etc., and that the upholsterer turns it into stools, etc., and I have not forgotten that yet. My father has told me that the Romans used to oil their bodies and make them active, and I have not forgotten that, neither. In the Latin language thousands more are of the feminine gender than I knew. Some are masculine, some neuter. I know a good deal of geography, and I shall be very glad, too, when I know a good deal more: for geography, I find, is a very clever thing for me to know. I know a good deal of Latin. I think I know a little French, but no Welsh. I know no Greek, neither. God bless you, my dearest father and mother, and I hope you may see many happy days. I find in the 10th vol. of those books—('Museum Florentinum,' explains the father)—the figures are very fine of Hygeia, Venus, Apollo, Minerva, etc., and other statues. I hope I shall be a clever man."

But this was not to be. How could it? No child's brain could have received, unharmed, the flood of knowledge which was being poured into this thirsty little cranium,—geography, natural history, science, art; his native English, with French, Latin, and Greek; all of which studies were, if not encouraged, at any rate not prevented by the mistaken father. "It seemed," writes Mr. Malkin—

"It seemed to be a leading object of his ambition to make himself master of the dead languages...... It was with the utmost avidity that he looked for my assistance in comparing the idiom and construction of the Latin Syntax used at Eton, with the idiom and construction of his own and the French languages. Indeed, his acuteness in tracing the etymology and reducing to their elements the component parts of words, pursuing them through English and French, and inquiring after their forms in Greek and Italian, ground as yet untouched by him, evinces a mind more than commonly fitted for philological pursuits."

I wonder whether, after the boy's death, the father ever suspected that he might as well have fed his five-year-old son with poison as with philology.

But even when the poor little head took a rest, there was still work for the busy little hands. Thomas began map-making and drawing. He copied Raphael's heads, and even the cartoon of Paul preaching at Athens. He "had a remarkable habit of inventing little landscapes; for which purpose he was accustomed to cut every piece of waste paper within his reach into small squares. These he filled with temples, bridges, trees, broken ground, or any other fanciful and picturesque materials that suggested themselves to his imagination."

Of these, six are given in the book, accompanied by the following criticism by William Blake:

"They are all firm, determinate outline, or identical form. Had the hand which executed these little ideas been that of a plagiary who works only from memory, we should have seen blots, called masses: blots without form, and therefore without meaning These blots of light and dark, as being the result of labor, are always clumsy and indefinite: the effect of rubbing out and putting in, like the progress of a blind man, or of one in the dark who feels his way but does not see it. These are not so. Even the copy from 'Paul Preaching at Athens,' is a firm, determinate outline, struck at once, as Protogenes struck his line, when he meant to make himself known to Apelles. All his efforts prove this little boy to have that greatest of all blessings, a strong imagination, a clear idea, and a determinate vision of things in his own mind.

Here is another birthday letter—the last—which has in it less learning than usual, but a strange seriousness and tenderness. It is addressed to Cambridge, whither the parents had gone on his father's "University business."

"Hackney, Oct. 30, 1801.

"My dearest Mother,—Next time you go to Cambridge, if you will allow it, I should be very glad to accompany you there, for the sake of having a ride. I hope before you return you will be so good as to write to me a letter, and I shall be most happy to receive it. As you one day said you hoped I would hear Benjamin read and spell to me, I promise to do it sometimes when I have leisure to hear him, and when he is in a humor for it, and I shall teach him as near as I can to the manner in which you do. I am in great hopes you will think well of this letter, for I am sure I do all I can to put it in your power to do so. I hope you will trust that the great and good God will make us both better still, though, I assure you, I have this morning had very serious thoughts of being much better now I am six. However, I still think there is much room for improvement in us both, especially me, if God spares our lives, that we improve in them still more. I hope that you think all this about improvement is a very good subject. Till you return it is my intention to do, as near as it is in my power to, what I imagine you would like. I trust Cambridge is a healthy place for you and my father, and when you write to me I should hope you will tell me in what state of health you are. I should rejoice most amazingly to know how you was. At first you told me you would excuse the drawing and every thing of that sort: but I went to business on my birthday and did first the drawing. When you are from home it is always a pleasure to me to think you are in good health, and that you have met with no misfortune any way at least. Ben, I trust, will read and spell to me well, for you know the more improvement he will gain by it and the more useful it will make him. He seems to me to be a very good little boy altogether while you are gone. I hope you will believe me,

"Your most affectionate son, T. W. Malkin."

A touching letter, in spite of its painful self-consciousness, its obtrusive morality, and its tone of patronizing superiority over the junior Benjamin. What a curious contrast there is between this child and that other long-dead child—lately held up to modern criticism by Dr. John Brown—Pet Marjorie, with her premature flirtations, her unconscious coarseness, and her innocent "naughty" words; what a foil she is to this preternaturally good little boy, so quiet, so clever, and so pretty behaved! We hardly know which of the precocities is most objectionable, or rather most pitiable; for, does it ever occur to any body that for a child's faults the person most to be blamed is *the parent?* Do parents consider—would that they did!—how the most blessed or most fatal instruction they can bestow is the silent teaching of personal influence? It is not the slightest use in the world for a father to chastise his son for giving way to wrath, when, in inflicting the punishment, he is seen to be in a passion himself. Vainly does a mother preach to her girls the beauty of gentleness, sweetness, truthfulness, when they hear her every day giving sharp speeches to husband, children, or servants, and telling white lies of politeness to friends and visitors. The verbal instruction passes away, and is forgotten; but the unconscious effect of the permanent home atmosphere lasts in the individual throughout life.

Poor Thomas Malkin!—poor Marjorie Fleming!—there must have been something amiss in the bringing up of both of them. And when we reflect what very unpleasant people, as man and woman, they might possibly have become, we think almost with satisfaction of the two little graves.

I was once walking in her pleasant garden with a mother—the mother of ten children, all of whom had grown up to be a blessing to herself, to themselves, and to every body who knew them. Many sorrows they had, and she had for them; but only sorrows: no dissensions, no bitternesses, no sins. In the whole ten was not a single "black sheep." I said to her, talking about them, and the difference between them and most other families I knew, "How did you ever manage to bring them up so well?" "I did not bring them up at all," said she, smiling. "I did with them as I did with that apple-tree there—I let them *grow* up."

Ay, that is the secret, which parents so often miss.

They will not let their children grow. They must keep lopping them and propping them, training them after some particular form, forgetting that every human being, like every tree, has a growth of its own—ay, even though it may not be after the parental pattern; that the wisest thing in the end, seeing that the best of parents are not infallible, is just to treat young folk like young trees—removing all harmful influences, and bringing them under the reach of good; giving them plenty of earth and sun, freshness and dew, and then letting them alone.

Alas! this doctrine of "let alone" was apparently far too simple for Benjamin Heath Malkin, Esq., M.A., F.R.S.

In one thing, however, he must have been wise. The following letter, which in other points is almost pathetic in its simplicity, shows that there was dawning in the mind of little Thomas—he never could have been called plain "Tom,"—that strong religious sentiment common to precocious children. But it also shows that the pure heavenly light was never smothered in a fog of theological instruction upon subjects which no infant mind could understand:—

"GROVE PLACE, HACKNEY,
"Sunday evening, Jan. 22, 1802.

"MY DEAR MOTHER,—My anxiety of writing to you has proved the action quite necessary, having a good deal to say about the little child which the incomprehensible Almighty has, with all His wonderful works, given you reason to know will come. I certainly think it exactly true that it will come, by your saying so, though I should not have, of course, believed it so steadfastly if you had only thought so; but now I will return to the subject, not of your thinking that it will come, but of the infant itself. What use can it be of either to you or to me if I do not love it? But I shall love it, as much or more than I did Benjamin, when he first came, if I am not too much concerned about any thing—especially Allestone—to think of it at all, which, I dare say, I shall not be. I should love it whatever sex it was of: but I should love a sister rather the best, as you know I have a brother already.

"Indeed, I find that in another case this address to you is necessary, for in it I would tell you many subjects which I want to hide from any other person but yourself. I dare say the letter which my brother and you read, and also you alone, will in the end prove very entertaining and instructive, and will cause me to make very good resolutions. I promise you henceforth to read and study a great deal in that Holy Book, and also make a constant, and, perhaps, everlasting, resolution of attempting to receive instruction from the Bible. Henceforth this resolution will for a long time get the better of me, perhaps for all my life. I wish it may be long"—(poor boy, it was only to be six months more)—"hardly at all for the sake of fortune, being so much less important than piety and goodness; and as God cares so much more about it, that I may have time to fulfill my resolution, which, I dare say, is in yours, and I am sure in our Heavenly Father's opinion, good. But I will not get into that conceited way of thinking my own promises good; I had much rather have a better subject, as you say. I think myself happily circumstanced to have such a good mother and father. I think I could not have a better one. I also confess that I ought to think myself in the same happy state that I do. God grant that your life may be long—that you may keep your disposition towards us and the next little child that you have! In trouble I intend to attempt in future to console myself if I can with the thoughts of your tender disposition towards us, if, as I have great confidence it will, it lasts forever...... I from henceforth also promise to do your will always in every thing, and to obey the Almighty's will the same.

"Believe me, my dear mother, yours ever, T. W. MALKIN."

About this time the child writes a rough rhymeless paraphrase of Psalm cii., and a prayer. These are the only indications of that most questionable thing, "infant piety," except one little letter of much earlier date, in which the simple childish notions are touching enough:—

"The praise of God is great love. Well, I should like to go to heaven very much. Then you know I should see my little sister Mary and my little brother John, that are dead. So, they go to be buried. I think it is a very nice thing to go to heaven. Well, and then we should see our Heavenly Father and our Saviour. He has got a light round his head, our Saviour has. When we go we shall see Judas who brought the soldiers to seize our Saviour and put him to death—and so he went. There was St. Bartholomew, St. John, St. Peter, St. Matthew—but these were all the saints that I knew of."

During the last year of his life the little fellow must have kept up a large correspondence among aunts, uncles, cousins, and friends. One letter he writes

"to inform you of the coming of a little boy who was born yesterday. My mother has been long expecting it, and also hopes you will write her and me also a nice long letter soon...... The child is a very healthy little boy, and my mother, of course, hopes that it will live...... You would gratify me if you would describe your thoughts of the little boy just born yesterday, and also tell me how you would like a first sight of it. In my opinion it is a very fine child, and I also with pleasure hope and trust that it will, from its appearance, both live and form a good life,—also be obedient to its good, kind, and attentive parents."

This baby seems to have been a subject of intense interest to the elder brother. He refers continually to "the dear little Frederic," minutely describes his state of health, and makes plans for his education. Meantime, his own seems to have been going on with terrible rapidity. He writes essays, fables, and poems, sometimes of his own accord, sometimes at the instigation—oh, how cruel and unwise!—of friends and relatives. One instance the father mentions, of his "complying with his usual alacrity" with a request to write a poem, sitting for several minutes with the pen in his hand, then bursting into tears, and declaring "he was a stupid fellow, and could write no more verses that day." Doubtless, the overstrained brain was already beginning to give way. Indeed, in most of his productions of this last year there is a wildness of imagination and a slight incoherency, which looked ominous enough for the future.

But the most curious relic of this brief life, so soon to come to an end, was that referred to in a former letter as "Allestone." Allestone was the name Thomas gave to a visionary country—a sort of Utopia, of which he fancied himself king. He made a map of it, and lists of its cities, towns, rivers, all of his own invention. He wrote for it an imaginary scheme of government, an imaginary history, and numerous accounts of the imaginary Allestonians—their manners, customs, dress, and domestic adventures. Some of these are very quaint and ingenious:—

"The first king of Allestone had no father or mother, as he was the first Allestonian born. He could not certainly receive great instruction being without parents; but as soon as ever he was able to begin learning he practised as much as he could. He, by his diligence, attentive thought, and industry—also well-timed magnanimity, generosity, etc., acquired wonderful instruction...... By this time the kindness of manners of the Allestonians was fortunately increased. The then present king (George the First) was of a good, amiable disposition, and placed himself upon the throne when he was about ten years of age—and a very proper time too...... The Allestonians lived in good houses. They were very clever people. The dress of the Allestonians was, and is, very commodious. They in their houses wear nothing on their heads and no cravats. In their walks they have a little flapped hat, with a ribbon almost at top, and a buckle to keep it on. The men have a small head. They wear no waistcoats, have linen shirts, and quartered shoes, one flannel shirt, and brown breeches...... The Allestonian women dressed themselves in a commodious way. They wear their hair with a *toupée:* hoops are usual here: the ladies wear a shift and two dimity petticoats, and a long gown. When they go to church a fan is necessary to their dress. Allestone increased with numbers of Allestonians. They were all of a good character and inclined to generosity. One of their principal acts of generosity was that one of them gave the other a telescope, and the other said, 'I'll give it back to you again, sir.' That was when king James the Third was present—a good king he was. He placed himself upon the throne directly he was born, which was in 288."

Then ensue a series of imaginary biographical adventures and domestic historiettes, all concerning the inhabitants of the island of Allestone. One of these is enough to give:—

"Once upon a time, in a pleasant street of Countib (the capital city of Allestone) there lived a young lady...... As soon as ever she grew up old enough to be able to look for a house for herself, she settled a plan of doing it, and began to look out for one as fast as she could. After searching over a great many towns for one, at last she got to Countib, and went into a house from fatigue, to see if it was empty. She looked all about the house and found it so. Nobody can think how glad she was that she did find it, having taken so much trouble before. As soon as ever she had searched the house, she went to the parlor in great sorrow, took place of an arm-chair that was thereabouts, and begun to reflect on her offenses to her parents, whom she lost when about eleven years old: and after she had reflected about a quarter of an hour, she began to think of one, that in a few moments was so deeply impressed upon her mind, that she was almost ready to faint. She began in a few days to think that she chose to look out for a husband, and presently set about it, and though this was with a great deal of trouble, it was with less than her house. She took her husband with her to the house which she had with so much trouble chosen for herself. 'Do you know, sir,' says the lady, 'that a few days before this I have been reflecting on my offenses to my parents, whom I have long ago lost, and one was so deeply impressed upon my mind, that I was almost ready to faint.' 'Oh!' replied he, surprised. Some children were presently born to them, at first two at a time, and a few hours after that, one more. Their name was Malysbeg."

Alexander, Septimius, Adoleo, Ophelius, and Ablyth, are other names which figure in these odd little tales:—

"Septimius was most inclined to be good concerning humility and respect to the Divine Being; Alexander concerning generosity; Ophelius concerning wisdom; and Adoleo concerning virtue: in that they were all very good in all ways, but Alexander had the mildest disposition...... Though Adoleo had no wife, he was very happy with these relations of his. He loved his two brothers so much that he thought he could not be any happier with a wife: for they consoled him so much when he was in perplexity or trouble, that they served as one: and they were both of them ready to give up all consultation for their safety that they might busy themselves about his. Adoleo was always ready to do the same for them."

But I will quote no more from this curious production, which, and the letters also, the father says are printed *literatim.*

As if he must try his hand at every thing, little Thomas also began the composition of a comic opera, entitled "The Entertaining Assembly," and a canzonet, on the back of which he put in printed letters, "What the maker of the music means. The thing on the other side is only imaginary music made by Thomas Williams Malkin, who does not understand real music."

Invention seems to have been the most prominent characteristic of this boy's mind; likewise an originality of ideas, and a persistency in carrying them out—which, had he lived, might have made him a remarkable man. And under all the little fellow's priggishness there runs a current of steady conscientiousness, of earnest desire to do right, and strong home affections, which might also have made him a truly good man. The father's lengthy praise of him and trivial anecdotes about him, give not half so clear an impression of what the child really was, as the bits that peep out in his own innocent letters. Witness this—to an uncle in Quebec:—

> "Now for an account of the little baby. He grows very much, and talks in near the same quantity; he has just been inoculated for the cow-pox, which has proved very successful towards him: he has been christened Frederic, and I love him very much...... Now for a little information concerning Benjamin. He is but very slow in learning to write, and not much quicker in his Latin. I am sorry to give you an account which is at all unfavorable; but as it was my proposal to tell you of Benjamin, I could not give you a true account without making it as I have. I have made an undertaking to teach him to write, and also to teach him Latin gradually as I learn myself. It is hard to say which I shall succeed in, if in either; but it is uncertain if I shall succeed in either."

To this child-like statement Mr. Malkin adds three or four pages, apologizing for poor Benjamin's incapacities, and saying what a clever boy he is now turning out; how he is "learning French rapidly;" "reads the best English authors on polite and entertaining subjects with a due share of discrimination;" "is capable of carrying on in his head, without noting them down, a considerable series of arithmetical computations;" how "his temper is generous and affectionate, his manners open and engaging." Not bad for a child "just eight years old." One wonders if this Benjamin lived—if he be even yet alive, as is not impossible. He would be now an old man of seventy-six, who must long ago have forgotten all about the brother Thomas, that grieved so over his slowness in Latin.

But the short life was fast drawing to a close. The father declares that Thomas was always exceedingly healthy, and that he had no illness from his birth until the one of which he died. The only forewarning given might easily have been recollected, with exaggerations, after the event had happened: namely, that his mother having been talking with him about "the world to come," he exclaimed with animation, "Do you know, mamma, that what we have been talking of makes me almost wish not to live long, that I may have the pleasure of mounting?"

On the 1st of July, 1802, he complained of his throat, but continued his studies and play. The second day a shivering fit came on, and on the third the boy took to his bed, which he never again quitted.

His illness lasted a whole month. Its progress is described by the father with scientific minuteness. There seems to have been a combination of diseases, dropsy being the most prominent. Even through the cloud of verbiage under which Mr. Malkin relates his story, the boy's patience and sweetness are plainly discernible; also, his great love for his mother, who used to be with him all day, but could not remain at night, on account of his little brother, who was still a baby at the breast. He used to let her go quite cheerfully, only saying, "I shall be glad when it is morning, that you may come to me again." Those weary night-watches—longing for the morning! who does not know them? Only once the poor child is said to have complained—"I wonder when the time will come for me to have a settled sleep all through the night again!"

He does not seem to have had any idea that he was about to die. A week before his death he asked, "Do you think my illness is half over, mamma?" She answered, "Yes, much more than half. Did he think it long?" "No, not very long." And he said no more.

Up to the last he took pleasure in his books, which he insisted on having beside him on the bed; and in his maps, one of which he was trying to play with half an hour before he died. But, curiously enough, he seemed to have forgotten all about his fancied kingdom, Allestone, and only mentioned it once during his illness. His mind was wandering a little, and he talked about a certain King James. They asked if it were King James of England. "No; the King James of my imaginary country." Poor child! slipping away fast into the unknown country, the mystery of which eye hath never seen nor ear heard!

Sickness seemed only to strengthen his strong household affections. Every day he used to ask after his two little brothers, wanting to know what Benjamin was doing, and insisting on baby Frederic being brought to his bedside, for him to talk to and play with. "Pretty Frederic," he always called him. And the last night of his life he had Benjamin brought to take tea in his room, and watched his mother standing at the foot of his bed with baby in her arms —watched her, and the baby too, very earnestly; then tried to speak as usual, but could not. After two or three efforts he just managed to articulate "Frederic"—the last word he ever uttered. About midnight he "sank in the arms of his mother, without a struggle or a groan."

The day after, some medical friend hinted, as was most natural, that water on the brain, produced by over-study, had been the cause of death. The father, angrily disclaiming such an accusation—which all through the memoir he has repelled with a suspicious eagerness—states that on the 3d of August—the child died on the 1st—"Mr. Clive, Dr. Lester, Dr. Pett, Mr. Toulmin, and Mr. Smith met; when Mr. Clive opened the head." The brain was found to be unusually large, but perfect and healthy. The body was afterwards opened, when "the general organization was so complete as to have given the fairest promise of life and health."

How far this medical opinion was accurate we can not now judge; nor does it very much matter. The little life was ended. Only six years and nine months, and to have left so many memorials behind!

But the question still remains, whether in this present day, when the intimate connection between mind and body, physical and mental soundness, is so much better understood than it was sixty years ago, the verdict on this poor precocious child would not assuredly have been "Died from preventible causes." And causes, the prevention of which was given by Providence *into the parents' hands.* A very solemn thought, and worth the consideration of parents.

Mr. Benjamin Heath Malkin gives us a great deal more of sermonizing, but no other facts. He does not even tell us where his little son was buried. Probably, some inquisitive archæologists, searching over Hackney churches or churchyards, might find the tomb—no doubt a very elegant one, with a flowery epitaph in the most admirable Latin. But beneath it—whatsoever, and wheresoever it is—little Thomas sleeps well. And somewhere—though where, I have not the remotest idea—sleeps the father: who, for all his pedantic long-windedness, may have loved and mourned his little son, and mourned too perhaps even his own mistake concerning him—more deeply than any of us know.

* * * * * *

When I wrote this paper, and for some time afterwards, I had—as I say—not the remotest idea who the Malkin family were, or whether there were any of them surviving. I have since, by a curious chance, discovered all about them; which I think it is but just to append here—more especially as I have passed a rather severe judgment on the long-dead father of this painfully precocious child.

That judgment I can not conscientiously rescind. The harm frequently done by learned fathers to over-clever children is so great that it ought to be protested against in every possible way. Indeed, generally speaking, the less any father has to do with his children till past infancy, the better; for hardly any masculine mind has the tenderness, the patience, the power of ignoring self, and seeing only the child's good, which seem to be almost an instinct with mothers. And the pride—quite distinct from love—which a father feels in clever children, is a sore temptation to him to spur them on, instead of holding them back in every possible way. I may have been too hard upon this father in particular; but, as a rule, I believe the evil and cruelty of over-stimulating an already precocious brain can not be too strongly pointed out to parents, and therefore I let my words stand.

But concerning the Malkins, let me add a few more, which trench upon no privacy, since the family must all have been in a sense public characters—and a very remarkable family to boot.

Mr. Benjamin Heath Malkin (or Dr. Malkin, as he afterwards became), the father of little Thomas, was head-master of Bury Grammar School for a number of years, until about 1825, when he gave up his post, and retired to a quiet Welsh village, where he occupied himself with his studies to the end of his life. He was a kindly, courteous, and genial man; he had a handsome person, excelled in music, singing, and acting, and though gifted with no particular originality of mind, had a great faculty for absorbing every sort of knowledge.

Of his sons, Benjamin (the little Benjamin so slow at his Latin), afterwards Sir Benjamin Malkin, became a barrister, went to India, and was appointed successively Recorder of Penang, and one of the Puisne Judges of Calcutta. He was remarkable for his mental power, high character, and charm of disposition. Everywhere he won warm friends—some very distinguished ones. He died at Calcutta, in 1838, in the prime of life, and in the midst of a most useful career, leaving a widow and two children.

Frederic (the "baby" in whom little Thomas took such interest, and whose name was the last word he was heard to utter) was also an author, writing a History of Greece, and other solid works. Indeed all Dr. Malkin's sons were more or less connected with literature. Arthur, the only one now surviving, has written "Pompeii," "Historical Parallels," etc.

With such descendants to cast a halo round it, I may leave safely the memory of their father—as well as that of their little brother who died at seven years old.

HIS YOUNG LORDSHIP.

A STORY FOR GREAT AND LITTLE PEOPLE.

IT was a pat of butter—only a pat of butter, a small, silly thing, and yet it made me feel, as the children say, "like to greet." For I knew the spot it came from,—a lovely nook in a lovely land. I could picture the narrow valley, so rich and green, over which the huge gray granite mountains watched, frowning or smiling, but still watching, like faithful parents over their children; reflecting the sunshine, gathering the rain, and sending both down alternately upon the fertile tract below. I could summon up its "pastures green," not like English meadows, hedged and ditched, but divided angularly by stone dikes, among which grew innumerable ferns and accidental clumps of heather and whin; while here and there in damp places were queer bog-plants; butter-wort with its flat leaves and tall-stemmed blue flowers; the white tufts of the cotton-plant; the aromatic bog-myrtle. Nay, as I looked at my pat of butter, I could almost see the cows that originated it,—small, shaggy, active, Highland beasts, or the dainty little Ayrshire breed, the prettiest of cattle, moving about their restricted lot of pasturage under the shadow of these same mountains which—whom, I was nearly writing, they felt so like living friends—any one who knows, loves: and once loving, loves forever.

"Yes," said my hostess, whom I had better call by the good Scotch name of Mrs. Burns, "it is real Scotch butter; we in London don't get any thing like it. It was sent to me from ——," naming the place, to which I mean to give an imaginary name, and call it the Laighlands.

For upon it, and the butter, hangs a story, which Mrs. Burns immediately began to tell me: a story true and simple as that of Jeanie Deans—of which, while she related it, we were both strongly reminded. I asked her leave to write it down, just plainly as it was, with no elaborations or exaggerations,—for indeed it required none; only disguising the names and the places, so that while the truth remains—the internal truth, which is the real life and usefulness of fiction—the bare outside facts may be quite unrecognizable by the general public. And I wish I could give to the written tale any thing like the simple graphic power with which it was unconsciously told.

"Yes," said Mrs. Burns, looking me through with her clear kind eyes; "I must tell you all about that butter, and how we got it from such a distance. You know the Laighlands? Isn't it a bonnie place? Such a sweet, quiet, out-of-the-way farm. We lived there a whole summer. We had come to the neighborhood, and did not know where to get lodgings; so they took us in at the Laighlands, eight in all,—papa, and me, and our six: and we lived there for ten happy weeks. That was nine years ago."

It was not nearly so long since I had seen the Laighlands myself; and though I was only there for one day, I could still remember it. Especially the garden, wonderfully neat and well-stocked for that part of Scotland, where the lazy Highland nature has not yet arrived at the difficult science of horticulture: and among the common people life implies mere living, without any attempt to adorn existence with even the beauty of a cottage flower-border, or the small luxury of a dozen gooseberry bushes, and a row of beans or peas. Therefore, I had noticed this farmhouse, for it had a capital garden, and an upland orchard behind; and its orderliness within was equal to its picturesqueness without, which is a great deal to say for such dwellings in the Highlands of Scotland.

"Yes," continued Mrs. Burns (I will go straight on with her part in the conversation, and omit my own, which indeed consisted merely of a few questions), "we lived there for ten weeks, and during that time we got to have quite an affection for our landlord and his wife. They were such simple people, and so honest, so painfully honest. Of course, in country lodgings, where the people can only make hay while the sun shines, and that is for about two months in the twelve, one almost expects to be cheated, or at least made the most of in the same way; but these good folk only cheated themselves. For instance, we had the run of the garden, and you can imagine what a raid my six children would make upon the gooseberry bushes. Besides, we had an unlimited quantity of vegetables. But when, at the first week's end, I looked to see what was put down in the bill, there was nothing at all! 'Oh,' said the mistress, a tall, handsome Highland woman, much younger than her husband, and speaking English with a quaint slow purity of accent that you often find among those who have to learn it like a foreign language—'Oh, I hope ye'll use your freedom with the garden—we'd never ask ye to pay.' But when I remonstrated—for I don't like that Celtic fashion of being too proud to receive honest payment, and yet expecting always an equivalent in kind—Mrs. Kennedy (I will call her Kennedy) assented, with a sort of dignified acquiescence that had a touch of condescension in it, begging I would put my own price on the things we took, for she really did not know what they were worth. Which doubtless was the truth, for you are aware how little actual coin is current in that district, and how people there often live half a lifetime without ever having seen a town street, or the inside of a moderate-sized shop.

"This woman, Mrs. Kennedy, was a case in point. She was about forty, her husband being somewhat over sixty; yet neither of them had ever travelled twenty miles from their own farm, which had been rented by Kennedy, and his father before him, for the best part of a century, from the one great landholder of these parts.

"'And his lordship kens us weel,' said the gudewife to me one day, when my children had been describing a grand-looking gentleman whom they met riding over the hill-side. 'He's a fine man, and a gude friend to us. Many's the day I hae seen him stand and crack wi' the auld gudeman—that's Kennedy's father; and he never meets Kennedy himsel' but he'll stop and shake hands and ask for the wife and bairns. He's a fine man,—his lordship—and a gude landlord; he kens a' that's done on the property. Though I'll no say but that he might hae waur tenants than oursels: for my man and his father before him hae lived at the Laighlands, and paid their honest rent, every term-day, for seventy-five years.'

"I remember this little incident," continued Mrs. Burns, "because I remember the woman's face as she spoke—full of that honorable pride which is as justifiable in a farmer as in a duke; and, also, because circumstances brought it to my mind afterwards.

"Well, we staid at the Laighlands all summer. It was a glorious summer to my young folks—and a sorrowful day when we left the place. We had to start about four in the morning, in Kennedy's cart, which had been our sole link with the civilized world, and in which he had conveyed to us daily—for this absolutely refusing payment to the last—all provisions which the farm could not supply; and the few extraneous necessities—letters, newspapers, linen-drapery, etc.—which we indulged in at this primitive place. He brought them from the nearest town, or what flattered itself was a town, several miles off. We had given him a deal of trouble, and now he had taken for us the final trouble of all, by bestowing endless pains on the arrangement of seats and mattresses, so as to make the rough jolting cart a little comfortable for me and the children. They cried as they said good-bye to the pretty place where they had been so happy, and the good folk who had been so excessively kind to them. And I own I was half inclined to cry too, when Mrs. Kennedy, who had been rather invisible of late—she brought her gudeman his seventh child while we were at the Laighlands—appeared, weak and white-looking as she was, in the cold dawn of the morning, and gave me a basket neatly packed with all sorts of good things—eatables and drinkables. 'It's for the weans on their journey,' she said. 'We'll no forget the weans.'

"And it was a very long time before the weans forgot her or the Laighlands. Of winter nights they used to go over every bit of our blithe time there—from the first day we came and settled ourselves in the small but tidy parlor, in the clean bedrooms, full of furniture that looked as if it had been bought in the last century—as possibly it had—up to the final day when old Kennedy (he was quite an old man, though hale and hearty), drove his cart into the sea almost—for the waves were running high—and carried the children through them into the boat by which we had to reach the steamer that was to bear us far away—to horrid London, to streets, and squares, and work, and school. And over and over again I had to describe to the little ones, whose memories were fainter than they cared to confess, the figure of the good old man in his gray kilt, bonnet, and plaid, with his white hair flying in the wind, as he stood making his last signals from the shore, and shouting out his last Gaelic farewells, for he could speak but little English; the boys answering him in the few words he had taught them, which they remembered for ever so long, till Gaelic was rubbed out by Latin and Greek. I, too—with the warm heart that a mother can not help having towards any one who has been kind to her children—kept for a long time in my store-cupboard the basket Mrs. Kennedy had filled for the bairns on their voyage. And every New Year for several years, we sent books and other gifts to the little Kennedys, hoping each summer that we should manage to go back to the Laighlands. But we never did; and in process of time our connection with the place slipped by—perhaps our interest likewise in this busy London life it is so easy to forget.

"It was last New Year, or possibly a few days after then, that I was sitting just here—in this drawing-room"—(which was a very nice one, for Mrs. Burns's husband has honorably worked his way to a handsome house in one of the best streets in London)—"I was sewing by myself, and the young folks were down below in the school-room. It was one of those terribly cold black days that we had last winter, the wind howling in the chimney, and the snow falling or trying to fall, for it was too cold almost to snow. I was sitting with my feet on the fender, and with the feeling of intense thankfulness which always comes to me in such weather, that I have a good house over my head and all my dear ones about me,—when a message arrived that some one below wanted to speak to me.

"'Who is it?' asked I; for such messages are endless in our house, and generally prove to be applications for charity. It was a poor woman, my servant said; a woman with a little girl, and she would not send up her name, but insisted upon speaking to me myself.

"I thought it was one of the ordinary genteel London beggars, and you know what London begging is, and how, after being taken in over and over again, one has to harden one's heart"—(a process which, judging from Mrs. Burns's face, in her case would not be sudden or easy). "Of course, I could not refuse to see the person; but I went down to her, looking, I dare say, as cold as a stone.

"She was a tall, thin woman—remarkably tall for a woman; and her long straight black dress, and clinging black shawl, no thicker than yours to-day, though it was mid-winter, made her seem taller and thinner still. I looked in her face, which was sharp-featured, worn, and elderly, but I could not remember ever having seen her before. So I just asked her her business, very freezingly I suppose, for she drew back at once towards the dining-room door.

"'Ye'll no mind o' me, ma'am. I'm troubling ye, I see; so I'll just be gone. It's no matter.'

"It was a Scotch voice, and a Scotch manner; the air of quiet independence that, I am glad to say, even the very lowest of us seldom quite lose. We Scotch, if we are ever so poor, don't beg like your London beggars. So, of course, I asked her to wait a minute, and tell me her name.

"Do ye no ken?—Eh, Mrs. Burns? I must be sair changed—and nae wonder—if ye dinna ken me. I'm Mistress Kennedy of the Laighlands.'

"'Mrs. Kennedy of the Laighlands!' You will guess how in an instant the face of matters was entirely changed, and what sort of a welcome she got—she and her daughter, for the little girlie that hung by her gown, and peered from behind her with shy, dark eyes, must be hers—possibly the baby that was born while we were there.

"Ay, so she was. 'She's the youngest; and I could na leave her behind: though it's a very sad journey I come on to this awfu' London. Oh, it is an awfu' place, Mrs. Burns! And ye're keeping weel yoursel', and the gudeman and a' the bairns?' added she, with the instinctive tact and courtesy which one sees almost universally among Highland people, and which we had always noticed so much in Mrs. Kennedy. Though only a farmer's wife, her manners were as good as if she were a lady born. But she looked so ill, so depressed, so actually weighed down with care, that I shrank from asking her the especial trouble which had brought her hither. By-and-by she poured it out.

"'No, the gudeman's no deid, Mrs. Burns, though sometimes he almost wishes he were. He has got notice to quit the Laighlands. Just think!—the Laighlands! Where he was born, and his father likewise—and where he has paid his rent—never behind a day—for fifty year. Isn't it hard, ma'am?'

"It was hard. We folk who live in streets and houses all just like one another can scarcely recognize how hard. Besides, as Mrs. Kennedy went on to explain, and which I myself knew well, in that thinly-populated district an eviction meant actual turning out; with small prospect of finding another home. Houses were very scarce, and the farms few and far between, being mostly held by tenants who had held them for generations. A notice to quit implied not merely a flitting but a complete uprooting. No wonder the poor body spoke of it as we speak of some heavy calamity.

"'But your factor is a good man,' said I. 'Did you not appeal to him?'

"Mrs. Kennedy shook her head. 'I'm no saying aught against the factor, but he's my lord's servant, and they say my lord wants money, and they're wishing to feu the estate. Ah, they micht hae let my man keep the Laighlands a bit while langer. It'll no be unco lang—he's ower seventy, ye ken. It's breaking his heart.'

"I asked her why she did not write to the young lord; for the old lord, as he was now called, though scarcely past middle age when he died, had, I knew, been dead a year or more.

"'We did think o' that. His young lordship—do you ken him, Mrs. Burns?'

"That was not likely; but I had heard about him—a promising lad in his teens, left sole master of one of the finest properties in Scotland. He was too young for people to know much good about him—but nobody knew any harm: he was a college youth, frank and lively, given to all the amusements of his age and rank—not much of a student, but that could hardly be expected of the heir to indefinite thousands a year. Still, as I told Mrs. Kennedy, a young man scarcely twenty, in any rank of life, is apt to be thoughtless, and in his rank great people often do little people a deal of harm without in the least intending it.

"'That was just what the lawyer said—the lawyer I went to in Edinburgh, yesterday.'

"'Yesterday!' I exclaimed.

"'Ay, ma'am, though it seems a year sinsyne. The gudeman could na stir, being laid aside with rheumatism, so I just thought I would gang to Edinburgh mysel', and see Mr. Campbell, a friend o' mine that's a writer there. And he said to me—"Mrs. Kennedy, if I was you I would gang up to London and speak wi' his young lordship face to face." That was yesterday, as I said: there was na a day to lose—in a week's time the notice we got to leave the Laighlands was due; and we would be turned out. So I wrote to my husband frae Mr. Campbell's office; I put mysel' in the train—me and the bairn, for I could neither send her hame nor leave her in Edinburgh; and we travelled a' the night and reached London this morning, just as we were.'

"Just as they were!—in those thin clothes, and such a terrible cold night as it had been! No wonder they looked as wretched as they did, and that my servant had made such a mistake about them and their condition in life. Very much surprised she was when I rang the bell and desired her to take the little girl and make her comfortable in my children's nursery; and bring up breakfast at once for 'my friend Mrs. Kennedy, who had come all the way from Scotland last night.'

"Mrs. Kennedy said nothing, nor resisted in the least; she was utterly exhausted. She sat by the fire with her hands on her lap, and her sad eyes looking straight before her, scarcely noticing the things around her, as if she had been familiar with them all her life. And when at last she got a little strengthened by warmth and food, and was able to tell me her story, she did so with a composure and quiet dignity that would have surprised any one who did not know how the Jeanie Deans nature, fearless, self-reliant, yet absolutely without self-consciousness, is not exceptional, but lies dormant in many and many a Scotchwoman, ready to appear at once when circumstances require it, as in this case. For you and I, I suppose, can hardly realize what such a sudden journey to London must have appeared to Mrs. Kennedy—almost like a journey to the Antipodes.

"'Were you not afraid?' I asked her.

"'Maybe,' she answered, faintly smiling. 'But somebody maun do it, ye ken, and there was naebody but me.' By-and-by she told me how she had done it.

"Poor body! only imagine her, dropped in the gloomy winter morning at the terminus in Euston Square, not knowing a soul, having but one place to go to in all London;—and with her Scotch directness of purpose she had gone right to it—his young lordship's town-house, the magnificent mansion in —— Square.

"It was partially closed, as most great houses are in the Christmas recess. Mrs. Kennedy merely thought, 'the London folk are awfu' late of rising,' and, unwilling to disturb the family, sat down on the lowest stone step, with her little girl beside her. There she waited, pinched with cold—but she was well accustomed to cold—until there should be some sign of life in the house within. Presently came 'a braw sogerly young man, wi' a bag o' letters,' and rang as if he, at least, had no fear of disturbing his lordship's slumbers, but he poked his letters in at a slit in the door—and still it was not opened. At last Mrs. Kennedy took courage and rang the bell likewise, and begged the footman who opened it to tell his lordship that she had come all the way from Scotland to speak to him, and could he see her for five minutes on private business, as soon as he rose?

"But the footman only laughed, and called another footman who laughed too, and they told her it was a capital story, but that if she didn't go away they would send the Mendicity officers after her. 'I did na ken what the young man meant,' added Mrs. Kennedy, 'but I tell't him (ceevilly enough, for I was sure he was only doing his duty) that his young lordship would mind me weel;—I was Mistress Kennedy o' the Laighlands. But what do you think, Mrs. Burns?' and she looked at me with a grieved simplicity, 'he had never heard tell o' the Laighlands!'

"There must have been some uncomfortable passages between her and these grand footmen, though with her natural dignified reticence, which did not like even to own that she had been insulted, Mrs. Kennedy avoided particularizing them. Besides, the feudal reverence in which the young lord was held everywhere on the estate was such, that under the shadow of it even his domestics were exempt from blame. I could only gather that she was turning to quit the house, when up there came a young man, or, as Mrs. Kennedy pointedly put it, a young gentleman.

"He entered with an air of authority, so that she might have taken him for her landlord, only it had been plainly said that the young nobleman was absent from home; 'and,' reasoned she in her simplicity, 'his lordship must be far too great a gentleman to bid his servants tell a lee about himsel'.' But the new-comer was of some importance in the establishment. When he perceived the confusion in the hall, he asked imperatively what it was all about; and so he learnt Mrs. Kennedy's name, and where she came from.

"'He was a Scotsman—I'm gey sure he was a Scotsman,' she said: but at any rate he was a kindly-hearted young gentleman, and evidently held some good position in the establishment; for when he spoke and listened to her answers, the servants ceased interfering, and hung back respectfully. At length he asked her to walk into his 'study,' a little room leading off the hall, and then told her who he was.

(Mrs. Burns gave me the gentleman's name and position in the young lord's household; but neither are of consequence to my story. If he ever reads it, he may take the reward of one of those small kindlinesses which cost so little and are worth so much, and recognize himself.)

"He placed the weary woman in his own arm-chair, and shut the study-door. Then, before he allowed her to speak another word, he opened a cupboard, and took out a bottle of wine and a bag of biscuits, with which he put a little life into her and the child,—the good bairn, her brave mother's own daughter, who had stood silent and sleepy and hungry, but had never once shed a tear. Then he bade Mrs. Kennedy tell him her whole case from beginning to end.

"It was very simple; and he, of course, must have seen it clearly enough,—probably much clearer than the poor woman herself saw it. It was the common story of the different way in which the same things affect big folk and little. Probably nobody was to blame; or the whole was a matter of mere carelessness. In all likelihood the young nobleman knew nothing whatever about it, and never would, unless some one specially told him. 'You can not see him,' said Mr. ——, 'he really is not here, but you might write to him. If you like I will sketch out the letter.'

"'But,' continued Mrs. Kennedy, 'I tell't him that I was ill at the pen, and gin I wrote maybe his lordship could na read it; and if I could only see him, just for five minutes. I hae seen him mony a time—riding up our hill-side by his father's big horse—on his wee Shetland pony. Oh, gin I could but see his lordship!'

"Probably the young gentleman thought as I did then —oh, if his lordship could but see this woman!—one of the sort of women who bore the sons that followed and fought for his forefathers; with her strong, earnest, and yet not unbeautiful Highland face; her complete self-forgetfulness, and absorption in the work she had before her. So, after a little consideration, he agreed with Mrs. Kennedy that a personal interview would give her cause the best chance. But it could only be accomplished by her going to the college where the young lord then was; and which, to avoid all recognition, I will call St. Cuthbert's Hall, Oxbridge. Would she do this? Could she do it? For it was a considerable journey from London, and it would cost a good deal more money. She asked how much; and then inwardly reckoned her purse. It fell short by at least twenty shillings.

"This was a hard discovery, but she kept it to herself. She had never borrowed a half-penny in her life, and would not begin now,—certainly not from a stranger. The only thought that occurred to her was to sell something, perhaps a little cairngorm brooch she had; but how to set about it she did not know. And then, in answer to the young gentleman's question, had she any friends in London? she suddenly thought of us.

"She did not know, or if she ever did know, had forgotten, our London address, and our name was a common one enough. The Directory, which her friend took down and diligently searched in, scarcely helped her at all; till, at length, she recollected my husband's profession and somewhat peculiar Christian name. 'That's him,' she cried; and found to her comfort that Mr. —— knew him, at least by reputation. Most young Scotsmen in London know my husband. So, without more ado, Mrs. Kennedy took a grateful leave of the gentleman, put herself into a cab by his advice, and drove to our door.

"While she rested, for she absolutely refused to go to bed or to sleep, I went in to consult with my husband.

But when I saw him I was so excited by the story I had heard, by the old remembrances which the sight of Mrs. Kennedy had revived, and by things in general, that I could not speak a word, but fairly began to 'greet.' He, too, was in no small degree affected by what at last I managed to tell him; even so much that he had to take refuge in the study of *Bradshaw*, and discovery of the Oxbridge trains.

"We found the only available one now would take Mrs. Kennedy into the town about eleven that night—an impossible time to see a young undergraduate. So we persuaded her with great difficulty, for it seemed to be like losing time, that her best course was to sleep at our house, she and Jessie, and take the earliest morning train, which was at six A.M. To this she consented; seeing, with her clear good sense, that nothing better could be done, and being withal greatly comforted by perceiving how happy Jessie was with our children.

"The children—or rather the young people—were in great excitement all day. It was such a romantic story: Mrs. Kennedy was such a remarkable person, and Jessie (who, being left behind with us in awful London, was at first very unhappy—then being taken to the Zoological Gardens, found consolation in a ride on the big elephant), Jessie was such a quaint sort of child, speaking little English, yet full of Highland grace and Highland intelligence, that she amused us much. Late at night Jessie's mother came back, and then we all thronged round her, eager to learn how she had fared; in fact, greedy over every word of her story.

"It was told in her face. Never was there such a sad face. I wish his young lordship could have seen it.

"Understand, I don't mean unwarrantably to blame the young nobleman. He was but a boy—careless as boys are: and upon him had fallen, much before his time, the solemn responsibilities of property. I do not suppose he meant any harm, or had the least idea he was doing an unkindness. Only, he did it.

"When Mrs. Kennedy reached Oxbridge at about nine in the morning, she was told that his lordship could not be seen; in fact, he had not long gone to bed. This his valet informed her confidentially; adding, for he seemed a kind young fellow, and knew his Lordship's Scotch property, and even thought he remembered the farm at the Laighlands—that as soon as his master waked he would tell him that there has a woman waiting, who had come all the way from Scotland to see him.

"She did wait—hour after hour—wandering forlornly about the college gardens and quadrangle—going into the town for a little food—then walking hurriedly back again, lest by chance she should miss the happy moment when his young lordship should condescend to open his eyes; afraid to intrude, and yet trembling lest she should be forgotten and overlooked. It was now nearly three in the afternoon. Then, in despair applying again to the valet, she heard that his lordship was at breakfast; some friends were breakfasting with him; he could not possibly be disturbed.

"Nevertheless, the kindly valet took in a message, imploring that she might see his lordship just for one minute; she would not trouble him longer. He surely must remember the Laighlands; he had ridden there many a time on his little pony. His lordship sent out word that he did remember the Laighlands, and that though he could not see her now, he would do so on the Monday following, at his house in London.

"But Mrs. Kennedy knew that Monday would be too late. If she could not leave London on the Saturday evening, she would not reach home in time to prevent the notice from taking effect, and the ejection being accomplished. She urged this upon the valet, who was daring enough to go in and speak to his master a second time. Then one of the guests, a merry-looking young gentleman—they seemed a merry set, Mrs. Kennedy thought, for she heard their shouts of laughter through the door—came out and spoke to her, quite civilly, but with exceeding amusement at the idea of her thinking it was possible she could see his lordship. But, nevertheless, he told her to make her mind easy, for that a telegram should be sent to the factor, desiring him to pause in the ejection until he heard further.

"With this Mrs. Kennedy was forced to be content; but she left Oxbridge with a very heavy heart.

"She staid with us until the appointed Monday: and we took her about and showed her and Jessie the wonders of London, and diverted her mind as well as we could from the painful suspense under which she was laboring. She tried to enjoy herself—she was touchingly grateful. But still the heavy sense of what was hanging over her—hanging upon half-a-dozen words from a youth's careless lips—seemed to cloud over every thing. I never spent a more restless, uncomfortable Sunday than the one before that Monday, in thinking and wondering what would be the result of her application: a result of such slight moment to the young nobleman—of incalculable importance to the old farmer and his family.

"'I hope I'm no wicked, Mrs. Burns,' said the poor woman, looking at me pathetically on coming home from church—we had taken her to hear our own dear minister, though he was Free Kirk and she Established, to prove that there were good 'soun'' Presbyterian clergymen even in London—'I did na mean to be wicked or unthankfu'—and I likit the look o' him, and his sweet voice and kind eyes—but I did na hear one half o' the minister's sermon.'

"Neither did I, so I could say nothing. It was no use to begin moralizing to Mrs. Kennedy about the relations between class and class, and the respective duties that each owes to the other. It is just what I notice in my own household, that what seems a small thing to me may be a very great one to my servant: and that it behooves all who are put in authority to take the utmost pains to look at every question from the under as well as the upper side.

"Eleven in the forenoon was the hour fixed for the interview. We dressed Mrs. Kennedy for it with great care, and helped her out with some few things; for she had hardly any clothes with her; and we thought it advisable that his lordship's tenant of fifty years' standing, and representing a tenantry of fifty years previous to that, should appear before him as respectable as possible. To this end, it being a fearfully wet morning, we sent her off in a decent cab, which my husband gave orders should wait for her at the corner of the square.

"This done, we, too, waited, in a suspense that to my young people was very exciting, and to me actually painful. We had given her a full hour, indeed I expected a much longer absence, for I thought she would likely be kept waiting; people whose time is of little value never reckon the value of time to others. So if she were back by one, I should have been well pleased. But long before the clock struck twelve the cab drew up to the door, and Mrs. Kennedy stood in the hall. The moment I saw her face I was certain all was lost.

"'Come in,' I said, and drew her into the study, and shut the door, to keep the children out awhile. 'Come in and sit down.'

"She sat down, and then lifted up to me the forlornest face! 'Ye're vera kind, ma'am; I'll tell the gudeman ye've been wonderfu' kind. My puir auld man!—and he past seventy year!— It's awfu' hard for him.'

"I took her hand—poor soul! and then she shed one or two tears, not more, and rose.

"'I maun gang hame as soon as I can, Mrs. Burns, to look after the auld man.'

"'Then there is no chance? What did his lordship say to you?'

"'Naething. He gaed to Paris yestreen.'

"'And did he leave no letter—no message?'

"'Ne'er a word. He's clean forgotten me. Young folks hae sic short memories. Maybe he meant nae harm.'

"This was all she said. Not a word of blame, or reproach, or bitterness. The instinctive feeling of feudal respect in which she had been brought up, or perhaps a higher feeling still, sealed her tongue even then. Nor did I—indignant as I was—desire to be more severe upon the young man than he deserved. I only wished that he, who had such an infinite power of good in his hands—such an unlimited possibility of experiencing the keenest joy of life, that of making people happy—could have seen the misery on this poor woman's face, as she thought of all her weary journeys thrown away—of her returning journey to tell the bitter tidings to her old husband, about whom she seemed to grieve far more than for herself.

"'If his lordship wad hae let us bide at the Laighlands while the auld man lived,' she said, 'we wad hae paid a better rent—as we tell't the factor—and new stockit the farm, and Kennedy wad hae done his best wi' the new-fangled ways, though he hates them a'—and it wad na hae been for more than ten years at most: and what's ten years to his young lordship, that will scarce be a man when my auld man's in his grave? Ochone—ochone!' And she began rocking herself with a low moan, and talking in

Gaelic to Jessie, who had run in eagerly with several of my children. I took them all away, and left the child and mother together.

"There was no more to be done. To apply to Mr. ——, who had been so kind, was also useless; he had told her he was only in London for two days. Besides, he could not interfere openly in her affairs, with which, from his position in the household, he had nothing whatever to do. The only thing was to accept passively things as they were, and trust to the chance that the telegram sent had stopped present proceedings at the Laighlands. While in the mean time Mrs. Kennedy might take the course which had at first been intended, of addressing his lordship by letter.

"We wrote the letter for her, putting the case in her name, but in as strong terms as we could; and my husband took care it should be so forwarded that it was almost impossible his lordship should *not* receive it. This done, we sent the poor woman away by the night-train to Scotland—for she was most eager to be gone—making her and Jessie as comfortable as we could; earnestly hoping, and with perhaps an allowable hypocrisy trying hard to persuade her, that, after all, things might turn out less sad than she feared. We assured her—and ourselves in doing so—that the telegram would make all safe for a few days to come; and in the mean time her letter—that momentous letter, the invention and inditing of which had cost us, as well as herself, such a world of pains—might, nay, must, not only appeal to the young landlord's sense of justice, but touch his heart, even in the midst of his Paris enjoyments; so that he would immediately send back word, confirming the Laighlands Farm to poor old Kennedy for his lifetime. My young folk, full of youth's romance and inherent belief in goodness, felt quite sure it would be so; nay, I think the younger ones actually imagined his lordship would do all manner of noble and generous actions—even to driving to the farm in a coach and six, personally to express his regard for the Kennedys—the very next time he happened to be on his property.

"We started her off—poor body!—with many good wishes on both sides: talked of her very often for a week or so, and then, hearing no more, we concluded all was well so far; the whirl of London life swallowed us up, and the subject dropped out of our memories.

"It might have been February—no, I have the letter here, and it is dated 12th March—that my husband got the following from Mr. Kennedy, written in a feeble old man's hand, but carefully composed and spelt, as became one of the well-educated peasantry of the North; one, too, who though only a farmer, could count his forefathers for more generations than many an owner of a magnificent 'place.'

"'DEAR SIR,—I beg to return you my sincerest thanks for your unremitting kindness to my wife and daughter when in London: when they came home and told us, the whole family were delighted to hear of such kindness being shown them. Before Mrs. Kennedy came home, a friend got a paper made out in our favor, to prevent any thing being done against us: this friend was home in the boat along with Mrs. Kennedy, also officers from ——, to get us put out. I went in the morning to call upon the factor, and see if he had got the telegram from his lordship, but I could not see him, and I asked his clerk if he knew if he had got it, but he said he had heard no word about it. I told him the telegram was certain sent, for that Mrs. Kennedy saw the valet go to the telegraph office at Oxbridge with it. The officers came to the farm, but this friend of ours got them stopped. We learnt afterwards that the telegram had been misdirected, and so it went to another place, and did not reach the factor till too late. We have got no answer from his young lordship to the letter you was kind enough to help Mrs. Kennedy write. We have sold part of our sheep in order to get some better kind, as we have been hearing that it has been said we were turned out because our farm was not fully stocked; but the Order in Council about the cattle disease, preventing cattle being removed from one place to another, and the uncertain situation we are placed in, has hindered this being done. But if we get encouragement from his lordship, we will stock the farm, and get on as soon as possible. If you will be kindly pleased, say in your wisdom, if any thing can be done, and if we need to write his lordship any more till we hear from himself. I am, dear sir, your most obedient servant,

"'ANDREW KENNEDY.'

"On receipt of this letter, we all laid our heads together to consider what had best be done. The result was that Mr. Kennedy wrote a second letter to the young nobleman—sufficient, we thought, to have moved a heart of stone—and my husband got it forwarded immediately by what he believed to be even a surer channel than the first one had gone by. And, meantime, we made private inquiries as to what sort of young fellow he really was: and, I must confess, we heard nothing ill of him: nothing but faults of youth—which a few more years may mend, and cause him to grow up a man worthy of his important destiny; worthy of his ancestors and himself. Oh, that he may!—for many sakes besides his own,—this poor lad, left orphaned at a time a lad most needs a father's care, and pinnacled on a height where the bravest and steadiest could hardly walk without tottering.

"After sending this letter, for two months more we heard nothing from the Laighlands. Then came the following, headed by another date, which the minute I saw, I knew the poor old farmer's fate was decided:—

"'Fairbank Cottage, May 3d.

"'DEAR SIR,—I am sorry to say that we never received any letter from his lordship; and we had to submit to be ejected from our farm and home, so that we are now for a short time in a little cottage belonging to my brother, James Kennedy. I called upon the factor to-day, to see if he had any place for us now; but I got no encouragement. He had said the family could make us comfortable with another house if we left the Farm; but there is no word of that now. We would have written to you sooner, but Mrs. Kennedy has been so grieved in her mind, and she had no time to spare, being busy removing and packing up furniture until we get some home elsewhere. She still remembers the kindness shown her by you and your kind family, and bids me say she has a small box preparing with a few articles to send to Mrs. Burns, as a small token of her gratitude for the kindness shown her. You can let Mr. —— know how we have been used, and how the young lord forgot us in our distress. If his lordship would have given us a small lot of ground and a house, we should have taken it kind, though we lost our farm: and so we would now—but, in the way he forgot us, we have no encouragement to ask any other favor. I am, my dear sir, your sincere well-wisher, ANDREW KENNEDY.'

"That was all. No more complaints: no blame: no wild democratic outcry against the lord of the soil. The old man had been brought up to respect 'the powers that be,' and to submit, unmurmuring, in his stern, patient, unquestioning Presbyterian faith, to the ordering of Providence. Unto human injustice it is possible to submit too much: and yet there is a submission which is not merely wise, but heroic. I own, Mr. Kennedy's letter—in its brevity involving such a world of grief and loss, and that, too, at the close of life, when loss is quite irreparable—touched most deeply both my husband and myself. And —well, there lies before you Mrs. Kennedy's butter."

I tasted it, for the second time feeling "like to greet," but with a far deeper emotion than the mere remembrance of the lovely country about the Laighlands.

* * * * * * *

I should like to end this tale—a true tale, be it again understood—with the bright winding-up exacted by "poetical justice." I should like to state how—"better late than never"—his young lordship had recognized his responsibilities; and though the carelessly worded telegram did fail of its object, though the promised appointment was broken, and the humble entreating letters left unanswered, possibly even unread, still some good angel had brought the matter to the young man's memory, with favorable results for poor Kennedy's few remaining years. So that, though he could not be reinstated in his farm—nay (for let us hold the balance of justice fairly between poor and rich, the rich who are often in reality so painfully, humiliatingly, poor), although it might even be inevitable, for some recondite reason, that he should have been removed from it—still there was found for him that "little lot of ground" hard by somewhere, where the old man could live comfortably and content until the end of his days.

But nothing of this sort has happened, or seems likely to happen, so far as I know. I can only tell the story, and leave it; as we are obliged to leave so many things in this world—sad, unfinished; unable alike to see the reason of them, or the final settlement of them. Only there is One above us who sees all.

ELIZABETH AND VICTORIA.

FROM A WOMAN'S POINT OF VIEW.

"Uneasy lies the head that wears a crown."

WE women have a voice in the nation—let the men say what they will. Nor, I think, will any good man say aught unkind of it, or of us, so long as we take care to keep this voice what it should be—what God and nature meant it to be—low and sweet in their ears as the voice of Eve in Adam's; yet clear, firm, and never to be silenced or ignored, like the voice of conscience in their hearts. For the condition of a nation where it has ceased to speak and to be listened to—this soft utterance, appealing less to reason and expediency than to instinct and feeling—would be analogous to that of a strong, bold, active man, with every physical and mental power in full perfection; only—without a conscience.

It can do no harm to speak a little, in this said woman's voice, upon a subject which has been very much discussed of late, in newspapers, social circles, and, since it touches on family and fireside things, at almost every family fireside throughout the kingdom. We shall come to it by-and-by; but previously let me refer to two other subjects which drew my thoughts towards this one, and are, in fact, illustrations of it. The first was a book—the second a picture.

The book was Froude's history of the reign of Queen Elizabeth. What a wonderful history it is! Not written after the ancient pattern, viz., laying down the law: stating certain received facts, concerning which no evidence is either given or expected to be required. Such and such events happened—there is no doubt of it—every body believes it, dear reader, and so must you; thus and thus were people's actions, characters, and motives—we are quite sure of all, there is no room for either dispute or inquiry. This was the old style of writing history: but Froude does it on a totally different principle. He rarely gives any individual opinion, and as seldom makes any statement without proving it or making it prove itself. He does not trust to chance at all. He hunts out from every available source a series of well-authenticated data, which he lays clearly and impartially before you: and then leaves you to form your own conclusions. Sometimes in a few vivid touches—(witness the opening sentence of vol. i.: "The breath was scarcely out of Queen Mary's body," etc., etc.)—he gives you a picture of incidents or characters, interesting as a novel, and vivid as life; but, generally speaking, he allows them to make pictures for themselves on your mind. His part is to place before you, as perfectly and truthfully as he can, the people and the events of the period, which you then judge for yourself. If he assists your judgment by any personal bias of his own, it is concealed so artistically that you never discover it. And you become so deeply interested in these historical personages—these long-dead men and women, once so living and warm—that you scarcely think of the historian at all; which is the highest compliment you can pay him.

Most life-like among all these portraits—now reproduced almost in flesh and blood, after being mere historical shadows for three centuries—is the young Queen. Not as yet the Queen Elizabeth of our school-days, who cut off the heads of Mary Stuart, her cousin, and Essex, her supposed lover—(wicked lie!)—whose terrible death-bed scene fixed itself on our youthful imagination, as she lay raving on her palace floor, with her gray hair torn, and her three hundred dresses, stiff with jewels, all disregarded. Not this Elizabeth, but Elizabeth, still not much over twenty, the learned, accomplished, handsome princess—with qualities sufficient to exact personally the homage necessarily given to her station: acute, determined, liking to rule and quite capable of doing it: given to "indirect, crooked ways" and diplomatic deceits—rather, perhaps, from the excessive cleverness of her scheming brain than from any absolute untrueness of heart. For she had a heart—this poor Elizabeth—a heart as passionate, proud, capricious, artful, and yet sincere, as ever tormented a woman.

To students of human nature, there is hardly a more pathetic picture than England's favorite "virgin Queen"—Shakspeare's

> "Fair vestal, throned in the West,"

at whom throughout her long and glorious reign Cupid shot unheeded—

> "And the imperial votaress passed on
> In maiden meditation, fancy-free."

So the poet puts it; but history records, from undeniable evidence, that restless, solitary, unloved life—that miserable death. And the root of all, as we now know, was what is at the root of most women's characters and lives—love; her persistent, imprudent, and yet most pitiable attachment to Robert Dudley, Earl of Leicester. A passion which, however unworthy (that it was actually guilty, is impossible to believe), was yet deep and sincere enough to contrast strongly with the falseness, vanity, and ambition which made up the other half of her character: and which, in after days, combined with outward circumstances, brought her, from her youthhood of promise and brightness, to be that wretched, old, forlorn, and dying Queen, upon whom the sternest judge can not look without a certain compassion.

True, she had earned her fate, the inevitable fate of a woman who fixes her affections upon an unworthy man; she is dragged down to his level; or else, undeceived at last, she lives to unlove him and to despise him—happy for her if she does not at the same time, and by the same lamentable process, learn to despise and to deny love itself!

But, nevertheless, as Elizabeth passes from the scene, as her brilliant reign closes, and the curtain falls upon that busy, troublous, splendid, empty life of hers, wherein this combination of a man's brain and a woman's heart brought upon her the faults, weaknesses, and sufferings of both, and the happiness of neither—our strongest sensation towards her is absolute pity.

Glorious as the Elizabethan era was, we can not but draw a parallel between it and what we are now thankfully and proudly beginning to call "the Victorian Age." Alike they are in many points, especially in one—that in both the centre and nucleus is a regnant queen. Two queens, belonging to two as different types of womanhood as could well be found: yet both stamping their own individuality, not only on their personal court, but on the country at large. What strongly contrasted figures they will make in future history! Elizabeth, with her masculine intellect, and iron will, masculine also, yet often womanish in its fitfulness; her stately court, all etiquette and outside show; and the utter blank of her domestic life, a hollow crater wherein burnt fiercely the ashes of one consuming passion, which first conscience and then ambition forbade should ever become holy, peaceful, wedded love;—Victoria, gifted only with moderate talent, who if not born a queen might have been much like an ordinary gentlewoman; refined, accomplished, sensible, and good: in every thing essentially womanly, and carrying in her bosom through life a woman's best amulet, the power of giving and of winning affection. Loving and fortunate in her love; a happy daughter, wife, mother—ay, and happy widow, to whom even the memory of her dead is a crown of honor; for it was a love wise and worthy, and lasting until death. And this brings me to the picture I spoke of, which contrasted so vividly with the imaginary picture I had formed of Queen Elizabeth—Froude's Elizabeth.

It is a very small thing, only one of the studies for an unfinished painting. A mere sketch in crayons, and with nothing either tragic, dramatic, or even picturesque about it: simply the portrait of a woman, no longer young, and who even in her youth could never have been beautiful. One of those faces, the most trying to artists and most unsatisfactory to friends, in which the principal charm lies in expression, and that expression so fleeting and variable that it is almost impossible to catch. But here, by a rare chance, this is done: and the imperfect outside forms are idealized by a certain spiritual grace, which in these sort of faces is continually seen; the momentary outward shining of the inward light, which friends recognize, strangers never.

Yet it is not a plain face. The features are delicate, with a clear cut nose, finely formed brow, and honest eyes, but with a soft, sad droop of the mouth, round which touching wrinkles are already forming—nay formed. The hair, which looks as if it were slightly gray, is put back under a widow's cap, and round the throat is a neat close widow's collar. But it needed no dress to indicate one of those who are "widows indeed."

In spite of this excessive simplicity, there is an inexpressible benignity and sweetness about the face. A something better than beauty; a quiet motherliness, a composed sorrow—sorrow not succumbed to, but struggled with, as only a woman can struggle. Yes, that is the heart of the portrait,—its exceeding womanliness. It is the sort of portrait which, whether met with over a family hearth, or on an Academy wall, you would involuntarily stop before, and say: "I am *sure* that is a good woman, one whom I should like to know and make a friend of." But you can not, dear reader, for she happens to be Victoria, by the Grace of God, Queen of Great Britain and Ireland; placed by her high estate above all friendships, and all equal bonds of every sort, except one, which it has pleased Heaven now to remove from her forever.

This picture, and Froude's book, I take in connection with that subject on which the entire country is now talking—a certain paragraph in the *Times.* Every body has read it: but I re-copy it, for it is one of those bits of human nature which spring up here and there in the arid deserts of courtly formalities and State history, touching —and they ought to touch—the whole heart of a nation:

THE QUEEN.

The following communicated article appeared in the *Times* of Wednesday:—

"An erroneous idea seems generally to prevail, and has latterly found frequent expression in the newspapers, that the Queen is about to resume the place in society which she occupied before her great affliction; that is, that she is about again to hold levees and drawing-rooms in person, and to appear as before at court balls, concerts, etc. This idea can not be too explicitly contradicted.

"The Queen heartily appreciates the desire of her subjects to see her, and whatever she can do to gratify them in this loyal and affectionate wish she will do. Whenever any real object is to be attained by her appearing on public occasions, any national interest to be promoted, or any thing to be encouraged which is for the good of her people, her Majesty will not shrink, as she has not shrunk, from any personal sacrifice or exertion, however painful.

"But there are other and higher duties than those of a mere representation which are now thrown upon the Queen, alone and unassisted—duties which she can not neglect without injury to the public service, which weigh unceasingly upon her, overwhelming her with work and anxiety.

"The Queen has labored conscientiously to discharge these duties till her health and strength, already shaken by the utter and ever-abiding desolation which has taken the place of her former happiness, have been seriously impaired.

"To call upon her to undergo, in addition, the fatigue of those mere State ceremonies, which can be equally well performed by other members of her family, is to ask her to run the risk of entirely disabling herself for the discharge of those other duties which can not be neglected without serious injury to the public interests.

"The Queen will, however, do what she can—in a manner least trying to her health, strength, and spirits—to meet the loyal wishes of her subjects; to afford that support and countenance to society, and to give that encouragement to trade which is desired of her.

"More the Queen *can not* do; and more the kindness and good feeling of her people will surely not exact from her."

Strange and touching words! Here is the highest, loneliest woman in the land, appealing, with a sad gentleness, to the sympathy of her people. Pleading, without State reserve, and with a pathetic simplicity that feels no shame to confess either love or grief, her "former happiness," her "ever-abiding desolation." Nevertheless, she "will do what she can." Surely there is not a man in the nation, a real man, father, husband, or brother, who would not respond loyally to such an appeal?

And yet there have been many hard things said of her, this Queen of ours, in speech or print, and especially by men; words which, if spoken of any other woman, a widow too, her "next friend" would have been justified in fiercely resenting. But she, in her splendid isolation, has no next friend. She has to take the unprecedented step of writing a letter—for in point of fact it is that—through the *Times* newspaper to her people.

There are people who doubt the wisdom of this—people who regard royalty as a mere State machine, to which forms are indispensable. They could hardly imagine a queen without a crown on her head and a sceptre in her hand, making due public appearances, and fulfilling to the last iota all ceremonial observances. They require, in this as in all else, not merely the thing itself, but the outward demonstration of it, almost at any personal cost. And in a sense, they are right. Such persons are always to be esteemed, for they are very conscientious. They keep society safe and smooth, and contribute greatly to maintain that fair conservatism without which it would soon crumble away into anarchy, disorder, and misrule. And they are very loyal too. It is in sad and sore earnestness that they believe the Queen, in giving up State etiquette, is perilling the life of the nation.

But they forget one thing—that the life of a nation is not its ceremonial but its moral life, to which such a letter as this, out-spoken, honest, and free, from the Sovereign to the people, contributes more than the holding of a hundred drawing-rooms. And why? Because it is a true thing, a real thing. Because it sets forth, the more strongly because unconsciously, the fact that womanhood is higher than queendom. Even though never a queen did the like before, it is well done in this our Queen—loved and honored as such for twenty-seven years—to have the courage to stand forward, quite by herself, and in her own identity, without intervention of ministers, or councillors, or parliament, and say to the country, "I am only a woman, I have lost my husband, my one love of all my life; my heart is broken, but I will try to do my duty. Ask of me no shows or shams, and I will try to fulfill all that is real and necessary. 'The Queen will do what she can.'"

Surely, when we consider what courts are, what queens are, and what they have been in our own past history and that of foreign countries, there is in the simple sincerity of this letter, with its open recognition of two things, only too much ignored—the reality of love, the reality of grief—an influence which can not fail to affect strongly our own and other nations. It is the woman's voice, speaking, neither loudly nor dictatorially, but with that sweet humility which is the best persuasion.

But still a word may be said on the other side, and it should be said, with very great earnestness.

There is something in our strong, reserved Saxon nature which recoils exceedingly from much outward demonstration of grief—indeed of every kind of emotion. We do not beat our breasts or tear our hair. We follow our best beloved to the grave in composed silence. We neither hang *immortelles* on their tombs, nor wreathe their memorial busts with flowers. Not that we condemn these things, only they are not our way. After any great affliction we rarely speak much about it, but as soon as possible go back to our ordinary habits, and let the smooth surface of daily existence close over the cruel wound. We bury our dead in our hearts; there they soon arise and live, and live forever. And we believe it is best so.

It would make us only the more tender over her, our widowed Queen, if she would try as much as possible to remember this. Englishmen would esteem her all the more for making her sorrow a silent sorrow. And English women, so many of whom are also widows, or childless, or solitary and forlorn, would like to see her suppress, in every suitable way, all outward tokens of suffering. We suffer too, and are obliged to bear it; we can not mourn externally, at least not for long; some of us, after the very briefest season of that death-like passiveness which nature itself allows to a great sorrow, have to rise up again and resume our daily burden, fulfilling unremittingly, and at any personal sacrifice, all the duties of our station, be it low or high.

We are compelled to do this: and we should love her all the better, and revere her all the more, if, so far as she can, our Mistress, God bless her! would do the same. He would have done it—the husband, whose highest praise it is that all his virtues were so silent; and who, for this very reason, has been taken into the deepest core of the strong, silent, British heart. For his sake we ask this, and for the upholding after his death, as during his life, of that truth which *we* know to be true—that as men are what women make them, so women are what men make them; that every one of us grows more or less after the pattern of the man we love. In his name, therefore, who was so perfect a man, we would appeal to our Queen, as honestly as she appeals to us, that she should do her best to overcome her grief, and to rejoice in the many comforts that are left her. We would cry to her as with one voice—the echo of her own—"Be strong! You do but love as we love, suffer as we suffer. We understand it all, but still we ask you to bear it. Live through it, as many of us have done, expending wholly for others the life which is no longer sweet to ourselves: until there comes a time, when it pleases God to send you the peace which is securer than joy, the blessedness which is better than happiness." In words which —to so truly religious a woman—must be far more precious than any words of ours, "Be strong, and He shall comfort thine heart. Put thou thy trust in the Lord."

A WOMAN'S BOOK.

"WHAT!" lately said a certain young American, entering a London bookseller's shop, and laying his hand, a little contemptuously, on a newly-published volume—simple enough to look at, having on its plain green binding neither coronets nor coats-of-arms—nothing but a monogram, "V.A."—the entwined initials which we English used to see familiarly everywhere for so many years, and now see only there—"What! do you call that a Queen's book?"

"No," replied the bookseller, with an honest dignity, "we call it *a woman's book.*"

And this is the true way in which to look at them, both the present and the previous volume, which go by the name of "the Queen's books," as if her Majesty were trying to place herself among the ranks—sparse and small—of royal authors. Not at all. The very name—"royal author"—is a double misnomer, especially with regard to the second work. The worthy bookseller—we would it were fair to give his honest name—was quite right. "Leaves from the Journal of our Life in the Highlands" is essentially a woman's book. There is little of "the Queen," and almost nothing of "the author" in it. They who look for either, but especially the last, will assuredly be disappointed—as disappointed as they might be, and would deserve to be, if in reading the home-letters of their wives and daughters they expected to find them *Saturday Review* essays or *Times* leading articles. Such a thing is not likely, nor would it redound much to the credit of the wife or daughter, if instead of being a simple woman, writing her natural home-letter, just as will please them all at home, she were to soar into grand literary composition, compiled, as some celebrated authors do their most familiar epistles—with an eye to posterity.

This, our Queen's book, is, in a sense, no book at all—only a letter. A General Epistle, as it were—addressed to all her people, who in some things have rather misunderstood and wronged her of late—opening to them her whole heart, and appealing to their good hearts to try and understand the depth of her sorrow by measuring it with what she now reveals to them of the high perfection of her vanished joy. This utter candor—this wonderful absence of reticence, under circumstances when a nature so womanly would ordinarily grow reticent in the extreme—is of itself the strongest testimony in favor of the book, and the advisability, nay, necessity, of publishing it. Another woman has said, speaking of grief:—

> "Judge the length of the sword by the sheath's,
> By the silence of life, more pathetic than death's;"

and so it usually is. But our Queen was in perfectly exceptional circumstances. She could not keep silence; her position did not allow it: and this was the only way in which she could speak.

It was becoming high time she should speak. The dissatisfied half of the nation was already murmuring against her bitter and unjust things. And here, in their climax of dissatisfaction, appears this book, proving by its straightforward unconscious evidence—circumstantial evidence, the strongest of all—that every disloyal allegation was inherently and ludicrously false. That, so far from being absorbed in a morbid selfish sorrow, there is probably not a woman in the three kingdoms more utterly unselfish, or freer from that most unpleasant form of egotism, self-consciousness, than herself. That she is also a busy woman—fulfilling her many duties, harder than any of us know, with earnest conscientiousness; a wise woman—ordering her household and family, and acquainted with all that happens therein; an affectionate woman—beloved by, and cordially appreciating every worthy servant of the crown, from the great Duke of Wellington to the Highland gillie who runs along by her pony's side. That instead of rejecting her people's love, and being careless of their sympathy, she is touchingly, sensitively eager for both.

There is nothing worse for a nation than the habit of carping at its rulers; of slandering and backbiting; "speaking evil of dignities," merely because they are dignities; of being ever ready to carry from mouth to mouth defamatory or ludicrous stories. Now, as our widowed Lady passes on her lonely way, surely the silliest, wickedest tongue will be ashamed to wag about her any more.

Though neither of these books can be rated high as literary productions, nor judged by the strict canons of the art of authorship, they are in one sense remarkable contributions to literature, and especially to historic literature. What would we not give for a dozen pages of such fragments out of the reign of Queen Elizabeth, or any other English sovereign! Two hundred years to come how valuable they will be! Even now it is curious to read them—and think how they will be read by posterity.

But they have an interest and value of their own already. However we may gossip about it, and try to pry into it, we middle classes know very little of the inner life of royalty. We have still in our secret hearts a dim suspicion that if

"Uneasy lies the head that wears a crown"—

it must be because her Majesty is in the habit of sleeping in it—and that had we the honor of meeting her in private life, she would certainly carry a golden sceptre instead of a common parasol or umbrella. In fact our ideas are very misty about court life altogether. We do not fall before it on our bended knees, as we did in the time of the Georges, when Sunday after Sunday a loyal adoring crowd followed down the slopes of Windsor that good, jolly, farmerlike man, his plain, prim wife, and their tribe of commonplace sons and daughters. Nor do we, as a staunch Tory once observed, "revere the crown though it hung upon a bush." We have ceased to believe in the divine right of kings; but we believe all the more earnestly, as perhaps no generation ever did before, in the divine right of all humanity.

And this is what makes these books so valuable in themselves, and likely to do so much good—they are intensely human, especially the last one.

To begin from the outside—the widest circle of interest before it narrows down to the pure, fine point of conjugal and parental love, the central star of the whole. For twenty years we had been accustomed to read in journals, and brief court circulars, and lengthy articles by "Our

Own Correspondent," of the Queen's progresses, entertainments, ceremonials; ponderous accounts of the crowds, the processions, etc.; and minor details, whenever they could be gleaned, of the royal personages, their looks, sayings, and doings—notably few, and generally rather apocryphal. Now, after this long interval we see the picture from the other side.

Take, for instance, her Majesty's account of what was a vivid public interest at the time—the first royal visit to Scotland.

Now many Edinburgh people will remember the incidents of that landing—how there was some unfortunate hitch in the ceremonial, causing much trouble and confusion, and bringing a shower of abuse and quizzing and disparaging criticism upon the luckless bailie whose fault it was. But not a word of this does the gentle diarist record. She sees only the pleasantness and the loyalty. And when, at last, these two young people—we must remember they were young people, not above a year or two married, and dearly loving each other's society—escape, "feeling dreadfully tired and giddy," from the endless ceremonial of welcome, to reappear in an hour or two after, as the cynosures of a large dinner-party, there is still not a word of complaint; only "every body was very kind and civil." Perhaps one of the most touching things in the book is the half-surprised gratefulness—actual gratefulness—with which this simple-natured, high-hearted woman, accidentally born a queen, takes every demonstration of royalty.

Again, it may be good for the many lady-grumblers, "bored" or "worn to death" by their burdensome and mostly self-imposed social duties, as they call them, to read the story of two days during her Majesty's visit to Dublin, on a tour supposed to be a tour of "enjoyment:"—

"*Wednesday, August* 8.—At twenty minutes to one o'clock we left for Dublin, I and all the ladies in evening dresses, all the gentlemen in uniform. We drove straight to the Castle. Every thing here as at St. James's Levée—the staircase and throne-room quite like a palace. I received (on the throne) the addresses of the Lord Mayor and Corporation, the University, the Archbishop and Bishops, both Roman Catholic and Anglican, the Presbyterians, the non-subscribing Presbyterians, and the Quakers. They also presented Albert with addresses. Then followed a very long levée, which lasted without intermission till twenty minutes to six o'clock! Two thousand people were presented.

"*Thursday, August* 9.—There was a great and brilliant review in the Phœnix Park—six thousand one hundred and sixty men, including the Constabulary. In the evening we two dined alone, and at half-past eight o'clock drove into Dublin for the drawing-room. It is always held here of an evening. I should think, between two and three thousand people passed before us, and one thousand six hundred ladies were presented. After it was over, we walked through St. Patrick's Hall, and the other rooms; and the crowd was very great. We came back to the Phœnix Park at half-past twelve, the streets still densely crowded. The city was illuminated."

Verily the poor young Queen was a hard-worked woman.

It is an open question how far the abolition of even cumbrous and vexatious state ceremonials is desirable. They are a link with the past—an inferior past, may be, to our present: for it is a mistake to suppose that parents are necessarily wiser than their children; often quite the contrary. Still, as we advance in life, we cling tenderly to old things simply because they are old. The pomps and splendors of stately royalty are not to be despised, being the outward and visible sign of a much higher reality. Thus there is some justice in the grumblings of those good "auld-farrant" souls who mourn over the annihilation of the Lord Mayor's Show—or the eight cream-colored Hanoverian horses, "eating their heads off," unseen, from year to year, in the royal stables; and especially the unworn royal robes, thrown ignominiously over the back of a chair. Mere forms these things may be, child's play, transmitted to us from barbaric ages, when the national eye loved to be dazzled with outside show, and very irksome they must have been to those engaged therein. Still, we all have to go through a good deal for the benefit of society. And royalty has its duties, too, even ceremonial duties, from which it can not escape without perilling a little of the patient self-denying dignity, which adds lustre to any throne. The crown may be more or less thorny than one of our every-day bonnets: but we are apt to forget that while we wear only this bonnet, one queenly head wears not merely the ordinary matron-coif (alas, the widow's cap now!) but *also* the crown.

These "Leaves" ought to serve as an admonishment to authors in general and travelling authors in particular, of the graphic effects produced by extreme simplicity; that we have only to go to Nature, and reproduce her faithfully, and as Ruskin would say "lovingly," in order to arrive at results more telling than the most labored art. Little thought the royal journalist, setting down in the simplest language her "visits to the old women," that she was furnishing a subject which the hand of a future Sterne, Wilkie, or Wordsworth may do into endless poems and pictures for the benefit of posterity. Undoubtedly the last thing her Majesty thought of was painting her own portrait; yet she has done it, and in colors vivid and true beyond the touch of time to efface. Therein the most prominent characteristic is the one already noticed—the very last we would expect in a queen—an absence of self-consciousness; in fact, a total abnegation of self so pathetic as to be often almost sublime. There follows, as a natural consequence, an unlimited sympathy with other people. From the highest to the lowest every one seems to have a place, small or large, in this warm heart—this tenacious and accurate memory. Even persons casually met, such as "Mr. Taylor, mineral agent to the Duchy of Cornwall, a very intelligent young man, married to a niece of Sir Charles Lemon's;" "Mr. Fox, a Quaker, who lives at Falmouth, and has sent us flowers, fruits, and many other things," will feel something better than mere curiosity in seeing themselves thus remembered.

Besides her friends, the Queen seems to exercise a peculiar care over her servants. It should be a sharp example to those fine ladies among the middle classes who treat their domestics as automatons or slaves, and then complain that good servants are impossible,—to see what a thoroughly feudal relationship seems to subsist between the highest lady in the realm and *her* servants. "Jane Shackle," "the good Grant," Brown, "handy and willing to do every thing and any thing, and to overcome every difficulty, which makes him one of my best servants anywhere;" nay, even "poor Batterbury," the English groom at Balmoral, of whom his mistress relates, with a gentle drollery, that "he followed me about in his ordinary dress, torn boots and gaiters, and seemed any thing but happy"—all share the same kindly remembrance. Indeed it is touching in going through the book to mark note after note respecting these and other faithful servants, and, incidentally, what has been done for them by her Majesty or the Prince Consort in acknowledgment of their fidelity.

Another lesson this book unconsciously teaches—indifference to personal luxury. No one can read of the Queen's life in the Highlands without feeling that what she and her husband enjoyed most in it was its excessive simplicity—at times almost amounting to hardship. And when one thinks of the *blasé*, grumbling, self-indulgent tourists who go about the beautiful world, seeing nothing in it, or only things to complain of—the picture of this young Queen and Prince cheerily enjoying their mutual journeyings, making the best of every thing, always ready to be grateful and pleased with what was done for them and shown to them, and, best of all, always content with what was their stronghold of happiness—their own companionship and that of their children—this, though a picture now mournfully curtained over, is yet a bit of Arcadia which will remain for generations.

No pure happiness ever dies, or becomes any thing but happiness. The sharp sense of loss may darken it for a time, but can never wholly annihilate it. Days may come—from the evidence of this book the nation affectionately trusts they are coming now—when the mother of her people may feel that the noblest tribute to him whom we shall forever venerate as

"The silent father of our kings to be,"

is for her to assume in its utmost responsibility that regal motherhood; to show herself just as she is, in her sacred sorrow as in her youthful bliss, unto her myriad children; every one of whom holds out to her—not unmingled with few contrite tears—earnestly-longing, reverent arms. She has opened her heart, and confided herself to the heart of the nation; it acknowledges and respects the trust, and will ever be faithful to it.

What further need be said? if indeed there was need to say any thing, when by this date the book will have been read universally wherever English is spoken throughout the wide proportion of the earth's surface which owns as sovereign and queen, this—woman. Mere *woman;* she could not have a higher or better title; it will last her longer than her crown.

One word more—which we are sure the royal lady would be the last to wish left unsaid—even though the interest of the work itself a little blinds one to that of the preface which introduces it. In a most difficult and delicate position, as a gentleman and an author advising a *not* literary lady; as a subject giving both wise counsel and valuable assistance to a sovereign, Mr. Arthur Helps, in his own manly, simple, independent fashion, has done exactly what he ought to have done, and said exactly what he ought to say.

THE AGE OF GOLD.

BUT not that precious metal with a queen's head upon it, which you, O anxious-eyed Paterfamilias, shovel up on a copper scoop from the Bank counter; or you, bare-armed and be-jewelled Materfamilias, stop to fasten somewhere about your elegant evening dress, in passing from your nursery-door to your carriage. The gold here referred to is none of yours. You have forgotten you ever had it, or maybe you never had it at all; for it does not fall to the lot of every one, even in childhood. But your little, quiet, pale-cheeked boy, crouching in a window-seat with his knees up to his chin, and a book upon them; or your bright-eyed, clever girl, the Dinarzade of the nursery, sitting in the gloaming with the little ones round her, spinning "stories" without end: they know all about it. They are in the very midst of the treasure: it lies about them in ungathered heaps; morning, noon, and night. They eat of it, drink of it, wear it, play with it; it is their own rightful property in fee and entail—and as such will descend through generations to the last child that ever is to be born upon this earth. A possession in one sense unalienable; for though it, and the very memory of it, may fade—the influence which it has unconsciously exercised remains, and remains forever. Every good thought and noble act of after life may, nay must, have originated in the Age of Gold.

By that phrase is not implied the age of innocence. Much poetic nonsense is talked concerning the "innocence" of children. Taking a sober, candid revision of our own childhood, or that of our "co-mates and brothers in exile," still left on pilgrimage beside us, and therefore not exalted as we are fain to exalt into angelic perfection those children who remain children always—few of us can remember being very good or very happy in those early days. Most of us, we confess—or rather, we hope—were a great deal naughtier then than we are now. Otherwise, what would have been the use of our remaining on probation here? we should have assumed our wings, and mounted direct to paradise.

But we were any thing but infantile angels, and we know it. We recall with contrition our affectations, conceits, jealousies, selfishness, meannesses—not to count those fierce angers and revenges—excusable, perhaps in degree inevitable, when the blood is hot, and quick, and young. Nor do we remember being so very happy. Then, as now—nay, far more, thank Heaven, then, than now—did we

"Look before and after,
And pine for what is not:
Our sincerest laughter
With some pain was fraught;"

—pain, sharpened by the fact that it was new and incomprehensible; that we either fought furiously against it, as an injustice and a wrong, or hugged it to our hearts with a kind of morbid pleasure; thereby laying the foundation of that diseased state of mind, which out of an over-sensitive child, makes a nervous, fretful, useless woman, or a discontented, egotistic, miserable man.

Surely, considering how vividly all impressions must come to a child, a being so new to this world, and how the balance of mental sensations and emotions must necessarily be as undecided and untrue as that of the physical powers, the happiness of childhood becomes almost as doubtful as its innocence. We believe in neither. And yet we believe, solemnly, pathetically, thankfully, in the Age of Gold.

It does not, as was said before, come to all children. Human beings are not—though many good deluded people, try to make them—all of one mould and one pattern: to be reared in shoals, like tadpoles, each with the prescribed head, body, and tail, out of which it is to emerge into a uniform maturity of perfect froggism. Not so. Apparently, Omniscient Wisdom, at least in us, His immortal creatures, wishes to combine infinite unity with infinite variety—a law we can not too early recognize, especially concerning children.

Thus the boy being "father to the man," possesses even in babyhood the germ of that individuality which is to distinguish him from other men. We can not conceive Benjamin Franklin, that prince of practicality, with his immemorial recipe, "Honesty is *the best policy;*" or that "Successful Merchant" who began his career with buying a lollipop for a penny, and selling it for twopence—we can not, I say, imagine these notable characters ever to have had an age of gold. They would probably deny that there was such a thing. And yet it is the truth, just like first love or boyish friendship, or many another thing that some of us grow out of and live to laugh at; until possibly in old age it may rise up and stare us in the face as the one reality of our existence. However the fashion of them may alter and pass away, woe be to us, if we have been false to the dreams of our youth! ay, or of our childhood either; and should come to despise or offend one of these little ones, delighting itself in the impossible happiness, indescribable lovelinesses, and never-to-be attained virtues, that constitute its age of gold.

This age, and the sort of children who enjoy it, may be indicated by one word, Imagination,—that strange faculty which rationalistic philosophers present as the solution of many difficult problems, but yet which is itself the greatest problem of all. What is it—this power, which enables the human mind to *create?* not merely to put together certain known facts or materials, and derive therefrom certain conclusions or results—but to originate, to make something out of nothing, to transform intangible fancies into credible or at least credited realities? To which question the answer is probably as difficult as it must be for the conscientious atheist—and there is such a thing—to explain away by logical induction, how it was that the first idea of a Divine Being (granted any sort of God, Hebraic, heathen, or Brahminical), ever entered into the mind of any being merely human, and subject to all the laws and accidents of change, decay, and death.

Curious, wonderful, almost awful, is it to watch and investigate this faculty of Imagination, the first to be developed in nearly every child, and lasting during the whole period of infancy and adolescence; either passively, in the universal delight with which, from the earliest dawn of intelligence, a child listens to "a 'tory"—or actively, when it begins to invent one for itself. What astonishing historiettes result!—queer mingling of the real and the ideal, till you hardly know whether it would be wiser to smile at the eccentric fancy and brilliant invention of the prattler at your knee, or gravely to admonish it for "lying." There are many children of vivid imagination, who, even to themselves, can hardly distinguish between what they see and what they invent, and have to be taught, by hard and patient lessons, the difference between truth and falsehood. For instance, a little fellow I knew, scarcely past the lisping age, used day after day and week after week to relate to mother and nurse continuous biographies of his "brother William," and a certain "Crocus bold" (both equally fabulous characters); how he used to meet them on the sea-shore, and go sailing with them—how "the Crocus bold" fell out of the boat, and "my brother William" jumped overboard and fished him up again; and how they two lived together in a bay—a real bay—and "sold lobsters," etc., etc. Amidst all the laughter created by this story, told with the gravest countenance by the young relater, who was exceedingly displeased if you doubted his veracity for a moment—it produced an uneasy sensation, not unlike what one would feel in listening to a monomaniac, who tells you earnestly how he

"Sees a face you can not see,"—

though perhaps it is, he avers, looking over your shoulder at this very time. Or, rather, one listened to it with the sense of curious bewilderment with which one hears the statement of a modern Spiritualist, probably in all respects but this a very sensible, rational person, who relates "communications," as lengthy as they are ludicrous, from the invisible world; informs you, and expects you to believe, that he has seen spirit-wreaths moved from head to head by spirit-hands, and felt soft dead-cold fingers clasping his under his respectable dining-table. You can not deny those things, without accusing good people of voluntary mendacity: you have, therefore, no resource but to set it all down to "the force of imagination."

But what is imagination?—None of us on this side immortality are ever likely to be able satisfactorily to answer that question.

It remains, therefore, only for us humbly to accept the manifold developments of this faculty, the nature and causes of which we can never demonstrate. We can but use it as we are meant to use all our faculties—reverently, judiciously, cautiously. And as to those who are given to our charge—those helpless little ones, who, so far as we see, will owe it *to us* whether they grow up to be, unto themselves and society, a blessing or a curse—we can but attempt wisely to guide that which we have no power either to annihilate or to repress.

A few serious thoughts of this kind, consequent on going through a course of what may be termed Infantile Imaginative Literature, resulted in the present paper, which, however, only offers the merest and vaguest suggestions on a subject daily becoming more important—viz., the character, tone, and matter, most suitable for children's books.

On this question there is one wide split between "the parents of England." We find them divided into realists and idealists—the one faction going the whole length of fairy tales, "Arabian Nights," etc. etc.,—the other protesting that no book which is not strictly and absolutely true should ever be placed in a child's hands. To argue this question would be idle; though it may be just hinted in passing that we have the Highest authority for the presentation of truth through fiction, and that the fiercest realist would hardly venture to accuse the Divine Relator of the Gospel parables of *lying*.

Let us grant, then, that imagination is a child's natural birthright, its strongest tendency, its keenest enjoyment. No person will doubt this who has ever been told or heard of any sort of tale, from the most ordinary reproduction of ordinary infant life—"There was a little boy and he had a garden"—to one of those wildly improbable romances about fairies and genii, and what not—winding and unwinding, without connection or plot, the most confused succession of events and characters, and combining all that the child has ever read or heard of with original ideas of the most extraordinary kind, of which you wonder how they ever got into its head at all! And all the while the wide-open eyes are fixed on yours, and the grave little voice goes on with a quiet conviction of its own veracity, which at times perfectly staggers you. You can not help feeling, though you may be the mother who bore it, that there is something in the creature which you can not understand, something above you and beyond you, which tells you that this little one, created of your flesh, is yet a separate existence, immortal, with all the needs, instincts, and responsibilities of mortally-invested immortality. How awful this makes *your* responsibilities, is there any need to urge?

So, in swift and sure succession, like heirs coming into their inheritance, do individuals out of all generations enjoy the age of gold; some of us entering upon it so early that we never remember the time when it was not ours. All the personages in the Arabian Nights, and in the classic old fairy-tales, together with Lemuel Gulliver, Robinson Crusoe, and a few more, seem to have been with us, and to have gone along with us during all our childhood, co-existent companions, as real as any of our living playmates, most of whom have now become as unreal characters as they.

And yet it is curious, in thus attempting to analyze our old selves, to find what a duality of nature there was in us, and what a distinctly double world we lived in; half of it being composed of strong realities—breakfasts, dinners, suppers, school, play, and bed-time,—wherein we fed and quarrelled, hated spelling and adored mince-pies, with true animal intensity: while the other half was a region of pure imagination, in which we roamed and revelled, unfettered by any moral consciousness, or indeed any mundane necessities whatsoever. How the seven brothers were turned into swans, and the white cat into a princess; whether it was right of Puss-in-boots to tell such atrocious falsehoods about "my Lord, the Marquis of Carabas;" and for young Hop-o'-my-thumb to cause that simple-minded Ogre to commit unintentional suicide by the delicious deception of the leathern bag and the hasty pudding—were questions that never troubled us. We believed it all—that is, our fancy did; and fancy alone is the first shape assumed by that strange quality which we here term Imagination.

This fact may serve as a hint to those who write for children. All a child wants, at first, is "a story:" about good or bad people matters not,—whether with or without a moral, 'tis all the same. Every impression must be conveyed in the broadest coloring and simplest outline. The young mind instinctively refuses to perplex itself with nice distinctions of right and wrong. Brave little Jack attacking the cruel giants, Cinderella's unkind sisters punished by seeing her exaltation, and, in fact, the general tenor of old-fashioned fairy-lore, where all the bad people die miserably, and all the good people marry kings and queens, and live very happy to the end of their days, furnish as much moral teaching as can well be taken in at the age of six or seven. And the intellectual, like the physical appetite, is not a bad indication of its own capacity of digestion.

Therefore, we can not help suggesting that there may be some little mistake in the flood of moral and religious literature with which our hapless infants are now overwhelmed: where every incident is "usefully applied," and the virtuous and the wicked walk about carefully labelled, "this is good," "this is bad:" so that no child can possibly mistake one for the other. And, without wishing to blame a very well-meaning class of educators, it may fairly be questioned how far it is wholesome to paint children going about converting their fathers and mothers, and youthful saints of three and a half prating confidently about things which, we are told, "the angels themselves desire to look into," yet can not, or dare not. We honestly confess that we should very much prefer "Jack the Giant-killer."

However, in spite of all these modern instructors of youth, we delight to find the old non-moral—let us not say immoral—literature still flourishing. Witness a one-volume family edition of the "Arabian Nights," illustrated by W. Harvey; and a still more charming volume, adorned by even better artists—to wit, Absolon, Harrison Weir, etc.—who, undisdaining, have taken our ancient friends Mother Hubbard, Little Bo-peep, Poor Cock Robin, the Babes in the Wood, etc.; with prose favorites, the two heroic Jacks of glorious memory, Cinderella, Whittington, Goody Two-shoes, and Tom Thumb; also the modern Three Bears and Andersen's Leaden Soldier; and pictured them all with a poetic feeling and a true high-art fidelity to nature which can not be too highly praised. No child in the three kingdoms could have a better birthday present than this pretty book. Or, another, the "Children's Pilgrim's Progress." An allegory out of which centuries of older Christians have drawn more truth and consolation than out of any book, except the Holy Bible. But to children it is, and ought to be, merely "a story." These, to whom the perplexities of doctrine must be wholly unintelligible, may yet receive Christian and Faithful, the Slough of Despond and the Celestial City, as ideal pictures—first strongly impressed on the fancy as pictures only; to be afterwards vivified with that glorious reality—that truth of God, with which He inspired old John Bunyan; which makes children of a larger growth read, with tears in their eyes, and a yearning unutterable at their hearts—of the "burthen" which fell from Christian at the foot of the cross: of the Shining Ones, who walked in the Land of Beulah; of the river which was "very deep;" of the city which "shone like the sun."

In a child's book no "preaching" should be admissible. The moral of it should always be left to speak for itself, for the silent truth-telling of fiction is one of the strongest agencies that can be set to work upon the human mind, at any age. I could speak of a precocious little damsel, who, put in charge of a younger child, was made a miserable martyr—being waked regularly at four A.M. by the obstreperous infant to "tell stories." She told them—and remonstrated, begged to be allowed to sleep, and was roused up again—till at last it struck her that, entreaties being wasted, she would weave the moral—"selfishness" —into her tale! How she managed it, memory fails to recall; but it so subdued her young tyrant, that in the dim light of the dawn repentant arms were thrown round the narrator's neck, with an earnest promise "to be a good little girl, and not tease you any more;" which promise was faithfully kept. The twelve-year-old story-teller has "preached" through a good many three-volume novels since, and the small listener, if still alive, is probably a comely mistress of a family, with

> "Twa weans at her apron and ane at her knee."

—but this true incident may suggest to both mothers and tale-writers for children how much power they have to teach, if they take care that their lessons be conveyed, as life's lessons invariably are, by implication rather than direct admonition.

As an instance where this is done, and well done, we may give "Princess Ilse," a German translation;—by-the-by, there needs an earnest protest against the injustice of putting only the translator's name, and not the author's. It is a charming specimen of this kind of legendary allegory: the outward design being worked out with true poetic unity of detail, and the under meaning conveyed with such clearness, that even a child could hardly miss it.

"Princess Ilse" is a personification of the stream so named, which we conclude to be a real river in the Hartz mountains. She is first presented as "a youthful streamlet, wrapped in a white veil, lying on the ground and weeping bitterly," on an Alpine summit, whence she had refused to descend, after the Deluge, to the "green bed" prepared for her by the angel of her course.

"'Poor child,' said the good Angel; 'why are you remaining here all alone on the rugged mountains? Are all the others gone, and none remembered to take you with them?'

"The little Ilse, however, tossed her head quite saucily, and said, 'I am not forgotten. Old Weser waited long enough, calling and making me signs to go with him; and both Ecker and Ocker tried to seize me. But I did not choose to go; nothing would induce me; I would rather perish here. Was I to descend into the valley, and traverse the plain like a common brook for menial service, to slake the thirst of cows and sheep, and to wash their plebeian feet?—I, the Princess Ilse! Look at me, and see if I am not of a noble race! A ray of light was my father, and the clear air my mother; my brother is the diamond, the dewy pearl in a rose my beloved little sister. The billows of the Deluge bore me high aloft: I played on the snowy summits of the most lofty mountains, and the first ray of sunshine which broke through the clouds embroidered my dress with glittering spangles. I am a Princess of the purest water, and I really can not descend into the valley! I therefore preferred hiding myself, and pretended to be asleep; and old Weser, with his train of sluggish brooks, who have nothing better to do than to rush into his arms, was at last forced to pursue his course grumbling.'

"The Angel shook his head sadly at this long speech of little Ilse, and looked gravely and searchingly at her pale face; and as he gazed long and steadily into her childish large blue eyes, which to-day emitted angry flashes, then he saw in their clear depths a dark spot moving, and he knew that an evil guest was harbored in the head of little Ilse. A little Demon of Pride had entered there, and driven away all pious thoughts, and looked mockingly at the good Angel out of the large blue eyes of poor little Ilse......

"'Dear Ilse,' for thus spoke the Angel, 'as you remained here from your own choice, and considered it beneath your dignity to descend into the plain with the other streams, surely you ought to be quite contented, and I can not understand why you choose to weep and lament.'

"'Alas!' answered Ilse, 'when the waters were all gone, dear Angel, the stormy wind came to sweep the hills, and when he found me here, he was quite furious; he roared and raged, and scolded and shook me, and threatened to dash me from this rock into a deep black abyss, where no ray of light ever shines. I wept and prayed, and pressed myself trembling against the sides of the rock; at last I succeeded in escaping from his strong grasp, and hid myself in a fissure of the precipice.'

"'But as you can not always succeed in hiding yourself,' spoke the Angel, 'for the Storm-wind sweeps clean, and keeps good order up here, you must see, dear Ilse, that it was foolish of you to remain here all alone; and I think you will gladly follow me, when I offer to lead you to the good old Weser and your young companions.'

"'On no account whatever!' cried the little Ilse; 'I will stay up here,—I am a Princess!'

"'Ilse!' said the Angel, in his gentle soft voice, 'dear little Ilse! I like you, and therefore you will, I hope, oblige me and be a good child. Do you see that white morning cloud sailing in the spacious blue sky? I will hail it, and it will descend on this spot; then we will both take our places in it. You shall lie down on the soft snowy cushions, and I will be beside you; and the cloud will quickly transport us to the deep valleys where the other brooks are. There, I will place you gently in your pretty green bed, stay with you, and relate stories, and bestow pleasant dreams on you.'

"Princess Ilse was, however, incurably perverse; she called out again, more crossly and imperiously than before, 'No! no! I won't go down—I don't choose to go down!' And when the kind Angel approached her, and wished to take her in his arms, she tried to push him away and dashed water in his face!

"The Angel seated himself sorrowfully on the ground, and the little headstrong Princess crept back into the crevice of the rock, quite proud that she had shown so much decision of character; and though the Angel repeatedly endeavored to persuade her to go with him, she only gave him short repulsive answers.

"When the good Angel at last saw that, in spite of all his love, he had no power over little Ilse, and that the little Demon of Pride had got complete mastery over her mind, he turned away from the perverse child, sighing heavily, and sought out his own blessed companions, who were still busily engaged below.

"When Princess Ilse found herself once more alone on the summit of the Alps, she wished to enjoy her lofty position. She crept forth from the crevice of the rock, placed herself on a jutting crag, spread out her vaporous drapery in wide folds, and waited to see if the other hills would not bow down before her, and the clouds approach to kiss the hem of her garment. Nothing of the kind, however, occurred, notwithstanding the dignified air of the lofty little lady; so at last she became weary of remaining in one place, began to feel very desolate, and said with a low sigh, 'I could have borne a certain portion of ennui, befitting my rank, but so much of it is more than even a Princess can be expected to endure!'"

But evil comes—in the shape of the Demon of the Brokenberg, who persuades her to slip into a shining shell, and be transported to his witch-festival on the Hartz mountains, where she hears herself called "a tea-kettle" princess, and learns that she is to be boiled in the unholy caldron. Nevertheless, she contrives to escape to the "green forest," and there flows calmly and safely on; notwithstanding that the demon sends the north wind and the winter frost to bring back to his clutches the "ethereal child." But in vain; and she lives on her peaceful, happy life of many hundred years.

How, afterwards, becoming subject to advancing civilization, which converts the forest into an iron-works, and makes it populous with toiling and suffering humanity, the little stream condescends to turn a mill, to wash poor folk's clothes, and even to be boiled on the household fire, careless of the obnoxious title "tea-kettle princess,"—all this, readers may learn for themselves.

Another book of somewhat similar character, where lessons of the purest Christian morality gleam like threads of gold through the web of a beautiful story, is "the History of Sir Thomas Thumb:" in which Miss Yonge has woven together the old familiar nursery tale, the poetic legend of King Arthur, and the Shakspearian fairy-lore, in a manner that will charm old and young.

Frances Freeling Broderip, daughter of him who so exquisitely sang the "Plea of the Midsummer Fairies," has surely been gifted by them with the faculty of delighting children. No "Little Folk," and few great ones, could fail to appreciate the "Snail who came of a Distinguished Family."

"'May I ask whom I have the honor of speaking to?' asked a large Snail, with a fine ring-marked shell, who was leisurely feasting on a low branch of a very fine crop of green peas.

"'My name is Atalanta,' quietly replied a sober-looking Caterpillar of a greenish-black color, with a spotty yellowish band running along its sides.

"'Dear me, what a ridiculously fine name for such a dingy creature; "Deadleaf" would be far more consistent with the faded color of your vestments, which seem to have seen better days. I hope you are not hungry, my good fellow, and that you have not come on a foraging expedition; because I must tell you that this row of peas is especially the peculiar property and feeding-ground of my family, and our own cousins, the Slugs.'

"'Don't alarm youself,' said the Caterpillar, 'I don't care for peas. I always prefer something more highly seasoned; indeed nettles are my principal food.'

"'Indeed,' said the Snail, patronizingly; 'and I dare say, now, you consider them good eating. What a bountiful provision there is for the lower orders! How many more nettles there are than rows of peas or beds of strawberries! We, more delicate and refined beings, who are particular in our fare, are not so bounteously provided. For myself, I prefer early green peas; I don't care about them when they get the least old and hard. I am partial to strawberries, when ripe and full-flavored. When I am really pushed to it for food, however, I *can* make a meal on the heart of a young mild cabbage-lettuce.'

"'You are easily satisfied, then,' remarked the Caterpillar; 'not *very* dainty in your eating, seemingly.'

"'Yes,' said the snail, with a virtuous air; 'I am, alas! used to the ups and downs of life, and have known times of great scarcity. Why, do you know, I have really passed one or two summers almost without tasting an apricot or peach?'

"'You must have suffered much, then,' said the Caterpillar.

"'Indeed I have,' sighed the Snail, 'for a member of such ancient lineage. We are of as good family as any in the land, being cousins only once removed from the fat white Dorking Snails. They, as you have doubtless heard, are illustrious exiles from the sunny land of France. Still, even the highest and noblest meet with occasional misfortunes, and I have had my share. I have been tormented by those obnoxious articles called gardeners, to a fearful extent; in fact, they only seem made to be a perpetual penance to us. The trouble they have given *me*, I am sure, no one would believe. Many times have I snugly established myself in a pleasant grove of ivy, intending to make my winter residence there; but no! the perverse wretches would not let me alone, but must send me flying over the railings into the road. Fortunately my house is strong and well built, so I have never come to any material harm. The greatest annoyance, besides flying through the air in that breathless way, has been from being obliged to walk back over the dusty, gritty road, through the garden gate again.'

"'You are not very easily daunted, then,' said the Caterpillar, who had listened with amusement to all this pompous oration.

"'Oh dear, no!' said the Snail, affectedly; 'we must not let a little daunt us, and deter us from our purpose. And so, when I am sent flying thus, as I am obliged to change my residence, I do so for the better, and locate myself in the middle of a clump of nice choice carnations, or a blooming pansy.'

"'But suppose the ruthless gardener should find you there, and crunch you without remorse,' suggested the Caterpillar.

"'Why, then, "I shall have lived my life," and leave my children to carry on an illustrious line. By the way, I have a most promising family of this season, feeding yonder on those young shoots. Their shells are almost hard already.'

"'They seem to have voracious appetites for such small creatures,' observed the Caterpillar; 'notwithstanding their delicate rearing.'

"'They are young,' said the Snail haughtily, 'and require plenty of nourishment to sustain their delicate nervous systems. By the way, where do you lodge for the night? I suppose you are obliged to put up with any thing.'

"'Why, I generally curl myself up in a leaf,' said the Caterpillar. 'I find it very airy and well ventilated in the warm weather.'

"'Ah, poor fellow!' said the Snail, compassionately; 'what a vagrant, gypsy sort of life. You should have a house like mine; it is so much more respectable to be a householder.'

"'I should think such property must bring its own responsibility, and often become burdensome,' said the Caterpillar. 'Don't you find it a great load to carry?'

"'Oh dear, no! answered the Snail; 'and only consider the comfort of being able to draw in your head in safety from your enemies.'

"'Thrushes manage, though, to demolish your mansion sometimes, don't they?' asked the Caterpillar, mischievously.

"'Sometimes, but not very often; and then one must put up with a few dangers on account of one's dignity and exalted situation. Take my advice, and get a house: I dare say you can find a few empty ones lying about, quite good enough for your limited wants. And now, as I see my friend, Sir Helix, coming this way, I must leave you; and I will beg of you to go a little farther off, my good fellow, as he is not very fond of new acquaintances, unless they are extremely select.'

"Some time after, while our Snail was slowly creeping along on his way to a fine fruit tree, richly laden, he beheld not far above his head a gorgeous creature. Its wings, of a rich velvet-like black, were edged with the most brilliant blue; splendid scarlet bands that seemed robbed from the poppy itself, were, as it were, embroidered upon them, studded with snowy spots of pure white. On the underneath these lovely wings were painted, as if in imitation of an Indian shawl. Rich shades of golden brown were mingled with delicate patterns of red, amber, and blue, in the most harmonious manner.

"'Good-morning, your Royal Highness,' said the Snail, obsequiously; 'we are deeply honored by your condescending visit.'

"'And who may you be?' inquired the lovely creature, languidly. "You seem a slow, humble sort of body; and your bundle on your back, too: how very amusing.'

"The Snail was deeply mortified at the ridicule of the Butterfly, but did not presume to reply, for fear of giving offense. Those who are most overbearing to their inferiors, are generally servile enough to those who are above them in station.

"'Do you carry your food in that funny sort of cupboard on your back?' inquired the Butterfly; 'pray, what do you live on, you grovelling creatures?'

"'Please your Highness, this is my house, my little cottage; and as for food, we snails live on peas, lettuces, or strawberries, when we can get them.'

"'Oh, you coarse things,' said the Butterfly, 'how very unpleasant! But all you lower orders are so uncouth in your habits. I suppose you have no idea what the taste of honey is like?'—that is the nectar upon which *we* feed.'

"The Snail professed his ignorance very humbly, hoping to get an invitation to the Butterfly's domain.

"'Poor drudging thing!' said the Butterfly, with an air of supreme pity, toiling along the dusty road with all your goods and chattels on your back. Now, when we are tired of reposing in a lily, we spread our light wings and go next door to a rose. We feed on the sweetest dews and the purest and finest honey. We soar into the air on our jewelled wings, and fly hither and thither over garden and meadow, wheresoever we will.'

"'Oh, your Highness,' said the Snail, envyingly, 'what a charming existence! How flattered I feel by the honor of your conversation!'

"'Do you?' said the Butterfly; 'I am sorry I can not return the compliment. I suppose in this gay attire you don't recognize the Caterpillar you once patronized and insulted?'

"The horrified Snail fairly drew into his shell with dismay, but speedily recovering his presence of mind, he began a sort of apology.

"'Pray, don't say another word,' said the Butterfly, unfolding his beautiful wings, and preparing for flight. 'Such blindness as yours is not confined to the snail tribe; there are many greater and wiser, who can find no beauty or virtue under a humble exterior. Had you been only commonly civil to me when I was a humble, crawling creature like yourself, I should not now disdain your acquaintance; but your present respect is only paid to my gay attire. You disowned me in my lowly, early days, and despised me; consequently, now my wings are grown, I leave you to your own sordid pursuits, and soar far above you in the sunny air.'"

From an equally pleasant book, "Little Estella," we take this picture of the deep sea world, to which has been brought a stolen mortal child.

"At first little Viola wept, for she remembered her sweet mother's face, but soon she learnt to love the sea-nymphs and their Queen, and became like one of them.

"In the mornings, when the sun's rays pierced through the crystal water, and fell upon the steps of yellow marble, and into the bright hall of the palace, Coralline and Sepiola, seating themselves on either side of her, taught the child to weave the beautiful green and purple tapestry destined for the Queen's new grotto, and which was embroidered all over with seed-pearl; whilst the Queen reclined on a couch near them, issuing her orders, or telling such incidents of the previous day as were most likely to amuse little Viola, and to teach her what was good and lovely.

"When the time came to gather up the embroidery threads, and fold together the tapestry, Pearl came by on her way to the palace of green marble. Pearl was Viola's favorite friend; she was young and full of mirth and frolic; but she could be grave too. None had so sweet and sad a voice to pity the little injured fish, so gentle a hand to bind their wounds, or such patience to hear their sorrows, and Viola liked to share in her labors.

"It was a great delight to both, when their recovered favorites were able to leave the hospital and return to their native haunts. Often as they sat at work in the mornings, the little fish, grateful for so much kindness, came waving their fins, and sporting about before the steps of the palace, to catch a glimpse of Pearl and Viola, or see their Queen. Sometimes she would bid them tell her where they had travelled, and what curious things they had seen; this they thought a great honor, and sometimes had the most amusing adventures to relate, so that Viola learned to watch for the glancing of their silver scales, and the twinkling of their bright eyes, as one of her pleasures.

"The most tiresome of all the Queen's subjects were the crabs and lobsters, who were always bent on seeing and touching every thing; but being too heavy and idle to swim in pace with the rest of the train, they used to hold on by their claws to the flowing robes of the sea-nymphs, thereby impeding their progress. They had very little sharp eyes, and were extremely curious; they were, moreover, very quarrelsome, and were perpetually pinching and fighting each other, especially the lobsters, who would poke their long feelers into every body's way, and often got them broken in consequence; upon which they used to run off to the hospital in a miserable plight, and nobody but the gentle Pearl would ever have had patience to nurse them.

"The Queen used often to punish them by having them tightly wound up in sea-weeds, so that they could not use their claws; after which, they became very penitent, and were glad to be allowed to carry on their strong backs all the food and other things which Pearl needed in her labors.

"Viola used to look forward with great pleasure to the approach of evening, when Ulva came with Doris and Lorea, to take her abroad with the Queen. At first, Ulva used to lift the child in her arms; but soon she learnt to ride a quiet old Dolphin, who was too old to gambol and curvet as the Queen's sea-horse did, while Doris and Lorea held the bridle-rein, and taught her to manage it."

Alack, and well-a-day! where are the fairies of our youth? We believe in them no longer. We create them no more. But Heaven forbid that they should not exist still for others, and for years to come delight the little children now growing up around us,—the dear ones unto whom we look with unutterable love and longing, praying that in them our childhood and youth may be renewed, only that they may prove infinitely better and happier than we.

But after the first craving of infantile imagination has satisfied itself with its natural food, namely, mere amusement, there usually comes a new development, without which the liveliest fancy is mere fantasy, vague, unsubstantial, and utterly insufficient for the yearnings of a human soul. This is ideality—the nearest word we can find to express that thirst for ideal beauty and ideal good, which, more or less, exists in every immortal soul—may it not be, as the intuitive instinct of its immortality?

When the child-nature first wakes up to this, how the whole world becomes transformed, full of a glorious mystery, glowing with unutterable beauty! How the little heart beats, and the bright eyes glisten, at tales of heroic virtue or pathetic patience! How nothing seems too mighty to achieve or to endure, in this wonderful new world, of which the gate is just opened; an ideal earth, beautiful as Paradise, and yet it is this very earth of ours.

This is the first great crisis in youthful life. On the use that is made of it, the influences that surround it, depends frequently the bias of the whole character. Parents can not be too careful of the books they then give their children to read, of the tone of the conversation they let them hear, and of the associates with whom they surround them. In many children, especially those of imaginative temperament, no after impression will ever efface those received at this age. Therefore it is good to furnish either boy or girl with such strengthening food as this history, by Sarah Crompton, of the old man who waited fifteen years for leave to sail from Spain in search of a New World.

"Though each day, as they sailed on, must bring them nearer to land, yet each day the fears and conduct of the crew became worse. The signs so full of hope to the mind of Columbus did but add to the fears of the men.

"Some of them laid a plot to throw their leader into the sea, and turn back. Columbus knew of all this bad-feeling, but still bore all in patience, and spoke wisely and well to each man in turn. On the 25th of September the wind was due east, and took them onwards. Once the cry of land was heard, but the daylight put an end to this fresh dream of hope. They still went on. Dolphins played around the ships, and flying-fish fell upon the decks. These new sights kept the sailors amused. On the 7th of October some of the admiral's crew thought they saw land in the west, but before the close of day the signs were lost in the air. They had now sailed 750 leagues, more than 2000 miles, from any known land. Flights of small birds came about the ships; a heron, a pelican, and a duck were seen; and so they went on, till one night, when the sun went down on a shoreless sea, the crew rose against Columbus, to force his return. He was firm as ever, but spake gently, and prayed them to trust that all would yet be well. It was hard work to make them submit and obey, and the state of things for Columbus was bad indeed.

"Next day brought some relief; for the signs of land were more and more sure. They saw fresh weeds, such as only grow in rivers, and a kind of fish only found about rocks. The branch of a tree with berries on it floated past, and they picked up a piece of cane; also a board and stick, with strange things cut on them. All gloom and ill-will now cleared away. Each man hoped to be the first to see the new land, and thus to win the large reward in money which was then to be given him. The breeze had been fresh all day, and they sailed very fast. At sunset their course was due west. Every one was on the alert. No man on board the three ships went to sleep that night. Columbus took his place on the top of the cabin. He was glad to be alone just on the eve of the long-looked-for event. His eye was keen, and on the strain, through the deep, still shades of night. All at once, about ten o'clock, he thought he saw a light far off. Lest hope should mislead him, he called up a man to his side. Yes—there again—it surely was a light. They called the mate. Yes; he, too, was sure of the same: and then it was gone, and soon they all saw it again. It might be a torch in the bark of some fisherman, rising and sinking with the waves, or a light in the hand of a man on shore, moving here and there. Thus Columbus KNEW that land was there, with men upon it. What words can tell the joy of his brave and noble soul!"

The boy who could read this passage (told so graphically that we wish many a historian would take a lesson from Sarah Crompton's "short words") without a thrill of emotion that may give the first impulse to the chance of becoming himself a great man, must be a very common-minded boy indeed.

A less complete, and yet very pleasant book, is "Days of Old:" though, as a child's book, not quite satisfactory. We should say, from internal evidence, that the writer has not so long passed the season of childhood as to be able clearly to see its requirements. She—for the style is essentially feminine—falls into the common error of "writing down to children:" that is, of presenting the ideas of a grown-up person in the language of a child. Now the first necessity to secure the attention of little people, is to make yourself a child—not in a condescending, carefully-acted fashion, but by coming down, literally and entirely, to their level, and trying to see every thing from their point of view. Their interests must be your interests, their reality your reality. It is this which forms the charm of the old-fashioned fairy tales—the exceeding gravity and verity with which they are related, the relator seeming no more to doubt than the child-readers, that Jack did really cut off all the giant's three heads; and that it was perfectly natural and probable for Puss to put on boots and converse with every body he met in that extremely gentlemanly manner.

With this suggestion, that the author would do well to avoid "poetical" language and recondite moralizing, and study that perfect simplicity of conception, action, and diction, which is quite compatible with perfect ideal beauty, nay, forms the chief element therein—we can give warm praise to the "Days of Old."

It consists of three tales, each illustrating a principle. The first is "Self-sacrifice." A little British child, Deva, daughter of Caswallan, or Cassivelaunus, hearing that once a brother died to save a brother, offers herself to the Druid god, hoping thereby her sick brother may be spared, and live to become a hero. The sacrifice is not completed, but she learns from Otho, a Christian convert, of "the only perfect Man and perfect Sacrifice," and recognizes in Him the story of the brother who died. Less intelligible to children, we fear, and yet worked out with exceeding beauty, is "Wulfgar and the Earl," a story of pride broken by sorrow, of the will of man forced to submit itself to the will of God. The third tale, "Roland," is that of a younger brother, "the scholar of the family," with "more friends among his books than among his fellows," who, under a strong impulse, follows his elder brother to the Holy Land.

There Gerard applies himself to acquire glory, and gains it; but Roland, touched by the anguish of a mother whose son had been tempted over to Saladin's camp, devotes all his energies to recover the apostate; whom meeting at last in battle, he will not slay, preferring to be branded as a coward rather than murder the widow's son. His generosity is the sinner's redemption.

The tone and spirit of this story can not better be shown than by extracting its conclusion, beginning with part of Roland's last conversation with the monk whose preaching had induced him to embark for the Holy Land, which he was now quitting forever:—

> "These two were walking together within sight of the sea that would take one back to his own land, and separate the other from him.
>
> "'My son,' the monk asked abruptly, 'are you content?'
>
> "'I am.'
>
> "'You have gained no renown.'
>
> "'I came not for that, father.'
>
> "'Nor riches.'
>
> "'I did not expect them.'
>
> "'What, then, have you gained?'
>
> "'A brother!'
>
> "'Yet you did not come for that. Why, then, are you content?'
>
> "'I came not for that, indeed; I came to do my own work; but God gave me His to do instead. He gave me the work, the will to do it, and the power to succeed. Have I not cause to be content?'
>
> * * * * * *
>
> "This is all the story.
>
> "Gerard went on fighting, and men called him a good soldier; and Roland went home. He took with him no golden spurs, but he had a friend and brother by his side who would never be unfaithful.
>
> * * * * * *
>
> "When that generation had passed, though Roland's name was remembered, it was not as a crusader; but Gerard's fame and prowess were talked of and sung of for many a day.
>
> "That he, the elder brother, was 'fit for a soldier,' no one ever doubted; indeed, a tangible proof of the same remains to this day in the shape of a yellow banner laid up somewhere as a memento of the past—at least, if it does not remain to this day, it is only because it has dropped away thread by thread; for Time must have worn it a long while, and perhaps by this time has worn it out.
>
> "That Roland was 'fit for a soldier,' *no* proof remains—on earth. But perhaps it is not only here that brave soldiers are known from cowards, and that mementoes of great deeds are laid up."

This book speaks for itself. It appeals instinctively to what is highest in child or man—that struggle after something better than any thing we possess or behold, which, beginning in this Age of Gold, is never to be ended on earth. But what matters it unto those who recognize themselves as mere travellers, bound for another Country brighter than even the Celestial Country of which Bunyan's little readers are taught to dream? Ay, and it is good for them so to dream, and good to read stories such as this we have been quoting from, wherein the actual is elevated into the ideal, and by means of its imagination the child is taught lessons, the influence of which may be needed in after life, who knows how often or for how long? Until at last we cease to crave after the ideal, merely as such, and recognize in it the spirit's blind groping after that faith which is "the substance of things hoped for, the evidence of things not seen."

Possessing this, need we mourn that the season is gone by, for us grown people at least, when glamour was over all our world, when every body seemed so good and so beautiful, and from others as well as from ourselves we expected the noblest deeds, the most impossible perfections? If they have somewhat failed—and we also—if, instead of walking this poor earth in stature greater than men, and speaking,

> "With the large utterance of the early gods,"

we see ourselves and our friends the pigmies that we really are, let us not repine; nor, because we have come short of it, let us deny the truth we once held, for it *was* the truth. Happy are we if we can still recognize, in spite of all mutations, that the Age of Gold has never become dim—that we still believe in the same good and lovely things that we believed in when we were young.

ON

LIVING IN PERSPECTIVE.

AN enterprising artist once painted a picture, after the fashion of that school which, with all its exaggerations, has done much for the reformation of modern art;—ay, as much as Wordsworth's startling simplicities once did for that of modern poetry. Not a bad picture, though *very* pre-Raphaelite. Two decidedly plain young people leaned against a wall, or rather seemed growing out of it; and the wall itself was painted minutely down to the last brick, over which a large green beetle was meditatively walking. The landscape beyond rose almost perpendicularly up to the sky, against which, sharply outlined on the top of a very verdant tree, was a solitary black crow—so large, that if seen on the ground he would have been as big as a sheep. He and the green beetle together quite distracted one's attention from the melancholy lovers; and though many parts of the picture were well painted, still there was a lack of proportion which marred exceedingly the general effect. It was unlevel, irregular; a sacrifice of the whole to particular parts, which were carefully "worked up," while others were totally neglected. In short, it made one feel, with a sad moralizing, what a fatal thing in pictures, books, or human lives, is a lack of proportion.

It is a plausible theory that neither good nor evil is absolute; that each vice is the exaggerated extension of a virtue; each virtue capable of being corrupted into a vice; so that the good and wise man becomes simply the man with acuteness enough to draw the exact line between either, and then to obey the advice—*In medio tutissimus ibis.* If this be a sophism, there is yet truth in it. Undoubtedly the best man, the man most useful to his species, is he whose character is most equally balanced; and the most complete life is that which has been lived, so to speak, in perspective. People with enormous faults and gigantic virtues may be very interesting in novels, but they are exceedingly inconvenient in real life. An equable person, with no offensively exaggerated qualities, is by far the safest to have to do with, and especially to live with. My friend Juventus, when you marry, be sure you choose a woman with no strong "peculiarities;" let her soul, like her form, be without angles; above all, take care that she has, in all her doings and thinkings, a clear eye for the fitting relations of things which make up what I call the perspective of life.

How shall I explain it? Perhaps best by illustration, beginning with the root of all evil, and of a very great deal of good—money.

It may be a most immoral and unpoetical sentiment, but those are always the best people who have a carefulness over, and a wise respect for, money. Not *per se*—not the mere having it or amassing it, but the prudent using of it—making it our servant and not our master. As a test of character, perhaps *£ s. d.* is one of the sharpest and most sure. A man who is indifferent and inaccurate in money matters, will rarely be found accurate in any thing. He may have large benevolence—externally; you will see him throw half-a-crown to a beggar, and subscribe to every charity list in the *Times;* but if he forgets to pay you that five shillings he borrowed for cab-hire, you may be quite sure that the beggar's half-crown and the twenty pounds in the printed subscription will have to come out of somebody's pocket—probably *not* his own; for there is nothing like the meanness of your "generous" people—always robbing Peter to pay Paul. A liberal man is a glorious sight; but then he must be "liberal in *all* his ways"—even-handed as well as open-handed. His expenditure must be, like his character, justly balanced and in due proportion. And since how to earn and how to spend, are equally difficult arts, and that a large part of our usefulness, worthiness, and happiness depends on our learning them—ay, and they can not be learnt too soon—is it wrong to put money as the crucial test of what we term living "in perspective?"

For example: Smith has exactly five hundred a year.

We all know this fact—we can not help knowing it, he being a salaried official of Government. We also know—somehow, every body does know every thing—that he has no private fortune, and that he had the courage and manliness to marry a woman without a half-penny to hers. Nevertheless, when he married he took a house, which, being in our own street, we are aware must cost him, rent and taxes together, at least £70 a year; this leaves him, for all other expenses, just £430. A very comfortable sum if fairly divided among the moderate necessities of life, but which, in these modern days, will certainly allow no extraneous luxuries.

Yet we meet Mr. and Mrs. Smith continually in "society"—he well-dressed as usual, she in her beautiful marriage gowns, which would be ruined by a common cab or omnibus; so we must conclude they come to these elegant parties in a fly—(10*s.* per night; say, at lowest calculation, 30*s.* per week of carriage-hire. Poor Smith!) In process of time we are invited to Smith's own house, to meet "a few friends at dinner." And every dinner—counting the wine, the hired cook, the two waiters, and all the inevitable extraneous expenses of a small household giving a large entertainment,—must, we are certain, have mulcted our poor friend of at least £15. If he gives three of them—there, at one fell swoop, goes £45 out of the £430 merely eaten and drunk, with nothing to show for it. And Smith being an honorable fellow who *will* pay his tradesmen, though he starve for it, we shrewdly suspect there will be sharp economies somewhere; that the Gruyère cheese may result in family butter frightfully salt, and that these elegant desserts will cause Smith to go puddingless for days. Also, that the tall green-grocer in white gloves, who didn't a bit delude us into believing that our friends kept a footman, will dwindle in daily life to a slatternly Irish girl, who, being paid half the wages of a good housemaid, is so incompetent a servant that poor Mrs. Smith has to do half the work herself. Yet there she sits, pretty young creature! wan, but smiling; anxious to keep up the dignity of her husband's table, but enduring agonies lest all should not go on rightly in the kitchen,—which, in that household of £500 a year, aping for one day only the luxuries and conveniences of £5000, is nearly impossible. We are so sorry for her, our gentle hostess; and as for our host, though we laugh at his jokes and praise his wine, we feel as if all the time we had our hand feloniously in his pocket. But why—oh! why was he so foolish as to invite us to put it there?

Why? Because he can not see that he is living out of perspective. That if he asked really "a few friends"—not acquaintances—to share the wholesome joint and nice pudding which, I doubt not, Mrs. Smith gives him every day, with perhaps a cozy "crack" over walnuts and wine afterwards, we should not only enjoy our entertainment, but respect our host a great deal more. For we should feel that he was giving us real hospitality—a share of his own bread and salt—the best he could afford: and, therefore, just as valuable in its way as our best:—though, we being richer men, this may consist of turtle and champagne, which, if he honors us by sharing, we are honored; for he and his wife are well-born, well-bred, and altogether charming and acceptable guests. Why should they not believe this, accept our invitations, and take their stand in society upon higher ground than petty rivalry in meats and clothes? Why not say, openly or tacitly, "We have just five hundred a year, and we mean to live accordingly. We enjoy society, but society must take us as we are. We will attempt no make-believes; we will not feast one day and starve another; appear finely dressed at our neighbor's house, and lounge about our own in shabbiness and rags; have a large, well-furnished, showy drawing-room to receive our company in, and let our family sleep in upper chambers, bare, comfortless, dirty—something between a workhouse ward and a pigsty. Whatever we spend, we will spend levelly; then, be our income large or small, we shall always be rich, for we shall have apportioned our spendings to our havings. The nobleman who is said to have an income of a thousand a day can do no more."

Not less unreal than the Smiths, or more devoid of that fine sense of the proportion of things which distinguishes a wise man from an unwise, is our other friend Jones.

Jones is a self-made man. He and his wife began life in a second-floor over their shop in the High Street. There, by steadfast industry, he developed from a tradesman to a merchant—from a merchant to a millionnaire. Now, in all—stop!—let me not name the city,—no house is more palatial than the one built by Thomas Jones.

When he gives a dinner-party, his plate, glass, and china dazzle your eyes; and his drawing-room—on those rare occasions when you are allowed to behold it—is the very perfection of the upholsterer's art. But, ordinarily, its carved marble chimney-pieces gleam coldly over never-lighted fires: its satin damask is hid under brown holland; its velvet pile carpet you feel, but can not see it—not an inch of it!—under the ugly drugget that covers all. The chandeliers, the mirrors, and picture-frames, nay, the very statues, are swathed in that dreadful gauzy substance, sticky, flimsy, and crackly, which must have been invented by the goddess of Sham—as if any thing not too good to buy were too good to use!

Yet, even in this their dreary condition, the splendid apartments are seldom opened. Jones and his wife live mostly in their little back parlor, where are neither books, pictures, statues, nor handsome furniture; nothing pretty to delight the eye, nothing comfortable or luxurious to pleasure the old age of Jones himself or of excellent Mrs. Jones, who was such a faithful, hard-working wife to him in his poverty days, and who now richly deserves all that their well-earned wealth could give her. But, alas! both had grown so used to narrowness, that when good fortune came they could not expand with it. Save on show occasions, they continue to live in the same unnaturally humble way, approaching actual meanness; as much below their income as Smith lives, or appears to live, above his; and both are equally wrong.

The poor Joneses!—they can not see that riches were given to a man richly to enjoy, and, what is higher still, to help others to enjoy also. How many a young fellow, with a full brain and an empty purse, would keenly relish those treasures of art which the merchant prince buys so lavishly, just because other people buy them, but does not understand or appreciate one jot! How often some sickly invalid would feel it like a day in Paradise to spend a few hours in Mrs. Jones's beautiful country house and delicious garden, or to take an occasional drive in her easy barouche, which six days out of seven stands idle in the coach-house! For she, with her active habits, prefers walking on fine days; and on wet days, afraid of spoiling the carriage or harming the horses, she takes a street cab—nay, she has been seen tucking up her old black silk gown and popping surreptitiously into an omnibus. A noble economy, if there were any need for it, but there is none. The childless couple had far better spend their income in making other folks' children happy. As it is, for all the use or benefit their wealth is to them, they might as well be living in those two little poky rooms over their first shop; and that heap of countless guineas, which they can neither spend nor carry away with them, is, for all the enjoyment got out of it, of no more value to them than the dust-heap at their stable door. Their folly is, in its way, as foolish as the folly of the spendthrift, and only a shade less sinful.

Far wiser are the Browns, whom I went to see the other day, and talked over old times and new. "Yes," said Mrs. Brown—commenting, smiling, upon "now" and "then,"—"our great secret has been, whatever our income was, we lived within it." That income, as I knew, began at £300, out of which two households had to be maintained. At present, it is probably over—it can not well be under—£3000 a year. And I like to see Mr. Brown drive off in his well-appointed brougham, and Mrs. Brown sit cheerful in her pretty drawing-room, resplendent in rich black silk and delicate lace caps, even of a morning. How nice she always looks! yet not nicer than she used to do in the neat muslins and warm merinos, made every stitch by her own hands. She never makes her own dresses now; she employs a Court milliner, and sometimes appears at dinner-parties in attire quite gorgeous. But do I admire her the less for this? Do I not feel that such lawful and pleasant extravagance is the natural outcome of those simple days when she was her own milliner, and went to evening parties hooded and cloaked, in an omnibus? Now, as then, she lives in proportion to her means, fully using and enjoying her income, and, I am certain, taking good care that others shall enjoy it too. For the true root of generosity is carefulness; and if in the omnibus times she managed to spare out of her slender wardrobe many an old gown, and out of her small store-cupboard many a half pound of tea, to people poorer than herself, depend upon it, out of the £3000 there is still a large item left for "charity." For true charity consists, not in slap-dash acts of astonishing liberality, but in persistently managing one's expenses so that one always has a margin left wherewith to do a kindness.

Money is, I repeat, the point upon which this system

most plainly breaks down; but there are many other sad ways in which people may live out of perspective.

Your great philanthropist, for instance, who devotes himself to one or more pet schemes for the improvement of the race, firmly convinced that his scheme is the only scheme, until it absorbs his whole time, and becomes, like the big black crow on the tree-top, a mere blot in the otherwise fair landscape of his life, and out of all proportion to the rest of it—how can he condescend to such small duties as to be the kind husband, whose smile makes the evening sunshine of the fireside; the affectionate father, who is at once the guide, the companion, and the confidant of his children?

Your great author, too. It is a pathetic thing to see a wife sit smiling under the laurels of an illustrious husband, and

"Hear the nations praising him far off,"

while, near at home, she knows well that the praise never warms the silent hearth, from which he is continually absent, or, if he comes to it, only brings with him sulkiness and gloom. Alas! that shadow of fame rather blights than shelters the weak womanly heart which cares little, perhaps, for ambition, but is thirsting for help, comfort, and love. Doubtless many a time that great man's wife envies the lot of a woman married to some stupid respectable spouse who goes to his office at nine and returns at six—goes with the cheerful brow of the busy, active man, and comes back with the kiss and the smile of the honest man who has done his work and got it over, and has room for other cares than bread-winning—other thoughts than of himself and his celebrity.

And the "auri sacra fames" is as great a destroyer of all domestic peace, as great a blot on the level landscape of a man's life, as the "cacoëthes scribendi." See it in all its madness, in our poor friend Robinson. He has made one fortune, but did not consider it large enough, and is now busy making another. He is off to the city at 8 A.M., never returning till 8 P.M., and then so worn and jaded that he cares for nothing beyond his dinner and his sleep. His beautiful house, his conservatories and pleasure-grounds, delight not him; he never enjoys, he only pays for them. He has a charming wife and a youthful family, but he sees little of either—the latter, indeed, he never sees at all except on Sundays. He comes home so tired that the children would only worry him. To them "papa" is almost a stranger. They know him only as a periodical incumbrance on the household life, which generally makes it much less pleasant. And when they grow up, it is to such a totally different existence than his that they usually quietly ignore him—"Oh! papa cares nothing about this!" "No, no, we never think of telling papa any thing,"—until some day papa will die, and leave them a quarter of a million. But how much better to leave them what no money can ever buy—the remembrance of a *father!* A real father, whose guardianship made home safe; whose tenderness filled it with happiness; who was companion and friend as well as ruler and guide; whose influence interpenetrated every day of their lives, every feeling of their hearts; who was not merely the "author of their being"—that is nothing, a mere accident:—but the originator and educator of every thing good in them: the visible father on earth, who made them understand dimly "our Father which is in heaven."

One of the saddest forms taken by lives lived out of perspective is one which belongs not so much to men as to women, and that is with regard to the affections. We laugh at the lady with whom every second person she chances to name is "my very dearest friend." We know there can be but one "dearest," or else the phrase means nothing at all. We take these demonstrative people for what they are worth: extremely obliged for their friendship, but not breaking our hearts about them, and well assured they will never break their hearts about us.

But while we smile with a sort of half-contemptuous pity at those who have such shallow and thinly spread affections, such small capacity of loving, we are forced to admit that it is possible to love too much—I mean, to allow one passion or affection, of whatever kind, to absorb so much of a life that the rest of it, with all its duties, tendernesses, and responsibilities, becomes dwindled down into unnatural proportions. Who has not seen, with sorrowful bitterness, some woman—it is usually a woman—wasting her whole time, thoughts, and feelings upon one individual, friend or relative (we will not add lover, because that is, at all events, a natural engrossment, leading to natural and righteous duties), and sacrificing to this one person every thing in life? An unholy sacrifice, and generally to an unworthy object, or it would not have been accepted. Gradually, this influence narrows the worshipper's whole nature. She, poor voluntary slave, can not see that the essence of honest love is perfect freedom, exacting no more than its just rights, and being delicately careful of the rights of others. No friend ought to be the only friend; no tie of blood, the only tie; our affections, like all else, were meant to be fairly divided. When they are concentrated upon one object, a wholesome attachment becomes a diseased engrossment, which, instead of elevating, deteriorates the character, and makes an all-absorbing love more injurious than many an honest hate.

Ay; for love itself may be degraded from a religion into a mere superstition. Sometimes even a mother will neglect her other children to waste her substance upon an undutiful scamp, whom every body knows to be a scamp, and treats accordingly. And continually one sees sisters condoning and palliating in some ne'er-do-weel brother, errors which in any other man they would condemn and scorn. Worse still—how many a wife, who has unhappily borne children to a man whom it is ruin for them to have as a father, hesitates and quails before her conflicting duties—God help her! Yet how can He help her unless she sees clearly what is her duty,—which is not to let even the tie of marriage obedience blind her so that she compromises with sin? There may be cases in which the only salvation is escape. It is possible to love, not only father and mother, but husband or wife, more than God, and so be led astray from His absolute right and unalterable truth.

And this brings us to the last and most fatal phase of lives out of perspective. There are people who to one special duty, which by some morbid exaggeration of fancy they have been led to believe a duty paramount, will sacrifice every thing else. The balance of conscience is in them quite lost. They see all things in a distorted light. They are unable to take a just estimate of either their own rights or those of others—nay, their very moral consciousness becomes diseased; all the more so, because these victims are generally among the best and noblest of natures—the most single-minded, devoted, and self-sacrificing. While the mass of the world is made up of exceedingly selfish people, passionately pursuing their own interest, there is a proportion in whom the element of self seems to be altogether and fatally absent. I repeat, fatally; because a certain quantity of it, just sufficient to make one weigh one's self, one's own capabilities and rights, in equal measure with those of other people, is not only beneficial but necessary. Nothing is more hateful than the egotist, whose one little "I" is the centre of his universe. Yet, on the other hand, it is sad to see a person, man or woman (and here again it is generally a woman), in whom the quality of self-esteem or self-respect is so totally wanting that she allows herself to be continually "put upon;" follows every body's advice, succumbs to every body's tyranny, is the victim of all the injustices of friends and the caprices of acquaintances. Sadder still, because the woman is almost invariably a very good woman; only devoid of that something, intellectual or moral—which is it?—which forms, so to speak, the centre of gravity in a character—enabling the individual to see clearly and decide fairly the balance of duties and the relative proportions of things.

Otherwise, as continually we see, many a noble and useful life is actually wrecked for the sake of some self-created or, at best, strongly exaggerated duty, into which circumstances had drifted the individual, and for which all other duties (including the one, not to man but to God, to preserve for His utmost service the mind and body which He bestowed) are completely neglected. A mother will sacrifice all her children, and herself, upon whom her whole family depends, to some one child who happens to have more influence over her than the rest; a sister will strip herself of every penny, and perhaps come to subsist upon charity in her old age, to supply the wanton extravagances of some scapegrace brother, for whom a workhouse crust of his own earning would be a salutary lesson; or—though of this evil let us speak with tenderness, for it verges on the noblest good—a daughter will waste her health, her strength, all the lawful enjoyments of her youth, perhaps even sacrifice woman's holiest right—love and marriage—for the sake of some exacting parent or parents, who consider that the mere fact of having given life constitutes the claim to absorb into themselves every thing that makes life pleasant or desirable. These are hard words, but they are true words; and though it may be a touching sight to see one human being devoted—nay, say sacrificed—to another, woe be to that other—ay, even though it were a parent—who compels the sacrifice!

Ay, even as Nature made this tree—at which, while I write, I sit looking—in such marvellous proportion as well as perfection: the strong rough trunk, the slighter boughs, the slender branches and twigs, all hung with green leaves and rosy blossoms, foretelling wealth of fruit; so she created our lives to be lived in perspective, and our duties to be fitted into one another, or rather to grow out of one another—none taking an exaggerated size, or assuming a false relation, to the injury of the rest. And truly, the great art of living is to learn this secret.

What is it? Where is the one point from which, speaking geometrically, we may safely "describe" all lines, so as to make our confused lives into that divine, harmonious figure which alone constitutes completeness, rest, and peace? Not self, certainly. However conceited and egotistic we are in our youth, we rarely grow to middle age without discovering that egotism, *per se*, is a huge mistake—not merely ugly, but ridiculous. He who dwells wholly in himself, who sees all things with reference to himself, makes a blunder as patently ludicrous as he whose feeble self-dependence and low self-esteem cause him to lean always on the judgment and be guided by the opinion of others. Both err in precisely the same way as our friend the pre-Raphaelite painter, who took his point of sight anywhere, or nowhere in particular, and so lost altogether his power of comparison between objects; made his crow as large as a donkey, and his green beetle a more interesting personage than his unfortunate lovers leaning against the wall.

One last word, and a solemn one, for life is a sad and solemn thing.

In this strange landscape of our mortal existence there is but one true and safe point of sight, and that is neither from self within us nor from the world without us, but *from above*. The man who feels, humbly yet proudly, that his life is owed to Him who gave it, to be fashioned according to the clearest vision he has of His pattern, possesses in himself a permanent centre whence he can judge of all things with an equal eye. He is like what David says of "a tree planted by rivers of water:" he grows firmly on his own root, and every development of his character, every act of his life, is in due proportion. Consequently, season by season, he will bring forth, in sight of all men, his buds, leaves, blossoms, and fruit: even like my apple-tree there, which stands steadfast in its place, while the bees come humming about it, and the birds sit and sing in the branches, as they will do to its very last summer—its very last day. Such a man, who, whatever sort of life it may please Heaven to give him, carries it out to the full, so far as its possibilities allow, bears with him to the end of his days the blessing of the tree—"His leaf also shall not wither; and look, whatsoever he doeth, it shall prosper." And be his life short or long, lofty or lowly, it is sure to be a complete life, inasmuch as, whatever its proportions, it was lived "in perspective."

SERMONS.

LET us consider the question of Sermons, not in any controversial or doctrinal, or, what is mournfully different from both, in any religious point of view, but simply regarded as sermons—*sermo*, a discourse—to be judged as we judge any other discourse on any other subject, literary, scientific, or political. Is this allowable? Some may say decidedly no. There are those who believe that every word which drops from the lips of any youth consecrated episcopally is altogether sacred, and beyond the pale of criticism. Others, while denying the doctrine of apostolic succession, deem their own "gospel preacher"—that is, the man who preaches their own particular gospel, however incoherently, illogically, and ungrammatically—to be a "teacher sent from God." And a large intermediate portion of the decently religious community view "the clergyman," or "the minister," with a sort of respectful indifference, as a decorous necessity, whose discourses, like himself, are to be taken for granted, but neither judged nor investigated.

But does not the truth of the question lie far below—or above—these various opinions? The more earnest is our belief in, and reverence for, the minister of divine things, the sharper must be our judgment upon every man who assumes such an office, until, or unless, he has proved himself consecrated to it by the only true consecration—the Spirit of God burning within him and shining without, in all his words, and works, and ways. Otherwise, whether he wear Geneva bands, Episcopal apron, or the fustian jacket of John Jones, bricklayer and Methodist preacher, he is still no more than "the man in the pulpit," whom it is lawful and right for us to judge as we judge any other man; or rather, not him but his sermon.

Thus I mean neither offense nor irreverence, if I speak out plainly a few things which many persons must have inwardly thought, regarding the discourses that we all hear Sunday after Sunday, in our various churches and chapels of England, Scotland, or Ireland. It would be easy to make an amusing article of thinly-disguised personalities, but the subject is too serious to be "amusing" upon. Besides, there is a certain text, "He that is not against us is for us." The very poorest soldier who wears our Master's cloth, and fights, ever so feebly, in our Master's army, deserves respect, and shall have it here.

A sermon, then—what is it? Among Episcopalians it usually means an original discourse about twenty-five minutes long, read carefully, but unimpressively, and listened to with civil indifference, as an excrescence, often unwelcome, upon the noble and beautiful liturgy which is the pride and bulwark of the English Church. In Scotland it is different: the mere phrase "between sermons" implies the difference. South of the Tweed it is always "between service." There, the service is every thing, the sermon of comparatively little moment. Mingle in an English congregation, passing out, wearily maybe, but reverentially, into the open air, and you will rarely hear the slightest comment on the preacher. He and his sermon are taken as a matter of course. But at the "skellin" of a Scotch kirk, almost before the congregation have quitted their pews, you may catch the eager buzz of conversation on the merits of the discourse and the peculiarities of the minister. He knows this only too well—is aware that each hearer is a sharp critic, and possibly a sharper theologian; that every fragment of the worship—prayer included—will be assuredly commented upon by every worshipper present, with that keen earnestness that the national mind brings, proverbially, to every thing with which it comes in contact.

This is the weak point of the Church of Scotland—that where the weight of the service falls on one man, it is apt to become a service directed unto men, instead of a worship offered unto God. And though in its highest sense all worship ought to be extempore, the voice of one man lifting up the praises and supplications of the rest, in the language of the moment, and suited to the present needs of the people; still we all know into what this is apt to degenerate. Many, nay the most of Presbyterian prayers are mere doctrinal disquisitions; or, worse, harangues addressed to the Almighty, informing Him, in a tone little less than blasphemous, of what He is, what He has done, and what He ought to do.

To any one familiar with this peculiarity of the Scottish Kirk, and of many English and Irish Nonconformist sects, there will appear nothing extraordinary or incredible in the story of the minister who, in giving thanks for the good harvest, stopped and carefully excepted "a few bad fields between here and Strathbyres;" or the Baptist elder, who, in earnest supplication for an erring brother, explained that "he wears a blue coat, and lives at the corner of the lane."

The same irreverent ignorance affects the sermon. It ceases to be a gospel—a message—in which the speaker feels himself to be the mere deliverer of truths which have been put into his mind and heart to say, in the simplest, clearest form, so as to carry the strongest conviction to his hearers. He becomes the exponent, not of his Master, but of himself: considers what effect he can produce, and what the congregation will be thinking of him. For he is fully aware that on his sole individuality the whole attention of the congregation, and the whole weight of the service, depend.

Whatever other errors, such as dry formalism and wearisome monotony, the English Church falls into, it escapes this. You never hear from English clergymen those flowery discourses, delivered with set changes of voice and rhetorical action, which are the pride—and shame—of youthful Scotch ministers: those elegant extempore rhapsodies which we are well aware have been "got" by heart, and "studied" before the looking-glass all the week. Happily, however, the practice of first writing sermons, and then committing them to memory, is being gradually discontinued. Its patent folly and falseness are such that one wonders it was not long since resisted and put an end to by all sensible and spirited ministers of the Kirk of Scotland.

To this may be mainly attributed the great bane of that Church—"show" sermons. The preacher—he is usually young—mounts the pulpit, every hair in every curl, and every motion of hands or eyes, being arranged with a view to effect. He then begins, gets quickly through the hymns, Scripture-reading, and prayer, and girds himself for the grand achievement—the sermon. It has a text certainly, which he delivers with energy; then bursts into a continuous stream of language. Mere language—nothing more; a farrago of similes, epithets, adjectives, quasi-soliloquies, and scenery pictures (oh, what daubs they are!) heaped together in unconnected confusion; sentence after sentence threaded on, bearing not the slightest relation to each other or to the text. And often, though headed with a text, it is scarcely a religious discourse at all, but a string of sentimental nonsense, into which is dragged, for illustration or embellishment, every conceivable subject in art, literature, or science, with which the young man is acquainted. At last he stops, wipes his damp brow, and sits down, congratulating himself, and deluding a portion of his hearers, that he has preached a very "powerful" sermon. And by a series of such, he will very likely "lead captive silly women," and become for a time a popular preacher.

"Unhappy is the nation whose king is a child," says the wise Solomon. And unhappy is the Church whose clergy are raw boys, eager to display themselves and their cleverness, and believing that the whole duty of a minister of the Gospel is to preach "popular" sermons.

At the opposite pole of inefficiency is the sort of clergyman whom one continually finds in English country parishes, where he has been located by hereditary influence as the squire's younger brother, son, or nephew; or has settled down into the Church because he was not considered clever enough for any other profession. In the Presbyterian, and most other forms of unliturgical worship, a man must possess a certain amount of original talent; but in the Church of England talent is not indispensable. Education is, and corresponding refinement. You will rarely find the poorest curate, or the richest and dullest rector, who is not, in degree, a gentleman; but a gentleman is not necessarily a clever man, and certainly not a clever preacher; nay, sometimes quite the contrary. You may get interested in Jack the blacksmith, with his wild, uncouth bursts of passionate piety, in which, like all intensely earnest things, there is something pathetic, something that at times rises almost into poetry. But in the Reverend Blank Blank, with his Oxford or Cambridge learning, his unblemished Johnsonian English, and his grave, decorous, and wholly unobjectionable delivery, you never get interested at all. You can but sit in passive patience, listening to those vapid periods which compose a moral essay as mindless and commonplace as the school-theme of a lad of twelve. Yet he writes such, week after week, as a duty and necessity; and his congregation listen to them with the same feeling: "He is not much of a preacher, to be sure;" but then he is such a worthy man in his parish—a real pastor, as, God bless them! most of the English country clergy are, only—would that he were a silent shepherd! One would respect him exceedingly could he only be persuaded to confine himself to the district and the reading-desk, and never mount the pulpit more.

But there is a class of preachers more trying even than he—for they do not leave us at peace in that lowest deep of "the intense inane," where even the tenderest conscience is satisfied that to listen is impossible, and we take refuge in blissful repose or in thinking about something else. In these other sermons there is a degree of pretension and even accomplishment. They rise to the level of mild mediocrity. They are well written and scholar-like, and delivered with that quiet, gentlemanly elocution which, in strong contrast to the Scotch and Irish habit of thundering and cushion-thumping, is the especial characteristic of the English clergy. As to matter—there is, without doubt, a certain substance in the discourse—a degree of steady connectedness and logical induction; only, unfortunately, all the premises are taken for granted, and all the arguments we think we have somehow heard before. The whole sermon is, in fact, not so much an elucidation as an expansion of the text. Or else it is a familiar fragment of Bible story, reproduced with amplifications innumerable, imaginary conversations, soliloquies, and descriptions, until the anecdote or parable is diluted from its original Saxon brevity—touching and beautiful—into a long-winded history of which every body knows beginning, middle, and end—moral included; which last is tacked on to it with remorseless accuracy, and often with exaggerated applications for which the original text has not the slightest warrant. But the good man must say something—and he says it: though at the close we can not but think he has left his subject precisely where he found it. He had much better have read in his impressive, sonorous voice, the chapter or parable, and closed the book.

Would that there could be impressed upon half the preachers of the day this wholesome doctrine of silence! As said one of them lately—a noted man too—to the present writer, who desired to come and hear him preach: "You had better stop at home. What do people come to hear me for? Most of them know every thing that I can teach them." "Then," replied his interlocutor, "why do you preach at all?" "Well," said the other, half sadly, "I sometimes do ask myself that very question. Why should we parsons be expected and obliged to preach, Sunday after Sunday, whether or not we have got any thing to say?"

Ay—that is the question. Two sermons per week: one hundred and four sermons a year: such is the average produced by, and expected of, almost every clergyman in the United Kingdom. One hundred and four discourses on one subject to be extracted from one human brain in the course of a twelvemonth! Why, if the same were demanded of any other literary worker—say a quarterly reviewer, an essayist, a lecturer on science, or a writer of political leaders—he would answer, if he had a fairly humble estimate of himself and his own powers, "It is impossible. That is, I may do it somehow; but the work will not be good. I shall drift into prosy expansions—feeble repetitions; reproductions in my own words of other men's ideas; or, be my own ideas ever so original, they will be presented crudely, roughly, and imperfectly. No. If I am a worker at all, I must have time to do justice both to myself and to my labors."

Yet if one were to suggest to any preacher that, be his sermons good, bad, or indifferent, if he were to write two per month, instead of eight, they would likely be much better; or if, instead of wearying his soul out every Friday and Saturday, to concoct a given number of pages of his own, he would sometimes substitute the same quantity of some body else's, how horrified and offended our reverend friend would be! Yet why? We all are sometimes ill, or worried, or overdone with business. Why should our rector or curate have more immunity than his neighbors from the weaknesses of humanity? Why, instead of cudgelling his brains Saturday after Saturday, in spite of sickness, business, or worry, to compose a discourse for which nobody is the least the better, does he not occasionally stand up calmly in his pulpit with a preface after this kind:—"My brethren, this week I could not write a sermon worth your hearing, so I will read you one that is worth hearing."

Ay, and suppose he then opened a volume of Jeremy Taylor, or Tillotson, or Ken, or of our many excellent modern preachers whom it would be invidious to particularize: —reading it with his heart and soul, and sympathy; perhaps pausing here and there to discriminate and explain some little point wherein the two minds of writer and reader differed; what a blessing it would be! For he would have given, humbly and honestly, another man's wheat, instead of his own bran; and sent his flock away full, not empty; well-fed, not choked with the poor refuse of what, properly administered, might have been good and substantial pabulum for many a day.

If many of our clergymen would have the moral courage to do this, surely, after the first shock of surprise at the innovation, their congregation would acquiesce gratefully in a proceeding so much to the advantage of both preacher and hearers. Especially as it would only be attempted by a very honest man, whose humility equalled his honesty: who had the sense to take that conscientious estimate of himself and his productions, which insures the only real respect, and constitutes the only true dignity.

It remains to speak of one more class of sermons, which are, for many things, still more objectionable. Worse than the dullest written discourse that one ever dozed over, on a sleepy Sunday in June, with the church-doors open, and the "baa" of the sheep in the churchyard, or the faint warble of the skylark on a level with the steeple weathercock, coming in at every pause, inclining us to believe that the Reverend Dr. Laverock is the best minister after all.

These really extempore preachers, different from the pseudo-extempore Scotch preachers before described, are usually Irish. Who except an Irishman possesses that wondrous "gift of the gab," that frothy facility of speech, and that unfailing confidence in the same, which enables him to stand up in a pulpit, armed only with a pocket

Bible, and pour forth by the hour a stream of disconnected rubbish—clever rubbish it may be—gilded and filigreed over with apt illustrations, picturesque phraseology, and passionate exclamatory devotion, but still devoid of substance, purpose, or argument; a sermon, in short, which, though it may interest for the moment, contains not an atom of truth which the hearer can take hold of, or carry away with him? No doubt it sounded very fine at the time, but when he comes to think it over, he can not in the least remember what it was about—can recall at best but a few stray passages, or a brilliant thought, brilliantly expressed, sticking in the midst of a heap of verbiage, like a fire-fly in a negro's hair.

No wonder. Among our reticent and self-contained Northern races, the power of extemporaneous fluency is extremely rare. Very few even among educated men can put six consecutive ideas into as many sentences, without muddling all up together, falling into nervous repetition or stilted declamation, and ending by a conviction that they have made thorough asses of themselves, said a great deal that they never meant to say, and nothing that they did. So much for ordinary public speaking. As for the great gift of oratory, it does not, either in pulpit or public rostrum, fall upon three men in the course of a century.

Among the lay community these would-be Demostheneses find their level, are hissed from platforms and hustings, or coughed down in Parliament: but in the church there is no remedy against them. And yet a section of the young and foolish is caught by the clap-trap of such sermons; believes that "the Gospel" consists of a number of texts strung together without meaning or consistency: and that a mere fluency of speech, a fatal facility of adjectives, and the power, by means of repetitory verbs, of spinning out a sentence to the last extremity of tenuity, is indeed the divine eloquence of one whose lips are touched as with the prophet's living coal.

But the very lowest of all sermons are "sensational" sermons. It is just the same whether they are preached by the Reverend Boanerges Wakesouls in the pulpit of a legitimate establishment, or by Mr. Apollos Groanall, in his hot, musty, and not over-clean conventicle, or by the before-mentioned Jack Blacksmith, tossing his brawny arms and shouting out "Glory! glory!" from his improvised cart or tub; all are equally obnoxious, equally dangerous to the cause of religion.

First, because, like all extempore sermons, they are such a personal display. A read sermon obliges the reader to keep his eye on his MS., the matter of which must consist of what he has of necessity previously thought of, be his thoughts ever so commonplace, and written down, be his language ever so barren or diffuse. But the preacher without notes throws himself in all his individuality upon the (audience, I was going to write) congregation; attitudinizes, cultivates droppings of voice, and peculiarities of gesture; becomes, in short, as much of an actor as any on the stage. Many of us must know such; men whom we go to hear and are much entertained by, but, somehow, come away with the involuntary feeling that they have mistaken their vocation, and that their proper place ought to have been before the footlights instead of under the ecclesiastic chandelier. And when, in addition, they are not merely actors, but clap-trap actors, using all the lower emotions and passions of men as instruments to produce an effect, stirring up hatred not only against heresy but heretics; taking advantage of that eager craving for the terrible—the same which makes children scream with awful delight at ghost-stories—to treat grown children with vivid pictures of hell, and threatenings of the near approaching day of judgment; when they use all these elements of excitement to effect one grand purpose—their own glorification—do they not deserve the strongest condemnation that tongue or pen can give? Ay, though crowds may fill their churches—exactly as they would the pit of a theatre, and with the same purpose; though there may be power, passion, and even genius, in these discourses; still, it is the misuse of power, the pretense of passion, the prostitution of genius. Worse than all, it teaches men to substitute excitement for devout impression, showy talent for earnestness, and the tickling of the ears for the solemn instruction in righteousness which is an essential part of the service of God.

And now let us consider for a moment what a sermon ought to be. In its highest sense a message—the "glad tidings of good things"—delivered by a man who believes, in all devout humility, that his utmost honor is to be such a messenger: who in his noblest inspiration never forgets that he is only a messenger, the mouth-piece of the Divine Spirit, by whom, as in his consecration vow he believed and declared himself, he is called to be a chosen priest, and yet a minister. Yes, whether Episcopalian, Presbyterian, or dissenting Nonconformist, still a mere minister: elected to teach the laity, that is, those who are more ignorant than he is himself, what he can, and as much as he can, of Divine truth. If he can not, and knows he can not, may Heaven have mercy upon him! for, like Ananias, he has "lied, not unto men, but unto God."

So much for the high ideal of what a sermon is or ought to be. Beneath this there are its commonplace practical necessities.

A sermon should be, as its name implies, a discourse—like any other discourse on a secular subject: and from it should be exacted the same requirements. It should have one clear idea running through it—all the better if only one—of which its text should be the exponent and illustration; not, as is often supposed, the sermon being the illustration of the text. There is no commoner or more fatal mistake than choosing an accidental isolated verse, or clause in a verse, and building upon it a whole superstructure of theological fantasy—useless and baseless—and which, to any clear mind, on carefully examining text and context, is seen immediately to crumble into dust. A good preventive of this error, and an admirable means of elucidating dark passages of Scripture, is the form of preaching called "exposition," namely the reading of a chapter and expounding it verse by verse; a practice used and commended by the early Christians, and which might advantageously be adopted in many pulpits now.

That the sermon, to be worth any thing, must be the outpouring of the preacher's honest heart to the hearts of the congregation, no one will deny; and this is the reason why earnestness, however blended with coarseness, narrowness, and shallowness of argument, will always have a certain power over certain—nay, over all—audiences. It is their earnestness and not their rant, the true thing in them and not the false, which is the secret of the great influence of our Spurgeons, and Cummings, and Guthries; as it was of that of the Whitfields and Wesleys of the past generation. The first requisite, therefore, of a sermon is earnestness; that the congregation should feel, without one doubt, that the preacher means exactly what he says, and teaches what he himself entirely believes. Next to that, his discourse should have completeness. It should be a perfect whole, well fitted in all its parts: every one of which has been carefully thought out and clearly arranged. Not perhaps in hydra "heads" to "sixteenthly," but still artistically put together in fair logical sequence. Whatever opinion he holds—whatever doctrine he preaches—he should have the faculty of clearly expressing it, clothing it in a plain form of lucid language, so that no hearer can possibly mistake his meaning, but, whether agreeing or differing, may be able to carry away a distinct impression of the discourse—sound matter conveyed in sound words.

Then as to the manner. To any deeply religious mind, one fact is self-evident, as true as that the real Church is neither High, Low, nor Broad; Presbyterian nor Episcopalian; Catholic nor Protestant; Established nor Nonconformist; but the Spiritual Church of Christ, known to Him alone. The highest form of a sermon is *not* oratory. If the message be any thing, it is a divine message. No flowers of rhetoric can exalt, and may ignominiously degrade it. Intellectual dignity of style it should have—neither common colloquialisms, nor slipshod expressions; but a certain solemn musical flow, which springs natually out of the high beauty of the subject. That, and no more. The simplest sentences, terse and succinct—the fewest illustrations—the most careful avoidance of all clap-trap appeals to the sentiment, fancy, or emotion of the audience: in fact, a style pure, noble, and severe as those discourses which are chronicled in Holy Writ—this is the perfection of a Sermon.

THE HOUSE OF COMMONS:

FROM THE LADIES' GALLERY.

THIS does not pretend to be a political article. The writer has a decided objection to women who

"Talk of things that they don't understand;"

and seldom can any woman really understand politics. The cool, clear, large brain, the steady judgment, the firm, unimpassioned, yet not untender heart, is a combination of qualities which very few among men, fewer still among women, can boast. And this alone justifies an individual in taking part in, or even criticising those who do take part in guiding the vessel of the State and governing the destinies of nations. To be a truly great politician is so grand a thing, that to be a small one appears simply ridiculous: and perhaps a political woman is the most ridiculous of all. Unless, indeed—which is the only excuse for exceptional women—Providence has endowed her with a man's brain, and something of a man's nature. It is so often. As we see womanish men, so we sometimes see manly, nay "very gentlemanly" women: and then it becomes a question whether both they, and society, are not safest in following out, under certain limitations, the law of their individual natures, so far as it can be done without injury to the general well-being of the community. This, possibly, is the golden mean into which the great contest now pending between the total repression and unlimited emancipation of women will subside.

But to our article: which assumes—shall we say presumes?—to give a woman's view—unbiased, and absolutely unpolitical—of that great deliberative assembly, perhaps the greatest in all the world—the British House of Commons.

Our Saxon ancestors evidently thought that this feminine view was quite unnecessary; that our sex's opinion concerning them, or our presence among them, was a matter to be tacitly ignored. Our business as *ladies*—(the Saxon word means "loaf-givers")—was to rule the household, to rear the children, to instruct duly the dependent maidens, to look after the poor and the helpless, and especially the sick; enough, one would think, to occupy fully any woman's life. They—our forefathers—certainly did not contemplate our doing as some of us nowadays are understood to desire—take our seats and make speeches in Parliament. Nay, they only in later times allowed us even to hear their speeches; and Sir Charles Barry, carrying out this ungallant tradition, has made the Ladies' Gallery of the House of Commons very comfortable indeed within, but without, not much better than a wire cage. Let us flatter ourselves that this is a matter of self-preservation, lest honorable members should be led astray from their duties, blinded by the blaze of beauty, or beguiled by the tenderness beaming from sympathetic eyes. In the mean time here we are; enclosed like beautiful but obnoxious animals, and tamely investigating through our bars the nobler animals below.

But before reaching this elegant den we have had various long galleries to traverse, and staircases to climb, where every accidental masculine eye regards us doubtfully and condescendingly, as if to say—"Ladies, you must be aware that you are here quite on sufferance." We did not mind. Armed with an honorable ticket of admission, we penetrated, glad and grateful, to our sanctum, and there prepared to spend an evening, which was expected to be, and has since become, a matter of history.

It was the night—now some years ago—when the British Goverment made its manifesto on the subject of Italian liberty. Every available space that could afford a hearing for man or for woman, was eagerly sought; and though we ourselves—let us contritely confess—cared but little for the great question of the night, still there was a pleasurable excitement in feeling ourselves part and portion of the national assembly, and in peering down through our gilded bars at the gradually filling House, and the already crowded Strangers' Gallery opposite. The Ladies' Gallery, whatever it may look from thence—within, be it known to all inquirers, is exceedingly comfortable. It consists of three divisions—two public boxes, to which every Member of the House has the privilege of giving a limited number of admissions, and the Speaker's box, which is private, like a *loge* at the Opera. Behind it is a small, well-appointed sitting-room; and farther away, for general benefit, is—oh, let us thank the lords of creation for this!—a kitchen, whence comes the refreshing clatter of tea-cups and saucers. We consoled ourselves that the long evening we were prepared to spend—it was then six P.M., and the House was not expected to rise till three A.M.—would not be spent in total starvation. But—alas for another feminine weakness!—we saw inscribed in every available position, the ominous, not to say impertinent, words, "*Silence is requested.*" Could we—I put it to the sympathizing public—be expected to hold our tongues for nine mortal hours?

However we determined to try; and took our places, so as to obtain the widest and most satisfactory view possible of the scene beneath.

A large, well-proportioned, simply yet tastefully decorated hall, through the colored windows of which the April sunset glow streamed down on to "the floor of the house," where a notable Irish member once expressed his intention to die. He might have died in a more uncomfortable place; for it is well matted and broad, while from either side of it rise in tiers the well known "benches"—"Ministerial" and "Opposition." They are of green leather—comfortable, well stuffed; with plenty of room for honorable gentlemen to lounge and loll in, as some hundred or so were now doing. In this intermediate space a few figures moved about—Members taking their seats, or officials carrying messages to and fro. The business of the night had begun, and there was a certain vocal murmur floating about, but if any particular Member were then speaking, neither we, nor apparently the House, much noticed him. Our first attention was caught by the sight directly opposite us—the Strangers' Gallery.

Probably on every night, but especially on an important night like this, there are few places in London which afford a better study of character than the Strangers' Gallery of the House of Commons. The variety of heads would have delighted a painter. There was the sharp Londoner, free and easy, well accustomed to this, as to most other sights, and taking it merely as a matter of business. There was the sober, stolid country visitor, a good deal awed, but full of importance; who, no doubt, had hunted out and worried "our member" no little, to get admission to this privileged spot, where, after being wedged in tightly and uncomfortably for a whole night, he might attain the honor and glory of taking back to "our borough" a full, true, and particular account of what the member did and said, and how he looked, and how exceedingly attentive or inattentive, as might be, he was to his constituent. Sprinkled among these, the middle class—or rather below the middle class—of metropolitans and provincials, were a few heads of higher order, acute, intelligent, refined, appertaining, you saw at a glance, to scholars and gentlemen, who had friends in the House, in whose success, or in the success of the cause, they were vitally interested. And one small atom in the audience, specially noticeable because his light-colored feminine petticoats broke the monotonous line of masculine costume, was a pretty little boy, placed beside a fashionable, handsome young man, who guarded him paternally, and pointed out every thing to him in a way that was charming to witness. Who knows but that the mighty brain of some great statesman, who,

"When we all lie still,"

shall wield the destinies of Europe, may lurk undeveloped under those soft shining curls and intent childish eyes?

But from this pleasant sight (to a woman at least) we turned our gaze to what we had especially come to see—the House, the legislative assembly of our native land. Externally, there was no call for enthusiasm. Not even the memories of a generation hung about these glaringly new walls. This was not the classic spot whence Chatham was borne out dying: where Fox and Pitt, whose wonderfully characteristic statues now stand in ever-silent opposition in the gallery below, fought out their never-ceasing battles; where Burke rolled out his sonorously elegant periods, Sheridan startled and dazzled with his useless ephemeral brilliance, and Canning charmed both friends and enemies, by the polish and grace of an eloquence, remembered lovingly by many still alive. No—here was nothing to awaken either archæological or historical fervor. Here was merely a well-adorned, very comfortable modern hall, where an assemblage of very comfortable-looking gentlemen disposed themselves in all varieties of attitude. Every costume, from the easy morning-coat to the full-dress black suit—from the stylish attire of the young man, whom the detestable slang of the day would term "a swell," to the solidly-respectable dress of the old-fashioned English gentleman,—was represented here. Every age, too, from twenty-five to eighty; and almost every class—educated, uneducated; stupid, intelligent; patrician, plebeian; for the one leveller—money, which only too often brings a man into Parliament, ceases its power when the glory of election is over, and he comes to sit on these formidable green benches —a single individual, upon whose personal talent it alone depends whether he shall become of any weight in the House and the world, or sink ignominiously into a mere "Ay" or "No" of a division. Still, taking the average of these men, and judging them—utterly unknown to us as they were—only by their externals, there seemed a fair proportion of honest-looking, intelligent, and truly gentlemanly English gentlemen, such as could fairly be trusted with that responsibility which the British House of Commons has wielded, in all generations, as almost the strongest, perhaps the very strongest, power in the nation.

As our perceptions, at first slightly confused by the novelty of the scene, began to right themselves, we caught certain sonorous sounds arising from below, and distinguished, among the moving figures in the centre of the House, one stationary figure, which, gesticulating slightly, tried to make itself heard. We became aware that an honorable Member was "on his legs"—is not that the phrase?—and striving to gain "the ear of the House"—which mysterious organ appeared to suffer from chronic neuralgia. Nevertheless the present speaker—I omit his name—seemed a worthy gentleman, very much in earnest; and this earnestness won, from his most uproarious opponents, a certain genial personal respect. Still, his whole speech of—how many? —hours' duration, could, we solemnly aver, have been easily condensed—facts, arguments, applications and all—into one half-hour of blessed brevity; or, to put the thing professionally, into four printed pages large octavo, or two of ordinary Magazine type. Repetitions innumerable, every idea reappearing again and again, clothed in slightly altered phraseology; assertions given for arguments, and invective for simple statements; involutions and divergencies interminable, till the original subject was buried under one mass of inextricable confusion—this was the impression his speech made upon the unprejudiced feminine mind. It grieves us to have to say it, but so it was. The advisability of first knowing clearly what one had to say, of saying it as tersely, lucidly, and briefly as possible, and then sitting down again, never seemed to present itself to the honorable gentleman's imagination. And yet he was a most honorable and sincere gentleman, and it was quite pathetic to see the mingled dignity and patience with which he bore the House's ironical cheers or laughter at his various blunders and hesitations. If a wrong-headed, he was certainly a much-enduring man, with courage and self-possession worthy of a better cause.

What—are we turning political? Does the strong revulsion which the House evidently shows against a speech defending pope and tyrant, Pio Nono and Bomba of Naples, rouse in us a spirit of partisanship? We fear so. We begin to feel our hearts warm in the contest—our staunch, liberty-loving, Protestant hearts; and we listen to this not too dangerous champion of a creed outworn, who has just thrown down the glove of the evening, with an angry intentness equal to that of Parliament itself.

Nevertheless, after its occasional but unmistakable expression of opinion, the House seemed to take the matter very quietly, as if well accustomed to that sort of thing. It suffered the honorable Member to go mildly meandering on, while it listened or lounged, exchanged messages, notes, or *sotto voce* conversation, with a nonchalance that in most public meetings would be considered, to say the least, rather peculiar. Occasional murmurs of "Hear, hear," "Oh, oh," "Order," were the only signs that Parliament was condescending to pay any attention to business. In truth, it somewhat surprised us ignorant women, who expected to behold a body of men concentrating every energy of their powerful minds on the government of their country, to see the easy, not to say "free-and-easy," demeanor, the want of dignity and gravity, and the total absence of any thing like Areopagite solemnity in the British House of Commons.

When the long-winded gentleman at length concluded, a sigh of relief seemed to flutter through the House, and was undoubtedly echoed in the Ladies' Gallery. Then, after a slight confusion, unintelligible save to parliamentary ears, another member rose to speak. Rose—first placing his stalwart figure in an apparently well-considered oratorical attitude—like a man who was, or, at any rate, believed himself to be, perfectly master of his subject and of himself; and, certainly, his first sentence made it apparent that, if not an orator, he was a capital speaker, with the faculty of lucidly expressing original and valuable thoughts. He began composedly, but gradually waxed more and more vehement; clenching each of his arguments—and they were terse and clear, fortified by a ground-work of apt and well-put facts—by striking his two hands together with a noise that resounded through the whole House, causing us continually to lose the thread of discourse in counting the minutes that would elapse before the next blow came. If this periodical manual exercise is the constant habit of the honorable member—the uninitiate female mind would humbly suggest that it does not in the least improve his oratory, and is very disturbing to the nerves of his listeners.

Another fact, which in this and in succeeding speeches struck us with considerable amazement, was the extreme latitude with which M.P.'s abuse and insult one another. Any thing short of actually giving the lie seems to be quite "parliamentary." Scarcely less than this was both expressed and implied by the two honorable gentlemen aforesaid; yet the latter one contented himself by ejaculating, with a stolid obstinacy truly British, the customary "No, no," and only once rose to explain, in the meekest manner, that, despite his political opinions, he was not an absolute ruffian, deaf to all considerations of common sense and common humanity. Indeed, when we had recovered from the effect of his prosy speech, our advocate of popes and tyrants displayed himself in such an amiable light, so patient of contumely, so steadfast to his own convictions, so forbearing to those of his opponents, that the respect with which the House regarded him, despite his little peculiarities, was not surprising to his audience in the Ladies' Gallery.

Our box was now filled. With whom, does not matter to the public. Suffice it that they were high-born beauties, bearing historical names; ancient ladies, also beautiful, with that loveliness of matronly old age which is met nowhere as it is in England; and other honorable women—having a woman's interest in the House, which, as was natural, concentrated itself in one especial member thereof. Alack! it will be so to the end of time. We of the weaker sex—ay, the very best of us—will always have our deepest interests rooted in and our strongest opinions governed by—not something, but *somebody*.

After an energetic speech, the last M.P. sat down, and another M.P. rose—who shall be also left unrecorded, trusting that his oration was as satisfactory to himself as it undoubtedly was to other people. For it gave the house an opportunity for unanimous evasion. In a miraculously short space of time, yard after yard of empty green benches was ominously displayed, till only a few members and the hapless Speaker remained as listeners. Uncheered by friends, unhissed by foes, the honorable member blandly continued his speech, as if emulating Tennyson's brook—

> "For men may come and men may go,
> But I go on forever."

For how long he did go on this deponent can not say, since we also took the opportunity of disappearing to—our tea! What private alarms beset us because spoons would strike resonantly against saucers, and knives would clatter down to the ground with a noise that we feared might be heard by the whole British Parliament, who had so imperatively commanded our "silence,"—need not here be confessed. Enough, that we subdued our terrors, took our meek and blameless repast; and much invigorated—as we trust were the nobler feeders below—we settled to the serious business of the evening.

The House, having dined, began to reassemble. One member, unknown to fame, who seemed of a practical turn, delivered himself of a few harmless remarks, chiefly arithmetical; and then another—not unknown—in a few brief, but telling sentences, given with classic grace—spoke out his honest mind. Afterwards came a comic interlude, carried on between a large impulsive gentleman, who used language of the sledge-hammer style, and a mild, spare, politely irate partisan of the first speaker. These two fell upon one another so fiercely that at last they were decided to be "out of order"—which phrase seemed, in parliamentary etiquette, to allow of any vituperation short of one gentleman's calling another gentleman "a"—euphuistically speaking, a person who is not too particular in his attention to veracity.

This storm abated; with one or two more of a similar nature, for indeed they apparently formed part of the House's nightly entertainment. Another was, that several members should get "on their legs" at the same time, when there would ensue vociferous and contradictory calls for each, until the Speaker's fiat decided the matter. One member, who was always "rising," seemed an especial pet of the House, and was continually called for; but whether to be listened to or laughed at we could not determine. Parliament clearly liked to be amused, and darted upon the merest shadow of a joke with boyish avidity. Indeed, there was a strong school-boy element in this dignified assembly; and those whom nature or chance forbade to use their lungs for the benefit of the Reporters' Gallery and the public, evidently took a secondary pleasure in merely making a noise.

And now the full House settled itself into post-prandial ease; ay, even the member round whose devoted head had hurtled the chief artillery of the evening. He sat in his place, honest man! and gave no sign of nervousness, save an occasional patting of the back of his bench. He had faced his foes like a Briton: but perhaps he knew—what we did not—that of all his enemies "the greatest was behind."

A little man—or he seemed little, viewed from the altitude of the Ladies' Gallery—rose from the Government benches, and leaning his arm on the table before him, began to say a few words.

"Saying a few words" best expresses this commencement. So unobtrusive was it, that, until we noticed the sudden silence of intent attention which fell upon the House, we scarcely noticed *him* at all. Then we did.

Neither you nor I, good reader, ever heard Demosthenes or Cicero. Other lights of later date—Burke, Fox, Pitt, Sheridan, etc.—are likewise to us little better than myths of a departed age. Oratorical, like musical and dramatic glory, must always be taken by after generations entirely on trust. Daniel O'Connell is almost forgotten; and yet he was dubbed "orator" widely enough in his day. Not undeservedly. Even though you believed in your conscience that he was one of the greatest humbugs alive, and that three words out of every six he uttered were tainted with Irish "imaginativeness," still those words fell so honey-sweet that you caught yourself listening with moist eye and beating heart, as if every syllable were true. Nay, his voice—just the mere organ—so thrillingly musical, so deeply pathetic—haunted you for hours after; even like that of the present Bishop of Oxford, which—

"A lyre of widest range,"

possesses the same inexplicable fascination, and can invest the commonest language, the dryest, most uninteresting topic, with a charm all its own. He, like O'Connell, could almost "wile a bird off a bush."

But this man, *my* orator, the nearest approach to my ideal —that ideal which we most of us have, and never expect to see realized, does not attempt to wile. He scarcely even condescends to persuade. He appeals simply to your reason, or rather, without any direct appeal, he lays before you what your reason at once acknowledges to be the truth, thereby, if he has any victory to gain, making yourself, not himself, your conqueror. Nor in the conflict does he use any ungenerous weapons. His fiercest anger is but the indignation of an honest man.

And an honest man both friends and enemies know him to be. Beyond this, the present writer, in no way a political partisan, does not presume to judge him. Posterity will decide in what niche of his country's history to place the name of William Ewart Gladstone.

He began, as has been recorded, so unobtrusively as to be scarcely recognized; then, with a grasp, ruthless as it was firm, he seized his adversary and smote him hip and thigh with a great slaughter. Quite impersonally, the man being the mere embodiment of the cause; but he did it. Point by point he anatomized his whole speech, its contradictory facts and weak fallacious arguments; then caused the speaker to annihilate himself, to put the torch of truth to his own funeral pile, and reduce his speech, his principles, and all his surroundings to ignominious ashes. This done, the victorious orator went on his way amidst a storm of applause, for the House was now warmed up to the highest pitch of enthusiasm.

He let it subside a little, and then he burst—though still with calmness and dignity—into the free tide of an eloquence—

"Strong without rage—without o'erflowing, full."

That line best expresses the peculiar character of his oratory. Strictly classic it is not, yet it has a flavor of Attic salt befitting one of the ripest scholars of the day. Nor is it plain Saxon, though fraught with a Saxon directness, simplicity, and earnestness, that none of your florid Southern or Celtic orators ever attain. Its grace is not injured, while its force is increased, by a slightly provincial tone—scarcely an accent—which sometimes intrudes upon what would be otherwise the purest academic English. His voice, without being noticeably mellifluous, strikes one as emphatically a sincere voice: firm too—the voice of a man who possesses that strongest element of governing others—the power of being "fully persuaded in his own mind." You feel by instinct that whatever be his opinions, or by whatever process he has arrived at them, they are his real opinions, and will be abided by to the end.*

The House listened to him—as the House always does—with an intentness that his mere diplomatic position, and the importance of his speech, as the mouth-piece of the Government, could never have won. How we listened—we in the Ladies' Gallery—those present will long remember and rejoice. When he ended, the sudden silence felt like an actual pain; we knew well that never in all our lives might we hear the like again. The pause of regret, however, was broken by a naïve exclamation near us—

"Only look! —— —— has actually crossed the House and put his arm upon his shoulder."

And so it was. "He," the great orator, and evidently the one "he" in the world to his affectionate listener, sat in amiable confabulation with his late enemy, who had come over to him and laid his hand upon him—in amicable, not inimical intent. There they were, chatting and smiling together as if they had not been all this time at open warfare, tearing one another to pieces in the most gentlemanly manner—which manner long may they and

* This sentence, written years ago, the author records unhesitatingly; being of the same conviction still.

the whole House retain! No harm can come if each valorous M.P. keeps up a true Briton's hearty respect for another equally true Briton who happens to hold a different opinion from himself.

With this little episode, characteristic in itself—touching, too, if one could dare to put into public print such sacred things as the tender pleasure of a woman's talk, the glad proud light beaming in a woman's eyes—our share in the night's proceedings unhappily terminated. It was long past midnight, and we were very weary, yet we shall always regret that we did not stay to hear the short decisive speech of Lord Palmerston, whose setting sun outshines many of the most brilliant luminaries of Parliament. But the life of the debate seemed to have ended with Gladstone; and besides, we little cared to hear any other speaker: we rather wished to carry away with us, sharp and clear, the recollection of that wonderful speech which has now become matter of history, and which to us personally will always remain as our ideal of oratory—and an orator.

The Abbey towers showed distinct in the moonlight, and London streets were silent and empty, as we drove through the sleeping city into the region of green fields and gardens. Alas! we fear we shall never become politicians, or cease to take a much more vital interest in the destinies of our family and friends than in those of nations; yet we never see the debates (which, contritely be it owned, we seldom read) in *The Times* newspaper, without a vivid memory of our night in the Ladies' Gallery of the House of Commons.

A FEW WORDS ABOUT SORROW.

OF which it is rather venturesome to say any thing in this Democritan age, which boasts so many laughing philosophers. Our forefathers sentimentalized over and dwelt upon their feelings—we are somewhat ashamed of having any; they made the most of all afflictions, real and imaginary—we are often disposed to turn grief itself into an excellent joke. A "broken heart" is a stock subject for humor; yet some have known it; and the worthiest of us have at one time or other caught ourselves making a jest about funerals, just as if there were no such thing as dying. It is good to laugh,—good to be merry; no human being is the better for always contemplating "the miseries of human life," and talking of "graves and worms and epitaphs." Yet since sorrow, in its infinitely varied outside forms and solemn inward unity, is common to all, ought we not sometimes to pause and look at it, seriously, calmly, nor be afraid to speak of it, as a great fact—the only fact of life, except death, that we are quite sure of? And since we are so sure of it, will a few words, suggesting how to deal with it in others, and how to bear it for ourselves, do us any harm? I think not.

For, laugh as we may, there is such a thing as sorrow; most people at some portion of their lives have experienced it—no imaginary misery—no carefully petted-up wrong; no accidental anxiety, or state of nervous irritable discontent, but a deep, abiding, inevitable *sorrow*. It may have come slowly or suddenly; may weigh heavier or lighter at different times, or according to our differing moods and temperaments; but it is there—a settled reality not to be escaped from. At bed and board, in work or play, alone and in company, it keeps to us, as close as our shadow, and as certainly following. And so we know it will remain with us; for months, for years—perhaps even to the end of our lives.

Therefore, what can we preach to ourselves, or to our fellows, concerning it? Perhaps the best sermon of all is that of the ancient Hebrew, who laid his hand upon his mouth, "because THOU didst it." For sorrow is a holy thing. The meanest mortal who can say truly,

"Here I and sorrow sit,"

feels also somewhat of the silent consecration of that awful companionship, which may well—

"Bid kings come bow to it,"

yet elevates the sufferer himself to a higher condition of humanity, and brings him nearer to the presence of the King of kings.

Grief is a softening thing, from its very universality. *Ex uno disce omnes.* Your child, my neighbor, may be dying, or giving you anguish sharp as death; my own familiar friend may have lifted up his heel against me, causing me now, and perhaps forever, to doubt if there be such a thing as fidelity, or honor, or honesty in the world; a third, whom we all know and meet daily, may have received yesterday, or last week, or last month, some small accidental stab, altogether inward, and bleeding inwardly, yet which may prove a death wound; a fourth has sustained some heavy visible blow or loss, which we all talk of, compassionate, would fain comfort if we could, but we can not. These various shapes which sorrow takes compose a common unity; and every heart which has once known its own bitterness, learns from thence to understand, in a measure, the bitterness of every other human heart. The words, "He bore our griefs and carried our sorrows," —"in all our afflictions he was afflicted," have a secondary and earthly as well as a Divine significance; and to be "acquainted with grief," gives to any man a power of consolation, which seems to come direct through him from the great Comforter of all. The "Christus Consolator" which Scheffer painted,—the Man Divine, surrounded by, and relieving every form of human anguish, is a noble type of this power, to attain which all must feel that their own anguish has been cheaply purchased, if by means of it they may have learned to minister unto all these.

This ministry of consolation is not necessarily external, or intentional. We must all have sometimes felt, that the people who do us most good are those who are absolutely unaware of doing it. Even as "baby-fingers, waxen touches," will melt into flesh and blood again a heart that has seemed slowly turning into stone, so the chance influence of something or somebody, intrinsically and unconsciously good, will often soothe us like a waft of sweet scent borne across a dull high-road from over a garden wall. It may be the sight of peaceful, lovely, beloved old age, which says silently and smilingly, "And yet I have suffered too;" or the brightness in some young face, honest and brave, which reminds a man of the days of his own youth, and shames him out of irresolution or cynical unbelief, daring him, as it were, to be such a coward as to let his after-life give the lie to the aspirations of his prime. Nay, perhaps the influence, more fugitive still, comes from a word or two found in a book, or a look in a stranger's face, which, however inexplicable, makes us feel at once that this book or this stranger understands us, refreshes and helps us—is to us like a flower in a sick-room, or a cup of water in a riverless land.

It would be curious to trace, if any but immortal eyes ever could trace, how strongly many lives have been influenced by these instinctive sympathies; and what a heap of unknown love and benediction may follow until death many a man—or woman—who walks humbly and unconsciously on, perhaps, a very obscure and difficult way, fulfilling this silent ministry of consolation.

We are speaking of consolation first, and not without purpose; let us now say a little word about sorrow.

It may seem an anomaly, and yet is most true, that the grief which is at once the heaviest and the easiest to bear is a grief of which nobody knows; something, no matter what, which, for whatever reason, must be kept in the depth of the heart, neither asking nor desiring sympathy, counsel, or alleviation. Such things are—oftener perhaps than we know of; and, if the sufferer can bear it at all, it is the best and easiest way of bearing grief, even as the grief itself becomes the highest, we had almost said the divinest, form of sorrow upon earth. For it harms no one, it wounds and wrongs no one; it is that solitary agony unto which the angels come and minister—making the night glorious with the shining of their wings.

Likewise, in any blow utterly irremediable, which strikes at the very core of life, we little heed what irks and irritates us much in lesser pain—namely, to see the round of daily existence moving on untroubled. We feel it not; we are rather glad of its monotonous motion. And to be saved from all external demonstrations is a priceless relief; neither to be watched, nor soothed, nor reasoned with, nor pitied: to wrap safely round us the *convenances* of society, or of mechanical household association: and only at times to drop them off and stand, naked and helpless as a new-born child, crying aloud unto Him who alone can understand our total agony of desolation. But this great solitude of suffering is impossible to many; and indeed can only be sustained without injury by those strongly religious natures unto whom the sense of the Divine presence is not merely a tacit belief, or a poetical imagination, but a proved fact—as real as any of the facts of daily life are to other people. With such people it is impossible to argue. Let him that readeth understand, if he can understand, or if it be given him to understand, these great mysteries.

But one truth concerning sorrow is simple and clear enough for a child's comprehension; and it were well if from childhood we were all taught it; namely, that that grief is the most nobly borne which is allowed to weigh the least heavily upon other people. Not every one, however, is unselfish enough to perceive this. Many feel a certain pride in putting on and long retaining their sackcloth and ashes, nay, they conceive that when they have sustained a heavy affliction, there is a sort of disgrace in appearing too easily to "get over it." But here they make the frequent error of shallow surface-judging minds. They can not see that any real wound in a deep, true, and loving heart is *never* "got over." We may bury our dead out of our sight, or out of our neighbor's sight, which is of more importance; we may cease to miss them from the routine of our daily existence, and learn to name people, things, places and times, as calmly as if no pulse had ever throbbed horribly at the merest allusion to them—but they are not forgotten. They have merely passed from the outer to the inner fold of our double life—which fold lies nearest to us, we know; and which are usually the most precious, the things we have and hold, or the things we have lost—we also know.

It may seem a cruel word to say—but a long-indulged

and openly displayed sorrow, of any sort, is often an ignoble, and invariably a selfish feeling; being a sacrifice of the many to the few. If we look round on the circle of our acquaintance, with its percentage, large or small, of those whom we heartily respect, we shall always find that it is the highest and most affectionate natures which conquer sorrow soonest and best; those unselfish ones who can view a misfortune in its result on others as well as on their own individuality; or those in whom a great capacity of loving acts at once as bane and antidote, giving them, with a keen susceptibility to pain, a power of enduring it which to the unloving is not only impossible but incredible. It is chiefly the weak, the self-engrossed, and self-important, who make to themselves public altars of perpetual woe, at which they worship, not the *Dii manes* of departed joys, but the apotheoses of living ill-humors.

An incurable regret is an unwholesome, unnatural thing to the indulger of it; an injury to others, an accusation against Divinity itself. The pastor's reproof to the weeping mother—"What! have you not yet forgiven God Almighty?" contains a truth which it were well if all mourners laid to heart. How hard it is to any of us to "forgive God Almighty;" not only for the heavy afflictions which he has sent to us, but for the infinitude of small annoyances, which (common sense would tell us, if we used it) we mostly bring upon ourselves! Yet even when calamity comes—undoubted, inevitable calamity—surely, putting religion altogether aside, the wisest thing you can do with a wound is to heal it, or rather to let it heal; which it will, slowly and naturally, if you do not voluntarily keep it open into a running sore. Some people, with the very best intentions, seem to act upon us like a poultice laid over gaping flesh; and others again officiate as surgical instruments, laying bare every quivering nerve, and pressing upon every festering spot till we cry out in our agony that we had rather be left to die in peace, unhealed. Very few have the blessed art of letting Nature alone to do her benign work, and only aiding her by those simple means which suggest themselves to the instinct of affection,—that is, of affection and wisdom combined; which nothing but tender instinct, united to a certain degree of personal suitability, will ever supply. For, like a poet, a nurse, either of body or mind, must be born, not made.

We all know many excellent and well-meaning people, whom in sickness or misfortune we would as soon admit into our chamber of sorrow as we would an amiable elephant or a herd of wild buffaloes.

Perhaps (another anomaly) the sharpest affliction that any human being can endure is one which is not a personal grief at all, but the sorrow of somebody else. To see our dearly beloved writhing under a heavy stroke, or consumed by a daily misery which we are powerless to remove or even to soften, is a trial heavy indeed—heavier in one sense than any affliction of our own, because of that we know the height and depth, the aggravations and alleviations. But we can never fathom another's sorrow. Not even the keenest-eyed and tenderest-hearted among us, can ever be so familiar with the ins and outs of it as to be sure always to minister to its piteous needs at the right time and in the right way. Watch as we may, we are continually more or less in the dark; often irritating where we would soothe, and wounding where we are longing to heal.

Also, resignation to what may be termed a vicarious grief is cruelly hard to learn. We are sometimes goaded into a state of half-maddened protestation against Providence, feeling as if we—kept bound hand and foot on the shore—were set to watch a fellow-creature drowning. To be able to believe that Infinite Wisdom really knows far more than we do what is best for that beloved fellow-creature, is the highest state to which faith can attain; and the most religious can only catch it in brief glimpses through a darkness of angry doubt that almost rises at times into blasphemous despair. From such agonies no human strength can save: and while they last every human consolation fails. We can only lie humble at the feet of Eternal Wisdom, yielding into His hands not only ourselves but our all. And surely if there be such a thing as angelic ministry, much of it must needs be spent not only on sufferers, but on those whose lot it is to stand by and see others suffer, generally having all the time to wear a countenance cheerful, hopeful, or calmly indifferent, which in its dreary hypocrisy dare give no sign of the devouring anxiety that preys on the loving heart below.

Mention has been made of those griefs, wholly secret and silent, which are never guessed by even closest friends;

the sacred self-control of which makes them easier to bear than many a lesser anguish. In contrast to these may be placed the griefs that every body knows and nobody speaks of,—such as domestic unhappiness, disappointed love, carking worldly cares, half-guessed unkindnesses, dimly suspected wrongs; miseries which the sufferer refuses to acknowledge, but suffers on in a proud or heroic silence that precludes all others from offering either aid or sympathy, even if either were possible, which frequently it is not. In many of the conjunctures, crises and involvements of human life, the only safe, or kind, or wise course is this solemn though heart-broken silence, under the shadow of which it nevertheless often happens that wrongs slowly work themselves right; pains lessen to the level of quiet endurance; or an unseen hand, by some strange and sudden sweep of destiny, clears the dark and thorny pathway, and makes every thing easy and peaceful and plain.

But this does not always happen. There are hundreds of silent martyrs in whom a keen observer can see the shirt of horse-hair or the belt of steel-points under the finest and most elegantly-worn clothes; and for whom, to our short-sighted human eyes, there appears no possible release but death. The only consolation for such is the lesson,—sublime enough to lighten a little even the worst torment,—which is taught by that majestic life-long endurance, sustained by strength celestial that we lookers-on know not of, and for which in the end await the martyr's bliss and the martyr's crown.

These "few words about sorrow" are said. They may have been said, and better said, a hundred times before. There is hardly any deep-thinking or deep-feeling human being who has not said them to himself over and over again: yet sometimes a truth strikes truer and clearer when we hear it repeated by another, than when we listen to its dim echoes in our own often bewildered mind. To all who understand the meaning of the word sorrow, we commend these disjointed thoughts to be thought out by themselves at leisure. And so farewell.

A HEDGE-SIDE POET.

"A poor, tired, wandering singer, singing through the dark."

WE hear a good deal now of poets of the people. The days are gone by when glorious ploughmen and inspired shepherds were made much of at noblemen's tables, and treated by noblewomen with something of the magnificent protection which the great Glumdalclitch accorded to Lemuel Gulliver. We no longer meet them led about as tame lions by an admiring yet patronizing host, who hints "hush!" at the least prospect of their roaring; and they are expected to roar always at the keeper's will —never against it. But if in these times they are more independent, they are much less rare and majestic creatures. They haunt every literary drawing-room by twos and threes,—the mud of their aboriginal fields still sticking to their illustrious boots,—pleased, but awkward; trying hard to tone down their native accents, manners, and customs, to the smooth level of what is termed "good society." Or else, taking the opposite tack, are forever thrusting forward, with obnoxious ostentation, their "origin;" forgetting that the delicate inborn refinement which alone can save a nobleman from being a clown, is also the only thing which can make a clodhopper into a gentleman. If it has not made him such—in manners as in mind—he may be a poet, but he remains a clodhopper still.

But, happily, many of these poets of the people are likewise of the true "gentle" blood; and thus, be their birth ever so humble, they rise, step by step, educating themselves—heaven knows how—but they are educated: acquiring, as if by instinct, those small social *bienséances*, which are good as well as pleasant, being the outward indication of far better things. Men such as these, wherever met, are at once easily recognizable, and quickly recognized; society gives them a cordial welcome; they are neither merely tolerated nor insultingly patronized: but take by right their natural place in the world, as its "best" portion—its truest aristocracy.

There is yet another class of born poets, whom the muse finds at the plough, the loom, the forge, the tailor's board, or the cobbler's stall,—and leaves them there. This, from various causes. First, because genius, or talent—call it which you please—is infinite in its gradations; the same amount of intellectual capacity which, found in an educated person, will enable him to take a very high place among "the mob of gentlemen who write with ease," will not enable a common-day laborer to teach himself every thing from the alphabet upwards, and raise himself, of his own strength, from the plough-tail to the Laureateship. Secondarily, because, almost invariably, the organization, mental and physical, which accompanies the poetic faculty is the one least fitted for that incessant battle with the world, for which a man must arm himself who aims to rise therein. Therefore it is, that while our noble Stephensons, and the like,—men who live poems instead of singing them,—move grandly on through their brave career, which may begin in a hut and end in Westminster Abbey,—these, who may be called our "hedge-side poets," never rise out of the station in which they were born. Unless some Capel Lofft or Savage Landor should catch them and exhibit them, they probably flutter on through life, singing their harmless songs to themselves, or to a very small audience; far happier in many things than if they had been set up to plume and strut their little day in the gilded cage of popularity.

Yet, hear them in their native meadows, expecting from them neither epic hymns nor operatic *fioriture;* and we are often charmed and amazed to find how exquisitely they sing: with a note as sweet and unexpected as a robin's warble out of a yellowing hedge, when leaves are falling, and flowers are few.

Such as this is more than one lyric, which we have discovered in two humble-looking volumes, printed by subscription, and probably hardly known beyond the subscribers' drawing-room tables, which purport to be "Poems" by a Cambridgeshire laboring man, James Reynolds Withers.

Let us take the first that offers, a "Song of the Butterfly:"

"I come from bowers of lilacs gay,
With honeysuckles blending;
And many a spray of willows gray,
Above the waters bending.

I flutter by the river side,
Where laves the swan his bosom;
And o'er the open common wide,
Where yellow ragworts blossom.

Away on downy pinions borne,
With many a happy rover,
I skim above the rustling corn,
And revel in the clover.

I laugh to see the frugal bee
For others hoard her treasure;
From morn till night a toiler she,
But mine's a life of pleasure.

* * * * *

The truant schoolboy loves to chase
Me through the winding mazes;
I lure him on a merry race,
O'er meadows white with daisies.

He creeps and crawls with cat-like tread,
When I'm on cowslip rocking;
Then up I flutter o'er his head,
His vain endeavors mocking.

And when the bee is in her cell,
And shrill-tongued cricket calling,
I sleep within the lily's bell,
Whilst nightly damps are falling.

There round my clean white-sheeted bed,
Are pearly dews distilling;
And nightingales, above my head,
Their sweetest notes are thrilling.

I dance, I play, make love, and sleep,
This is my whole employment;
For men may smile, or men may weep—
My life is all enjoyment."

Now to take a working man from his inherited calling, and exalt him into a poet, is a difficult and dangerous thing. But when an English agricultural laborer, at seven shillings a week, writes such verses as these, those acquainted with the normal condition of the race are naturally somewhat surprised. If a Wordsworth, descending from his height of gentlemanly scholarship to this sweet, simple chronicling of simple nature, fresh as a breezy June morning,—if a Wordsworth had done it, we should have set down this poem as "charming;" but when it comes from the brain of uneducated Hodge, to whom even decent English must have been a difficult acquirement, we are forced to reflect, "This man must have something in him: who and what is he?" Let him answer for himself. A letter of his, which has fallen under our notice, is so simple and touching an expression of the man, James Reynolds Withers, that it is a poem in itself. We feel we are not breaking confidence, nor infringing on the right of every author to be known only by his published writings, if he so chooses, in giving it here, entire and unaltered:—

"I was born in the year 1812, on the 24th of May, at Weston Colville, in Cambridgeshire—a village with about 400 inhabitants. My father was a shoemaker there, but had failed in business before I was born. I am the youngest of four children, and the only son, born almost out of due season, a sort of Benjamin to my parents, being a child of their old age. They could not afford to send me to school, so my mother taught me to read and write a little. At an early age, I was employed at picking stones, weeding corn, and scaring birds, and part of one year I was a keeper of sheep, when I was much alone, and from that time I date the first awakening of a poetic feeling. I had a book of old ballads, and Watts's Divine Songs for children, that I used to read a great deal, and many I committed to memory. After that, I began to like to be alone, and preferred, when unemployed, strolling in the woods, and rambling in the meadows amongst the trees and flowers, to joining in the games of my playmates. My father had some knowledge of a market-gardener at Fordham, and wishing to get me into some way of getting my living, at twelve years old I was put to this man for three years. The first two years I had only my board and lodging; for the last year I received thirty shillings. I staid my time, but I learned but little—in fact, there was nothing to learn but what any one might do—plain digging, hoeing, and weeding. After my time was out I went to lodgings and continued to work for my old master at seven shillings per week. When I was about nineteen years old my second sister married and was living at Cambridge, and she hearing that an under-porter was wanted at Magdalene College, succeeded in getting the place for me, but I did not stay more than five months. I felt like a caged bird, and sighed for the freedom of the fields again. I returned to Fordham again, to my old place and old wages, but I could study nature in the day and books in the evening, and write my jingling verses without interruption; but I was often in straitened circumstances in the winter; perhaps, for two months I had nothing to do. At such times I visited my mother; my father was still living, but it was my mother that I always clung to the most. When I was about twenty-four years old, my mother had a small sum of money left her by her mother, who died at the age of ninety-six, and then it was that I thought I should like to learn the shoemaking; and my mother, wishing always to benefit me all she could, paid a small sum to the successor of my father to instruct me for one year, and in that year my mother died, and I never learned the trade. After two years' absence I returned to Fordham again, and soon married, and have got a livelihood by mending shoes and sometimes working in the fields, always going to harvest work. It was while reaping for R. D. Fyson, Esq., about six years back, that I was so fortunate as to be introduced to Mrs. Fyson, who first brought my works before the public, and has been my constant friend ever since.

"I have had four children, three of whom are living; the eldest a girl, eighteen years, and two boys, one seventeen, the other fourteen years old. The girl belongs to the 'stitch, stitch, stitch' sisterhood: the boys I am anxious to get out to something where they may get a living. They go out to work in the fields when they can get work to do, but I should rejoice in the hope of being able to give them some trade.

"Yours truly, J. R. WITHERS."

A simple story; yet what a picture it gives of this poor man's life, outwardly not different from the lives of thousands of East-Anglian peasants; the only difference was in *the man*, to whom nature gave a portion—great or small, time will show, for he is still not old—an undoubted portion of that strange gift called the poetic faculty. He therefore sees things with other eyes, feels things in another way, than his fellows; has pleasures they know not, struggles and pains which they can not comprehend. Whether this has been good for him or ill, God knows; but it is the necessary lot of all who have ever so small a share of the gift of genius,—God's gift, and therefore never to be undervalued or denied.

In going through these two volumes, with their occasional errors of rhyme and rhythm, their conventional phraseology, and commonplaceness of subjects; the author, like all uneducated rhymers, choosing themes and thinking thoughts which scores of poets have lighted on before him,—it is curious to see the *mens divinior* cropping out, as geologists would say, through the commonest stratum of style and ideas. Such as—

"Away, away, through valleys fair
 Where flames the mustard bloomy,
*As if the sun was shining there,
 When all around is gloomy."*

Or this picture of the baby year, out of a series of many equally good, which form a poem, rough and careless in diction, but vivid and beautiful in imagery, entitled, "Reminiscences of the year 1855."

"Wrapt in robes of snowy ermine,
At first I saw thee slumbering lie,
Calm, quiet, still, and beautiful;
But soon thy chubby dimpled hands
Were playing with the crocus cups,
And gingling silver snowdrop bells.
And now a toddling fair wee thing,
Dressed in a frock of palest green,
All sprigged with pinky hawthorn buds,
And bordered with hepaticas.
Thou lov'dst to tease old Father Frost,
Pulling his grizzly crispy beard,
Shaking the powder from his locks,
Spoiling with fingers moist and warm
The pictures of his palsied hand."

A tender, close, and minute observation of nature is the strongest peculiarity of Withers's poetry. There is not much of the hot current of human emotion in it; little sentiment, and no passion; a gentle, moralizing, thoughtful nature, an eminently religious mind, and a shy retiring temperament, characterize it; as we doubt not, they are the characteristics of the man himself; for with small demonstration, there is yet no pretense or affectation in his verses: all he does is essentially real. Such poems as "The Fire of Sticks," "The Old Well," "The Old Lane," indicate what a true "poet of the people" he might have become—nay, might yet become, had he the power to concentrate into careful study of the art of poetry—for it is an art, as well as a native faculty—his delicacy of fancy, accuracy of perception, and truth of delineation. A man who could do this—enbalming in real poetry the rural life of England—the poor man's life—would do for it, and us, a thing which has never yet been done. The southern half of our island may boast its Clare and its Bloomfield—with one or two lesser singers—but it has never produced, perhaps never may produce, a Hogg or a Burns.

One may naturally ask, how is it that a man like Withers, with qualities, intellectual and moral, sufficient to raise him into a much higher and more congenial sphere, should, at forty-eight, remain still a common agricultural laborer? Possibly the explanation of this fact he has himself unconsciously given us in a little poem, called "Solitude the best Society."

"I was not formed to stem the tide,
  Or ride the stormy waves of strife:
My little bark can only glide
  Along the shallow streams of life.
Whilst bolder spirits fearless roam,
  And ocean's wildest tracks explore,
I linger like a drone at home,
  And play with pebbles on the shore.
    Whilst some are proudly gaining
    A name for valiant deeds,
    Here lonely I only
    Gather shells and weeds.
I know 'tis called a weakness
  'Gainst which I ought to strive;
And if I had less meekness
  Perhaps should better thrive.
Why should I feel so shrinking,
  So timid and unwise,
Whilst many men unthinking
  By boldness gain the prize?
I see them how they toil and scheme,
  And plan from day to day;
By grove and stream I muse and dream,
  Thus pass my time away,
I would not be a senseless clod
  To only eat and sleep:
Thou knowest me, my Father God,
  Though I can only creep.
Towards thee still my heart doth tend
  Though pressed with sorrow down;
To thee, my everlasting Friend,
  Are all its struggles known.
    Let bold blind bigots wrangle,
    And think they only see,
    I care not, I fear not,
    I dare to hope in Thee."

There is something deeply pathetic in all this; and one can easily understand the "struggles" which a man so gentle and refined, must, in his position, have had to bear. But Withers is no prater of his own personality; even the incidents of his outward life are rarely more than hinted at: some lines "On the Death of my Child," being almost the only instance of what may be termed personal poetry. Except one, "Written from Newmarket Union to my Sister in Cambridge."

A poet in a workhouse! Yes, it was so. In the year 1847, when, during very severe weather, he could get no work, rather than run into debt or subsist upon charity, this honest Englishman had the courage to ask the help which every Englishman, unable to find work or to do it, may claim, not so much as an alms, but a right—he dared to go with all his family, for a few months, into the union workhouse. And this little song he sung there, in its cheerful patience and self-respect, deserves to be quoted here, if only to shame all maudlin, egotistic, hypochondriac rhymsters, who think that genius warrants a man in being, not a man at all, but only a poet.

> "Since I can not, dear sister, with you hold communion,
> I'll give you a sketch of our life in the Union.
> But how to begin I don't know, I declare:
> Let me see; well, the first is our grand bill of fare.
> We've skilly for breakfast; at night bread and cheese,
> And we eat it, and then go to bed if we please.
> Two days in the week we've puddings for dinner,
> And two we have broth so like water, but thinner;
> Two, meat and potatoes, of this none to spare;
> One day bread and cheese—and this is our fare.
>
> And now then my clothes I will try to portray;
> They're made of coarse cloth, and the color is gray;
> My jacket and waistcoat don't fit me at all;
> My shirt is too short, or else I am too tall;
> My shoes are not pairs, though of course I have two,
> They are down at the heel, and my stockings are blue.
>
> But what shall I say of the things they call breeches?
> Why mine are so large they'd have fitted John Fitches.
> John Fitches, you'll say, well, pray who was he?
> Why one of the fattest men I ever did see.
> To be well understood, dear, they ought to be seen;
> Neither breeches nor trowsers, but something between;
> And though they're so large, you'll remember, I beg,
> That they're low in the waist and high on the leg,
>
> And no braces allowed me—oh dear, oh dear;
> We are each other's glass, so I know I look queer.
> A sort of Scotch bonnet we wear on our heads;
> And I sleep in a room where there are just fourteen beds;
> Some are sleeping, some snoring, some talking, some playing,
> Some fighting, some swearing, but very few praying.
>
> Here are nine at a time who work on the mill:
> We take it by turns, so it never stands still:
> A half an hour each gang; 'tis not very hard,
> And when we are off we can walk in the yard.
> We have nurseries here, where the children are crying;
> And hospitals too for the sick and the dying.
>
> But I must not forget to record in my verse,
> All who die here are honored to ride in a hearse.

I sometimes look up to the bit of blue sky
High over my head, with a tear in my eye,
Surrounded by walls that are too high to climb,
Confined as a felon without any crime;
Not a field, not a house, not a hedge can I see—
Not a plant, not a flower, not a bush nor a tree,
Except a geranium or two that appear
At the governor's window, to smile even here."

A noticeable trait in Withers is his exceeding refinement of sentiment and expression. While far loftier versifiers seem to think it poetical to be coarse, and hold that gorgeous diction atones for any sensuousness, or even sensuality; — this man whose life has been passed in the sphere where the grossness of human nature rarely attempts to disguise itself, never pens a verse which a good man, when grown an old man, might regret having once written, and blush to see one of his own growing-up daughters read.

"Tea-table Talk,"—a conversation between a Dock and a Nettle, in which these two vegetable scandal-mongers tear to pieces a number of floral reputations; "Retaliation," where the same thing is done by a certain quick-witted Mrs. Sparrow, perched on the—

"—— green-budded thorn,
Where the birds were assembled on Valentine's morn;"

and the "Toper's Lament," prove that Withers has a spice of humor in him: though, on the whole, he has too much of the meditative, didactic tone, to be capable of the strong contrasts of fun and pathos which constitute the dramatic element in poetry. In short, he is more of a dreamer or a moralizer than an emotionalist. But, as we said, he is still far from being an old man; there may be much undeveloped power in him yet. A late MS. poem, not included in these volumes, is better than any thing they contain.

As to the man himself—for the core of all a man writes or does, the root and indication of every thing he may live to be, is his ego, his essential manhood,—let us quote what his minister, the clergyman of Fordham parish, has written of him:—

"Although Withers is in a very humble position of life, his mind is so well stored with valuable information on a variety of subjects, that with the greatest delight I spend much time in his company. I would also add that his character is irreproachable, and that he delights in doing good."

Will no one, who also "delights in doing good," try if a little good can not be done in some way, by raising into a position more suitable for him, our poor hedge-side poet, James Reynolds Withers?

THE

LAST GREAT EXHIBITION.

ITS BEGINNING.

FIVE shillings' worth! Yes, and full worth too: though, according to statistics at the doors, the public in general do not seem to think so. Only season ticket-holders as yet throng the great World's Fair, that magnificent piece of daring incompleteness, which has lately been the talk of London, as if it were a sudden only half-comprehended fact which had just started up under one's very eyes. For, in truth, whatever might be the excitement in the provinces and abroad, the general body of working London had taken the International Exhibition very quietly. After the great gloom of Christmas-time, the Christmas marked by the death of the good Prince who had planned it all, every body said that of course it would be put off, must be, ought to be; till every body acquiesced in the wiser judgment and deeper tenderness which made the accurate and sacred carrying out of the wishes of the dead the best tribute to his memory. Afterwards "every body" seemed to think very little about the matter. Hundreds and thousands of the middle class, living within an easy radius of five miles, had actually never seen more of the Great Exhibition than those two ugly domes, that rose month by month, and week by week, first as skeleton scaffolding, and then as dazzling crystal, catching the sun's rays from over the house-tops and the park trees. Country cousins alone, who seem to have the constitutions of elephants, the legs of camels, and the eyes of Argus himself, went to see it, and brought back wonderful stories of that town under glass, with its myriads of workmen, running to and fro along the ground like ants, clustering like bees over the galleries, or dangling perilously from the roof like spinning caterpillars; creating around them an atmosphere which might truly be considered "the dust of ages," and a Bable-like noise of unwearied hammers, and tongues! As to the building itself—its beauty, convenience, desirability, payability, or the contrary—there were disputes and arguments without end: —ending, as most arguments do, in each side sticking only the firmer to its own opinion. But on one point every body was agreed, namely, that it could not possibly be finished by the first of May.

Consequently London, as a whole, cared very little about it; and even up to the middle of April it was a rare thing to find an acquaintance who had done the desperate deed of buying a season-ticket, and actually meant to be present at the opening. Rumors were rife, to the very last, of that opening being quite impracticable: of the infinite difficulties, perplexities, and hindrances which beset the hapless contractors: how more than even at first feared, was felt, day by day, the want of that guiding Head, to whose clear, calm wisdom, unbiased and universal kindliness, and decision at once acute and rapid, every doubtful point could be brought, and was brought—in 1851, but, alas! not in 1862. Now, though no trouble nor exertion was spared, though the Commissioners almost lived in the building, still there were incessant complaints on the one side, incessant changes of purpose on the other. There was no definite ruler to pronounce distinctly of any disputed question, "It had better be so and so;" no dignified autocrat to settle differences by a gentle word or two, being universally obeyed, because universally trusted.

It is a strange comment on the text: "Death is better than life, and the end of a thing better than its beginning" —that until we lost him we never knew what we lost in that good man, true man, true gentleman, true Christian, whom all England now glories in, with affectionate remembrance. Deep, inexpressibly deep and tender, is now the thought of him: especially among the British middle classes, by whom a character like his, the beauty of which takes half a lifetime to find out, when once found out, is cherished forever. The regret for him, an almost household regret, was probably at the root of the great indifference with which most people viewed the Exhibition. Many, both men and women, said outright, "No, they should not like to go; they had seen the '51 Opening, with the Queen and Prince Albert there, and—and"—with a quiver of the lip—"they would rather not see this one; they did not like to make fools of themselves in public."

Even to the very last week of April, when the *Times* told us daily of the almost miraculous exertions that were being made to get the Exhibition open, nobody seemed to heed, or to believe that the event would really come to pass. And those who took the trouble to make the circumbendibus down Exhibition Road, along Cromwell Road, and up Prince Albert's Road, into the main western thoroughfare, shook their heads ominously, and declared it was all nonsense to expect it: the thing was impossible.

As the day arrived, however, the public found to its intense amazement that this resolute body of Englishmen were working on the polite Frenchman's principle: "Madam, had it been possible, it would have been done already; and if it is impossible, it shall be done." And now stories began to grow concerning the throng gathering from all parts of the world to see the grand show—itself the grandest part of it; of the terrific rush for season-tickets; of the despair of Sir Richard Mayne, to whom the Lord Mayor had sent word that he was coming with "six hundred carriages," and who was reported to have answered a nobleman who asked, if he started from May Fair about 9 A.M. on Thursday, what time he might expect to reach the Great Exhibition?—"On Saturday, my lord; or, perhaps, if you are very lucky, by Friday afternoon."

These tales, gently irritating, tickled the public ear; but the general mass of society, living only a few miles from the scene of action, was very little disturbed thereby; read its *Times*, and congratulated itself that it was "out of the way." A few, who, sitting in their parlors, or walking in their gardens that bright May morning, heard the distant sound of the Park guns, stopped to think, "Oh, this is the Great Exhibition day!" and in every heart—every woman's heart assuredly must have been a stab of pain to remember how heavy a day it must be to another widowed woman, and be thankful that she was distant from the scene of such saddened festivity.

"I'm glad of it," one house-mother was heard to say with a sob, as she read aloud the brief intimation of the Queen's having that morning reached Perth to breakfast. "I am glad she is far away. I care more for those two lines than for all the rest of the newspaper." And such was the universal feeling.

But grief has its blessed side. How good it has been for the general community to discover, as death only fully could have discovered, such virtues in high places,—virtues based on the inward conviction and outward recognition of the one great truth of Christianity, self-abnegation, "I will spend and be spent for you." How much good may not unconsciously be done to many careless, unloving heads of families, in all ranks, to find that the head of the first Family in the realm was, voluntarily, as hard-working a man as if he had had to earn his daily bread in a profession or trade: that he was a scrupulous paymaster, a wise, prudent, exact governor of his household; a liberally educated gentleman, who by his methodical use of talents and opportunities, in spite of his innumerable occupations, found time for every thing and every body. Ay, every body: from his own loyally cherished wife, to the poorest author or artist who came to him for a little help, or a few kindly words. And all this, this noble, admirable, heroic life, was lived with such a simple, silent, and reticent humility, that the nation, much as it respected him, never really knew what he was, till he was gone.

No more—for it is only saying what every body has said and felt, and will feel while this generation lasts—this generation, which remembers the familiar face, so sweet and grave, the graceful figure, gradually changing from boyish slenderness into the stateliness of fatherly middle age,—then suddenly missed from among us, out of all our pomps and shows and ceremonies. But I think any one, joining in that May-day festival, must have felt, as the long-drawn hallelujahs pealed down the crowded aisles, and up to the glittering roof, that it was still better to be away. Better than all this turmoil of jubilee, to be where he is; among those who, all life's duties done, and burdens borne, and sorrows perfected, sit down among the saints at the feet of "the mighty God, the everlasting Father, the Prince of peace."

Of the opening of the Exhibition I have nothing to say, being among the innumerable number who contented, or discontented, themselves with the columns of the *Times* newspaper on the day following; having not even attempted to get within sight of that wonderful crowd—a crowd is always wonderful—which "Our own Correspondent" describes so graphically: which for hours listened outside for the music, and at the faint echoes of "God save the Queen" tried to take off its honest, loyal, British hat, and repeat, with true British warmth, the cheers within, until street after street caught the sound, and carried it even to Hyde Park Corner. Yes, it must have been a grand thing,—that crowd. We shall always count it as one of the "mistakes" one makes sometimes, and repents of too late, that we spent May-day, 1862, at least a day's journey distant from the International Exhibition.

But time has its rewards as well as revenges. The 6th of May found us bound, resolutely, in defiance of all impediments, to get a good, honest five shillings' worth out of the commissioners.

"Well, I wish you joy," observed a consolatory friend. "If you go every day regularly for two months, perhaps you may contrive to see the whole of it."

"Still, on the principle that faint heart never won—never any thing in this world; also, that half a loaf is better than no bread, we'll see as much of it in one day as we can."

But the strict regulation of "no change given," was near stopping us on the threshold. I beg to confess, for the information and warning of future visitors, that my five shillings—was, from the melancholy but utterly unavoidable circumstances of my having "no change," and Government declining to give me any, composed of a borrowed half-crown, a florin, a "threepenny bit," a penny, and four halfpennies. Consequently, Government—in the shape of one of these commissionnaires, invalided soldiers, whom one is so glad to see filling useful positions about London—hesitated a little at taking such eccentric payment; but finally consented, and we passed in.

No—there may be substitutions—higher and better things even than the things gone; but in this world there are no repetitions. As well might a man expect to find a second first-love, as a second Crystal Palace of 1851. It was quite *per se;* a fairy-land; a dream. Who does not recall his or her first entrance into its exquisite transept, with that lovely vista of trees and fountains, gleaming statues, gorgeous carpets and fabrics of all sorts, making every conceivable combination of form and color? Also the perpetual under-tone of music; organs, pianofortes, and instruments of all sorts, sufficiently apart not to jar unpleasantly on the ear, and yet producing an incessant, circumfluent harmony; an atmosphere of sound, soothing as that of a wood full of birds?

Oh, how delicious it was! the like of it can never be again; nor would we wish it. Let it vanish, like a dream of youth, into the immortality of the past.

And now, let us take a fair, wide, unprejudiced view of the Great International Exhibition of 1862; making no comparisons; for indeed there are none to be made. Here is no fairy-land, but a gigantic building, whose very size alone is impressive. Overhead is an enormous glass dome —they say as large as that of St. Peter's at Rome—and opposite stretches the long aërial nave, ending in a second dome, the counterpart of the first. On the right hand and the left run other avenues, the north-west and south-west transepts, both terminating in curved arches; but the whole three lines of view melt into such shadowy distance, that one can at first hardly distinguish how they end. There is no glow or glare of color: and, on the whole, the effect is extremely subdued; the chief thing that catches the eye being the inscriptions, in sufficiently large, legible letters, which run along under the rim of the dome, and are formed into arches over the entrance, and at the termination of either transept:—

> "Tua sunt Domine, regnum, magnificentia, et potentia et gloria atque victoria; et tibi laus: cuncta enim quæ in cœlo sunt et in terra, tua sunt."
>
> "Gloria in excelsis Deo, et in terra pax."
>
> "Domini est terra et plenitudo ejus."
>
> "Deus in terram respexit, et implevit illam bonis suis."

This silent recognition, in the grand old Latin tongue common to all nations, of Him who is the Father of all the nations of the earth, is very impressive. It contributes much to the feeling which many people have already expressed, that the difference between this second building and the first is exactly like that between youth and maturity—less of beauty, more of real greatness; the greatness of deliberate, perfected work. It is not a palace; but it gives in no small degree the idea of a temple—a true temple of industry;—*laborare est orare* being the motto thereof.

That is, it will be so—by-and-by—for now it is in such an incomplete state that no wonder the sapient British public declines to pay five shillings to behold the sight. However it might have been polished up for the opening day, at present the whole scene presented the appearance of a gigantic "flitting." Packing-cases everywhere; planks lying about to be tumbled over; nails ready to run into your shoes; rude calico hangings, confronting you with the warning, "No admission;" elegant furniture in haybands and Holland pinafores; statues swaddled in real drapery; china and ornaments dispersed about the half-empty, or wholly vacant glass cases in every stage of that pitiable confusion which all housekeepers, or rather house-quitters, understand. In fact, nothing in the building looking complete and comfortable, except the roof, and the clear glass dome, through which the blue May-morning sky smiled serenely and cheerfully.

Yes, every body seemed cheerful. Though every body was as busy as busy could be—workmen, attendants, exhibitors, policemen, commissionaires, running hither and thither, or gathered in little knots, talking vociferously in every language under the sun; still they all appeared quite at home, and in the best of spirits. The people who looked most uncomfortable and most "in the way," were the unhappy visitors or season-ticket holders, who were eyed much as a materfamilias would eye a select party of well-dressed guests coming in to spend a social evening on the very first evening of "flitting" into a new house. They swept the dust, nails, and packing-cases with their flounced trains; they brushed against the china with their tremendous hoops; they sat down where they had no business to sit, and stood where they ought not to stand, and altogether made themselves as elegantly inconvenient as might naturally be expected under the circumstances.

But we, who came on business, had no conscientious qualms. We determined to begin systematically, and see as much as we possibly could see in a given number of hours. So, to economize space, we walked through the north-west transept—where Austria appeared in a perfect chaos, a wreck of nations—to the north-west Annex—which is devoted to machinery.

There is something intensely British in machinery. One felt one's heart swell with true Anglo-Saxon pride as one walked down the long row of locomotive engines, painted in marvellous colors—bright blue, dark blue, grass green, sea green, and rifle green, and polished as to their brass and iron to the last extremity of glitter. In their very best coats—of varnish—they stood, these silent monsters,—the genii of our iron roads. There was one belonging to the Caledonian line, made by Neilson & Co., Glasgow—a very fine monster he or "she" was, too; and there was C. England's "Little England"—a brilliant dark-blue creature. Sharp, Stewart & Co., Manchester, furnished another, shining in the very brightest green; and there was one "designed by R. Sinclair," which was stated to have "run on the Eastern Counties line 44,450 miles, with no repairs except turning the leading wheels and painting."

On the other side was machinery of every sort: a paper-mill from George Bertram, Sciennes, Edinburgh, which "made paper from vegetable fibre, at the rate of 100 feet per minute," and various specimens of "mules," and other kinds of dumb factory laborers, attended by live laborers from the same region; a Manchester "chap" who stood patiently picking each thread as it broke; and two tidy Manchester lasses, working as briskly as if they were in their own factory. The centre of the Annex is occupied by a model of the great sugar-mill of Merrilees and Tait, Glasgow, and near it is a rival mill of Heckmann's, Berlin, where the brilliant copper and brass of the sugar-boiler is a perfect picture of mechanical elegance.

There is something strangely fascinating in fine machinery,—man's design and handiwork, yet in its accuracy, harmony, and, above all, in its invisible force, giving a sense of superhuman perfectness. Wheel upon wheel incessantly convolving, each acting on the other in such a slight and yet miraculous way; life-like motion; life-like perpetual sound, as if some spirit were at work in the inert mass which enabled it to go on forever and ever. Involuntarily, the mind reverts from this to the great mechanism of the universe, of which we know so little, and on that little seem so ready to dogmatize. Fools that we are! It is as if one of these ever-spinning reels, one of these threads which break in the instant, one of these tiny wheels whose small gyration influences so many more, were to stop and say to itself,—"This whole mechanism was made for me; and I—I understand it all."

But on; for time does not trot, but gallops in this International Exhibition; on, through chaotic Austria, bewildered Belgium, and sober Holland, which, like most sober people, is a little beforehand with its neighbors; on, between the two enormous mirrors that should have been; but, alas! one, broken in the transit, shows only the melancholy empty frame; past the wonderful diamond, "Star of the South," round which is a circle of those most annoyingly fashionable ladies in hoops and trains. Long may they remain there, staring at what looks to our unappreciating eyes no better than a large piece of cut-glass dangling in the centre of a case of other specimens of glass uncut, which look no better than pebbles on the road, but which we understand are of inappreciable value—worth a king's head or a queen's heart. Verily, the world is under some extraordinary delusion about jewelry, especially diamonds.

Now we come to something really beautiful. It is a group of statuary by Molin of Sweden, "The Grapplers." Two men, elder and younger, are wrestling; evidently for life or death; both being armed with short knives. If murder ever could be grand, it is made so here. The fierce intensity of the elder man's face, the wild fury of the younger, and the clasp of terrible hate, closer than of love, are absolutely sublime. Four bas-reliefs round the pediment tell the story: "Jealousy," "The dream of vengeance," "The contest of battle," "A woman weeping at the grave." It is awfully real; for as I watch two young men who stand gazing at it, I fancy I can read the reflection of it in one of their faces. Alas! human nature is everywhere the same. But is it not a question whether an artist who can so dignify evil, would not have done wiser in choosing a subject that should immortalize good?

Here is the French Court; our neighbors having invaded and appropriated about a fourth of the whole Exhibition. Well, let them! if they do it as charmingly as no doubt they will. Even now, in its imperfectness, our eyes are dazzled by half unpacked splendors; silks that "stand alone;" laces of fabulous value; diamonds which, as a busy but civil assistant of Jacta & Cie. pauses to inform us, "sont vrais—tous vrais, madame;" and certainly, arranged in tiaras, sprays, and wreaths, are *almost* as pretty as a common wild-flower. We could almost feel ourselves in Paris, so incessant is the clatter of French around, and so numerous are the specimens of the genus *ouvrier*, one of whom, complete in beard and blue blouse, and exquisitely worked slippers, is just descending from giving the last arrangement to a large plaster statue, on whose base is painted the characteristic translation, "Fondu d'un seul jet "—" Cast in *single spout.*"

From France—which, when finished, will likely be one of the most attractive regions in the building—we go on to Italy. There, scattered about in every phase of "pack" and disarrangement, are countless treasures of beauty, especially statuary. We can only stop to admire one, "The Daughter of Zion," by Salvius Salvini,—a grand-limbed, majestic matron, with overhanging brows, and lips protruding, sitting passive, sullen, and fierce with her wrongs.

Here, too, stands Gibson's tinted Venus. Much has been said about this statue, and much will be said. Yet, I doubt, most people will own regretfully that it is a great mistake. Marvellously beautiful; for this is no Venus Anadyomene, or Venus Aphrodite, but the "Alma Venus Genitrix," the fruitful chaste mother of gods and men. Had it been in pure white marble, the Venus de' Medici, even the lovely Venus of Milo, could hardly have equalled it; but as it is, it is neither classic nor human; it loses all the severe grace of colorless form, and yet approaches no nearer to life than a bad imitation of a wax-work figure. The tinted eyes, the slightly reddened lips, and the hue, certainly not that of flesh, which has been given to the marble limbs, produce an effect at once painful and unnatural. Some connoisseurs may admire, and antiquaries may argue that the Greeks are supposed to have tinted most of their statues; but a large portion of us fond ignorant art-lovers will always protest, that Gibson's fancy is not the advance but the decadence of true classic art.

But we must go back into the nave, and, consulting the plan, make a determined search after that ignominious necessity, food. Certainly here is plenty, but it is arranged in a hopeless manner in the shape of Trophies. There is one trophy entirely composed of pickles; another of sweetmeats; another, which looks, at a distance, like a Greek temple with alabaster columns, is fabricated of candles. There is an erection invitingly labelled "To the Juveniles," which consists of every sort of toy that can be imagined; and another, the centre figure of which is a light-ship, stuck round with telescopes, reflector, etc. All down to the eastern dome are dotted these abominations of bad taste, completely obscuring the perspective of the nave, and some of them in themselves grotesque to the last degree of imaginable ugliness. They ought to be swept away with the besom of destruction. May it speedily be done?*

The eastern dome, and the north-east and south-east transepts, have their corresponding inscriptions written in English:—

"The wise and their works are in the hand of God."

"Lord, both riches and honor come of thee: thou reignest over all; and in thy hand is power and might, and in thy hand it is to make great."

And two blank-verse lines (Query, from what author?) not too poetical—

"Each climate needs what other climes produce."
"Alternately the nations learn and teach."

The south-east transept is devoted chiefly to iron-work: the north-east, to the products of the colonies. Here is the only trophy which is endurable—a fine pile of ornamental woods from Tasmania. Near it is the Australian quarter, where our eyes were caught by a specimen of art, which proved that the antipodes can boast as bad painters as some of those who, under the wise selection of this year's hanging committee, we yesterday beheld on the Royal Academy's walls;—acres of canvas spent over full-length portraits, and pounds of good color lavished over what high art and anti-pre-Raphaelite painters consider flesh and blood, but which is in reality like nothing in nature,—or art either, for art is the highest nature. However, what care they, the ancient leaders of our R.A's—our illustrious Forty? Like Sir Godfrey Kneller, Nature always "puts them out."

It is to be feared that we are growing savage as wild beasts for want of food, so let us quit the obnoxious pictures, and proceed at once to the refreshment-room. In any place of public resort like this, there is always con-

* *N.B.* It *is* done. Hurrah!

siderable entertainment in watching the people feed. So much character peeps out, so many phases of domestic or social life, in the little groups that gather themselves round the table. You may, if you have quick observation, make up a whole novelette in ten minutes, or at least gain fragmentary studies of human nature enough to furnish half a dozen magazine tales. Of such was a trio beside us, finishing off with ices what had apparently been a very comfortable lunch.

I have said nothing hitherto of the visitors to the Exhibition, and yet we had noticed them a good deal. They consisted—besides the fashionable dames aforesaid, who were always annihilating us with their hoops, or turning round upon us with sudden fierceness, when we accidentally trod on their demi-trains—of people that you at once decided were "from the country;" healthy-looking squires, with stout matronly squiresses; magisterial county magnates; tall, aristocratic gentlemen, possibly peers; and a large sprinkling of clerical personages, with sedately clad wives and pretty daughters. Also, and they were a goodly sight to see, not a few ancient couples, just husband and wife alone, who took their quiet pleasure together in their life's decline, looking as happy and contented in one another's company as when they were young lovers. Such a pair we saw beside the Armstrong gun, and the elderly, rather military-looking gentleman, was explaining it minutely to his elderly wife. She listened, dear soul! with a devotedness of attention that indicated a habit, possibly thirty years old, of listening to all he said, admiring all he admired, and sharing with him every pleasantness, as doubtless every pain, in a fullness of love that shines out as sweetly in an old woman's face as in a young girl's. Perhaps more sweetly, because it has been tried—tried and *not* found wanting.

A second bit of nature, almost as charming, was beside us in the trio I have mentioned, father, mother, and growing up daughter. They were evidently country people; for he spoke with a slight provincial accent; and they were dressed—oh, how many thoughts and mutual consultations those splendid gowns and bonnets must have cost, after "papa" decided to take three season-tickets and come to London. And what plannings — what arrangements—what joyous anticipations, before they were fairly started, and had located themselves in some sober "family hotel," which the squire may have frequented in his young days, when George the Fourth was king. Thence, now, they doubtless emerge, every morning, to spend the day in the International Exhibition. And night after night, while poor mamma rests her wearied limbs, is benign papa coaxed by that coaxing girl—(what a winning way she has, and how mischievously she drinks up the remainder of his wine, which he himself holds playfully to her lips!)—coaxed into taking her to some theatre or other, where she will laugh, and cry, and look about her, with the intense enjoyment that no *blasée* London young lady ever knows. And how, when the week or fortnight is over, she will go home and tell all the village—the rector's daughter, her bosom friend—and old Betty at the lodge, her nurse—every single thing that has happened in every single day; and all will decide that there never was such a place as the International Exhibition.

Be it so. Even such little episodes—of which there must be so many now going on, and will be all this year—constitute the Exhibition a good thing, a source of wholesome natural enjoyment to thousands.

Enjoyment? Well, even that has its limits, and so have human powers of locomotion. The great drawback to the Exhibition—its enormous size. You may walk miles upon miles without recognizing the fact, until you suddenly stop, feeling that if your life depended on it, you could not proceed a step farther. And the staircases, when one has been on one's feet for half a day, are literally awful to contemplate! How we overcame them I hardly know, but at last we found ourselves on one of those delicious settees that some merciful and enlightened Commissioner has provided in glorious plenty—sitting in peace opposite to Gainsborough's "Blue Boy:" and vaguely staring alternately at the washed-out Reynoldses, Hogarths, and Laurences on the walls, and the living phantasmagoria of graceful figures, pretty—or occasionally pretty faces, and universally charming toilettes, which moved in a continuous stream up and down along the gallery of British pictures.

Dare we confess that among all these art-treasures, at first we principally studied nature—especially clothes? There can be no doubt that a thoroughly well-dressed, elegant Englishwoman is a very charming sight. These spring toilettes, in which, on the whole, was great simplicity, harmony, and above all, unity of color, were quite refreshing to behold. Nor, except the atrocious hoops, was there any great exaggeration or ugliness of costume. It is the underbred class of quasi-fashionables, who wear spoon-bonnets, with bushels of flowers stuck on the top, and gowns trailing in the mud, or kilted up over scarlet stockings and glaring petticoats, stiff and circular as an iron cage. But these gentlewomen, with their black or subdued-colored silks, their delicate muslins, their flowing white bournous, or dark rich Indian shawls, had, whether or not they possessed actual beauty, a general graciousness, dignity, and sobriety of mien, that I doubt if the Prado, or the Corso, or Unter den Linden, or even Longchamps itself, could rival. Excellent season-ticket holders! May they promenade there, gratifying their eyes, and improving their minds if possible, all summer, in this most perfect picture-gallery that England ever possessed.

It occupies the whole length of the part of the building parallel with Cromwell Road. Well lit, well ventilated; every picture hung where it really can be seen; no careless juxtaposition, whereby two equally admirable works of art are made actually to "kill" one another; arrangement without confusion; the different masters being, wherever it was possible, hung in groups, so that the eye easily takes in the distinctive peculiarities of each; no dust, no heat, no crowding;—it is little to be wondered at if all London makes for the next four months of this place its favorite promenade.

Of the two galleries, British and Foreign, it were almost invidious to decide which is the finer. Ours has decidedly, and especially among its living painters, the richest glow of color, the truest rendering of nature, the highest and purest moral tone. Our Continental brethren paint larger pictures, of gallery rather than cabinet size; are finer draughtsmen, and choose subjects of tragic and personal rather than domestic interest. Some of these are intensely painful. One could hardly find anywhere such a horribly well-painted collection of corpses as that which may be found along one wall of the Foreign gallery. One picture, representing the lying in state of two unfortunate gentlemen, Egmont and Count Horn, *after* their decapitation, is quite ghastly. The two bodies are stretched side by side on a bed, and the two heads, which, as is plainly perceptible, are only just stuck on to the bodies, lie loosely, each in its place, and look as if, with the least shake of the canvas, they would roll down upon the gallery floor. Query —What high purpose can be attained, or what good can possibly be done to any human being by such art as this?

On the whole, in spite of many excellent pictures in the combined foreign schools, our British artists may hold their heads honorably high. Setting aside all the elder painters, our Hunt, Millais, Noel Paton, Faed, Leighton, Hughes, Clark, M'Callum, Hook, and many others, who twenty, or even fifteen years ago, were mere "Academy lads," form of themselves a noble national school: a school that, whatever its shortcomings, is pure, refined, natural; free from every coarse, meretricious, or melodramatic taint; appealing to one's highest and tenderest emotions, and without being strictly religious art, having throughout a strongly religious and always moral tone. On pictures such as these, the eye, educated or uneducated, rests and lingers with an unconscious sense of refreshment and calm. They "do one good," so to speak; ay, down to the tiniest bit of green landscape, or the humblest cottage interior—J. Clark's "Sick Child," for instance; and what can the grandest so-called high-art painters desire more? Truly, as we walked slowly up and down the long gallery—not attempting to particularize or examine—only taking a fond look at long-missed familiar favorites, and a speculative glance at the very few, here and there, that we did not know, our British hearts thrilled with a not unnatural delight, to think that "our own" were the best after all.

Ay, without any obnoxious insular pride, we can not but feel, cursory and imperfect as has been our investigation of this magnificent building, that no other country in the world could in so short a space, or in any space of time, have erected such an one. No other race than the brave Anglo-Saxon, with its dogged perseverance, its untiring energy, and its strong, patient, passive rather than active will, could have so maintained its ground against insuperable difficulties, and finally carried out a purpose which even to the very last day, the last hour, appeared all but impracticable.

There is much to be done still. It will be weeks before the chaos settles into any thing like order; and even then, the daily working arrangements of such an enormous undertaking, must present difficulties, mistakes, mismanagements, perplexities without end.

But for all that, the thing is done, and done successfully. The building so much ridiculed for its external ugliness (and, perhaps, the less said on that subject the better, even by the most enthusiastic Briton), has been found substantial, convenient, and, within, not unbeautiful. The unpaid, unthanked Commissioners, have toiled early and late to accomplish their self-imposed duties. The whole country, let us say the whole world, has now before it for the next six months, a nucleus of interest, entertainment, instruction if they will, nay, almost whether they will or not; for the dullest clown, the most indifferent aristocrat, could hardly go through the International Exhibition without feeling his brains, or his heart, or some recondite portion of his common humanity, a little the better for it.

And one thing, the grandest thing about the whole, is the public acknowledgment of our nation, of all nations, both in the opening ceremonial, in the inscriptions I have copied, of the Source from whence all these good things do come. It is, more even than the former Exhibition, our confession of faith before the whole world. We owe this, doubtless, as we owe the pristine design of Industrial Exhibitions, to that deeply religious heart and active brain now at rest forever.

He sleeps, and others have completed his plans; he labored, and lived not to see the fruit of his labor. To us, this may seem infinitely sad: probably no one, gentle or simple, of the myriads that will visit this place, will do so without a sigh to the memory of our Prince Consort. But for him, who lived so much for others and so little for himself, whose almost perfect life was carried out without the smallest show, or vain-glorying, or personal assertion of any kind, for him it would be enough to know that what he wished done has been done, though done without his aid. What matter? The good servant desires only that his master's will should be accomplished, in his master's own way. He was that servant, and so thus early, the Master called him.

Coming away from this busy place, with its clang of incessant work, its tramp of innumerable feet, its confused mingling of all possible sights and sounds, one could not but think of him, the originator of it all, now a disembodied soul. Ay, so it is! We toil and struggle, wrangle and praise, enjoy and endure.

> "But thou, dear spirit, happy star,
> O'erlook'st the tumult from afar,
> And smilest, knowing all is well."

THE LAST GREAT EXHIBITION.

ITS END.

IT is all over. Last Saturday's foggy daylight shone for the last time on that wonderful crowd surging up and down the nave between dome and dome, on the still thicker mass moving—or moved, for volition was doubtful —inch by inch along the picture-galleries, on the quieter and more scattered groups that, in the various side courts delighted themselves once more over treasures and curiosities which they will likely never see again. True, for a "day after the fair," or even fourteen days, our six-months' friend, become such a familiar friend now, may drag on a sort of galvanized semi-existence; but his real life is ended: the Great International Exhibition of 1862 is no more.

De mortuis nil nisi bonum. There will be plenty of people to abuse it, this vanished show: let us speak only kindly of it: for, be it bad or good, successful or unsuccessful, it is probably the last of its race. Even should there be, in London, and during this generation, another Great Exhibition, that time is so far in the future that we ourselves shall have grown quite elderly people. The more reason, therefore, for us to remember this one tenderly, to count up all the good it was meant to do and did, all the innocent pleasure that we gained from it. Let us forget the aching heads, wearied limbs, pushing crowds, bad dinners, fights for omnibuses, and insane struggles after cabs, and only recall that bright pleasant place,—where, if there was a ray of sunlight to be found anywhere in London, it was sure to be caught by the great glass dome, and reflected upon the odious—well, we'll not call it odious now—Majolica fountain, and borne thence down the misty vista of the nave. Ay, it was a pleasant place, diffusing a general sense of beauty, both of color, form, and sound, which, we scarcely knew how, put us into a cheerful frame of mind. Probably, out of the multitudes that have visited it, there has not been one who did not carry away from it a certain amount of actual enjoyment, to be, as all pure happiness is, an eternal possession.

The humors of the Exhibition, its various phases, social, intellectual, and moral, from May to November, would make a curious book, even supposing all instructive views of it were carefully omitted. Regarded as a place of study and general information, its wonders never ended, its interest never flagged. Has not the *Times* found matter for one article, often two, *every day* for six months? And is not this present writer acquainted with an energetic juror who has visited it daily ever since it opened, yet on last Saturday was seen as brisk and beaming as ever, though with a certain tender melancholy overspreading his countenance, investigating something he had never seen before? Nay, putting aside those who went on business, or for scientific study, how continually one heard of people who, for mere entertainment, had been twenty or thirty times, or of whole families who located themselves for a month or two in Brompton, and spent every day, and the whole day long, in the Great Exhibition—dining, meeting their friends, and transacting their business; in fact, doing every thing but sleep there.

The mere chronicle of the crowd—as it changed from month to month, from the stately season-ticketers and five-shilling folk of June to the middle-class country visitors of July, and then again to the excursionists, charity-sent schools and workhouses, mechanics with their families, down to the ultra-agricultural element, which appeared in smock-frocks and clouted shoes just before or immediately after harvest—this of itself would be a curious record. What "odd fish" one used to see sometimes!—people who might have been unearthed from the most distant places and times, of whom you wondered what would have induced them to come here, how they got here, and, still more, how they would ever got home again? The sight of such as these, mingling in the ordinary crowd, was either intensely ludicrous or extremely pathetic. I remember one lady, whom I met at intervals during one five-shilling day, who might have been Dickens's study for *Miss Havisham*. Her costume, rich and good, must have been made, every item, at least twenty years ago. There she was, amidst all the modern crinolines, flowing *bournous*, and sweeping demi-trains, in her short-skirted gown, hanging in straight folds to the ankles, her little silk tippet, her large muslin collar, with a point on either shoulder, and her poke bonnet, exactly the attire of our mothers and aunts when we were little children. The sight of her brought back, with an instantaneous flash of memory, that strange, half-forgotten period of childhood, till it was impossible to laugh: one felt much more inclined to cry.

Besides apparitions like this, what queer people one used to see perambulating about—chiefly in groups, with a vague perpetual terror of being separated. I saw one day three big grown-up youths who went everywhere in a sort of string, never letting go of each other's hands; and one met continually little family knots, father, mother, and children, who kept as close as possible to one another, and in whose round healthy faces, full of mingled alarm and ecstacy, was "country cousin" written as plain as light. How amusing it was to listen to their naïve comments on the wonders about them, especially the pictures; and how strongly their broad provincial tongues and rough, rugged provincial manners contrasted with the genteelly-dressed and quick-spoken Londoners, who never seemed as if they could condescend to be surprised at any thing. Yet, sometimes one of these sharp Londoners—shopman or clerk—would be found benignly escorting two oddly-clad maiden aunts, or a tribe of blowsy cousins: to whom he was very patronizing and kind, though just a thought ashamed of his connections; busy imparting much—and perhaps learning more. For how pleasant and honest-looking were many of these country-folk—how intense was their enjoyment—how open their demonstration thereof! How they would fraternize with any body and every body: coming and throwing themselves upon one for information or sympathy, in the most innocent and confiding way! And, viewed as a whole, what a grand impression they gave—ay, with all their oddities, foibles, and simplicities—of the foundation-class of our empire—the strong, reliable, persevering Britons, that "never, never will be slaves."

As the year went on, what a year it became! London, in 1862, was a sight never to be forgotten; the streets, from being full, grew almost impassable, and a journey by cab or omnibus was an event to be contemplated with awe and doubt. Still, the state of things had its bright side. Be your own inconvenience ever so great, or your temper ever so bad, you could not help being struck with the extreme patience and good-humor of the tired-looking crowd, who thronged every omnibus terminus and railway station, making wild and vain rushes for seats. Especially you pitied the continuous stream that might be seen flowing daily between Brompton and Hyde Park Corner, vivaciously pouring along of mornings, and of evenings dragging itself wearily back; husbands helping wives, and wives carrying babies—for babies, as in '51, formed one of the grand features of the Exhibition. Then, about August, came the great influx of foreigners, who also went about in groups, or rather in lines stretching across the street pavements, smoking, jabbering, and gesticulating, perplexing omnibus conductors and squabbling with cabmen; but, on the whole, very civilly treated by the general British public, and behaving themselves civilly in return. Since—full as London was, so that how the extra population ever found food to eat and beds to sleep on, seemed a perpetual mystery—the crowd was a holiday crowd, disposed to be on the best of terms with both self and neighbor, the word "neighbor" being understood to bear, for this year only, the widest interpretation.

So much for the external aspect of London. Of its internal and social life, as affected by the International Exhibition, no doubt all householders could unfold volumes. Every body, in every class, seemed to keep open the doors of house and heart, to the last extremity of expansion. Rich and poor, idle and busy, all devoted themselves to the duties and delights of hospitality. Perhaps, in summing up the good done by the year departed, this one small item ought not to be omitted—that the number of old ties riveted afresh, broken ties re-united, and new ties formed by the holiday-making of the year 1862, will probably influence society for half a generation.

Summer ended, London went "out of town," though by the aspect of the streets you would never have thought it. And still at the Great Exhibition was found the same eager contented crowd, though it varied a good deal in its character, especially on shilling-days. Then, by far the greatest proportion of visitors was sure to be of the working-class — hard-handed, rough-headed, fustian-coated; or else clad sublimely in well-kept broadcloth, lighted up by a scarlet waistcoat, or a necktie of every color of the rainbow. Wives, daughters, and sweethearts emulated the same splendor, and the number of times one's teeth were set on edge by combinations of pink and crimson, blue and green, lilac and yellow, would defy calculation. Still, how happy they were! though they enjoyed themselves in a different way from the early frequenters of the place. They deserted the long fashionable promenade of the nave, and, except when the organs were playing, or there was a performance on Cadby's grand piano, or Distin's band, they scarcely lingered even under the pleasant domes. But they pressed eagerly to the picture galleries, and they haunted in banded multitudes the machinery annexe.

It was grand to watch them there—looking so thoroughly at home among the locomotives, mules, power-looms, steam-hammers, and sugar-mills — shaking hands with the smart Manchester girls or other operatives who attended to the various machinery: nay, sometimes even trying hard to enter into conversation with the queer foreign *ouvriers*, in blouse and mustache, who formed such a contrast to themselves. And their spirit of inquiry knew no limit — witness the tightly-packed circle, wedged as close as human beings could squeeze, that always surrounded the carpet-weaving, ice-making, printing, and other machines. They had a keen sense of fun, too—as you saw if you watched the faces round that eccentric machine, which could be made at will to puff out wind enough to blow a man's hair confusedly about, or waft his newspaper, or his pocket-handkerchief, right up to the ceiling. Nor could one mingle among this throng without being struck by the large average of intelligence that exists, and necessarily must exist, among their class. What cool, clear, clever heads they must have—those whom we are wont to term mere "hands." Most deft hands they are; but there must be a head to guide them; and a head sound and steady, endowed with both ingenuity and patience—

"Endurance, foresight, strength, and skill."

You could read it in their looks, oftentimes. One of the

finest faces I ever saw—as fine as that of the wife in Millais's "Order of Release," and of much the same character—was that of a young woman who stood at one of the power-looms, day after day—grave and busy—apparently quite unconscious of her own beauty: not merely prettiness, but noble beauty. And I never shall forget the face of a working weaver at, I believe, a Manchester loom. He was weaving a very common material for gowns, such as would be sold for seven-pence or eight-pence the yard—a plain fabric with a stripe at equal distances across it. In looking about (I fear—oh, pardonable weakness!—it was at a very pretty girl who stood watching his labor), the poor man lost count of the times his shuttle should fly, and wove a double instead of a single stripe. A small error—but it could not be allowed to pass. Looking doleful but determined, he stopped his loom at once, and taking out his penknife, cut, thread by thread, and picked out, with pains and care, the superfluous stripe; refilled his shuttle with a different color; and then, after full five minutes' delay, he set the loom going and the shuttle flying. The web was all right—the error remedied—the victory won. A lesson, methought, for more of us than Manchester weavers.

Yes, it was worth being squeezed almost to a pancake, half deafened with the noise of machinery, and half suffocated by the smell of oil and hot iron—to see that earnest, eager, intelligent crowd. One ceased to wonder at those heroic, patient, silently-suffering Lancashire operatives—one saw here the sort of stuff they were made of. God help them!—and may their country-people help them too, out of their present straits, before the enormous amount of dormant power in the class, instead of working itself out healthily in honest labor, be turned by the force of starvation and misery into anarchy, confusion, and crime.

But I linger over these living memories of our lost friend, when I meant only to speak of his latter days. People began to say he was dying, and that it was time for him to die; that he ought to be put an end to, ere he faded out, the miserable ghost of his summer splendor, in the November fogs. There was truth in that. As the attendance lessened, the hour of "ringing out" was made earlier and earlier; yet still, before visitors departed, mists were seen gathering down the vaulted nave, and one gaslight after another—not unneeded—appeared like glow-worms about the darkening courts; one began to feel that our old friend had lived his life, and it was time for him to depart. Nevertheless, when we really knew that the 1st of November was to be his death-day, we all felt sorry. And it seemed, the final week, as if all the procrastinators in London, or Britain, had made up their minds at last, and come in a body to the Great Exhibition.

On the penultimate shilling-day, they streamed in a continuous flood, on foot or in omnibuses, down from Hyde Park Corner. Foggy the air was, muddy were the streets —to the heart's delight of many a busy shoe-black—yet the crowd rolled merrily on, past the shut-up Gospel Hall, the bureau for Bibles in all languages, the telegraph office, and the office for foreign newspapers—those temporary erections which will soon vanish like mushrooms. Once more the Exhibition doors opened, as if they were to keep open forever; and once more the people poured in by tens, twenties, hundreds, thousands, till in an hour or two the building was full.

Sixty-two thousand human beings collected under one roof is of itself a rare, grand, and touching show. As you sat on the benches under Dent's great clock, which goes solemnly moving on like the visible finger of Time, and looked down on the ever-stirring, yet ever-stationary sea of life below, you were filled with a sense of inexpressible awe. Your own individuality dwindled into nothing. Why, every monad before you was just as important as you; had its own pleasures, pains, and passions, no less keen than yours; must, like you, live alone, die alone, and pass into eternity alone. What were you, poor atom! to dare to dictate, criticise, condemn, or hate; or, indeed, to do any thing but love and have pity, even as may the Highest in His infinite pity have mercy on us all!

But it was necessary to cease moralizing, and rise from our seats, in order to wander for the last time through the already crowded picture galleries, full of riches that we shall never see again. The saddest thing about pictures is, that they are, to the many, such a fleeting possession; then vanish away into unknown galleries and rich men's drawing-rooms, to delight our eyes no more. It was grievous to bid good-bye to our familiar English favorites; and scarcely less so to part with those which, more than any other foreign painters, seemed to have taken hold on the British heart—the Norwegian, Danish and Swedish pictures, so pathetically simple and true in themselves, and so charming as indications of that Northern life of which we know but little. One can not turn from one to the other, whether it be Tidemand's "Haugians, a Religious Sect in Denmark;" or the same artist's exquisite "Administration of the Sacrament to Sick Persons in a Norwegian Hut;" the little cabinet pictures, so womanly and sweet, of Amalia Lindegren; or Exner's equally sweet "Sunday Visit to Grandpapa;" and Schiott's "Offer of Marriage"—nay, I might name a dozen more—without feeling what a fine race these Northmen must be; how essentially domestic, honest, and sincere. And we go away glad to think that our newly-betrothed Princess comes from this race; and that her pleasant girlish face, even in unflattering photographs, has in it all the strength and all the tenderness of the North.

On, past the Belgian horrors, grandly painted, but horrible still; and the gaudy rubbish of Southern art—how changed from mediæval Italy and Spain!—till we creep down stairs and refresh ourselves with the noble sculpture of the Roman Court, and with Magni's "Girl Reading," said to be a portrait of Garibaldi's daughter. Whether or not, it is enough to comfort us for walls full of bad Italian pictures—this almost perfect bit of sculpture, at once truest Nature and highest Art.

This is enough fatigue for one day, even though it be nearly the last day; so we will just sit quiet until the bells ring and we have to cast ourselves into that awful whirlpool of departure, thankful if we come to the surface somehow, without being engulfed in omnibuses, or dashed under cab-wheels, or meeting otherwise a summary and untimely end.

Every body said that Saturday, November 1st, would be a very quiet day; that, there being no ceremonial, the crowd would not be greater than on ordinary Saturdays. But every body was wrong. The public refused to part so easily from their six months' friend. Half an hour after opening, the picture-galleries were full to suffocation; not merely with the usual "half-crown people," but with many who, from their appearance, must not easily have scraped together their thirty pence, in order to see the Exhibition for, probably, the first and last time. In the nave the regular season-ticketers were in enormous force; not promenading, as usual, in slow lines, but collecting in knots, greeting and talking; every body seeming to meet every body they knew, and to unite in little condolatory chats, as they assisted at this farewell to the scene of so much enjoyment.

Still there was a change. No gay May and June toilettes; most of the visitors were in sober winter dress, suited for the day—a thorough November day. Many of the courts were half dark, and the dreary white fog, which Londoners know so well, began soon after noon to gather overhead in the arch of the nave. Ay, it was time for our friend to die; but we were determined he should die bravely, even cheerily, like a Briton.

Though there was no formal notification of the fact, it was understood that God save the Queen would be sung about four o'clock under the western dome; and thither about three o'clock, the visitors slowly pressed. Forty thousand of them, the *Times* stated next day, were gathered together at that one point, and we could well believe it. They filled area, staircases, galleries, thick as swarming bees. In the darkening twilight, they became a sight mysterious, nay, awful; for they were such an enormous mass, and they were so very still. That curious sound, familiar to all Exhibition-goers, almost like the roaring of the sea, only that it came not in waves but continuously, had altogether ceased. Wedged together in a compact body, the people waited silently for the first notes, which stir every British heart to the core, and ever will.

God save the Queen! Here, at closing of the building, which she must have thought of and looked forward to so long, yet where her foot has never been, who could help a thrill deeper than ordinary as the notes burst out thin and quavering at first—they were only sopranos in unison and unaccompanied—but gradually growing steadier and clearer, till the ending of the third line, when the organ took it up.

That was the moment—a moment never to be forgotten by any who were present. After a bar's pause, the people took it up too. From nave, transepts, and galleries, from the whole forty thousand as with one voice, arose the chorus—

"God save our gracious Queen,
Long live our noble Queen,
God save the Queen."

Again the shrill sopranos led the tune, and again the people answered it, louder, steadier than before:—

"Send her victorious,
Happy and glorious,
Long to reign over us,
God save the Queen!"

It was an outburst of popular emotion—actual emotion—for I saw many, both men and women—(better terms than "ladies and gentlemen," though they were such likewise)—stand singing out loud with the tears in their eyes. Such a sight was worth all the show ceremonials that could have been planned. Foreigners must have marvelled at it, and have seen in it some index of the reason why amidst crumbling tyrannies and maddened republics, we Britons keep our balance, with love and loyalty, that, we pray God, may never end.

As the anthem ceased, what a cheer arose! How interminably it lasted! And when, with a multitudinous roar, the public demanded it again, how it was chorused grander than before—the sound of it whirling and whirling almost like a visible thing up to the great glass dome, where used to be blue sky, but was now all but darkness.

Here I wish I could end. I wish I had not to record a sad anti-climax—a great mistake. The ill-advised organist, probably in compliment to foreign visitors, struck up "Partant pour la Syrie." The sopranos began to sing it, and failed; a few voices started it in the crowd, and also failed; there was a feeble cry for "Hats off!" but the British public unanimously refused. It would not—how could it?—take its hat off to any but its own rightful Queen. A generally uncomfortable feeling arose. There were outcries for "Yankee Doodle," and other national airs; a few hisses, cat-calls, and the like; and the public, which had taken the ceremony so entirely in its own hands, was becoming a very obstreperous public indeed. It evidently felt, and with justice, that it was not a right or decorous thing for the last notes heard in our great International and National Exhibition to be a foreign tune; nor that the farewell cheer given therein should be given for any body but our own beloved Queen.

It was a difficult position, for we could hardly have "God save the Queen" a third time; until some bold spirit in the crowd settled the matter by shouting out at the top of his voice, "Rule Britannia!" The crowd leaped at the idea. Overpowered by acclamations, the organist returned to his seat; once more the choir began, and the organ joined in chorus, together with the whole multitude below and around, who testified their not unworthy triumph by singing out, with redoubled emphasis, how "Britons never, never will be slaves."

So ended this strange scene, and with it the last day of the Great Exhibition of 1862. Slowly and peaceably the visitors dispersed; many pacing for a long time up and down the shadowy nave, and in the French or Italian courts, where the cases, already covered up, looked in the dusky light like gigantic biers, faintly outlined under the white palls. And in spite of the deafening clang of innumerable bells, many still lingered round the Majolica fountain—lingered till it was nearly six o'clock, and quite dark, taking their last look of the familiar scene.

Yes, it is all over; and the chances are many that we of this generation shall never see an International Exhibition again. Let us remember this one tenderly. Let us say "*Requiescat in pace*," and go our ways.

TO NOVELISTS,

AND A NOVELIST.

"To justify the ways of God to men."—MILTON.

THE history of a human life is a strange thing. It is also a somewhat serious thing—to the individual: who often feels himself, or appears to others, not unlike the elder-pith figure of an electrical experimenter—vibrating ridiculously and helplessly between influences alike invisible and incomprehensible. What *is* life—and what is the heart of its mystery? We know not; and through Death only can we learn. Nevertheless, nothing but the blindest obtuseness of bigotry, the maddest indifference of epicureanism—two states not so opposite as they at first seem—can stifle those

"Obstinate questionings
Of sense and onward things,
Fallings from us, vanishings,
Blank misgivings of a creature
Moving about in worlds not realized."

And continually in our passage through these "worlds not realized"—either the world of passion, or intellect, or beauty—do we lift up our heads from the chaos, straining our eyes to discern, if possible, where we are, why we are there, what we are doing, or what is being done with us, and by whom. Then if we think we have caught even the fag end of a truth or a belief, how eagerly do we sit down and write about it, or mount pulpits and preach about it, or get on a platform and harangue about it! We feel so sure that we have something to say; something which it must benefit the world to hear. Harmless delusion! Yet not an ignoble one, for it is a form of that eternal aspiration after perfect good, without which the whole fabric of existence, mortal and immortal, natural and supernatural, slides from us and there remains nothing worth living for, nothing worth dying for;

since the smallest animalcule in a drop of water—the meanest created organism which boasts the principle of life—is, in such case, as noble a being as we.

Now there is something in us which *will not* "say Amen to that." We will not die—forever: we will not, while any good remains in us, cease to believe in a God, who is all we know or can conceive of goodness made perfect. As utterly as we refuse to regard Him as a mere Spirit of Nature, unto whom our individuality is indifferent and unknown, do we refuse to see in Him a Being omniscient as omnipotent, who nevertheless puts us into this awful world without our volition, leaves us to struggle through it as we can, and, if we fail, finally to drop out of it into hell-fire or annihilation. Is it blasphemy to assert that, on such a scheme of existence, the latter only could be consistent with His deity?

No, human as we are, we must have something divine to aspire to. It is curious to trace this instinct through all the clouded wisdoms of the wise; how the materialist, who conscientiously believes that he believes in nothing, will on parting bid you "good-bye and God bless you!" as if there were really a God to bless, that He could bless and that He would take the trouble to bless *you*. Stand with the most confirmed infidel by the coffin of one he loved, or any coffin, and you will hear him sigh that he would give his whole mortal life, with all its delights, and powers, and possibilities, if he could only see clearly some hope of attaining the life immortal.

What do these facts imply? That the instinct which prompts us to seek in every way to unriddle the riddle of existence, or as Milton puts it,

"To justify the ways of God to men,"

is as irrepressible as universal. It is at the root of all the creeds and all the philosophies, of the solid literature which discourses on life, and the imaginative literature which attempts to portray it.

It were idle to reason how the thing has come about; but, undeniably, the modern novel is one of the most important moral agents of the community. The essayist may write for his hundreds; the preacher preach to his thousands; but the novelist counts his audience by millions. His power is three-fold—over heart, reason, and fancy.

The orator we hear eagerly, but as his voice fades from us its lessons depart; the moral philosopher we read and digest, by degrees, in a serious, ponderous way: but the really good writer of fiction takes us altogether by storm. Young and old, grave and gay, learned or imaginative, who of us is safe from his influence? He creeps innocently on our family table in the shapes of those three well-thumbed library volumes—sits for days after invisibly at our fireside, a provocative of incessant discussion: slowly but surely, either by admiration or aversion, his opinions, ideas, feelings, impress themselves upon us, which impression remains long after we have come to that age, if we ever reach it, which all good angels forbid! when we "don't care to read novels."

The amount of new thoughts scattered broadcast over society within one month of the appearance of a really popular novel, the innumerable discussions it creates, and the general influence which it exercises in the public mind, form one of the most remarkable facts of our day. For the novelist has in our day ceased to be a mere story-teller or romancist. He—we use the superior pronoun in a general sense, even as an author should be dealt with as a neutral being, to be judged solely by "its" work,—he buckles to his task in solemn earnest. For what is it to "write a novel?" Something which the multitudes of young contributors to magazines, or young people who happen to have nothing to do but weave stories, little dream of. If they did, how they would shrink from the awfulness of what they have taken into their innocent foolish hands; even a piece out of the tremendous web of human life, so wonderful in its pattern, so mysterious in its convolutions, and of which—most solemn thought of all—warp, woof and loom, are in the hands of the Maker of the universe alone.

Yet this the true novel-writer essays to do; and he has a right to do it. He is justified in weaving his imaginary web side by side with that which he sees perpetually and invisibly woven around him, of which he has deeply studied the apparent plan, so as to see the under threads that guide the pattern, keener perhaps than other men. He has learned to deduce motives from actions, and to evolve actions from motives: he has seen that from certain characters (and in a less degree certain circumstances) such and such results, which appear accidental, become in reality as inevitable as the laws which govern the world. Laws physical and moral, with which no *Deus ex machinâ* can interfere, else the whole working of the universe would be disturbed.

Enough has been said, we trust, to indicate the serious position held by what used to be thought "a mere writer of fiction." Fiction, forsooth! It is at the core of all the truths of this world; for it is the truth of life itself. He who dares to reproduce it is a Prometheus who has stolen celestial fire: let him take care that he uses it for the benefit of his fellow-mortals. Otherwise one can imagine no vulture fiercer than the remorse which would gnaw the heart of such a writer, on the clear-visioned mountain-top of life's ending, if he began to suspect he had written a book which would live after him to the irremediable injury of the world.

We do not refer to impure or immoral books. There can be but one opinion concerning *them*—away with them to the Gehenna from which they come. We speak of those works, blameless in plan and execution, yet which fall short—as great works only can—of the highest ideal: the moral idea, for which, beyond any intellectual perfection, a true author ought to strive. For he is not like other men, or other writers. His very power makes him the more dangerous. His uncertainties, however small, shake to their ruin hundreds of lesser minds, and

> "When he falls, he falls like Lucifer,
> Never to rise again."

If a mountebank at a fair plays his antics or mouths out his folly or foulness, we laugh, or pass by—he is but a mountebank: he can do little harm: but when a hierophant connives at a false miracle, or an eloquent, sincere apostle goes about preaching a bewildering lie, we shrink, we grieve, we tremble. By-and-by, we take courage openly to denounce, not the teacher but the teaching. "You are an earnest man—doubtless, a true man—but your doctrine is not true. We, who can not speak, but only feel—we *feel* that it is not true. You are treading dangerous ground. You have raised a ghost you can not lay, you have thrown down a city which you can not rebuild. You are the very Prometheus carrying the stolen fire.

See that it does not slip from your unwary hands, and go blasting and devastating the world."

Thoughts somewhat like these must have passed through the mind of many a reader of a novel, the readers of which have been millions. Probably the whole history of fiction does not present an instance of two such remarkable books following one another within so short a time as "Adam Bede," and "The Mill on the Floss." All the world has read them; and though some may prefer one, and some the other, and, in a moral point of view, some may admire and some condemn—all the world grants their wonderful intellectual power, and is so familiar with the details of them that literary analysis becomes unnecessary.

Nor do we desire to attempt it. The question which these books, and especially the latter book, have suggested is quite a different thing. It is a question with which literary merit has nothing to do. Nor, in one sense, literary morality,—the external morality which, thank heaven, our modern reading public both expects and exacts, and here undoubtedly finds. Ours is more an appeal than a criticism—an appeal which any one of an audience has a right to make, if he thinks he sees what the speaker, in the midst of all his eloquence, does not see—

> "The little pitted speck in garnered fruit,
> That, rotting inward, slowly moulders all."

Of "The Mill on the Floss," in a literary point of view, there can be but one opinion—that, as a work of art, it is as perfect as the novel can well be made; superior even to "Adam Bede." For the impression it gives of *power*, evenly cultivated and clear-sighted—the power of creation, amalgamating real materials into a fore-planned ideal scheme; and the power of selection, able to distinguish at once the fit and the unfit, choosing the one and rejecting the other, so as to make every part not only complete as to itself, but as to its relation with a well-balanced whole—the "Mill on the Floss" is one of the finest imaginative works in our language. In its diction, too: how magnificently rolls on that noble Saxon English—terse and clear, yet infinitely harmonious, keeping in its most simple commonplace flow a certain majesty and solemnity which reminds one involuntarily of the deep waters of the Floss. The fatal Floss, which runs through the whole story like a

Greek fate or a Gothic destiny—ay, from the very second chapter, when

> "Maggie, Maggie," continued the mother, in a tone of half-coaxing fretfulness, as this small mistake of nature entered the room, "where's the use o' my telling you to keep away from the water? You'll tumble in and be drowned some day, an' then you'll be sorry you didn't do as mother told you."

This is a mere chance specimen of the care over small things—the exquisite polish of each part, that yet never interferes with the breadth of the whole—which marks this writer as one of the truest *artists*, in the highest sense, of our own or any other age.

Another impression made strongly by the first work of "George Eliot," and repeated by "his" (we prefer to respect the pseudonym) second, is the earnestness, sincerity, and heart-nobility of the author. Though few books are freer from that morbid intrusion of self in which many writers of fiction indulge, no one can lay down "The Mill on the Floss" without a feeling of having held commune with a mind of rare individuality, with a judgment active and clear, and with a moral nature conscientious, generous, religious, and pure. It is to this moral nature, this noblest half of all literary perfectness, in our author, as in all other authors, that we now make appeal.

"George Eliot," or any other conscientious novelist, needs not to be told that he who appropriates this strange phantasmagoria of human life, to re-paint and re-arrange by the light of his own imagination, takes materials not his own, nor yet his reader's. He deals with mysteries which, in their entirety, belong alone to the Maker of the universe. By the force of his intellect, the quick sympathies of his heart, he may pierce into them a little way—farther, perhaps, than most people—but at best only a little way. He will be continually stopped by things he can not understand—matters too hard for him, which make him feel, the more deeply and humbly as he grows more wise, how we are, at best,

> "Like infants crying in the dark,
> And with no language but a cry."

If by his dimly-beheld, one-sided fragmentary representations, which mimic untruly the great picture of life, this cry, either in his own voice, or in the involuntary utterance of his readers, rises into an accusation against God, how awful is his responsibility, how tremendous the evil that he may originate!

We doubt not, the author of the "Mill on the Floss" would shudder at the suspicion of this sort of involuntary blasphemy, and yet such is the tendency of the book and its story.

A very simple story. A girl of remarkable gifts—mentally, physically, and morally; born, like thousands more, of parents far inferior to herself—struggles through a repressed childhood, a hopeless youth; brought suddenly out of this darkness into the glow of a first passion for a man who, ignoble as he may be, is passionately in earnest with regard to her: she is tempted to treachery, and sinks into a great error, her extrication out of which, without evolving certain misery and certain wrong to most or all around her, is simply an impossibility. The author cuts the Gordian knot by creating a flood on the Floss, which wafts this poor child out of her troubles and difficulties into the other world.

Artistically speaking, this end is very fine. Towards it the tale has gradually climaxed. From such a childhood as that of Tom and Maggie Tulliver, nothing could have come but the youth Tom and the girl Maggie, as we find them throughout that marvellous third volume: changed indeed, but still keeping the childish images of little Tom and little Maggie, of Dorlcote Mill. Ay, even to the hour when, with that sense of the terrible exalted into the sublime, which only genius can make us feel—we see them go down to the deeps of the Floss "in an embrace never to be parted: living through again, in one supreme moment, the days when they had clasped their little hands in love, and roamed through the daisied fields together."

So far as exquisite literary skill, informed and vivified by the highest order of imaginative power, can go, this story is perfect. But take it from another point of view. Ask what good will it do?—whether it will lighten any burdened heart, help any perplexed spirit, comfort the sorrowful, succor the tempted, or bring back the erring into the way of peace; and what is the answer? Silence.

Let us reconsider the story, not artistically, but morally.

Here is a human being, placed during her whole brief

life—her hapless nineteen years—under circumstances the hardest and most fatal that could befall one of her temperament. She has all the involuntary egotism and selfishness of a nature that, while eagerly craving for love, loves ardently and imaginatively rather than devotedly; and the only love that might have at once humbled and raised her, by showing her how far nobler it was than her own—Philip's—is taken from her in early girlhood. Her instincts of right, true as they are, have never risen into principles; her temptations to vanity, and many other faults, are wild and fierce; yet no human help ever comes near her to strengthen the one or subdue the other. This *may* be true to nature, and yet we think it is not. Few of us, calmly reviewing our past, can feel that we have ever been left so long and so utterly without either outward aid or the inner voice—never silent in a heart like poor Maggie's. It is, in any case, a perilous doctrine to preach—the doctrine of overpowering circumstances.

Again, notwithstanding the author's evident yearning over Maggie, and disdain for Tom, we can not but feel that if people are to be judged by the only fair human judgment, of how far they act up to what they believe in, Tom, so far as his light goes, is a finer character than his sister. He alone has the self-denial to do what he does not like, for the sake of doing right; he alone has the self-command to smother his hopeless love, and live on, a brave, hard-working life; he, except in his injustice to poor Maggie, has at least the merit of having made no one else miserable. Perfectly true is what he says, though he says it in a Pharisaical way, "Yes, *I* have had feelings to struggle with, but I conquered them. I have had a harder life than you have had, but I found *my* comfort in doing my duty." Nay, though perhaps scarcely intended, Bob Jakin's picture of the solitary lad, "as close as an iron-biler," who "sits by himself so glumpish, a-knitting his brow, an' a-lookin' at the fire of a night," is in its way as pathetic as Maggie's helpless cry to Dr. Kenn, at the bazar, "Oh, I must go."

In the whole history of this fascinating Maggie there is a picturesque piteousness which somehow confuses one's sense of right and wrong. Yet what—we can not help asking—what is to become of the hundreds of clever girls, born of uncongenial parents, hemmed in with unsympathizing kindred of the Dodson sort, blest with no lover on whom to bestow their strong affections, no friend to whom to cling for guidance and support? They must fight their way, heaven help them! alone and unaided, through cloud and darkness, to the light. And, thank heaven, hundreds of them do, and live to hold out a helping hand afterwards to thousands more. "The middle-aged" (says "George Eliot," in this very book), "who have lived through their strongest emotions, but are yet in the time when memory is still half-passionate and not merely contemplative, should surely be a sort of natural priesthood, whom life has disciplined and consecrated to be the refuge and rescue of early stumblers and victims of self-despair."

Will it help these victims—such a picture as Maggie, who, with all her high aspirations and generous qualities, is, throughout her poor young life, no stay or comfort to any human being, but, on the contrary, a source of grief and injury to every one connected with her? If we are to judge character by results—not by grand imperfect essays, but by humbler fulfillments—of how much more use in the world were even fond, shallow Lucy, and narrow-minded Tom, than this poor Maggie, who seems only just to have caught hold of the true meaning and beauty of existence in that last pathetic prayer, "If my life is to be long, let me live to bless and comfort," when she is swept away out of our sight and love forever.

True, this is, as we have said, a magnificent ending for the book; but is it such for the life—the one human life which this author has created so vividly and powerfully, that we argue concerning the girl as if we had actually known her? Will it influence for good any other lives—this passionately drawn picture of temptation never conquered, or conquered just so far that we see its worst struggle is but beginning; of sorrows which teach nothing, or teach only bitterness; of love in its most delicious, most deadly phase; love—blind, selfish, paramount, seeing no future but possession, and, that hope gone, no alternative but death—death, welcomed as the solution of all difficulties, the escape from all pain?

Is this right? Is it a creed worthy of an author who should have pre-eminently "the brain of a man and the heart of a woman," united with what we may call a pure sexless intelligence, clear and calm, able to observe, and reason, and guide mortal passions, as those may, who have come out of the turmoil of the flesh into the region of ministering spirits, and have become "αγγελοι," messengers between God and man? What if the messenger testify falsely? What if the celestial trumpet give forth an uncertain sound?

Yet let us be just. There are those who argue that this—perhaps the finest ending, artistically, of any modern novel, is equally fine in a moral sense: that the death of Maggie and Tom is a glorious Euthanasia, showing that when, even at the eleventh hour, temptation is conquered, error atoned, and love reconciled, the life is complete: its lesson has been learnt, its work done; there is nothing more needed but the *vade in pacem* to an immediate heaven. This, if the author so meant it, was an idea grand, noble, Christian: as Christian (be it said with reverence) as the doctrine preached by the Divine Pardoner of all sinners to the sinner beside whom He died—"To-day shalt thou be with me in paradise." But the conception ought to have been worked out so plainly that no reader could mistake it. We should not have been left to feel, as we do feel, undecided whether this death was a translation or an escape; whether if they had not died, Maggie would not have been again the same Maggie, always sinning and always repenting; and Tom the same Tom, hard and narrow-minded, though the least ray of love and happiness cast over his gloomy life might have softened and made a thoroughly good man of him. The author ought to have satisfied us entirely as to the radical change in both; else we fall back upon the same dreary creed of overpowering circumstances: of human beings struggling forever in a great quagmire of unconquerable temptations, inevitable and hopeless woe. A creed more fatal to every noble effort, and brave self-restraint—above all to that humble faith in the superior Will which alone should govern ours—can hardly be conceived. It is true that there occur sometimes in life positions so complex and overwhelming, that plain right and wrong become confused; until the most righteous and religious man is hardly able to judge clearly or act fairly. But to meet such positions is one thing, to invent them is another. It becomes a serious question whether any author—who, great as his genius may be, sees no farther than mortal intelligence can—is justified in leading his readers into a labyrinth, the way out of which he does not, first, see clearly himself, and next, is able to make clear to them, so as to leave them mentally and morally at rest, free from all perplexity and uncertainty.

Now, uncertainty is the prevailing impression with which we close "The Mill on the Floss." We are never quite satisfied in our detestation of the Dodson family, the more odious because so dreadfully natural that we feel we all are haunted by some of the race, could name them among our own connections, perhaps have even received kindnesses from a Mrs. Pullet, a Mrs. Glegg, or a Mrs. Tulliver. We are vexed with ourselves for being so angry with stern, honest, upright, business-like Tom—so contemptuously indifferent to gentle, unsuspicious Lucy, with her universal kindness, extending from "the more familiar rodents" to her silly aunt Tulliver. We question much whether such a generous girl as Maggie would have fallen in love with Stephen at all: whether she would not from the first have regarded him simply as her cousin's lover, and if his passion won any thing from her, it would but have been the half-angry half-sorrowful disdain which a high-minded woman could not help feeling towards a man who forgot duty and honor in selfish love, even though the love were for herself. And, last and chief perplexity of all, we feel that, granting the case as our author puts it, the mischief done, the mutual passion mutually confessed, Stephen's piteous arguments have some justice on their side. The wrong done to him in Maggie's forsaking him was almost as great as the wrong previously done to Philip and Lucy:—whom no self-sacrifice on her part or Stephen's could ever have made happy again.

And, to test the matter, what reader will not confess, with a vague sensation of uneasy surprise, to have taken far less interest in all the good, injured personages of the story, than in this mad Stephen and treacherous Maggie? Who that is capable of understanding—as a thing which has been, or is, or may one day be—the master-passion that furnishes the key to so many lives, will not start to find how vividly this book revives it, or wakens it, or places it before him as a future possibility? Who does not think with a horribly delicious feeling of such a crisis, when right and wrong, bliss and bale, justice and conscience, seem swept from their boundaries, and a whole existence of Dodsons, Lucys, and Tom Tullivers, appears worth nothing, compared to the ecstasy of that "one kiss—the last" between Stephen and Maggie in the lane?

Is this right? The spell once broken—broken with the closing of the book—every high and pure and religious instinct within us answers unhesitatingly—"No."

No! It is *not* right to paint Maggie only as she is in her strong, unsatisfied, erring youth—and leave her there, her doubts unresolved, her passions unregulated, her faults unatoned and unforgiven; to cut her off ignobly and accidentally, leaving those two acts of hers, one her recoil of conscience with regard to Stephen, and the other her instinctive self-devotion in going to rescue Tom, as the sole noble landmarks of a life that had in it every capability for good with which a woman could be blessed. It is *not* right to carry us on through these three marvellous volumes, and leave us at the last, standing by the grave of the brother and sister, ready to lift up an accusatory cry, less to a beneficent Deity than to the humanly-invented Arimanes of the universe.—"Why should such things be? Why hast thou made us thus?"

But it may be urged, that fiction has its counterpart, and worse, in daily truth. How many perplexing histories do we not know of young lives blighted, apparently by no fault of their own; of blameless lives dragged into irresistible temptations; of high natures so meshed in by circumstances that they, as well as we, judging them from without, can hardly distinguish right from wrong, guilt from innocence; of living and lovable beings so broken down by unmerited afflictions, that when at last the end comes, we look on the poor dead face with a sense of thankfulness that there at least,

> "There is no other thing expressed
> But long disquiet merged in rest."

All this is most true, *so far as we see.* But we can never see, not even the wisest and greatest of us, any thing like *the whole* of even the meanest and briefest human life. We never can know through what fiery trial of temptation, nay, even sin,—for sin itself appears sometimes in the wonderful alchemy of the universe to be used as an agent for good,—a strong soul is being educated into a saintly minister to millions of weaker souls: coming to them with the authority of one whom suffering has taught how to heal suffering; nay, whom the very fact of having sinned once, has made more deeply to pity, so as more easily to rescue sinners. And, lastly, we never can comprehend, unless by experience, that exceeding peace—the "peace which passeth all understanding"—which is oftentimes seen in those most heavily and hopelessly afflicted: those who have lost all, and gained their own souls: whereof they possess themselves in patience; waiting until the "supreme moment" of which our author speaks, but which is to them not an escape from the miseries of this world, but a joyful entrance into the world everlasting.

Ay, thank heaven, though the highest human intellect may fail to hear it, there are millions of human hearts yet living and throbbing, or mouldering quietly into dust, who have heard, all through the turmoil or silence of existence, though lasting for three score years and ten, a continual still small voice, following them to the end: "Fear not: for I am thy God."

Would that in some future book, as powerful as "*The Mill on the Floss*," the author might become a true "Αγγελος," and teach us this!

BODIES AND SOULS.

"BODIES" are in this title advisedly and intentionally placed first. Not, God forbid! in any materialistic denying of the soul, or sensuous Greco-heathenish exaltation of the body; but in simple, religious recognition of the fact that it has pleased the Maker of both to put the soul into the body; to cause the soul to be worked on through the body; and, whether we ignore it or not, to continue for good or for evil that intimate union until it is dissolved by the mysterious change which we call Death.

Mystics may deny and defy it; poets may despise it; devotees may ignore it; and some few saints and martyrs may rise superior to it, but there the practical truth remains. Our body is our body; to be made—very much of our own will, or what seems to be such—either a useful, suitable dwelling for the soul to live and work and do her temporary duty in, or a cumbersome, wretched, ruined mansion, in which she wanders miserably, capable of nothing, enjoying nothing, and longing only for the day when the walls shall crumble, the roof fall, and the prisoner be set free.

> "When languor and disease invade
> This trembling house of clay,
> 'Tis sweet to look beyond our cage,
> And long to fly away."

So it is, God knows; and He, who never leaves Himself without a witness, gives us continually noble instances in which the divine inmate has so completely triumphed over the frail and perishing tabernacle, as to make the sick-room the brightest room in the house. But there are also other cases when, *before* "languor and disease" invaded and took captive the entire domain, the wretched struggles of the ill-used and ill-regulated body were mistaken for the writhings of the soul; when many an "earnest student" —*vide* one lamentable instance in a book of that name—goes on half-killing himself with study, and then sets down what every sensible person would call dyspepsia, or liver disease, as "convictions of sin," the "wrestling of the flesh against the Spirit," etc., etc. Alternations of terrible religious doubt, and agonized remorse for the same. In short, all that morbid introspection by which a certain order of pietists who call themselves "miserable sinners" gratify at once their conscience and their egotism, by dwelling continually on these said sins; flaunting them, as the Irish beggars do their rags and wounds, in the face of society, by diaries, letters, conversations, instead of keeping them for the sole ear of Him unto whom alone we who know ourselves so little and our fellow-mortals still less, are—we thank and bless Him—however miserable sinners we be, wholly and perfectly and compassionately known.

It is, therefore, in no irreligious spirit, but the contrary, that we put forward a word or two for the doctrine too apt to be forgotten, of Bodies and Souls, which God has, in this state of being, so mysteriously joined together that no man can put them asunder; no more than we can, however some of us think we can, shut Him out of a portion of His own world by dividing it into secular and religious, sacred and profane. But this is not a question to be entered on here, where all that is wished is to throw out a few suggestions, and also state a few facts, on the great subject of taking care of the body for the sake of the soul, and of getting at men's souls in the way which Providence seems to point out as the true and lawful way,—*through* their bodies.

I have been led to these reflections by a few walks round about a city probably one of the most religious cities in the kingdom, at least externally. And why not in reality? since its population mainly consists of those to whom religion must necessarily be the sole consolation: the aged, who have lived long enough to see the vanity of all things; the infirm and feeble; and the incurable invalid, whose life is and must be passed, not in the wholesome sunshine of ordinary existence, but in a long pale twilight of suffering, slowly darkening into that solemn night of which the day-dawn is immortality.

For these, and such as these, the city I speak of opens her friendly arms, and extends to them all her comforts, physical and spiritual. Probably in no given area of town habitations are so many churches and chapels; all of which, it must be owned, are continuously and devoutly filled. And in many of the faces you there meet—queer, withered, and world-worn though they be—is an expression of earnest piety that can not be sufficiently respected, ay, whatever form it takes, High Church or Low Church, Methodism, Calvinism, Tractarianism, Unitarianism, or any other of the innumerable isms which, despite all their differences, include, to His eyes who seeth not as man seeth, His universal Church. You can not pass along the streets about eleven on a Sunday morning and mark the grave, respectable, decorous throng which defiles severally into its several places of worship, each ready, no doubt, to thunder anathemas on every other place of worship, yet devoutly and earnestly bent upon serving God in its own fashion, without feeling certain that somewhere, under or above all these jarring creeds, must lie His Divine Truth; which He is able to take care of, to impress upon every human soul according to its temporary needs, and ultimately to demonstrate, perfectly and everlastingly, in His own time and way.

One word about the city herself, as she appears on such a Sunday morning as this, when her clean pavements are covered with an ever-moving, decent church-going throng, and her bright, sunshiny atmosphere, rarely either foggy or smoky, is filled with the sound of the "church-going bell." Truly she is a fair city. She sits like a lady in the centre of her circle of protecting hills, white and smiling, aristocratically still and calm. No ugly trade defiles her quiet streets; in her green environs no chimneys blacken and no furnaces blaze. For she is a lady city. She does not work at all, or seems as if she did not. She sits at ease on her picturesque site; so small that almost at every street corner you can catch a glimpse of green hills; looking outward and upward from her pleasant nest upon a country that for richness is the very garden of England.

The West of England, for most people will have recognized this beautiful city as Bath. Our island can boast none fairer, except, perhaps, Edinburgh, which in degree she resembles, though with a difference. Edinburgh, bold and manly, sits throned on the hill-tops and commands the valleys; Bath, lovely and feminine, nestles down in her valley and looks up at the hills. But there is in both the same picturesqueness of situation, the same compactness and elegance, the same atmosphere of white quietness, idleness, and ancient, historical, dignified repose.

Many a mutation has Bath gone through since the days when she was no city as yet—but a mere morass, spreading over the bottom of that circular valley or basin, in which bubbled up—as they do still, without change of temperature or diminution of quantity—those mysterious hot springs, which always seem to the stranger as something "uncanny"—something unconsciously reminding us of that Abode beneath, which some people seem to believe in far more religiously and eagerly than in the Abode above. *Where* can be—*what* can be that wondrous, inextinguishable fire which boils this unlimited supply of hot water, as it has done for thousands and thousands of years?

Strange it is to picture this heated morass as, according to mythic legend, it was first discovered by the leper-prince, Bladud, and his leprous swine. More difficult still to conjure up the Roman city there built, and called by the foreign civilizers *Aquæ Solis*—a city coeval with Pompeii and Herculaneum, and, doubtless, equally perfect and luxurious, to judge by the fragments of pavement, the remains of houses, temples, baths, which are even yet disinterred from the buried town—buried many feet below the surface of this our modern Bath—Bath, which owed its name to Hæt Bathan, the substitution for *Aquæ Solis* by the plain, rough Saxon conqueror, who set up his barbaric state there on the relics of refined and poetic Rome. What stories could not these hills tell—the unchangeable hills—of all the grim Saxons who abode or visited here—Osric the Monk, Offa the Thane, Ethelstane and Edgar the Kings.

And so through mediæval centuries these hot springs kept flowing; used, as the names of the baths indicated, by kings, queens, abbots, and lepers; afterwards, as the "horse bath" implies, sinking to the use of brute beasts. But at this point of decadence, in the Elizabethan age, which had wisdom enough to care for bodies as well as souls, the queen elevated the half-forgotten city by granting her a charter, and assigning, "of her Majesty's abundant grace, certain knowledge, and mere motion," "all and singular such and the same waters, baths, etc." to the mayor, aldermen, citizens, and to their successors, forever."

Which "forever" still remains in force, one only exception being made—the Kingston or Roman bath, which is private property.

The next notice of Bath is by old Samuel Pepys—who certainly had no slight regard for *his* body, whatever he might have had for his soul—"Looked into the baths and find the king's and queen's full of a mixed sort of good and bad—and the cross only almost for gentry. So home with my wife; and did pay my guides, two women, 5*s.*, and one man 2*s.* 6*d.*" Henceforward Bath gradually became a fashionable resort: for the sick to gain health, for the sound to enjoy it. Every pains was taken both to preserve and to entertain those frail bodies, so troublesome yet so dear to us all. Souls, it is to be feared, were rather at a discount—at least to judge by Miss Burney's, Miss Austen's, and Miss Ferrier's novels, and by the historical and biographical records of the time—probably less veracious than these admirable fictions.

Yet even then and there—though society was at its lowest ebb of frivolity—must have existed much of that large, loving, noble human nature which is found everywhere indestructible. How many a touching and heroic episode may, nay, must have been enacted along these very streets, and within those squares and crescents of dignified old-fashioned houses—whose frontage of white Bath-stone is darkening slowly into sombre harmonious gray. Young gentlewomen, who, in spite of hoops, sacques, paint, and patches, made the tenderest of nurses to exacting old age; young gentlemen, who, under flowing wigs, and ruffled shirt-breasts, carried sound heads and faithful hearts—and made honest love to those said gentlewomen along Pulteney Street, the Circus, or the Paragon; yes, or even in the Pump-room itself—or opposite the wonderful "Jacob's ladder" which makes the curious ornamentation of the Abbey door.

All, all are away; dropped with their numberless, forgotten joys and sorrows into the peaceful dust. Their life is now—as each of ours shall soon be—

"No more than stories in a printed book."

But the city still remains—though changes have come over her too—and in the gradual ebbing of the tide of fashion, Bath has for many years been left, like a faded beauty, to devote herself no longer to the decoration and disportation, but to the sanitary preservation of bodies—and also souls.

For she is, as before stated—a most religious city. *Laborare est orare* is certainly not her motto. Most of her inhabitants have nothing in the world to do, except to pray. That they do pray, and very sincerely—none would wish to deny. But it might be as well for them, as for most other religious communities, if they would mingle with their orisons a little less of the sounding brass and tinkling cymbal, and a little more of that most excellent gift of charity. Then they would cease disputing about the respective virtue of closed pews and open pews, lecterns and reading-desks:—and a "kettle-drum" (an innocent afternoon party, in demi-toilette, for sociality, music, tittle-tattle, and tea) would be esteemed no more irreligious, possibly a little less so, than those extraordinary and anomalous dissipations—technically termed Bible routs—where the *élite* of pious Bath assembles in full dress for Scripture reading and expounding—and the entertainments are coffee, ices, conversation, psalms, and prayers.

Nevertheless, Bath is a virtuous, decorous city; containing the average, or beyond the average, of good and kindly people—or so it appears, to judge by her long list of charities. Rarely has any city, so small, so many apparent outlets for her benevolence. These comprise ancient foundations; Blue Alms, Black Alms, Grammar and Blue Coat Schools; hospitals, modern and mediæval, a penitentiary, and so on. Add to these, that every one of the numerous churches and chapels has its own working schemes of schools, district-visitings, Dorcas and other charities, and we may conclude that the poor of Bath are tolerably well cared for.

Shall we see how? It will take but a short walk, this sharp but cheery winter day; the narrowness and compactness of the city's limits being a great advantage to us as well as to its charities.

Let us begin at the very beginning. How shall we attack poor people's souls—*through* their bodies, mind—except by the first principle of purification—cleanliness, which is emphatically pronounced to be "next to godliness?"

I have always had a deep faith in cleanliness. I believe

earnestly the saying, "that a man is not near so ready to commit a crime when he has got a clean shirt on;" for the sense of self-respect which accompanies a well-washed and decently clad body, generally, more or less, communicates itself to the soul. A working-man is always more of a man, more sober and well-conducted, more fit to go to church, or go a-courting, after he has "cleaned himself:" and a working-woman—a respectable mechanic's wife, or civil maid-servant—will be none the less civil and respectable for assuming, toil being over, a tidy apron, face, and hands. So let our first peregrination be to certain baths and laundries, built close by the river side, in Milk Street —a street which might have been especially chosen for the purpose, as it and the adjoining Avon Street are principally inhabited by sweeps.

It was not always so. This region, now the lowest in Bath, was, not so very long since, noted for handsome residences. Kingsmead House, which still remains, forming one portion of Kingsmead Square, must have been the finest of all, and its gardens are said to have extended down to the river side, over the area now occupied by these low streets and a sort of quay. We knock at a humble door (a very humble door, for the originator of the scheme, Mr. Sutcliffe, was too truly benevolent to waste money upon architecture), with "Bath and Laundries" thereon inscribed. It is opened by an honest-looking, respectable man, as he has opened it for the last seventeen years—ever since its foundation, indeed.

He is the whole of the staff—governor, housekeeper, secretary, accountant. He lives in two or three small rooms attached to the establishment, and devotes his whole time to its management. He had a wife to help him, but she is no more; now he does it all himself. "Bless 'ee, I like it," says he. "It's busy work enough, for I never go out except a Sundays; haven't taken a walk three times these seventeen years. But I like it." Easy to see that this manager is a very intelligent man of his class; working with a will—the root of all really good work. It can do him no harm to set down here his honest name—Cox.

Cox is evidently a character. He takes us into his little parlor—very tidy, and adorned with all sorts of curiosities—and, as preliminary information, gives us a printed paper, on which we read as follows:

"Bath and Laundries, Milk Street.

"The Committee have adopted the following low scale of charges, being far below the rates in most places, with a view to extend the benefits of the Institution to the largest possible number of persons. Charges in the wash-house—For the use of a tub and boiler, one halfpenny per hour. Drying and ironing (small articles), one halfpenny per dozen; ditto, ditto, large, one farthing each. N.B.—One penny must be paid on entrance and the remainder before the clothes are taken away. Charges for baths—First-class (hot or cold), threepence; second-class (ditto, ditto), twopence. N.B.—The baths for women are in a separate part of the buildings, and are provided with female attendance. A female bather may take one child under seven years of age, into the bath with herself, without additional charge."

Very simple, cheap, and admirable arrangements—with which, on more investigation, we are the more pleased. The baths are as good as any ordinary bath-room in a private house. We inquire who are the sort of people that avail themselves of such an easy luxury? Sweeps? "No," replies Cox, gravely; "we had only two sweeps the whole of last season." "And the poor people in the streets hereabouts—do they come?" "Never. Our bathers are chiefly mechanics, shop-girls from Milsom Street, and domestic servants. Not at all the class for which the place was started. They won't come. It's a great pity. Still, one sort or other, we get about thirty bathers a day; an average of 6000 in the course of the year." Well, 6000 clean-washed folks are not a bad thing. But the other statement only proves more and more that the lower a human being sinks in moral and physical degradation, the greater is his aversion to water. Let the rising generation take from this a wholesome warning—and a daily bath.

But the laundry, Cox said with pride, is much more popular—and among the class for which it was intended. One can imagine the comfort it must be to any poor woman—whose whole establishment, perhaps, consists of but one room—to be supplied with all the materials for a family wash—except soap—and to be able to take back her poor bits of "things" at the day's end, dried, ironed, and aired; no encumbrance of wet, flapping clothes, or damp smell of hot water and soap-suds, to irritate the tired husband and drive him to the public-house. Those women—seventy I believe there were—upon whom we opened the door, and gradually distinguished them through the steaming atmosphere—each busy in her separate division—looked thoroughly comfortable, though many of them were very ragged, worn, and poverty-stricken. 8000, Cox informed us, was the yearly average who used these wash-houses; by which we may reckon 8000 little or large families made comfortable and decent, so far as clean linen will do it.

"And do they always conduct themselves decently—these women, who bring no certificate of character, no warrant of admission except their need and their entrance-penny? Do they never quarrel, or use ill-language, or steal one another's property—as must be so very easy to do?"

Cox shakes his head smiling. "We have had only two dismissions for bad conduct in my time. As for stealing—sometimes there are mistakes, but the clothes are always brought to my room for fair exchange. For bad words—I never hear nothing, except now and then one of 'em will be humming a little tune to herself; that's no harm, you know."

Certainly not, quite the contrary.

We do not stay long in our examination, the machinery of the place being much as it is in all public establishments—water heated by steam, stoves for the irons, and hot-air presses for the drying. Besides, we can not quite feel that we have any right to stare at or hinder these decent women who have paid their honest pennies for liberty to do their honest work. We pass on to the big coal-cellar, which feeds the big steam-engine, which supplies the working power of all these arrangements. And there we are considerably amused to find, lying on the warm roof of the engine, a very good plaster nymph, with several extrinsic arms and legs, the work of a sculptor—I think we may say *the* sculptor of Bath—to whom Cox has long allowed the liberty of drying his casts here. Cox has evidently a taste for art; for he takes us into another room—his own workroom—which contains the labor of his life; a gigantic chair all encrusted with shells, the two arms formed in imitation of the sea-serpent, and the back of an equally ornamental and original design; more original than comfortable, we should suppose. A chair not beautiful, but very curious, and exactly suited for a presidential chair of the Conchological Society, if there was one. Cox unveils it, and regards it with lingering affection.

"Yes, it took me many years and much labor, for which I shall never be paid, of course. I was advised to present it to the Prince of Wales, but bless you, he'd never have it. It, and the fountain you see"—another enormous specimen of this shell-work—"would do well in some big lord's conservatory; but who is to make 'em known, or who will come and buy them of a poor man like me? Well, I enjoyed working at 'em," says Cox with a patient sigh, as he covers up his labors of many years.

We hope he may find a purchaser, for really the lovers of the grotesque and ingenious might do worse than buy. And so with hearty good wishes we leave worthy Cox, his baths and laundries, and make our way through the cutting east wind, which rushes like a charge of bayonets at every street corner, to the next place for advantaging poor folks' bodies—the soup-kitchens, belonging to the "Society for Improving the Condition of the Working Classes in Bath." No doubt one of the best ways of doing this is by feeding them; not by promiscuous charity, which lowers independence—that honest independence which is the best boast of both poor and rich—but by some means of supplying want and obtaining for the same benefit fair payment. The soup-kitchens do this. At the head establishment, in Chatham Row, Walcot, and at the seven branch establishments distributed about the city, there is a uniform tariff of prices; one penny the half-pint, and so on, when paid by the working-man himself, which price is doubled, when the expenditure is made in tickets to be given away as charity. And the Society especially begs that purchasers will not distribute these tickets promiscuously to beggars, but to the needy and deserving poor of the town.

Any one who considers how extremely difficult it is for a poor laboring man, or even a respectable mechanic, to get a hot, wholesome, well-cooked dinner at all, will understand that it was a satisfactory sight, on this bitter winter noon, to see those long lines of decent-looking men eating their steaming portions off a clean, tidy board. A cheap dinner—a penny bowl of soup and a halfpenny roll—and yet it was substantial enough for any man's needs—any gentleman's either. "I assure you," said a very civil personage, who looked like a cook in his white apron and sleeves, but received us with an air of dignity and authority which betokened something higher, "I assure you, many a colonel and general have been here and made their dinners off it, and declared they never wished to dine better, and only hoped they might never dine worse." In which sentiment, having tasted the soup, we heartily agreed with those respected military officers.

The interior working of soup-kitchens is pretty well known—this of Bath is like most others. Meat is procured daily from six or seven of the most respectable butchers of the city, cut up in fragments, mixed with vegetables, and thrown into the great boilers, which, during the winters of 1861–2, engulfed—how much think you?—11,433 lbs. of beef, 35½ sacks of onions, 107½ sacks of peas, and of salt more than a ton. Out of this *matériel* how many a hungry mouth must have been filled, and how many a busy workman sent cheerily back to his work all the better fitted to earn the family bread. And if, in truth, the nearest way to a man's heart—not to say his conscience—is through his stomach, the police-sheets of the Bath magistrates may have been lightened according as these soup-boilers were filled and emptied. They are, the attendant told us, emptied every day, and newly supplied with fresh meat and vegetables, lest the poor should imagine—as they are so prone to do—"Oh, any thing is thought good enough for *us*."

. At this head kitchen all the soup is made, and thence distributed, in enormous cans, to the various branch depôts. People can either consume it on the spot, or carry it away with them. Last winter, from November, 1862, to April, 1863, the consumption was 73,080 quarts, and the number of consumers was 36,333—average 300 per diem: the greatest number who ever came in one day being 563. The receipts across the counter amounted to 90,945 penny pieces—that is, £378 18*s.* 9*d.*—while £163 19*s.* was realized by the sale of tickets for benevolent distribution. This combined sum is more than sufficient to defray all expenses, and, with the addition of subscriptions and donations, has enabled the Committee to lay by a savings-bank fund for future expenses.

These plain facts are better than any poetical descriptions, and so we may safely congratulate the fair city of Bath on the care she takes of bodies as well as souls—suggesting, *en passant*, to her pious inhabitants, the administration of soup-tickets at least as numerously as of tracts; and the advising of poor women to attend the baths and laundries as regularly as church, chapel, or prayer-meeting. "This do, not leaving the other undone."

And now let us see what Bath does for those frail and dilapidated bodies to which neither food nor water can give health or soundness—perhaps never again. There are several hospitals, but the Mineral Water Hospital, peculiar to this city, is the only one I can speak of here. It was meant "for the relief and support of poor persons from any part of Great Britain and Ireland, afflicted with complaints for which the Bath waters are a remedy;" and its foundation-stone was laid by the Honorable William Pulteney, afterwards Earl of Bath, in 1737, nearly a hundred and thirty years ago.

At that time there were in Bath three remarkable men —Richard Nash, Ralph Allen, and William Oliver. The first is known as Beau Nash, Master of the Ceremonies for many years: gifted with gentlemanly manners, somewhat lax principles, an easy conscience, and a very kindly heart. The second raised himself from very humble origin to be thus written of by his friend Alexander Pope:

"Let low-born Allen, with ingenuous shame,
Do good by stealth, and blush to find it fame;"

and to be likewise immortalized by his other friend, Henry Fielding, in the character of *Squire Allworthy.** The third has gone down to posterity as the originator of that excellent Bath food, Oliver's biscuits, and as the first physician of the Mineral Water Hospital. To these three worthies it owes its foundation. Beau Nash, whose liberal hand was always in his own or other people's pockets, collected large sums of money; Ralph Allen bestowed, out of his quarries on Combe Down, the stone for building, and £1000 besides; Dr. Oliver contributed all that a wise physician could—skill, advice, influence, and personal su-

* For this, and much other information, the writer is indebted to a recent valuable and exceedingly erudite "Historic Guide to Bath," by the Rev. G. N. Wright, M.A.

pervision. Thus, in May, 1742—that frivolous and yet stormy era—just before the memorable '45, was opened that admirable institution; and, from the date of its opening to its anniversary in May, 1862, it either relieved or cured, out of admitted patients, a proportion of 40,780 persons.

With a feeling of due respect, we stand before its door at the foot of Milsom Street, not the original door, but that of the new wing, which in 1861 was added to the original building. A hospital is never a cheerful place to visit: but this being for chiefly chronic diseases, such as rheumatism, gout, palsy, and cutaneous disorders, is less painful than most. For the inmates are rarely in their beds; the large, clean, lofty dormitories are nearly empty; and even in the day-rooms, the women's especially, we find many patient-looking patients, busily pursuing, with as much activity as their complaints allow, many useful avocations. Knitting and sewing with the one side, draught-playing, reading, and mat-making with the other, appear to be the favorite occupations. As we pass through them, guided by the resident surgeon, at whose coming all faces seemed to brighten as if he were a general friend, I noticed how much more cheerful the women looked than the men. Not wonderful, considering how many, nay, all of the latter, are taken from active trades or agricultural day-labor, and shut up here, helpless but not hopeless: for the deaths, or those dismissed incurable, bear an infinitesimal proportion to the number "discharged cured."

We heard many little episodes, more comical than doleful, of hospital life. How respectable elderly patients have sometimes, after leaving, evinced their gratitude by sending proposals of marriage, not invariably declined, to the equally respectable elderly nurses; and how other patients, suddenly inheriting money, have thankfully and gladly contributed portions of it for the benefit of the hospital. One man who was in this fortunate position, we passed, eagerly writing letters in the seclusion of the sleeping ward; while in another, by the quiet, solitary fire, sat another patient, and beside him his pleasant-looking wife, who, for six weeks, had been allowed to come every day and nurse him through some accidental, acute illness. "Do you often allow this, doctor?" "Always, when needed; it is such a comfort to them." It must be.

The doctor told us another episode of a very eccentric patient, by name Kihiringi Te Tuahu,—a New Zealander. He spoke not a word of English; but still he managed to make himself a general favorite in the ward. His chief difficulty was smoking. He would creep down to forbidden rooms, obtain cigars, and carry them, still lighted, under his sleeve all chapel-time, then exhibit his unlawful booty with an innocent pride which disarmed all punishment. He was indeed, like all half-savages, very much of a child; and when, much better, he left the hospital, it was with an outburst of perfectly childish tears. "In fact," added the doctor, "I never did see any man who cried so much."

Generally, no doubt, the tears are few; the patients have an aspect of quiet endurance and familiarity with pain. They are on the whole an extremely respectable class. And yet nothing is required for entrance, no presentation or applications through subscribers: simply a letter from any medical man, stating the case and its necessities, to which is returned a blank certificate, to be filled up and signed by the clergyman and others, in the parish to which the applicant belongs. Beyond this is required to be deposited a sum of three pounds, if the applicant comes from any part of England; five pounds if from Scotland or Ireland, to be kept as "caution-money," intended to defray the expenses of homeward journey, or possible death, or great destitution as to clothes. If not wanted for any of these purposes the whole sum is returned to the party or parties who provided it.

On this simple plan the hospital works, and has worked—these hundred and thirty years. We went all over it—the wards, baths (with most admirable and ingenious contrivances for the feeble and the crippled), the kitchens, laundries, cellars, up to the chapel, which is so beautiful as to be almost a flaw in the establishment. One can not but think that an additional ward would have served God much better than a richly-ornamental chancel and seven gorgeously-painted windows, illustrating, out of Bible history, the use and benefit of water. But let us not grumble. People have a right to confer their benefits in their own way. And certainly here bodies are never neglected for the sake of souls. Let us hope that to hundreds and thousands of poor men and women this brief haven of rest, in an admirably well-conducted hospital, may be good for both bodies and souls.

We end our investigations in the board-room, round whose oaken table a century's meetings have been held. What tales it could tell of those old worthies whose portraits alone now look down upon their successors' deliberations. Besides a very imaginative likeness of Hygeia, a buxom young woman who flaunts it over the fire-place, there is a curious picture of Dr. Oliver and Mr. Pierce, the first physician and first surgeon to the hospital, examining patients affected with paralysis, rheumatism, and leprosy—a subject that, in spite of its repulsiveness, is interesting, and well painted. The painter is W. Hoare, R.A., who also leaves his own portrait, a thoughtful head, somewhat after the manner of Opie. Others besides adorn the walls; Mr. Morris, the first apothecary, his father, mother, and wife—Mr. Morris, senior, being a meek old gentleman, and Mrs. Morris, senior, a large grim woman, in ruffles and mittens, who looked as if she had ruled with a rod of iron both spouse, son, and daughter-in-law. There, too, smirks poor Beau Nash's jovial countenance, with the round cheeks (nearly all the men of that period seem to have been jolly and round-cheeked) and the weak, irresolute mouth; just like him who was, as the saying is, "Nobody's enemy but his own." And there also is the thin, acute, kindly face of good Ralph Allen, who was every body's friend, and whose palatial home, at Prior Park, still remains as one of the most magnificent yet forlorn mansions in England. It and Beckford's Tower gaze at one another across Bath, from opposite hills, strange monuments of the passing away of all human things. As one looks round at these faded and fading portraits, and thinks of the living men who week by week assemble at this table beneath them, one by one disappearing thence, to reappear, if they ever reappear at all, but as silent portraits on the wall, the deep truth of the oft-quoted yet ever-beautiful rhyme forces itself for the hundredth time upon one's mind:—

"Only the actions of the just,
Smell sweet, and blossom in the dust."

BLIND.

I WAS walking along a rather lonely road, humming a tune to myself—a most indefensible habit, which I only mention as it accounted for my being suddenly stopped by a civil voice—

"Ma'am, if you please—"

I turned, and now first noticed a young man who had just passed me by. He was stepping out, quickly and decisively, with a stick in his hand and a bundle on his shoulder.

"Ma'am, if you please, would you direct me to ——?" naming a gentleman's house close by. I was proceeding to point it out to him, when I perceived that the young man had *no eyes.* It was a well-featured and highly intelligent countenance, with that peculiarly peaceful expression that one often sees on the faces of the blind; but of his calamity there could be no doubt: the eyes, as I have said, were gone: the eyelids closed tightly over *nothing.* Yet his step was so firm, and his general appearance so active and bright, that a careless passer-by would scarcely have detected that he was blind.

Of course I went back with him to the house he named —in spite of his polite protestations that there was not the least necessity—"he could find it easily"—*how,* Heaven knows:—also, I had the curiosity to lie in wait a few minutes until I watched him come cheerily out again, shoulder his big bundle, plant his stick on the ground, and walk briskly back, whistling a lively tune, and marching as fast and fearlessly as though he saw every step of the road he traversed.

"Have you done your business?"

My friend started, but immediately recognized the voice. "Oh yes, thank you, ma'am. I'm all right. Very much obliged. Good-morning."

He recommenced his interrupted tune, and pursued his

way with such determined independence that I felt as if more notice of him would be taking an unwarrantable liberty with his misfortune. But his cheerful face quite haunted me, and I speculated for a long time what "business" he could be about, and how he dared trust himself alone, in the great wilderness of London and its environs, with no guide except his stick. At last I remembered he might be one of the "travellers" belonging to an institution I had heard of (and the foundress of which, by an odd coincidence, I was going that day to meet)—the "Association for Promoting the General Welfare of the Blind."

I proceeded to pay my visit to this lady—whose name, having been often before in print, there can be no scruple in mentioning here—Miss Gilbert, the blind daughter of the Bishop of Chichester. To her superintendence and endowment, in conjunction with the design and practical aid of another blind person, Mr. W. Hanks Levy, this institution owes its existence.

Laudatory personalities are odious. To praise a good man or woman for doing what he, she, or any other good person recognizes as a mere matter of duty, which, when all is done, leaves us still "unprofitable servants," is usually annoying to the individual and injurious to the cause. And yet the root of every noble cause must be some noble personality—some one human being who has conceived and carried into execution some one idea, and on whose peculiar character the success of the whole undertaking mainly depends.

Therefore, without trenching on the sacred privacy which ought, above all, to be observed towards women, I may just say that it was impossible to look on this little, gentle-spoken, quiet woman, who, out of her own darkened life, had become such a "light to the blind," without a feeling of great reverence and great humility. We who can drink in form and color at every pore of our being, to whom each sunset is a daily feast, each new landscape a new delight, who in pictures, statues, and beloved living faces have continual sources of ever-renewed enjoyment—God help us, how unthankful, how unworthy we are!

Miss Gilbert and myself arranged that I should visit her institution, in order to say any thing that occurred to me to say about it in print. "For," added she, "we want to be better known, because we want help. Without more customers to our shop we must lessen the work we give out, and refuse entirely the one hundred and fifty applicants who are eagerly waiting for more, and meantime living as they best can, in workhouses or by street begging. And winter is coming on, you know."

Winter to these poor—not necessarily belonging to the hardened pauper class, in many cases neither unrefined nor uneducated, since of the thirty thousand blind in the United Kingdom nine-tenths are ascertained to have become so *after* the age of twenty-one. It was a sad thought—these one hundred and fifty poor souls waiting for work—not for wealth, or hope, or amusement—simply for *work:* something to fill up a few hours of their long day in the dark, something to put food into their mouths of their own earning, and save them from eating the bitter duty-bread of friends, or the charity-bread of strangers. I arranged to meet Miss Gilbert the next day, at 127 Euston Road.

It was a house in no wise different from the other houses in this neighborhood, except that outside its shop-door there hung a picture not badly painted, representing a room occupied by busy blind work-people. The shop itself was entirely filled with baskets, mats, brushes, etc. And there the only one of the four persons in the establishment who is not blind was engaged in serving a few—far too few!—customers.

No "sighted"—(to use the touching word which they have coined, these blind, in speaking of us who see, as if the use of the eyes were a great, peculiar gift)—no "sighted" person can enter this house of busy darkness without a strange, awed feeling. To be in a place where every body is blind! a blind housemaid to sweep and clean—and very well it is done too: a blind porter to carry messages: a blind attendant to show you through dim passages, where you meet other blind people quietly feeling their way, intent on their various avocations, and taking no heed of you. It is like being brought into a new kind of existence, in the which at first you doubt if you are not an unwarrantable intruder. You feel shy and strange. The common phrases, "Yes, I *see*," or "it *looks* so and so," make you start after uttering them, as if you had said something unnatural and unkind. Only at first. Soon you are taught to recognize that undoubted fact, recorded by both sufferers and observers, that of all God's afflicted ones, there are none whom His mercy has made so cheerful, so keenly and easily susceptible of happiness, as the blind.

We went to the little parlor, furnished, like the rest of the house, with the utmost simplicity—no money wasted, as charities often do waste it, in useless elegancies, or in handsomely-paid officials. The only official here is Mr. Levy, the director, to whose intelligence and ingenuity the working of the whole scheme—which, indeed, he mainly planned—is safely consigned. Under his guidance—the blind instructing the seeing—we examined various inventions, some of them his own, for conveying instruction in writing, reading, and geography, both to those born blind and to those who have since become so. He likewise showed us a system of musical notation, by means of which the blind can learn the science as well as the practice of this their great solace and delight. Simple as these contrivances were, they would be difficult to explain within the limits of this paper: besides, persons interested therein can easily find out all for themselves by application at 127 Euston Road, London: where, also, any collector of objects of science, fossils, minerals, stuffed animals, and the like—not subject to injury from handling—may give entertainment and information to many an intelligent mind, to whom otherwise the wonderful works of God in nature must forever remain unknown. The delight his little museum affords is, Mr. Levy told us, something quite incredible.

Beside it, and more valuable still, is the circulating library of embossed books, for the use of the blind; among these is an American edition of Milton. How the grand old man would have rejoiced could he have foretold the day when, without interpreters, the blind would be taught to behold all that he beheld when, although

"So thick a drop serene had quenched those orbs,"

he was able, perhaps all the more through that visual darkness, to see clear into the very heaven of heavens. And when, to show us how fast the blind could read by touch only, Mr. Levy opened at random a Testament, and read as quickly as any ordinary reader some verses—which happened to be in *Revelation*—one felt how great was the blessing by which this (to us) blank white page was made to convey to the solitary blind man or woman images such as that of the City "which had no need of the sun, neither of the moon, to shine on it, for the glory of God did lighten it, and the Lamb is the light thereof."

Passing from this little sanctum, the centre of so much thought and ingenuity, we went to the work-rooms of the men and women employed in the house from nine to six daily. In the latter were about a dozen women busy over brush-making, bead-work and leather-work. The brush-making was the most successful, since in all ornamental work the blind can not hope to compete with those to whom the glory of color and the harmonies of form have been familiar unrecognized blessings all their lives. But it was a treat to see those poor women, some old, some young, all so busy and so interested in their work; and to know that but for this Association they would be begging in the streets, or sitting in helpless, hopeless, miserable idleness—the lowest condition, short of actual vice, to which any human being can fall.

More strongly still one felt this among the men: in some of whom it was easy to read the history of the intelligent, industrious, respectable artisan, from whom sudden loss of sight took away his only means of subsistence, dooming him for the rest of his days to dependence on his friends, or on the honest man's last horror, the workhouse. One guessed how eagerly he would come to such an establishment as this in Euston Road, which, offering to teach him a blind man's trade, and to supply him with work after he had learnt it, gave him a little hope to begin the world again. The skill attainable by clever fingers unguided by eyes is wonderful enough: but then the learning of a new trade *in the dark* requires of course double patience and double time. Nay, at best, a man who has to *feel* for every thing can not expect to get through the same amount of work in the same number of hours as the man who *sees* every thing—his tools, his materials, and the result of his labor. The blind must always work at a disadvantage, but it is a great thing to enable them to work at all. No one could look round on these men, most of them middle-aged, and several, we heard, fathers of families, without feeling what a blessing indescribable is even the small amount of weekly work and weekly wage with which they are here supplied, to workingmen, the chief element in whose lives is essentially work: who, in that darkness which has overtaken them at noon-day, have none of those elegant resources for passing time away which solace the wealthy blind: to whom there is no pleasure in idleness—or, bitterer still, to whom enforced idleness is simply another word for starvation.

And here, to make clear the working of this part of the Association, let me copy a few lines from notes that were furnished to me by its foundress:

"Those workmen who know a trade are employed at their homes, and receive the *selling* price for their work, buying their materials of the Association. No extra charge is made to the public upon their work. . . . Those who are learning trades at Euston Road receive a portion of their earnings for themselves: the rest pays for materials and goes as profit to the Institution. The teaching of trades is a costly part of the work. Many of the learners can not be supported by their friends, and are therefore boarded in houses connected with the Association—the money being provided by those interested in the individual, or by his parish, or in both these ways. The weekly terms are 9*s.* for each man, and 7*s.* 6*d.* for each woman—at which rate the managers and matrons of each house undertake to make it pay. They have no salary. In proportion as the pupil's earnings increase, the sum contributed for his board diminishes. In some instances the Association bears the chief cost. When he has learnt his trade, the Association may or may not employ him, or he is at liberty to start on his own account: but practically he is sure to ask for employment.

"The great object is to enable the blind, as a class, to earn their own livelihood, and to elevate their condition generally. If the sighted would help the blind by acting to them the part of levers, to raise them out of their present state, rather than of props to support them in it—the blind would most thankfully recognize that aid which they can not well dispense with, but which they most prefer, because, in accepting it, they reduce their honest independence in the least possible degree."

This principle of the cultivation of independence is the greatest and best feature of the Association. Charity is a blessed thing, when all other modes of assistance fail: but till then, it should never be offered to any human being;

for it will assuredly deteriorate, enervate, and ultimately degrade him. Let him, to the last effort of which he is capable, work for himself, trust to himself, educate and elevate himself. Show him how to do this—help him to help himself, and you will every day make of him a higher and happier being.

So thought I, while watching a lad of only twenty-one, who three years before had lost first sight and then hearing. Totally deaf and blind, his only communication with the outer world is by the sense of touch. Yet it was such a bright face, such a noble head and brow—you saw at once what a clever man he would have made. And there was much refinement about him too, down to his very hands, so delicately shaped, so quick, flexible, and dexterous in their motions—the sort of hands that almost invariably make music, paint pictures, write poems. Nothing of that sort, alas! would ever come out of the silent darkness in which for the remainder of his days lay buried this poor lad's soul. Yet when Mr. Levy, taking his hand, began to talk to him on it—the only way by which the blind can communicate with the deaf-blind—he turned round the most affectionate, delighted face, and caught the sentence at once.

"P-l-a plane. Lady wanting to see me plane? I'll get the board in a minute."

The voice was somewhat unnatural, and the words slowly put together, as if speech, which he could still use, but never hear, were gradually becoming a difficulty to him. But he set to his carpentering with the most vivid delight; and having planed and sawed for our benefit, again lent himself to Mr. Levy's conversation.

"Lady wishes to see my toys? I'll get them for her." And as nimbly as if he had eyes, the lad mounted to a high shelf, where were ranged, orderly in a row, a number of children's toys, manufactured in a rough but solid style of cabinet-making—the last made, which he brought down and exhibited with great pride, being a tiny table with a movable top and "turned" feet—a table that would be the envy of some ambitious young carpenter of ten years old, and the pride and glory of his sister's dolls' tea-party; as it may be yet—to children I know. How its maker's face kindled at the touch of the silver coin, and the shake of the hand, which was the only way in which our bargain could be transacted.

"She's bought my table! Lady's bought my table!" And then, with a sudden fit of conscientiousness, "Who shall I give the money to?" evidently thinking it ought to be counted among his week's wages, paid by the Association.

I inquired how much he earned.

"Seventeen shillings a week, and could earn much more if we only had it to give him. But even that makes a great difference. When he came, he was so moping and down-hearted, chiefly, he said, because it grieved him to be dependent on his two sisters. Now he is all right, and the merriest fellow possible. I asked him the other day if he were happy. 'Happy!' he said, 'to be sure I am. What have I to make me otherwise? It would be a great shame if I were any thing but happy.'"

Poor soul—poor simple, blessed soul! the greatest man on earth might be less enviable than this lad, totally deaf and blind.

I have thus given a plain account of what I saw and heard that day. Any one with more time, more money, and more practical wisdom than I, could hardly expend them better than in becoming "eyes to the blind" by a few visits to 127 Euston Road.

CHILDREN OF ISRAEL.

"CHILDREN of Israel." The phrase bears one meaning when we see it in our Bibles, and another quite distinct and opposite when we use it of the very same people of whom we there read—that extraordinary people who remain to the present day living witnesses alike to Christian and to atheist, that there may be some truth in that curious old Book which contains the history of their nation, the warning and subsequent records of its fall, and the prophecies of its final restoration.

Children of Israel. Let me premise a few words about them. Once, remarking to a very worthy and exceedingly religious lady of my acquaintance that I had been to visit a Jewish school,—" O !" said she: and within the circle of that magical letter was expressed a whole volume of surprise, pity, and even a certain amount of blame. As she and I never should have agreed in our opinions, and our arguments would have been like those of the two knights over the double-sided shield, I quitted the subject immediately.

But it led me to ponder a good deal on the reasons why there is, and the secondary question, whether there ought to be, so strong a feeling still kept up among large masses of Christians against the Jews. Not merely against their faith, but personally against themselves. True, we do not now, like our mediæval ancestors, make raids into their dwellings, attack their flesh with pincers, bent on extracting teeth or money. We neither confine them within the limits of miserable *ghettos*, nor refuse them the protection of our laws. Nay, we are gradually allowing them to enter into professions, and take their fitting share in the machinery of the State. But, privately and socially, the sentiment of not a few of us towards them is much as it was in Shakspeare's time.

Excellent Will—in spite of his noble protest, " Hath not

a Jew eyes?" etc., wrung, as it were, out of his own manly honest nature, which not all the prejudices of his time would wholly subdue—did a cruel wrong to a whole nation when he painted the character of *Shylock*. Yet, in spite of himself, the poet, like many an intelligent actor succeeding, has contrived to put some grand touches into the poor old Jew. Mean as he was, you can not but feel that the Christians were meaner—that they returned evil for evil in most unchristian fashion; encouraged swindling, trickery, and domestic abduction, in a way that was not likely to advance their creed in an adversary's eyes: and even when *Doctor Portia's* quibble triumphs, and *Shylock* is dismissed to ignominy, the most excited playgoer can not but be aware, in that uncomfortable portion of his being called Conscience, of a slight twinge—suggesting that two wrongs will never make a right; and that a certain amount of injustice has been done to the miserable old man, cheated at once out of "his ducats and his daughter," nay, of the very ring that "he had from Leah when he was a bachelor."

Far be it from any one of us, earnest believers in whatever we do believe, to allege that creeds signify nothing; that Jew and Christian, Brahmin and Mussulman, have an equal amount of truth on their side, and can harmonize perfectly; working and walking together like those who are entirely agreed. The thing is impossible. In all the closest relations of life there must be, on vital points, sympathy and union—at least as much as is possible in this diverse world, where Providence never makes two faces exactly alike, nor two leaves on the same tree of the same pattern. But each tree is made "after its own kind," and each nation or person also; and it is the best wisdom of us all to seek out and hold fast our similarities, rather than our opposites. The grand harmonies of life are produced by all holding firmly our own individuality—keeping *in tune* ourselves, without intruding discordantly upon the individualities of our neighbors. And when we find it distinctly written, "*In every nation he that feareth God, and worketh righteousness, is accepted of Him*," we dare not judge our brother, who, for all we know, may be "accepted" as well as we.

Besides, is there not something unfilially profane—like the act of a man who delights in trampling on the graves of his forefathers—in the intense dislike entertained by many good Christians towards Jews? They may be, perhaps always might have been, a race no higher than other races, and inferior to some; but they are an eternal testimony to the truth of Holy Writ: the keepers of the Divine revelations of old. From them, and them alone, came the belief in one God, that in its sublime verity has outlived all pantheisms and polytheisms, and become a river of eternal life, which, however the corruptions of successive ages may have dammed it up, defiled it, diverted it into petty and ignoble channels, has flowed on, and will flow, to the end of time.

Surely it is strange—passing sad and strange—that the same excellent Christians who sing the Psalms of David, and believe implicitly in the Mosaic, historical, and prophetical books of the Hebrew Scriptures, should not feel a solemn interest in the poorest Hebrew who goes down our streets chanting his melancholy monotone, "Old clo', old clo'!" Is he not a perpetual monument of the dealings of the God of the Old Testament? Is not he, too, a son of Abraham? There must have been some extraordinary twist in the mind of that good lady who is reported to have said, looking at Holman Hunt's picture of the Finding of Christ in the Temple, "Dear me! how exceedingly profane! the painter has made our blessed Saviour *exactly like a little Jew boy!*" Why—He *was* "a little Jew boy."

But enough of this. The days of religious persecution are over: we are coming to a belief that if truth be truth, it will prevail, without being propagated by fire and sword. Liberty of conscience—that right of every human being to serve God in his own way, provided that in so doing he does not trench on the rights of his neighbors—is every day more understood. The world has crept out of its swaddling-clothes, has survived the tumults of its impetuous youth, and is slowly growing into the full stature of manhood, as was meant by its Divine Creator. The law of reasonable, open-eyed duty is substituted for that of blind obedience—the religion of love for that of fear—the worship of the spirit for that of outward forms. And this —let us urge upon those of our Hebrew brethren who still deny it—is true Christianity; the truth which originated with our Christian Messiah—which, though taught apparently by one poor carpenter's son and twelve ignorant fishermen, has proved itself sufficiently divine to revolutionize almost the whole world.

Believing in this truth—and that the children of Israel will see it one day, as well as many a Gentile, more hopelessly blind then they—we need not shrink from visiting Jewish schools, nor from holding out the warm hand of fellowship and sincere respect to those who support them—even though, as many bigoted religionists would say, they have "denied the Lord." Denied Him, in a sense; yet not more so than many of those same religionists who think that they only know Him, and that all the rest of the world are doomed to eternal perdition. Surely, a far deeper and higher faith is that which believes He is able to justify Himself, and manifest His own glory, as He is doing every day in His own way and time.

Christians generally know so little of the inner life of Jews, that they are unaware how very much of the Christian element has introduced itself gradually and imperceptibly into modern Judaism; not only as regards social possibilities, but in modes of thinking; in a general, liberal, enlightened tone of mind, which has grown up among them since wiser legislation allowed that a Jew might be fit for something better than making money by old clothes or usury. The once-despised nation has lifted up its head, and shown what an extraordinary amount of latent power still lurks in the seed of Abraham, only wanting proper cultivation to find its fair level among the races of the earth. And though we may not agree with Disraeli, that every wonderful genius—musical, artistic, histrionic, or literary—must be either a Jew, or of Jewish descent, still, that a great number are is undeniable.

In this imperfect world we can only judge men by their deeds, and things by their results—clinging to and upholding good wherever we find it, knowing the Source from whence alone all good can come; and therefore I think many devout Christians will be interested to hear of this school, concerning which my friend—who, I repeat, is a most generous-hearted and religious woman—gave such a doubtful if not condemnatory "O!"

It is the Jewish Free-School, at Bell Lane, Spitalfields, London—the very heart of the Jewish quarter, and therefore comparatively little known to us Gentiles. You approach it through a wilderness of narrow and not over-sanitary streets, over every shop of which are inscribed such names as Salomans, Levi, Jacobs, Emanuel; while peering out of every door are faces—I must own rather grimy—bearing the unmistakable Jewish physiognomy, as it is after centuries of degradation. They stare at you in unmitigated curiosity, as if wondering what on earth you are doing there; unless you happen to come in a carriage, and then they break out into grinning welcome, for they know that no carriages are likely to pass down those foul and narrow streets, except those of the wealthy and charitable among their own people. Some of these—so well known that I do not need to name them—gentle-hearted women, of gentle breeding, go about among the dark haunts of Houndsditch and Spitalfields as familiarly as City missionaries, devoting time, thought, and substance, in almost unlimited degree, to the poor and miserable of their nation; providing schooling, clothing, food; visiting from house to house the sick and the dying, and carrying on a system of unobtrusive, deliberate, personal benevolence, to an extent that would put to shame thousands of us Christians who consider ourselves followers of Him who said, "Go out into the highways and hedges, and *compel* them to come in."

Entering the school, the first impression is that of passing into an entirely new world, or rather the ancient world revivified. Such a sound of strange tongues—for every child is taught Hebrew as well as English; such a mass of strange, foreign features, from the strongly-marked, sallow, almond-eyed Asiatic countenance, such as, variously modified, we may trace on Egyptian sculptures and Nineveh marbles, down to what we are accustomed to class as "the regular Jewish face," with long nose, sharp, beady eyes, full mouth—as little like the original Hebrew type, in its purity, as the St. Giles's Irishwoman is to the thoroughbred Celt.

Great as was the mixture, and low the class, of these children of Israel, there were among them faces that absolutely startled one by their beauty: little Rachels, Abigails, Hannahs; youthful Samuels, Davids, and Isaacs—faces that you might have pictured playing about under the palm-trees of Mesopotamia; or else, in their half-melancholy sweetness, sitting by the waters of Babylon, trying in vain to "sing the Lord's song in a strange land." Nay, so fine was the expression of some of them, that they might have sat as models for Holman Hunt's "little Jew boy"—as divine a child's face as ever was painted by mortal man.

So much for the artistic and poetic phase in which the school first presented itself. Now to give some idea of its practical workings.

Its 1860 children are divided into three schools—infants', girls', and boys'; the two latter being again subdivided into classes, the higher ones studying in separate class-rooms; while the juniors are taught together in large, lofty school-rooms, of which the boys' is shortly to be enlarged, being found quite inadequate for the number of pupils who attend.

But to the infants first. As all must allow, the ideal infant-school is a village-common or field. One would always rather see the little people cramming their hands with massacred daisies than their heads with the alphabet. But we must take what we can get: and to see these tiny creatures, well washed, well fed, well looked after, in a warm and admirably ventilated room, was far better than to meet them crawling about London streets, run over by cabs and omnibuses, or burnt to death in locked-up rooms. Probably their learning—which was shouted out in true infant-school chorus, following the instructions of a twelve-year-old damsel, with a gigantic "A B C" and a wand—is not so deep as to endanger the health of the young students; and, I was glad to hear, they are allowed an almost unlimited amount of play.

The girls' school-room, in which the pupils number 800, is ingeniously divided into compartments; every alternate compartment being occupied by a sewing-class, so that the noise of those who are being taught orally is comparatively little disturbing to the rest. Hebrew, of course, forms a part of the instruction; but, as a curious involuntary indication of the different position of women in olden times, of which the shadowy reflection still remains in this school, it is not thought necessary to teach the girls more than what enables them to say their prayers—which must always be said in the original tongue—by rote. The boys acquire the language, as a language; the girls, merely the pronunciation, though they have the general sense of the prayers explained to them by an English translation. Still, grand as it sounds—this majestic Hebrew—the Hebrew of Moses and the prophets—we Christians felt that we would rather have the simple heart-cry of the poorest Christian child, who has been taught to say "Our Father, which art in heaven," or "Pray, God, bless papa and mamma, and make me a good child!"—ay, even though it dwindles down to what I once heard—the ridiculous, or sublime, prayer of infantile faith, "Please, God, cure poor mamma's headache, and give me a new doll to-morrow." Therein lies the great difference between the Jewish and Christian dispensations —the relation of God to us as *the Father*—not only the King, the Lawgiver, the just and righteous Judge, but the loving Father—as revealed in latter days through the revelation of Jesus Christ.

It was impossible to go through these classes of girls, both in the general school-room and the lesser rooms, without noticing how exceedingly well taught they were: solid teaching, in which the reflective powers, as well as the memory, were called into exercise. Though in each instance of our visits it was no planned examination, but an accidental breaking in upon the routine of the class, their answers rarely failed. In history, geography, grammar, dictation, they seemed equally at home. Their reading was especially good; and any one who can appreciate the difficulties of a Cockney accent added to that of the lowest English and foreign Jews, will understand how surprising and refreshing it was to come upon *h*'s and *r*'s always put in their right places. This is, doubtless, mainly owing to the care and superior education of the head-mistress and her subordinates; some of them, who, like the others, had entered the school not even knowing their alphabet, were as intelligent, ladylike young people as one could wish to behold. I saw one or two lithe, graceful figures, soft gazelle eyes, and exquisitely-shaped mouths, that irresistibly reminded me of Rebekah at the well, or Rachel when Jacob kissed her and served for her seven years; "and they seemed to him but a few days, for the love he had to her."

Besides needlework,—cooking, laundry, and housework are taught to the girls; successive relays being taken out of the school-room to be initiated in those indispensable home-duties which are worth all the learning in the world to us women. Perhaps these little descendants of Sarai and Rebekah are none the worse for being given less actual learning than the boys, and taught to imitate their wise ancestresses in being able to "make cakes upon the hearth," and "prepare savory meat" such as many a man besides poor old blind Isaac would secretly acknowledge that "his soul loveth." The eight hundred little black-eyed maidens who are to grow up mothers in Israel may effect no small reformation in the nation, by being able satisfactorily to wash their husbands' clothes and cook their sons' dinners.

The general school-room of the boys is much larger than that of the girls: in fact, it consists of two rooms, communicating by a sliding door, and capable of being made into one large area, which yearly, on the Day of Atonement, is used as a temporary synagogue, and accommodates nearly 3000 worshippers. Even this space is not now sufficient for the number of boys who attend. Undoubtedly, there must be an intense love of learning in the children of Israel; for many of these lads, some of whom enter the school without even a knowledge of the alphabet, come daily a distance of four, five, and six miles, from all the suburban quarters of London. It was strange to see them—not, I must confess, quite so clean and wholesome and nice-looking as the girls, but with sharp, dark, acute faces—poring over their books and slates, or else sitting in rows, with their caps on, headed by a teacher who was also covered, repeating, *ore rotundo*, lessons or prayers in the sacred language; for they are all obliged to learn A, B, C, and Aleph, Beth, Gimel together. This of itself shows how much vitality the school must possess. What would be thought of one of the English national schools, or even the Scottish parochial schools—where the educational standard is much higher—at which it was expected that the children of mechanics or farm-laborers should study Greek and English at the same time?

The exceeding discipline maintained among these small sons of Jacob (doubtless by nature as unruly as their forefathers whom Moses struggled with at the waters of strife) was very remarkable. At a signal from the head-master, all the hundreds of lads sank instantaneously into the most profound silence, which lasted until another signal bade them recommence their tasks—with a noise astonishingly like Babel.

Like the girls', the boys' senior classes have rooms to themselves. Here their education is carried on to a pitch which has enabled some of them to enter as undergraduates, and take their degree at the London University. The school has also been placed under Government inspection, and the Government system of certificated pupil-teachers is successfully carried out. These have extra classes, under the instruction of the indefatigable head-master; so that the establishment answers all the purposes of a normal school. Two scholarships are established; one in commemoration of the emancipation of the Jews—of which the last year's examination-papers in grammar, geography, history, Hebrew, social economy, arithmetic, algebra, Euclid, and natural philosophy, are enough to drive an ordinary Gentile head to distraction. There are also two annual prizes in money, given in memory of deceased supporters of the school; and a gift of fifty pounds has been bestowed yearly upon the cleverest, most diligent, and well-conducted girl in the establishment, by Sir Moses Montefiore, in remembrance of his late much-lamented wife. Such charities, which make the beloved memory of the dead a perpetual blessing to the living, might well invite us Christians to imitate these generous-hearted, wisely benevolent Jews. It prevented one's smiling at a fact that could not but be noticed in going from class to class of these very sharp boys, that their chief sharpness seemed to lie in figures. They did every thing else uncommonly well: wrote from dictation a somewhat unintelligible poem of Shelley's with scarcely an orthographical error; answered geographical questions, and a long catechism on the principle of direct and indirect taxation, in a manner that showed their intelligent comprehension of the whole subject; but, when it came to arithmetic, they took to it like ducks to the water. In lengthy and involved mental calculations, the acuteness of these young Israelites was something quite preternatural. You felt that they were capable of "spoiling the Egyptians" to any extent, not necessarily by any dishonesty, but simply by the force of natural genius. And charity—which would always rather see the bright than the dark side of an acknowledged fact—might well pause to consider whether that astonishing faculty for amassing and retaining wealth, which is attributed to the Jewish community, may not arise quite as much from this inherent faculty for figures, added to the cautious acuteness which an oppressed race must always learn, as from other and meaner qualities which exist no less in us than in the Hebrews.

The less abstruse and more superficially refining branches of education are not neglected. In the highest class the boys are taught drawing, and vocal music from notes—also physiology as applied to health. Poor things, they must have small opportunity of converting their theory into practice! But one of the most noticeable points of the school was the exceeding attention evidently paid to the two most important necessities of youthful well-being in physical and consequently mental development—cleanliness and ventilation. In this low Spitalfields—this worst of all bad neighborhoods—it was something wonderful to pass from room to room, and feel the air perfectly pure and wholesome, though with no more complicated system of ventilation than that very simple one which so few people can be got to understand—namely, of windows *always* kept a little way open at the top, so as to produce a gentle but thorough current—*not* a draught—above the children's heads. These little heads were well kempt, the faces clean washed, and the clothes decent, or at least well mended. To each boy and girl is presented annually, by the bounty of the Rothschild family, certain habiliments to help out the poor wardrobe, those of the girls being fabricated by themselves, in the hour each day which is devoted to sewing. There are made also, from the same source, occasional additions to the scanty dinners which each pupil brings, or is supposed to bring. But these charities are carefully administered, so that in no case should the self-reliance and self-respect, which are the greatest safeguard of the poor, be broken in upon by indiscriminate or dangerous benevolence.

The pupil-teachers, also, many of whom must necessarily know painfully the hard struggle it is for a girl to maintain a respectable and even lady-like appearance upon an income smaller than that of many domestic servants, receive annually, from the same generous hand, a serviceable, pretty dress: less as a bounty than as a kindly acknowledgment from the higher woman to the lower, of how exceedingly valuable is all true service in all stations of life. The cordial sympathy between the committee and the teachers, the ease of their relationship, and the heartiness with which all labored together, in the bond of a common interest and common faith, was one of the pleasantest facts noticeable in the institution.

But I think I have said enough about this remarkable school, which, neither asking nor expecting any support from the general community, confines its workings strictly to its own nation. To judge by the results since its foundation in 1817, when it opened with 270 boys, "to be instructed in Hebrew and English reading and writing, and the rudiments of arithmetic," its influence must be very great, and yearly increasing. How far it will aid, or is meant by Providence to aid, in that climax of the world's history believed in alike by Jew and Gentile—Sir Moses Montefiore and Dr. Cumming—when the chosen people shall be all gathered together at the Holy City, it is impossible to say. God works less by miraculous than by natural means, and it may be that the blindness shall be taken from the eyes of the children of Israel, not by a sudden revelation, but by the gradual growth of their nation, through the great remover of darkness and prejudice—education. Who can tell how soon they may be gathered, in the most simple and natural way, from all corners of the earth whither the Lord has driven them, and brought to Jerusalem "upon horses, and in chariots, and in litters, and upon mules, and upon swift beasts," or as Dr. Cumming insists the original word *Kurkaroth* should be translated, "upon chariots revolving with the swiftness of the clouds," which may probably—odd as the coincidence sounds—indicate the newly-planned Syrian railways.

At any rate, whatever be their future destiny, it was impossible, without a strangely solemn feeling, to contemplate the growing-up generation of this marvellous people, who, amidst all His chastisements, have held so firmly to their faith in the One Jehovah, and in his servant Moses. And when, having gone through the school, we paused again in the girls' school-room to hear their chanting—in which the well-known richness of the Jewish voice was very perceptible—we could not listen without emotion to the mystical music, which may have been sung in the Temple before King David, of the Twenty-ninth Psalm:

"Give unto the Lord, O ye mighty, give unto the Lord glory and strength.

"Give unto the Lord the glory due unto His name; worship the Lord in the beauty of holiness.

"The voice of the LORD is upon the waters: the God of glory thundereth; the LORD is upon many waters....

"The voice of the LORD breaketh the cedars; yea, the LORD breaketh the cedars of Lebanon....

"The LORD sitteth upon the flood; yea, the LORD sitteth King for ever.

"The LORD will give strength unto His people; the LORD will bless His people with peace."

And surely all good Christian souls may say, "Amen and Amen!"

GIVE US AIR!

THE following epistle and accompanying MS. speak for themselves:

"*TO THE AUTHOR OF*," etc., etc.

"HONORED SIR OR MADAM (whichever you be), — I understand you known writers are sometimes kind enough to read and criticise, and help to publication, us unknown scribblers, less fortunate, though possibly not less deserving, than yourselves. If, therefore, you consider the world would benefit by the inclosed paper, wrung from me by my intolerable sufferings of the last three months, may I beg of you to forward it to the editor of any publication with which you may be connected. I remain your obedient servant, JANE AYRE."

("N.B.—The recipient of this letter has accordingly done as requested.")

I am, I believe, no Sybarite, but on the whole a person of limited desires, nor overmuch the slave of luxurious habits. It troubles me little what sort of clothes I wear, so that they are clean, whole, and not ungraceful. I flatter myself I can dine upon any well-cooked food; and I am sure I can sleep calmly upon any couch not harder than a deal board. In short, my nature is accommodating, and my wants are few. But there is one thing I can not do without. It is to me more necessary than meat, drink, rest, leisure; and without it friendly and domestic companionship, intellectual and social pleasures to me are almost worthless. My mind gets soured, my temper aggravated, my brain obscured, and my moral sense altogether obliterated; in fact, I become an irrational and irresponsible being. This thing, this very simple thing, which yet I find such difficulty in obtaining, is fresh air.

Will any sympathizing soul, or body, which recognizes its woes in mine, yet perhaps is ignorant why it suffers, derive benefit from the indignant outcry, the piteous moan, which I feel impelled to make, after spending a summer in a region where, as to both the land and its inhabitants, one has every blessing which heart can desire, *except* fresh air?

This region, however, I decline to name; and though I protest that every lamentable statement concerning it is absolute truth, I mean to betray nothing that can identify places or people. Let those whom the cap fits wear it.

Nor does this pretend to be a scientific article. In my youth people were born and died, ignorant of physiology, social science, or the chemistry of common life. On such subjects my brain is exactly as useful as an apple-dumpling or a sieve; either nothing gets in, or whatever accidentally does get in, immediately runs out. Though, as a matter of conscience, before writing this paper I delved through three large volumes and five pamphlets on the science of ventilation, I understand it, theoretically, precisely as much as when I began to read. Nevertheless, practically— Stop a minute, while I open the window!

I breathe again. What a comfort it is to breathe! Alas, as Shakspeare says,

> "How many thousands of my poorer brethren"—

(or richer, rather; but I complain not of those who can not, but who will not, have fresh air)—

> "How many thousands of my poorer brethren
> Are at this hour"—

Not "asleep," but suffocating; breakfasting in close parlors where the windows have never been opened since yesterday; or drowsing heavily in closer bedrooms, with the shutters shut, the curtains drawn, the door fastened, the chimney stopped, and the gas slightly escaping. The atmosphere—alas! I know well what it is! Poor things; poor things!

I left my home for a season. Home is home, be it ever so homely, and I love it, though I do not set it up as a model dwelling. Its ceilings are low, its rooms small; from attic to basement it boasts no ventilating apparatus whatever; nay, when I came into it, half the doors declined to shut, and half the windows to open. Even yet, some corners remain smothery and others draughty, so that I have ingeniously to induct unconscious visitors into particular chairs, where I know they can not complain of the atmosphere around. Therefore, let it not be imagined that my own domestic advantages rendered me over-sensitive to the shortcomings of my neighbors, and the woes they unwittingly inflicted upon me.

The first woe came only too soon. Vainly had I guarded against it by weighing the merits of a first-class daylight journey, with easy springs and soft cushions, against heat, stuffiness, and a full carriage, subject to intrusions, at every station, of new comers, each of whom has his or her peculiar theory of ventilation. The result was, I armed myself with air-cushion and plaid, prepared to dash gloriously along, second-class, in the cool night-mail. Face to the "horses," of course, that my only two fellow-passengers, happily neither ladies nor invalids, but stout, middle-aged gentlemen, might interfere the less with my chance of fresh air.

They did not, for half an hour. Then one of them shut his window, and carefully closed the ventilator above it. I trembled, but determined to hold on like grim death to my rights with respect to my own window. The evening went by, sunset faded into a pale amber line along the western horizon, the stars came out, and the fresh breeze of the midsummer night crept across the long flats that we were sweeping through at the rate of a county an hour.

My fellow-passengers ceased talking: each took out—not exactly his night-cap, but an apology for the same—and prepared to settle to slumber. Each cast—I felt—an anxious glance at my half-open window, out of which I steadily and sternly gazed. At last the elder of them, with an abrupt—"I beg your pardon, but I'm apt to catch cold"—rose and shut it.

Alack-a-day! But he was an elderly gentleman, and I have a certain old-fashioned respect for age, and a dislike to make an enemy even for a railway journey; so I sat, patiently suffocating, for a good while—then opened my window about two inches—assuring my friend that it would not affect him in the least; and, lest it should, would he take my plaid? Grimly he rolled himself up in it, and went to sleep again.

Even with this compromise, the state of things was bad enough. Three people, in a July night, shut up in a small second-class carriage containing—how many cubic feet of atmospheric air? and how many more ought to be admitted therein, to replace the exhaustion of breathing, during a given time?—I'm sure I don't know, for I am not scientific. I only know I was choking: that when I happened to turn away from my two-inch-wide breathing-hole towards the inner air—pah!

"The mouth of every human being, and of every other animal, is pouring the refuse matter of the body into the air. From it ensue cases of discomfort, of disease, sometimes of direct death. The surface of every animal is exhaling matter: cases of this may be shown in the odor of even human animals—the scent of beasts," etc.

So writes science, and I was experimentalizing upon it now! Still, matters might be worse; and I contented myself with staring at the dense black square of the window, and speculating upon the dark star-lit landscape through which we were ignorantly passing. By degrees, the black square changed to gray, and, in spite of the carriage-lamp, a faint outline of the world without grew visible. We stop at one of our rare halting-stations. Woe is me! the second elderly gentleman wakes—rubs his eyes—shivers—rises up, and with the crossness of a half-awakened sleeper, shuts the window with a bang.

So, there we were. No help for it, but calm endurance. "The mouth of every human being—" But I might have preached a whole volume of science to deaf ears. No doubt the atmosphere was exactly what my two friends were used to. I hugged myself, with malign satisfaction, in the thought if they only knew how horridly ugly they looked when asleep! How their mouths opened inanely, and their foreheads knitted savagely; their breathing grew stertorous, two brick-red spots burned on their cheeks; big unctuous drops gathered all over their flabby, fat faces. How they tossed, and moaned, and fidgeted—even though extended comfortably along the cushioned seats—not so ill a bed for any healthy man; and at last sunk into a stupor so heavy and ghastly, that one would hardly have marvelled had it subsided into paralysis, apoplexy, or death. Of course not. They were sleeping in a "vitiated atmosphere." Therefore they looked—exactly as you look, my excellent luxurious friend, about two A.M., in your shut-up chamber, with your bed-curtains drawn, where, a few hours after, you are surprised to wake with a queer feeling on the top of your head, a heavy heat on your eyelids, and a sense of general lassitude, as if you had not had half a night's rest, and it were impossible to rise at all.

Morning broke. "My friends," thought I, in an agony of suffocation, "necessity has no law. I must save you and myself against your will." So, with the stealthiness of a burglar, I let down a few inches of the window. The natural result ensued. The pure air, rushing into such a foul and heated atmosphere, created that horror of every body—a draught, and the same ventilating current, which, if by means of only an inch-wide aperture it had been kept up quietly and steadily through the night, would have made us all comfortable, became so cold that even I began to shiver. For my adversaries — but their wrath was spared me; they had come to their journey's end, and left the carriage to solitude and me. What I did afterwards, how I opened the window wide, wide!—quaffed insanely the fresh, bright, balmy air, watched the outlines of the beloved hills sharpen in the dawn, and finally, with the wind fanning me, and the sunshine resting on my head like a welcome and a blessing, went peacefully to sleep—all this matters not. My first woe was ended.

The second was not long of coming.

If my wanderings had any definite personal plan, it was, to keep clear of cities. I always hated them. Now, dislike had grown into morbid terror. I never passed through a metropolitan street without feeling first nervously depressed, then irritable, then positively wicked. One fortunate day a scientific friend enlightened me as to the cause of this—it was the want of Ozone. If asked to describe what ozone is, I can only say as I was told, that it is the life-giving principle in the air, which in ill-ventilated places and in large towns entirely disappears; and is found in the greatest abundance on mountains and at the sea-shore. "Therefore," said I, "to mountain and sea will I go. My search after happiness resolves itself into a search after ozone."

And where should ozone be found if not in this nameless region, with its grand estuary, its lovely coast, its waves upon waves of heathery mountains? Here, at least, I shall get my fill of fresh air! Ay, I did,—*outside*. But *within* the houses!

Let me be just to my friendly hosts. They were far better in sanitary matters than most of their neighbors.

Their living-rooms were unexceptional: windows always open more or less, and no lack of that best of ventilators, all the year round, a good fire. During the day I was happy; but when I retired to my chamber at night, lo! the excellent domestic had, according to custom, closed the window, fastened the shutters, drawn the bed-curtains, and lit the gas. And in that all but hermetically sealed apartment, which, the gas being put out, would also be left in total darkness, I was expected to pass eight mortal hours.

"What! you are not going to open the window?"

"My dear friend, I must breathe—by night as well as day."

"But night air is so pernicious!"

"Not half so pernicious as the air of this room will be two hours hence, with the gas, my breathing, and the exhalations always going on from the very cleanest of carpets, clothes, and curtains." And I own to giving a rather savage pull to the beautiful moreen hangings under which I was intended to be entombed. "Why, if you were to hang up a bird in a cage within this four-poster, it would probably be dead by morning. I am not jesting: the experiment was tried. The foul air which kills a bird would likely not benefit me; so of two evils I prefer to choose the least."

And I undid the shutters, and threw the window open about a foot wide at top.

My friend regarded me as she would a person preparing to commit suicide.

"But the damp; the frightful night-damp?"

"I shall shut out the worst of it by drawing down the blind, which acts as a sort of respirator. Any how, the dampest night air that could be found, especially in July, is not half so injurious as foul air."

"Is it foul?" with a little indignation in the question.

Now, this is the greatest difficulty that, in my humble character of ventilating missionary, I have had to contend with; people did not actually recognize when the air *was* foul. They had been so long accustomed to live in bad air, that their physical (like, alas! many a moral) standard of purity had become degraded. Many a room that to me was stifling, was to them quite innoxious, or at least unnoticed. True, they felt its effects; they complained of headache, weariness, loss of appetite and spirits, and, above all, of the drowsiness which is the first sign of a vitiated atmosphere; but they attributed all these things to ill health or extraneous causes. It never entered their heads that the present evil was a want of fresh air. It never occurred to them that the reason why, enjoying life enough in the day-time, they yet complained of "such bad nights," and found such difficulty in rousing themselves of a morning, was because the air that circulates round a sleeper at night should be *exactly as pure* as that which he breathes during the day. He may defend his body with as many blankets as he likes, just as he would with overcoats by daylight; he may shelter his eyes from light, and his head from draughty currents; but he *must* have in the room a free circulation of absolutely pure air for his lungs to breathe; otherwise, during one half of his existence—the nocturnal half—he might as well be in a baker's oven, a coal mine, or a church vault. And that is the reason why so many of one's excellent friends, when they come down stairs in the morning, look exactly as if they *had* spent the night in either of these three rather undesirable apartments, instead of in an ordinary bedroom.

The substance of this long paragraph I preached to my amazed young friend, who yet could not reconcile herself to the fatal position in which she left me, as regarded the open window. "In our climate, too! Think of the lung diseases so prevalent here!"

"May not that be from the very reason I have been speaking of?"

"Because we do not sleep with our windows open?"

"No; but because, granted the severity or dampness of your climate, instead of hardening yourselves against it by lessening the transition between the in-doors and out-of-doors atmosphere, you make your houses perfect stoves of heated, gas-impregnated, impure air, and then you rush out from them into bleak mountain blasts and soaking rain. No wonder you catch colds, consumption, and all those sad diseases which, perpetuated in families, become the scourge of the whole country-side. No wonder so many bonnie faces and stalwart forms pass away in their bloom, even here, in a region richer than any place I know of in sanitary blessings, if only its inhabitants were acquainted with and would obey common sanitary laws."

"But how can we begin?" said my companion, hesitating. "I really never did sleep with my window open—should have been horrified at such a thing; but I have a great mind to try. How wide shall I open it? As wide as yours?"

"And then, from the sudden change, you will catch a severe cold, and say it was the result of my advice, and never open your window afterwards. No, my friend; sudden reformations are never to be trusted. Open your window one inch, and one inch only, for a week; two inches for the next week, and so on. The terrible punishment of any habitual infringement of physical as well as moral laws is, that habit itself being so powerful, even a change for the better, unless very gradual, sometimes, at first, does more harm than good."

Here, catching a politely suppressed yawn, I thought it time to end my sermon. Whether it ever did any good, I know not;—but that is neither here nor there.

Alas, wherever I went I found texts for more homilies! Not among the rural poor, who pass their lives almost entirely in the open air, except during the few hours that they retire to the universal bed-place in the wall; an ill sleeping-place for healthy folk, and how the sick ever manage to recover in it—goodness knows! Nor yet have I a word to say against the wretched city poor; God help them; they *can not* get fresh air. My complaint is lodged against higher sinners; people who ought to know better; mothers of families who keep their children in almost air-tight nurseries; mistresses of households who allow their young people to sit in the same parlor all day without once changing the atmosphere thereof; excellent old-school people who think an open window or a fire in a bedroom "a very unwholesome thing"—yet have no objection to send their delicate daughters from the warm parlor fireside to undress in an apartment that rivals in temperature the "frosty Caucasus."

Above all, I become fierce against the givers of evening parties; cruelly cramming a hundred people into a space which could only properly afford breathing-room for a score; of dinner parties, where, retiring from vinous and alimentary vapors below to the drawing-room above, we find it with fire and gas blazing, with every window, shutter, and door carefully closed, and in that atmosphere fifteen or twenty persons are expected to be "agreeable" for the rest of the evening!

Are they agreeable? answer, dinner-givers and diners-out. Think of the long "slow" hours where, with your head aching, your nerves unstrung, your brains just equal to giving a plain answer to a plain question, you, hostess, listened for the carriages being announced; and you, guest, enjoyed the fresh, cool walk home more than any portion of the entertainment. Not that the latter was dull, far from it; you may like your friends extremely, and own that they bring together most capital people; but somehow, they put you in an atmosphere where you can not enjoy any thing; where the brightest wit falls dead, the most intellectual conversation flags, where the mental pleasure is so overpowered by the physical annoyance, that every thing in you and about you becomes an effort and a bore.

Let me suggest the simple remedy of some friends of mine, who were telling me how amused they used to be with the remarks of *their* friends on their soirées. "'Really, how pleasant the evenings always are at your house; so different from other people's, even though one meets exactly the same set and stays the same time. Here one feels so light and cheerful and ready to be amused; there, bah! one often goes to sleep.'—They never guessed," added the lady, with a smile, "that the secret of our success was, because, hidden behind a venetian blind, for fear of alarming the good folks, we always kept our windows a little way open."

But I must shorten my plaint.

Although the horrors of large towns, theatres, concerts, and social entertainments may be eschewed by a devout disciple of ventilation, still there is one form of assembly which one can not or would not desire to avoid;—going to church. Now, let me not be supposed to speak lightly of church-going; the solemn gathering together of Christian brethren to worship God. But He has given them bodies as well as souls; and why they should be required to worship Him in a house—consecrated or not—which is so ill-constructed and ill-ventilated, that these bodies are exposed Sunday after Sunday to a system of slow poisoning, and these souls so weighed down by the oppressions of the aforesaid body, that they can neither comprehend instructions, nor join in prayer and praise as they ought to do; why this should be I can not understand. With all my love for the grand old Kirk of this land, its noble simplicity, its earnestness of devotion, I declare solemnly and sadly, during the last three months I have been in but one place of worship where a human being could sit through the prescribed hours of divine service without having devotion interfered with, temper tried, and health deterioated to a very serious extent.

Country churches were bad enough. You passed from the glorious, breezy mountain road, fresh with heather and fern, fragrant with bog-myrtle, honeysuckle, and the small white Highland rose, into a low-roofed, barn-like edifice, which had been shut up all the week, and even now had only a window or two opened, to be closed again before the congregation assembled. This congregation, accustomed to its ills, sat contentedly stewing. Sometimes it fanned itself surreptitiously with a book or the end of a shawl; sometimes smelled at its little nosegays of bog-myrtle, quickly withering in this hot, fetid air. And though the exhalations that arose made the place quite noxious, and the united breath of the congregation gathered in a dense mist on the window-panes, still it never occurred—not to the people, of course, poor dear souls!—but to minister or office-bearers, that three inches of open window *at the top*, not the bottom, on either side the little church, would have carried off foul air, let in fresh air, and prevented that sickly girl from fainting, that hard-worked, but delicate-looking man from dozing in his pew, getting a fierce headache, and being in a carping mood against the preacher and his doctrine for the rest of the day.

Town churches are little better. There is one, which I go to with the familiar love of many years—where the minister is a good man and an admirable preacher—yet I never "sit under" him, on afternoons especially, without having to resort to smelling-salts, frequent changes of position, and an agonized concentration of attention, in order to prevent going to sleep. My neighbors are no better off, they know not why; probably the pious of them blame themselves—the irreligious, the minister; while the real cause of blame is the noxious air. No wonder they never enter church till the moment before the psalm; and rush from it with that unseemly haste, pushing, scrambling, crushing—in a way that any English congregation, though perhaps not half so earnest, reverent, and sincere, would be ashamed of doing. In one church I went to—and never will again!—where the congregation were admitted by tickets, and stood thronging the aisles half an hour before the commencement of the—I was going to say the *performance*—the minister must needs be a great healer of souls, if he can answer to his conscience for the evil which he inflicts Sabbath after Sabbath upon a few thousand human bodies.

Surely, the Maker of both soul and body did not mean it so! Surely He who put the soul into the body, meant its temporary resting-place to be treated with deference and care. Surely, it must be pleasing to Him that we should learn how best to do this for ourselves and for others; that we should make our frames strong and healthy, our intellects clear and our spirits bright and brave, seeing that each and all are alike His giving, to be used for His service. We have, thank heaven, got over that false mysticism which believed that the enfeebling of the body was the enfranchising of the soul; we know now that the *mens sana in corpore sano* is the best offering we can make to God or man. And no waste labor is that which we spend, even in small matters, to attain this end.

But I am growing serious, if not stupid; probably because my fire has burnt low—the hour of the diurnal prandial meal approaches, and—and the atmosphere of my apartment is not quite so fresh as it ought to be. Let me obey the laws of nature, common sense, and experience; let me open all the doors and windows, and rush out into the glorious fresh air!

IN THE RING.

IT was a most difficult position. An invasion *vi et armis*, by six charming English girls, upon the house of an elderly Scotch doctor, of small practice, slowly diminishing, in an out-of-the-way uninteresting town, whose few inhabitants live upon any thing and do nothing. Yet, such was my fortune, I, Adam Black, commonly called Uncle Adam, probably for the excellent reason of my being uncle to nobody, and therefore to every body, including these charming girls who had now made a raid upon me. So happy, laughing, loving, were they; full of admiration at all they saw — Uncle Adam's house and garden, Uncle Adam's pony-chaise, and, they were pleased to say, Uncle Adam's agreeable society, that I should have been more than man if my heart had not speedily found itself riddled through and through.

"And now, uncle, since we mean to stay till to-morrow, how do you mean to amuse us?"

Of course, I would have done any thing in reason, have given them a tea-drinking; but that would have driven my housekeeper crazy. Or a picnic, but ours is not the climate for picnics; being that identical part of the country where the traveller, asking, "Does it always rain?" was answered, "Na, na,—whiles it snaws." Or I would have invited half a dozen young men for them to flirt with—but there never are any young men in our town—besides, I dislike flirtation. I like a man or woman to fall honestly in love and stick to it, quite ready either to marry or to die, as may be most expedient, But people neither marry for love, nor die for it, nowadays. Which is rather a falling off, I opine.

But to the point. I could not allow my visitors to waste their sweetness on my desert air, and gay and pleasant as they always were, I fancied towards nightfall they began to weary of my agreeable society.

"I'll tell you what, girls," said I, driven to sudden desperation by the youngest's proposing Readings from "Young's Night Thoughts," and "Pollok's Course of Time," by way of passing the evening, "I'll take you to the circus."

I saw a slight smile flit over three of the six pretty—well, the six nice-looking faces—for pleasant women always look nice to me. Certainly it was a long way to come from London to go to a circus in a small country town in Scotland.

But I assured them this was a most talented company, which had been in the town three months, and the troupe were highly respectable people (indeed, I had attended one of them professionally, but I did not think it necessary to state this). Moreover, I had been there myself, with a small patient who wanted a treat, and had enjoyed the evening as much as the child did. In short, as I told them, if my "nieces," though such stylish young ladies, would only condescend to make themselves children for the nonce, to take pleasure in innocent childish folly (there was a most capital "fool," by-the-by), I would answer for it they would be exceedingly well amused.

So they put on hats and shawls—no need of white gloves and opera-cloaks here—and off we sallied, through the cool bright autumn evening, to the quiet street where the circus was. A large wooden, temporary building. I had passed it often on my walks into town, but took little notice of it, and no interest in it—according to the commonly received fact, that one-half the world neither knows nor cares how the other half lives—till my accidental visit lately.

Since then I had often paused to listen in passing to the sounds within, the band playing and the horses galloping; to wonder if that bonnie bit girlie were still bounding through the flower-enwreathed hoops, and that agile boy turning somersaults after her, both on their "fiery steeds." Above all, what sort of thing was that "Wondrous Performance of Signor Uberto on the Flying Trapeze," which had been announced night after night as the climax of attraction.

Poor Signor Uberto! it was he whom I had been doctoring; he had had a sore hand, which incapacitated him from professional duty. He seemed a very quiet, respectable young fellow, and his name was William Stone. Of course I did not think it necessary to tell all this to my satirical young ladies; besides, a doctor's confidence should be always sacred, be his patient a circus performer or a king.

We produced quite a sensation when we entered; such a large and distinguished party, who monopolized the reserved seats, and represented seven half-crowns of honest British money. On the strength of which, I suppose, we received seven distinct bows from the gentleman who received it, a very fierce, be-whiskered, hippodramatic individual indeed. I knew him, though I hoped he did not recognize me. He was the Herr von Stein, proprietor and manager of the troupe, and Signor Uberto's father. It had been privately confided to me that "old Stone," as he was called in private life, was as hard as a flint, and he looked it. He grasped the half-crowns as if they were pound-notes, or twenty-pound notes, and crammed them into his pocket immediately.

The performances had already begun. From boxes and gallery were stretched out a mass of those honest eager faces which always make a minor theatre, or an accidental dramatic entertainment in the provinces, so very amusing. At least to me; for I have seen so much of the dark side of life, that I like to see people happy, even for an hour, in any innocent way. There is a strong feeling in Scotland against "play-acting," but apparently the prejudice did not extend to quadrupedal performances, for I noticed a large gathering of the working and trading class in our town, with their wives and families. All were intently watching the careering round and round that magic "ring" of two beautiful horses, ridden by a boy and girl in the character of the "Highland Laddie and Lassie."

Ridden, did I say? It was more like floating, flying, dancing—in and out, up and down—twirling and attitudinizing, in one another's arms—changing horses—galloping wildly—both on one horse. The boy was slim and graceful—the girl—nay, she was a perfect little fairy, with her white frock, her tartan scarf, and the hood tying back her showers of light curly hair, that tossed, and whirled, and swirled, in all directions. Whether she stood, knelt, balanced herself on one leg, or wreathed herself about, in the supple way that these gymnasts do, she was equally picturesque. Not over-like a Highland lassie, such as one sees digging potatoes in Perthshire, but still a most fascinating something else. The little creature seemed to enjoy it so herself; smiled, not with the dancer's stereotyped grin, but a broad honest childish smile, as she leaped down, made her final courtesy, and bounded along through the exit under the boxes.

There—among the group which seemed always hanging about there—the ring-master, the clown, and one or two young men—there crept forward a figure in black, a young woman, who met the Highland fairy, threw a shawl over her, and carried her off; a performance not set down in the bills, but which seemed to entertain the audience exceedingly.

The next diversion was a "Feat on Bottles, by Monsieur Ariel," who shall here go down to posterity as a proof of the many ingenious ways in which a man can earn a livelihood if he chooses. Two dozen empty bottles—ordinary "Dublin Stout"—are arranged in a double line across a wooden table. Enter a little fat man, in tights and an eccentric cap, who bows, springs upon the table, and with a solemn and anxious countenance proceeds to step, clinging with his two feet, on to the shoulders of two of the bottles. This is Monsieur Ariel. He walks from bottle to bottle, displacing none, and never once missing his footing, till he reaches the end of the double line, then slowly turns, still balancing himself with the utmost care, as is necessary, and walks back again amidst thunders of applause. He then, after pausing, and wiping his anxious brows, proceeds to several other feats, the last of which consists in forming the bottles into a pyramid, setting a chair on top of them, where he sits, stands, and finally poises himself on his head for a second, to the breathless delight of all observers, turns a somersault, bows—and exit Monsieur Ariel. He has earned his nightly wage, and a tolerably hard-earned wage it is, to judge by his worn countenance.

But I can not specify each of the performances, though, I confess, after-events photographed them all sharply on my mind. So that I still can see the "Dashing Act on a Bare-backed Horse," which was a series of leaps, backward and forward, turning and twisting, riding the beast in every sort of fashion, and on every part of him, except his ears and his tail; indeed, I think the equestrian gymnast was actually swept round the ring once or twice, clinging with arms and legs to the creature's neck. And the "Comic Performing Mules!" how delicious they were in their obstinacy! Perfectly tame and quiet, till one of the audience, by invitation, attempted to get on their backs, when, by some clever evolution, they gently slipped him over their noses, and left him biting the ignominious sawdust. One only succeeded—a youth in a groom's dress—who, after many failures, rode the mules round the ring; on which there was great triumph in the gallery, which felt that "our side" had won. For me—I doubt; since did I not in the next scene, the "Grand Hippodramatic Spectacle, entitled Dick Turpin's Ride to York," behold that identical youth, red-headed and long-nosed, attired, not as a groom of the nineteenth century, but as a highwayman of the seventeenth, and managing a beautiful bay horse, at least as cleverly as he did the Performing Mule?

This ride to York—my nieces remember it still—and declare that Robson—alas, poor Robson!—could not have acted *Dick Turpin* better. And for Black Bess, her acting was beautiful, or rather it was not acting, but obeying. The way the mare followed her master about, leaped the turnpike at Hornsey, crawled into the ring again—supposed near York—with her flanks all flecked with foam (and white chalk), drank the pail of brandy and water, and ate the raw beefsteak, was quite touching. When, at last, she sank down, in a wonderful simulation of dying, and poor Dick, in a despairing effort to rouse her, struck her with the whip—my eldest niece winced, and muttered involuntarily, "Oh, how cruel!" And when, after a futile struggle to obey and rise, poor Black Bess turned, licked Turpin's coat-sleeve, and dropped with her head back, prone, stiff, and dead—most admirably dead—my youngest niece, a tender-hearted lassie, freely acknowledges that—she cried!

The last entertainment of the evening was the Flying Trapeze.

Not every body knows what a trapeze is; a series of handles, made of short poles suspended at either end by elastic ropes, and fastened to the roof, at regular intervals, all across the stage. These handles are swung to and fro by the performer or his assistant; and the feat is to catch each one, swing backward and forward with it, and then to spring on to the next one, producing to the eyes of the audience, for a brief second or two, exactly the appearance of flying. Of course the great difficulty lies in choosing the precise moment for the spring, and calculating accurately your grasp of the next handle, since, if you missed it—

"Ah," said my eldest niece, with a slight shudder, "now I see the meaning of those mattresses, which they are laying so carefully under the whole line of the trapeze. And I understand why that man, who walks about giving directions, is so very particular in seeing that the handles are fastened securely. He looks anxious too, I fancy."

"Well he may. He is Signor Uberto's father."

"Then is it any thing very dangerous, or frightful? Perhaps we had better go?"

But it was too late, or we fancied it was. Besides, for myself, I did not wish to leave. That strange excitement which impels us often to stop and see the end of a thing, dreadful though it may be, or else some feeling for which I was utterly unable to account, kept me firm in my place. For just then, entering quickly by the usual door, appeared a small, slight young man, who looked a mere boy indeed, and, in his white tight-fitting dress, that showed every muscle of an exceedingly delicate and graceful frame, was a model for a sculptor. He had long, light hair, tied back with a ribbon, after the fashion of acrobats, and thin, pale features, very firm and still. This was the Signor Uberto, who was going once more to risk his life—as every trapeze performer must risk it—for our night's amusement.

He stood, while his father carefully tried the fastenings of each handle, and examined the platform on which were laid the mattresses. But the youth himself did not look at any thing. Perhaps he was so accustomed to it that the performance seemed to him safe and natural—perhaps he felt it was useless to think whether it were so or not, since he must perform. Or, possibly, he took all easily, and did not think of any thing.

But I could not help putting myself into the place of the young man, and wondering whether he really did recognize any danger; more especially as I saw, lurking and watching in the exit corner, somebody belonging to him—the young woman in black, who was his sister, I concluded, since when I visited him she had brought lint and rags and helped me to tie up his sore hand. Over this hand the father was exceedingly anxious, because every day's loss of performance was a loss to the treasury. This was the first day of the Signor's reappearance, and the circus was full to the roof.

Popularity is seldom without a reason, and I do not deny that the flying trapeze is a very curious and even beautiful sight. In this case the extreme grace of the performer added to its charm. He mounted, agile as a deer, the high platform at the end of the circus, and swung himself off by the elastic ropes, clinging only with his hands, his feet extended, like one of the floating figures in pictures of saints or fairies. His father, standing opposite, and watching intently his time—for a single second might prove either too late or too soon—threw the other trapeze forward to meet him. The young man dropped lightly into it, hanging a moment between whiles, apparently as easily as if he had been born to fly, then gave himself another swing, and alighted safely at the far end of the platform.

This feat he accomplished twice, thrice, four times, each time with some slight variation, and more gracefully than the last, followed by a low murmur of applause—the people were too breathless to shout. The fifth time, when one had grown so familiar with the performance that one had almost ceased to shudder, and begun to regard the performer not as a human creature at all, with flesh and blood and bones, but as some painted puppet, or phantasmal representation on a wall—the fifth time, he missed his grasp of the second trapeze, and fell.

It was so sudden;—one moment the sight of that flying figure—the next, a crash on the mattressed platform, on its edge, from which rolled off a helpless something falling with a heavy thud on the sawdust floor below.

I heard a scream—it might be from one of my girls, but I could not heed them. Before I well knew where I was, I found myself with the young man's head on my knee, trying to keep off the crowd that pressed round.

"Is he dead?"

"Na, na—he's no deid. Give him some whisky. He's coming to, puir laddie."

But he did not "come to," not for hours, until I had

him taken to the nearest available place—which happened to be my own house, for his lodgings were at the other end of the town.

All the long night that I sat by the poor young man's bedside, I felt somehow as if I had murdered him, or helped to do it. For had I not "followed the multitude to do evil," added my seven half-crowns to tempt him, or rather the skin-flint father who was making money by him, to risk his life for our amusement? True, he would have done it all the same had I not been there; but still I was there. I and my young ladies had swelled the number which had lured him on to his destruction,—and I felt very guilty. What the girls felt, poor dears, I do not know; it was quite impossible for me to take any heed of them. My whole attention was engrossed by the case. I wonder if people suppose us surgeons hardened because we get into the habit of speaking of our fellow-creatures merely as "a case?"

No one hindered my doing what I would with my patient, so I had him removed to my own room—the spare rooms being occupied—examined him, and set a simple fracture of the arm, which was the only visible injury. Then I sat and watched him, as conscience-stricken as if I had been one of the old Roman emperors at a gladiator show, or a modern Spanish lady at a bull-fight, or a fast young English nobleman hiring rooms at the Old Bailey in order to witness a judicial murder. For had I not sat calmly by, a spectator of what was neither more nor less than murder?

Somebody behind me seemed to guess at my thought.

"If he had died, doctor, I should always have said he had been murdered."

There was an intensity in the voice which quite startled me, for she had kept so quietly in the background that I had scarcely noticed her till now—the young woman in black. She was not a pretty young woman—perhaps not young at all—being so deeply pitted with smallpox that her age became doubtful to guess at; but she had kind, soft eyes, an intelligent forehead, and an excessively sweet English voice.

If there is one thing more than another by which I judge a woman, it is her voice; not her set "company" voice, but the tone she speaks in ordinarily or accidentally. *That* never deceives. Looks may. I have known fair-faced, blue-eyed angels, and girls with features as soft and lovely as houris, who could talk in most dulcet fashion till something vexed them, and then out came the hard metallic ring, which always indicates that curse of womanhood—worst of all faults except untruthfulness—*temper*. And I have heard voices, belonging to the plainest of faces, which were deep and soft, and low like a thrush's in an April garden. I would rather marry the woman that owned such a voice than the prettiest woman in the world.

This young woman had one, and I liked her instantaneously.

"Who are you, my dear?" I whispered. "His sister?"

"He has none—nor brother either."

"His cousin, then?"

"No."

I looked my next question, and she answered it with a simple honesty I expected from the owner of that voice.

"William and I were playfellows; then we kept company five years, and meant to be married next month. His father was against it, or it would have been sooner. But Willie wished to stop trapezing and settle in some other line; and Old Stone wanted money, and wouldn't let him go. At last they agreed for six more performances, and this was the first of the six."

"He'll never perform more," said I, involuntarily.

"No, he couldn't with that arm. I am very thankful for it," said she, with a touching desperate clutch at the brightest side of things.

How could I tell her what I began every hour more to dread, that the broken arm was the least injury which had befallen the young man; that I feared one of those concussions to the spine, which are often produced by a fall from a height, or a railway injury, and which, without any external wound, cripples the sufferer for years or for life?

"No, he never shall do any thing o' that sort again," continued she. "Father or no father, I'll not have him murdered." And there came a hard fierceness into her eyes, like that of a creature who has long been hunted down, and at last suddenly turns at bay.

"Where is his father? he has not come near him."

"Of course not. He's a precious coward is Old Stone, and as sharp as a needle after money, or at keeping away when money's likely to be wanted. But don't be afraid. I've myself got enough to pay you, sir. That's all the better. He is *my* William now."

This was the most of our conversation, carried on at intervals, and in whispers, during the night. My fellow-watcher sat behind the curtain, scarcely moving, except to do some feminine office, such as building up the fire noiselessly, coal by coal, as nurses know how, or handing me any thing I required of food or medicine. Or else she sat motionless; with her eyed fixed on the death-white face; but she never shed a tear. Not till, in the dawn of morning, the young man woke up in his right senses, and spoke feebly, but articulately.

"Doctor, thank you. I knew you, and I know what's happened. Only, just one word. I want Dorothy. Please fetch Dorothy."

"Yes, Willie," spoken quite softly and composedly. "Yes, Willie. I'm here."

It was a difficult case. The first-rate Edinburgh surgeon, whom, doubting my own skill, I called in next day, could make nothing of it. There were no injuries, external or internal, that could be traced, except the broken arm; the young man lay complaining of nothing, perfectly conscious and rational, but his lower limbs were apparently paralyzed.

We sent for a third doctor; he, too, was puzzled; but he said he had known one such case, where, after a railway accident, a man had been brought home apparently uninjured, though having received some severe nervous shock, probably to the spine. He had been laid upon his bed, and there he lay yet, though it was years ago; suffering little, and with all his faculties clear, but totally helpless; obliged to be watched over and waited upon like an infant, by his old wife.

"For he was an old man, and he had a wife, which was lucky for him," added the doctor. "It's rather harder for that poor young fellow, who may have to lie as he does now for the rest of his days."

"Hush!" I said, for he was talking loud in the passage, and close behind us stood poor Dorothy. I hoped she had not heard, but the first sight of her face convinced me she had; every syllable we had spoken; only women have at times a self-control that is almost awful to witness.

Whether it was that I was afraid to meet her, I do not know, but I stepped quickly out of the house, and walked a mile or more to the railway station with my two friends. When I returned, the first thing I saw was Dorothy, waiting on the stair-head, with my housekeeper beside her. For, I should observe, that good woman did not object nearly so much to a poor dying lad as to an evening party, and had taken quite kindly to Dorothy.

Yes, she had heard it all, poor girl, and I could not attempt to deceive her; indeed I felt by instinct that she was a person who could not be deceived; one to whom it was best to tell the whole truth; satisfied that she would bear it. She did, wonderfully. Of course I tempered it with the faint consolation that doctors are sometimes mistaken, and that the young man had youth on his side; but there the truth was, blank and bare, nor did I pretend to hide it.

"Yes, sir. Thank you, sir. Thank you for telling me all. My poor William!"

I took her into the parlor, and gave her a glass of wine.

"*I* don't need it, sir; I'm used to sick-nursing. I nursed my sister till she died. We were dressmakers, and then William got me as costume-maker to the circus. I can earn a good deal by my needle, sir."

This seemed far away from the point, and so did her next remark.

"His father won't help him, sir, you'll see, not a halfpenny. He's got another—wife he calls her, and a lot of other children, and doesn't care twopence for William."

"Poor fellow!"

"He isn't a poor fellow," she answered, sharply, "he's a very clever fellow; can read, and write, and keep accounts; he was thinking of trying for a clerk's situation. With that, and my dressmaking, we should have done very well, if we had once been married."

I hardly knew what to answer. I felt so exceedingly sorry for the poor girl, and yet she did not seem to feel her affliction. There was a strange light in her eyes, and a glow on her poor plain face, very unlike one whose whole hopes in life had just been suddenly blasted.

"Doctor,"—the voice went to my heart, despite its bad grammar, and horrible English pronunciation, dropped h's and all,—"may I speak to you, for I've nobody else, not a soul belonging to me, but William. Will you let him stop here for a week or two?"

"A month, if necessary."

"Thank you. He shall be no trouble to you; I'll take care of that. Only, there's one thing to be done first. Doctor, I must marry William."

She said it in such a matter of fact tone, that at first I doubted if I had rightly heard.

"Marry him? Good Heavens! You don't mean—"

"Yes I do, sir. Just that."

"Why, he will never be able to do a hand's turn of work for you—may never rise from his bed; will have to be tended like an infant for months, and may die after all."

"No matter, sir. He'd rather die with me than with any body. William loves me. I'll marry him."

There was a quiet determination about the woman which put all argument aside. And truly, if I must confess it, I tried none. I am an old-fashioned fellow, who never was so happy as to have any woman loving me; but I have known enough of women to feel surprised at nothing they do, of this sort. Besides, I thought, and think still, that Dorothy was right, and that she did no more than was perfectly natural under the circumstances.

"And now, sir, how is it to be managed?"

Of course the sooner it was managed the better, and I found, on talking with her, that she had already arranged it all in her own mind. She had lived long enough in Scotland to be aware that a Scotch irregular marriage was easy enough; simply by the parties declaring themselves husband and wife before witnesses; but still her English feelings and habits clung to a marriage "by a proper clergyman." She was considerably relieved when I explained to her that if she put in the banns that Friday night—they might be "cried" on Sunday in the parish kirk, and married by my friend the minister, to whom I would explain the matter, on Monday morning.

"That will do," she said. "And now I must go up stairs and speak to William."

What she said to him, or how he received it, is impossible for me to relate. Neither told me any thing, and I did not inquire. It was not my business; indeed, it was nobody's business but their own.

Now, though I may be a very foolish old fellow, romantic, with the deep-seated desperate romance which, my eldest niece avers, underlies the hard and frigid Scotch character (I suspect she has her own reasons for studying it so deeply), still, I am not such a fool as I appear. Though I did take these young people into my house, and was quite prepared to assist at their marriage, considering it the best thing possible for both under the circumstances, still I was not going to let them be married without having fully investigated their antecedents.

I went to the circus, and there tried vainly to discover the Herr von Stein, whose black-bearded head I was sure I saw slipping away out of the ring, where the "Highland Lassie," in a dirty cotton frock, and a dirtier face, was careering round and round on her beautiful horse, while in the centre, on the identical table of the night before—what an age it seemed ago!—a little fat man in shirt-sleeves and stocking soles was walking solitarily and solemnly upon bottles.

From him—Monsieur Ariel, who had been inquiring more than once at my house to-day, leaving his name as "Mr. Higgins"—I gained full confirmation of Dorothy Hall's story. She and William Stone were alike respectable and well-conducted young people, and evidently great favorites in the establishment. Then, and afterwards, I also learnt a few other facts, which people are slow to believe everywhere, especially in Scotland, namely, that it is quite possible for "play-actors," and even circus performers, to be very honest and decent folk; and that, in fact, it does not do to judge of any body by his calling, but solely by himself and his actions.

I hope, therefore, that I am passing no uncharitable judgment on the Herr von Stein, if I simply relate what occurred between us, without making any comment on his actions.

Finding he could not escape me, and that I sent message after message to him, he at last returned into the ring, and there—while the horses still went prancing round, the little girl continued her leaping, and we caught the occasional click-click of Monsieur Ariel practising among his bottles—the father stood and heard what I had to tell him concerning his son.

He was a father, and he seemed a good deal shocked, for about three minutes. Then he revived.

"It's very unfortunate, doctor, especially so for me, with my large family. What am I to do with him? What," becoming more energetic, "what the devil am I to do with him?"

And—perhaps it was human nature, paternal nature, in its lowest form, as you may often see it in the police columns of the *Times* newspaper—when I told him that the only thing he had to do was to give his consent to his son's marriage with Dorothy Hall, he appeared first greatly astonished, and then as greatly relieved.

"My consent? Certainly. They're both five-and-twenty—old enough to know their own minds—and have been courting ever so long. She's an excellent young woman; can earn a good income too. Yes, sir. Give them my cordial consent, and, in case it may be useful to them—this."

He fumbled in his pocket, took out an old purse, and counted out into my hand, with an air of great magnificence, five dirty pound notes. Which was all that I or any body else ever saw of the money of the Herr von Stein.

When I gave them, with his message, to Dorothy, she crumpled them up in her fingers, with a curious sort of smile, but she never spoke one word.

Uncle Adam has been at many a marriage, showy and quiet, gay and grave, hearty and heartless, but he is ready to declare, solemnly, that he never saw one which touched him so much as that brief ceremony, which took place at the bed-side of William Stone, the trapeze performer. It did not occupy more than ten minutes, for in the bridegroom's sad condition the slightest agitation was to be avoided. My housekeeper and myself were the only witnesses, and the whole proceeding was made as matter-of-fact as possible.

The bride's wedding-dress was the shabby old black gown, which she had never taken off for three days and nights, during which she, my housekeeper, and I, had shared incessant watch together; her face was very worn and weary, but her eyes were bright, and her voice steady. She never faltered once till the few words which make a Scotch marriage were ended, and the minister—himself not unmoved—had shaken hands with her and wished her every happiness.

"Is it all done?" said she, half bewildered.

"Ay, lassie," answered my old housekeeper, "ye're married, sure enough."

Dorothy knelt down, put her arms round her William's neck, and laid her head beside him on the pillow, sobbing a little, but softly—even now.

"Oh, my dear, my dear! nothing can ever part us more."

The wonderful circus of Herr von Stein has left our town a long time ago. It took its departure, indeed, very soon after the dreadful trapeze accident, which of course got into all the local papers, and was discussed pretty sharply all over the country. Nay, the unfortunate Signor Uberto, alias William Stone, had the honor of being made the subject of a *Times* leader, and there was more than one letter in that paper suggesting a subscription for his benefit. But it came out somehow that his father was a circus proprietor of considerable means, and so the subscription languished, never reaching beyond thirty odd pounds, with which benevolence the public was satisfied.

I believe William Stone was satisfied too;—that is, if he ever heard of it, which is doubtful; for during the earlier weeks and months of his illness his wife took care to keep every thing painful from him; and so did I, so long as they remained under my roof. This was a good deal longer than was at first intended, for my housekeeper became so attached to Mrs. Stone, that she could not bear to let them go. And the poor fellow himself was, as Dorothy had promised, "no trouble," almost a pleasure, in the house, from his patience, sweetness, and intelligence.

When they left me, they went to a small lodging hard by, where the wife set up dressmaking, and soon got as much work as ever she could do, among my patients, and the townspeople generally. For some enthusiastic persons took an interest in her, and called her "a heroine;" though, I confess, I myself always objected to this, and never could see that she had done any more than what was the most right and natural thing for a woman to do, supposing women were as they used to be in my young days, or as I used to think them.

But, heroine or not, Dorothy prospered. And in process of time her love was rewarded even beyond her hopes. Her husband's mysterious affliction gradually amended.

He began to use his feet, then his legs, and slowly recovered, in degree, the power of walking. Not that he ever became a robust man; the shock of his fall, acting on an exceedingly delicate and nervous frame, seemed to have affected all the springs of life; but he was no longer quite invalid and helpless, and by-and-by he began anxiously to seek for occupation. I hardly know which was the happiest, himself or Dorothy, when I succeeded in getting him employment as a writer's copying clerk, with as much work as filled up his time, and saved him from feeling, what he could not but feel—though I think he did not feel it very painfully, he loved her so—that his wife was the sole bread-winner.

When I go to see them now, in their cheery little home of two rooms, the one devoted to dressmaking, the other, half kitchen, half bedroom, in which William sits, and where Dorothy, with her usual habit of making the best of things, has accommodated Scotch ways to her English notions of comfort and tidiness—I say, when I go to see these two, so contented, and devoted to one another, I often think that among many fortunate people, I have seen far less happy couples than William and Dorothy.

A DREADFUL GHOST.

"SUCH a dreadful ghost! — oh, such a dreadful ghost!"

My wife, who was luckily sitting by me, was at first as much frightened as I was, but gradually she succeeded in quieting both herself and me, which indeed she has a wonderful talent for doing.

When she had learned the cause of my terrified exclamation, we discussed the whole matter:—in which we differed considerably; as on this subject we invariably and affectionately do. She is a perfectly matter-of-fact, unimaginative, and unsuperstitious individual: quite satisfied that in the invisible, as in the visible world, two and two must make four, and can not by any possibility make five. Only being, with all her gentleness, a little pig-headed, she does not see the one flaw in her otherwise very sensible argument, namely, the taking for granted that we finite creatures, who are so liable to error even in material things, can in things immaterial decide absolutely upon what is two and what is four.

> "There lives more faith in honest doubt,
> Believe me, than in half your creeds."

And it is just possible that when the devil tempted our forefather to eat of the tree of knowledge, he was laughing, as maybe he often laughs now, to think what a self-conceited fool a man must be, ever to suppose that he *can* know every thing.

When I preach this doctrine to my helpmate—who is the humblest and sweetest of women—she replies, in perhaps the safest way a woman can reply to an argument, with a smile; as she did, when, having talked over and viewed on all sides my Dreadful Ghost, she advised me to make it public, for the good of the community, which I consented to do—believing that it really would do good, though in what manner my wife and I differed still. She considered it would prove how very silly it is to believe in ghosts at all. I considered—but my story will explain that.

She and I were invited to a strange house, with which, and with the family, we were only acquainted by hearsay. It was, in fact, one of those "invitations on business,"—such as literary persons like myself continually get; and which give little pleasure, as we are perfectly aware from what motives they spring; and that if we could pack up our reputation in a portmanteau, and our head in a hat-box, it would answer exactly the same purpose, and be equally satisfactory to the inviting parties. However, the present case was an exception; since, though we had never seen our entertainers, we had heard that they were, not a show-loving, lion-hunting household, but really a *family;* affectionately united among themselves, and devoted to the memory of the lately-lost head. He was a physician, widely esteemed, and also a man of letters, whose death had created a great blank, both in his own circle and in the literary world at large. Now, after a year's interval, his widow and three daughters were beginning to reappear in society; and at the British Association meeting, held at the large town which I need not particularize, had opened the doors of their long-hospitable house to my wife and me.

Being strangers, we thought it best to appear, as I would advise all stranger-guests to do, at the end of the day; when candle-light and fire-light cast a kindly mystery over all things, and the few brief hours of awkwardness and unfamiliarity are followed by the nocturnal separation—when each party has time to think over and talk over the other—meeting next morning with the kindly feeling of those who have passed a night under the same friendly roof.

As my wife and I stepped from our cab, the dull day was already closing into twilight, and the fire only half illumined the room into which we were shown. It was an old-fashioned, rather gloomy apartment—half study, half sitting-room; one end being fitted up as a library, while at the other—pleasant thoughtfulness, which already warmed our hearts towards our unseen hosts!—was spread out that best of all meals for a weary traveller, a tea dinner. So hungry were we, that this welcome, well-supplied, elegant board was the only thing we noticed about the room;—except one other thing, which hung close above the tea-table, on the panelled wall.

It was a large full-length portrait, very well painted; the sort of portrait of which one says at once, "What a good likeness that must be!" It had individuality, character—the soul of the man as well as his body: and as he sat in his chair, looking directly at you, in a simple, natural attitude, you felt what a beautiful soul this must have been: one that even at sixty years of age—for the portrait seemed thus old—would have shed a brightness over any home, and over any society where the person moved.

"I suppose that must be the poor doctor," said my wife, as her eyes and mine both met upon the canvas face, which glimmered in the fire-light with a most life-like aspect, the gentle, benevolent eyes seeming to follow one about the room, as the eyes of most well-painted full-face portraits do. "You never saw him, Charles?"

"No; but this is exactly the sort of man he must have been."

And our conviction on the matter was so strong, that when the widow came in, we abstained from asking the question, lest we strangers might touch painfully on a scarcely healed wound.

She was a very sweet-looking little woman: pale, fragile, and rather silent than otherwise. She merely performed the duties of the tea-table, whilst the conversation was carried on with spirit and intelligence by her three daughters—evidently highly accomplished women. They were no longer young, or particularly handsome; but they appeared to have inherited the inexpressible charm of manner which, I had heard, characterized their lost father: and they had, my wife whispered me, a still greater attraction in her eyes—(she had, dear soul, two little daughters of her own growing up)—which was the exceeding deference they paid to their mother, who was not by any means so clever as themselves.

Perhaps I, who had not married a woman for her cleverness, admired the mother most. The doctor's widow, with her large, soft, sorrowful eyes, where the tears seemed to have dried up, or been frozen up in a glassy quietness, was to me the best evidence of what an excellent man he must have been: how deeply beloved, how eternally mourned.

She never spoke of her husband, nor the daughters of their father. This silence—which some families consider it almost a religious duty to preserve regarding their dead—we, of course, as complete strangers, had no business to break; and, therefore, it happened we were still in the dark as to the original of that remarkable portrait—which minute by minute took a stronger hold on my imagination; on my wife's, too—or that quality of universal tender-heartedness, which in her does duty for imagination. I never looked at her, without seeing her watching either our hostess, or that likeness, which she supposed to be the features of the lost husband who to the poor widow had been so deservedly dear.

A most strange picture. It seemed, in its wonderfully life-like truth, to sit, almost like an unobserved, silent guest, above our cheerful and conversational table. Many times during the evening I started, as if with the sense of a seventh person being in the room—in the very social circle—hearing every thing, observing every thing, but saying nothing. Nor was I alone in this feeling, for I noticed that my wife, who happened to sit directly opposite to the portrait, fidgeted in her chair, and finally moved her position to one where she could escape from those steady, kindly, ever-pursuing painted eyes.

Now I ask nobody to believe what I am going to relate; I must distinctly state that I do not believe it myself: but I tell it because it involves an idea and a moral, which the reader can apply if he chooses. All I can say is, that so far as it purports to go—and when you come to the end you will find that out—this is really a true story.

My wife, you must understand, sat exactly before the portrait, till she changed places with me, and went a little way down the oblong table, on the same side. Thus, one of us had a front, and the other a slightly foreshortened view of the picture. Between us and it was the table, in the centre of which stood a lamp—one of those reading lamps which throw a bright circle of light below them, and leave the upper half of the room in comparative shadow. I thought it was this shadow, or some fanciful flicker of the fire, which caused a peculiarity in the eyes of the portrait. They seemed actually alive—moving from right to left in their orbits, opening and closing their lids, turning from one to the other of the family circle with a variable expression, as if conscious of all that was done or said.

And yet the family took no notice, but went on in their talk with us: choosing the common topics with which unfamiliar persons try to plumb one another's minds and characters: yet never once reverting to this peculiar phenomenon—which my wife, I saw, had also observed, for she interchanged with me more than one uneasy glance in the pauses of conversation.

The evening was wearing on—it was nearly ten o'clock, when, looking up at the picture, from which for the last half-hour I had steadily averted my gaze, I was startled by a still more marvellous fact concerning it.

Formerly, the eyes alone had appeared alive, now the whole face was so. It grew up out of the flat canvas as if in bas-relief, or like one of those terribly painful casts after death—except that there was nothing painful or revolting here. As I have said, the face was a beautiful face—a noble face: such an one as, under any circumstances, you would have been attracted by. And being painted, it had the coloring and form of life—no corpse-like rigidity or marble whiteness. The gray hair seemed gradually to rise, lock by lock, out of the level surface; and the figure, clothed in ordinary modern evening dress, to become shapely and natural—statuesque, yet still preserving the tints of a picture. Even the chair which it sat upon—which I now perceived to be the exact copy of one that stood empty on the other side of the fire, gave a curious reality to the whole.

By-and-by my wife and I both held our breaths with amazement, nay, horror. For, from an ordinary oil-painting, the likeness had become a life-like figure, or statue, sitting in an alcove, the arch of which was made by the frame of the picture.

And yet the family took no notice, but appeared as if, whether or not they were conscious of the remarkable thing that was happening, it did not disturb them in the least—was nothing at all alarming or peculiar, or out of the tenor of their daily life.

No, not even when, on returning with a book that I had gone to fetch from the shelves at the farther end of the room, my poor little wife caught my hand in speechless awe—awe, rather than fear—and pointed to the hitherto empty chair by the fireside.

It was empty no longer. There, sitting in the self-same attitude as the portrait—identical with it in shape, countenance, and dress,—was a figure. That it was a human figure I dare not say, and yet it looked like one. There was nothing ghastly or corpse-like about it, though it was motionless, passionless: endowed, as it were, with that divine calm which Wordsworth ascribes to Protesilaus:—

> "Elysian beauty, melancholy grace,
> Brought from a pensive though a happy place."

Yet there was an air tenderly, pathetically human in the folding of the hands on the knees, as a man does when he comes and sits down by his own fireside, with his family round him: and in the eyes that followed, one after the other, each of this family, who now quietly put away their several occupations, and rose.

But none of them showed any terror—not in the slightest degree. The Presence at the hearth was evidently quite familiar to them—awaking no shudder of repulsion, no outburst of renewed grief. The eldest daughter said—in a tone as natural as if she were merely apologizing to us heterodox or indifferent strangers for some domestic ceremonial, some peculiar form of family prayer, for instance—

"I am sure our guests will excuse us if we continue, just as if we were alone, our usual evening duties. Which of us is to speak to papa to-night?"

It was himself, then: summoned, how or why, or in what form—corporeal or incorporeal—I knew not, and his family gave no explanation. They evidently thought none was needed: that the whole proceeding was as natural as that of a man coming home at evening to his own fireside, and being received by his wife and children with affectionate familiarity.

The widow and the youngest daughter placed themselves one on each side of the figure in the chair. They did not embrace it or touch it; they regarded it with tender reverence, in which was mingled a certain sadness; but that was all. And then they began to talk to it, in a perfectly composed and matter-of-fact way; as people would talk to a beloved member of a household who had been absent for a day, or longer, from the home circle.

The daughter told how she had been shopping in town; how she had bought a shawl and a bonnet "of the color that papa used to like;" the books she had brought home from the library, and her opinion of them; the people she had met in the street, and the letters she had received during the day: in short, all the pleasant little chit-chat that a daughter would naturally pour out to an affectionately-interested *living* father; but which now—as addressed to the spectre of the father many months dead—sounded so unnatural, so contemptibly small, such a mixture of the ludicrous and the horrible, that one's common worldly sense, and one's sense of the solemn unseen world, were alike revolted.

No answer came: apparently none was expected. The figure maintained its place, listening apparently, with that gentle smile—reminding one of the ghostly Samuel's rebuke to the Witch of Endor—"Why hast thou disquieted me, to bring me up?" or indicating that superior calm with which, after death, we ourselves shall surely view all the trifles which so perplexed us once.

Then the widow took up the tale, with a regretful under-tone of complaint running through it. She told her husband how dull she had been all day; how in the preparations for these strangers (meaning my wife and me—we shivered as the eyes of the figure moved and rested on us!) she had found various old letters of his, which vividly revived their happy wedlock days; how yesterday one of his former patients died, and to-day a professorship, which he meant to have tried for, had been given to a gentleman, a favorite pupil; how his old friends, Mr. A—— and Sir B. C——, had had a quarrel, and every body said it would never have happened had the Doctor been alive to make peace between them—and so on, and so on. To all of which the figure listened with its immovable silence; its settled, changless smile.

My wife and I uttered not a word. We sat apart, spell-bound, fascinated; neither attempting to interfere, nor question, nor rebuke. The whole proceeding was so entirely beyond the pale of rational cause and effect, that it seemed to throw us into a perfectly abnormal condition, in which we were unable to judge, or investigate, or escape from, the circumstances which surrounded us.

Nothing is known—absolutely nothing—except the very little that Revelation hints at, rather than directly teaches, of the world beyond the grave. But any one of us who has ever seen a fellow-creature die—has watched the exact instant when the awful change takes place which converts the body with a soul to the corpse without a soul, must feel certain—convinced by an intuition which is stronger than all reasoning—that if the life beyond, to which that soul departs, be any thing, or worth any thing, it must be a very different life from this; with nobler aspirations, higher duties, purer affections. The common phrase breathed over so many a peaceful dead face, "I would not bring him back again if I could," has a significance, instructive as true; truer than all misty, philosophical speculations, tenderer than all the vagaries of fond spiritualists, with large hearts and no heads worth mentioning. If I had ever doubted this, my doubts would have been removed by the sight which I here depict—of this good, amiable, deeply-beloved husband and father, returning in visible form to his own fireside; no ghastly spectre, but an apparition full of mildness and beauty,—yet communicating a sense of revolting incongruity, utter unsanctity, and ridiculous, degrading contrast between mortal and immortal, —spirit in the flesh and spirit out of the flesh.

That the dead man's family did not feel this, having become so familiar with their nightly necromancy that its ghastliness never struck them, and its ludicrous profanity never jarred upon their intellect or affections,—only made the fact more horrible.

For a time, long or short I can not tell, my wife and I sat witnessing, like people bound in a nightmare dream, this mockery of mockeries, the attempt at restoring the sweet familiar relations that had once existed, of the living with the living, between the living and the dead. How many days or months it had lasted, or what result was expected from it, we never inquired; nor did we attempt to join in it; we merely looked on.

"Will papa ever speak?" entreated one of the daughters; but there was no reply. The Figure sat passive in its chair—unable or unwilling to break the silent barrier which divides the two worlds, maintaining still that benign and tender smile, but keeping its mystery unbroken, its problem unsolved.

And now my wife, whose dear little face was, I saw, growing white and convulsed minute by minute, whispered to me:

"Charles, I can bear this no longer. Make some excuse to them—we will not hurt their feelings—only let us go. Don't let them think we are frightened or disgusted; but we must go—I shall go mad else."

And the half-insane look which I have seen in more than one of the pseudo-spiritualists of the present day—people who twenty years ago would have been sent to Bedlam, but now are only set down as "rather peculiar," rose in my wife's eyes—those dear, soft, sensible eyes, which have warmed and calmed my restless heart and unquiet brain for more than fifteen years.

I took advantage of the next pause in the "communications," or whatever the family called them, to suggest that my wife and I were very weary, and anxious to retire to rest.

"Certainly," politely said the eldest daughter. "Papa, Mr. and Mrs. ——," naming our names, "have had a long railway journey, and wish to bid us all good-night."

The Appearance bent upon us—my wife and me—its most benevolent, gentle aspect, apparently acquiescing in our retiring; and slowly rose as if to bid us good-night—like any other courteous host.

Now, in his lifetime, no one had had a warmer, more devoted admiration for this learned and lovable man than I. More than once I had travelled many miles for the merest chance of seeing him, and when he died, my regret at never having known him personally, never having even beheld his face, was mingled with the grief which I, in common with all his compatriots, felt at losing him so suddenly, with his fame at its zenith, his labors apparently only half done.

But here, set face to face with this image or phantasm, or whatever it was, of the man whom living I had so honored—I felt no delight; nay, the cold clearness of his gaze seemed to shoot through me with a chill of horror.

When, going round the circle, I shook hands with the widow and daughters, one after the other, I paused before *that chair;* I attempted to pass it by. Resolutely I looked another way, as if trying to make believe I saw nothing there; but it was in vain.

For the Figure advanced noiselessly, with that air of irresistibly charming, dignified courtesy of the old school, for which, every body said, the Doctor had been so remarkable. It extended its hand—a hand which a year ago I would have travelled five hundred miles to grasp. Now, I shrank from it—I loathed it.

In vain. It came nearer. It touched mine with a soft, cold, unearthly touch. I could endure no longer. I shrieked out; and my wife woke me from what was, thank Heaven, only a dream.

* * * * * * * *

"Yes, it was indeed a dreadful ghost," said that excellent woman, when she had heard my whole story, and we had again composed ourselves as sole occupants of the railway carriage which was conveying us through the dead of night to visit that identical family whom I had been dreaming about—whom, as stated, we had never seen. "Let us be thankful, Charles, that it was a mere fantasy of your over-excited imagination—that the dear old Doctor sleeps peacefully in his quiet grave; and that his affectionate family have never summoned him, soul or body, to sit of nights by their uncanny fireside, as you so horribly describe. What a blessing that such things can not be!"

"Ay," replied I—"though, as Imlac says in 'Rasselas,' 'that the dead can not return, I will not undertake to prove;' still, I think it in the highest degree improbable. Their work here is done; they are translated to a higher sphere of being; they may still see us, love us, watch over us; but they belong to us no more. Mary, when I leave you, remember I don't wish ever to be brought back again; to come rapping on tables and knocking about chairs; delivering ridiculous messages to deluded inquirers, and altogether comporting myself in a manner that proves, great fool as I may have been in the body, I must be a still greater fool out of it."

"And Charles," said the little woman, creeping up to me with tears in her eyes, "if I must lose you—dearly as I love you—I would rather bury you under the daisies and in my heart; bury you, and never see you again till we meet in the world to come, than I would have you revisiting your old fireside after the fashion of this dreadful ghost."

MEADOWSIDE HOUSE.

THIS is not a story, though the title looks as if it were. It is merely a few words meant to be spoken at Christmas time, when people's hearts are open—when their hearths are brightened and their tables filled with little children; for Christmas, so rarely a happy time for us elders, can be made, and always should be, an especial time of delight to children, if only in remembrance of Him who then became a little child. And the more we suffer—we others, to whom year after year has inevitably brought bitter anniversaries—the more we ought to try and spare the children from suffering, as long as we can; by making for our own, in every possible way, a "merry Christmas and a happy New Year;" and also by scattering abroad among others not our own a little comfort, a little pleasure, a little of that light-hearted mirth, which is all of the present, dreading no future and remembering no past. Ah, let us always try to make the children happy! they will not be children long.

It is with this feeling that I wish to say a few words for a few "puir wee bodies" who live, or rather suffer existence—for in many cases it can hardly be called living,—in Meadowside House, Lauriston Lane, lately converted into the Edinburgh Hospital for Sick Children.

There is a region, quite unfamiliar to passing strangers and superficial sightseers, and yet within five minutes' walk of the picturesque, historical, melancholy, noisome, abominable Old Town—with its Canongate, Cowgate, Lawn-market, Grass-market,—classic ground, investigated by flying tourists with mingled curiosity and abhorrence: for seldom does a canker so foul lurk at the heart of any city as of this, the flower of cities—beautiful Edinburgh. Still, for its salvation maybe, close at the back of it lies the other region known to residents by the name of "the Meadows." How the word suggests to the southern ear pictures of

English fields, knee-deep in growing May-grass, reddened with wavy sorrel-seeds and yellowed over with buttercups; or sunshiny meads, where, sitting down and stretching round a circle, arm-wide, you may fill your two hands with cowslips; mingled here and there with those Shakspearian lady-smocks that—

> "All silver-white
> Do paint the meadows with delight."

Alas! not these meadows. I have seen a daisy there—bless the gowans! like the poor little children, they grow anywhere—and one or two dandelions, and (I believe, but would not undertake to affirm the fact) a buttercup: but the principal feature of these meadows is simple grass. Very good grass, though; green and smooth; and one ought to be thankful for it, and for the fresh breeze that blows across it, and for the merry rustle of the two lines of lately planted but well-growing trees. A pleasant place, where the Edinburgh volunteers—honest lads!—come and do rifle-shooting of mornings, usually placing their target directly in the way of early pedestrians; where, later, the genteel nurse-maids from George Square, Buccleuch Place, and the houses round Heriot's Hospital, walk with their young charges, and the ungenteel, youthful fry from Newington and Morningside come out to play, healthy and strong, barefooted and rough-headed. But the children of a lower class still, abiding in that melancholy region just spoken of, in the tall "lands"—twelve stories high; the dark cellars, windowless, fireless; up the wynds and closes, stiflingly foul, so foul that one often inclines to believe the only cleansing would be a good wholesome fire, like the Great Fire of London,—alack! the children who live here, *they* never come near the Meadows. Their poor, weak, rickety limbs could never totter far enough to reach and roll on the green grass; their eyes, accustomed to dank, damp cellars, where the sun never shines and never shone, could hardly endure the bright, broad daylight; and their poor, thin, unwashed, unclothed bodies would shrink, withered up, from the first sweep of the healthy breeze that blows across Arthur's Seat and the Braid Hills. They scarcely know that such things exist, unless the angel of sickness—it is an angel, often—carries them away, some strange, miserable, wonderful day, and leaves them, half alive, or with only a few days or weeks of life before them, to lie clean and quiet, away from all noisome sights and smells and sounds, in the peaceful, tidy crib in one of the wards at Meadowside House.

It was a wise and fortunate choice which located the hospital here—its first step since its small beginnings in Lauriston Lane. Let us briefly recount them.

Four years ago* a few worthy Edinburgh doctors—(truly a large portion of the world's worth lies among doctors)—woke up fully to the alarming fact that one half of the children born in Edinburgh die before their third year. Also to a second fact, statistically proved, that this frightful mortality does not lessen the population; but that the half generation thus cut off is assuredly and immediately replaced by another, more puny, more unhealthy, less fitted both to struggle with the burden of life themselves, or to transmit it to posterity. Worse far than the sight of a race wholly swept away by pestilence, sword, or famine—or vanishing like snow, as the Indians do, before the hot breath of advancing civilization—is the spectacle of a race dying out by slow deterioration, and from apparently preventable causes, under the very eyes of their brethren. For, however strange and incredible it may appear—as it did when lately the two highest born in the land, the Prince and Princess of Wales, blest in youth and love and happy fortunes, drove through the High Street and Canongate, smiling gayly and graciously on the two lines of wretched faces that put on a weak, accidental, welcoming smile—still they are our brethren. And it is only the Cains of this world, with fraternal blood on their hands—or the Levites, who, "passing by" the afflicted, are haply Cains too, by omission if not by commission—it is only such as these who dare meet the one Almighty Father with the cry of "Am I my brother's keeper?"

The Edinburgh doctors—with other gentlemen out of the profession—felt that they were, in one sense, their brothers' keepers; and being honestly convinced of the two sad facts before named, they set about to remedy them by means of a third great fact—that prevention is better than cure. On the principle that Reformatories are wiser, perhaps cheaper—than Penitentiaries; Servants' Homes than Magdalen Institutions; decent, sanitary la-

* This was written in 1864.

borers' cottages than jails and workhouses—they thought they would do their best to establish a Children's Hospital.

Few things can be, or need to be, without secondary motives: and even charity itself is in one form an act of self-preservation. It does not detract from the benevolence of this scheme, that its originators felt also how valuable it would be in furnishing opportunity for the study of children's diseases—so important and difficult a branch of medical science. Also that by taking hold of sickness, especially infectious disorders, at the very beginning, the hospital might be efficacious in stopping the spread of those endemics and epidemics which, rooting themselves amidst the foulness of the beggar's home, spread secret devastation to that of his wealthy and prosperous neighbor. People do not consider—until neglect brings its own retribution—that death has entered many a palace door by the filthy alley left to fester unheeded beneath its shadow; and that many a landlord who will not build, or suffer to be built, decent cottages for his laborers to live in has to meet his reward in other ways—by poachers, night robbers, dishonest or corrupted servants, contagious diseases, and the still worse contagion of crime. For it is a law of nature to help us in the eternal struggle between good and evil, that we dare not leave the latter alone, turning our lazy or sanctimonious eyes from it, under the supposition that it will never harm us. It will. Even for the safety of his own family, every householder in Edinburgh were wise to lend a hand in the cleansing of that Augean stable which Doctor Guthrie and many others are doing their best for, by sermon, speech, and pen. And one of these means of purification is a Children's Hospital.

The one in Lauriston Lane found many opponents—some conscientious, some careless or prejudiced; but of all, the less here said the better, seeing the hospital has outlived its time of trial, and attained the grand secret for converting enemies into friends—success.

From the day—8th March, 1860—when it held its first annual meeting, with Dean Ramsay in the chair, and many more honorable and notable Edinburgh gentlemen surrounding him, it has steadily progressed, its directors acting with true Scotch caution, and spending their funds with honest Scotch economy; until lately they were able to purchase, enlarge, and occupy the pleasant old mansion called Meadowside House.

It is in exterior more like a family house than a hospital. Its three stories of cheerful windows imply equally cheerful rooms within, as any body may prove who calls there between three and five on a week-day afternoon. Its very simplicity, plainness, and *familiness*, so to speak, are a great charm. No money squandered over porticoes and cupolas, bas-reliefs and statues without, and throngs of well-housed, well-salaried servants within: here is just what is wanted and no more. The whole resident staff comprises a medical officer, a matron—who truly appears like the universal mother of this large and helpless little family—a few nurses and domestic servants. Two ordinary wards—one filled always, and a second just opened, in hope that the institution will be enabled to afford it; two fever wards, carefully shut off from the rest of the house; a few smaller rooms for domestic occupation; and two others, with a separate entrance, devoted to the daily crowd of out-door patients who come for advice and medicine,—this constitutes the whole of the establishment.

It would be very easy to write pages of argumentative appeal or of emotional pleading on that subject which goes to the heart of all women—nay, of all humanity—a sick child. But I shall not do it. I would that, instead of any writing, I could paint a picture—dumb as themselves—of the little white, thin faces, lying so patiently on the comfortable pillows. "It is wonderful how good our children are," said the matron. "We never have the least trouble with them, and yet no nurse is allowed either to scold or to punish them." Or, rather, I would that I could tell, to both old and young, as a simple fireside story, with the yule log blazing and the chestnuts crackling on the hearth, the histories, quite true, of some of the poor children who come to, and go, unless in another and often more merciful way they are taken—from Meadowside House.

Hear, for instance, a few anecdotes, chosen at random from the matron's talk, while she went from crib to crib, smoothing one pillow or altering another, administering a word of kindness, or a pat and smile,—small things to rich men's children in pleasant nurseries, sunned through and through with mother's love: but oh, what great and new things to such children as these!

Thomas Weir, admitted here 29th March last; dismissed, cured, the 21st May; seven years old; very small of his age. The mother had had eight children; all dead but Tommy. The father was in Perth prison—third committal, for wife-beating. Tommy was sent here by the police doctor, his mother being found dead drunk on a stair and the child beside her, ill with fever. For weeks he lay between life and death, neither speaking nor taking notice of any thing. His mother would sometimes come to inquire for him, but in such a state that she could not be admitted to the ward. Once she did get in, and Tommy said, "Mither, ye suldna come here when ye've had a dram, the mistress will see ye." One day another wretched-looking woman came, and he told her to go away, and afterwards said to the nurse, "Nurse, she's an awfu' bad one—yon woman. She pawned mither's plaid, and they both got fou, and were taken aff by the police, and I sat my lane on a stair a' the nicht—cauld, cauld!" Tommy afterwards, during his convalescence, told many like tales of his short seven years' life—his numerous wanderings, often walking twenty miles a day ("that's what gars me look sae auld, ye ken"): how the father and mother once left him and his wee sister at Mid Calder, a village ten miles from Edinburgh, and never came back: how a kind woman gave them a sack to sleep on in a shed, and a "piece" in the morning, and then the two forlorn bairns set off to walk into Edinburgh to their grandfather, who lived in the Grass-market. "He was weel aff ance, and a grand singer; that's how I can sing sae weel," as poor Tommy often did, to the great delight of the nurses. "Grandfather," it seems, went about the country with a show, of which he played the Merry-Andrew, till, getting aged, he took a room in the Grass-market, and held prayer-meetings, Tommy and his mother leading the psalmody. "But," he continued, "in the cauld winter grandfather deed, ye ken, and granny gaed to see a leddy that's kind to her, and whiles mither lifted the things fra grandfather's bed and sold them for whisky. Wae's me! father will be out o' prison soon, and then what'll I do, for him and mither's always fighting." Alas, poor little Tommy Weir!

There was another boy, whose name I forget, found lying on straw in a dark cellar, which had literally nothing in it but this one heap of straw. The parents were in the habit of going out for the day, and locking up the child there, without food, or fire, or clothes. He was brought in—a mere bundle of rags—quite paralyzed, and lay for a week on one of the hospital beds, without stirring or speaking, till they almost thought he was deaf and dumb. At last he did mutter out one word, and it was "whisky!" He afterwards tried, in his wretched faint voice, to begin singing a whisky song, and told the nurse he had hardly tasted any thing but whisky since he was born. Somehow his wretched mother found him out and came to see him. Immediately after she left, the miserable little creature was caught hiding its wizened face and still half-paralyzed hands under the bed-clothes, trying to undo the cork of a small bottle filled with whisky! But this child also recovered, learned to feed on and enjoy other food than drams, and left the hospital for a future of—God knows what! Still the life had been saved—so far.

And sometimes, when help comes too late, and the life is not saved, it is touching to hear the end of these prematurely old children. One little girl, Jane Mackenzie, used to say often before her death, "I did na think ony folk *could* be sae kind to ither folk's bairns." She took a fancy to one of the gentlemen who often visited the hospital, and asked him to come and talk to her. "I heard ye speaking to yon wee boy, and I thocht, may be, ye wad speak to me too." As he did—many holy and peaceful words; and when the child died, content and happy, he took the trouble of travelling some distance to follow her to her grave.

The little patients who do not die sometimes live for better things than once seemed possible. In January last, one Mary Cullen was brought into the hospital, having suddenly lost the use of her limbs, and a fortnight afterwards her speech. She lay for a long time totally helpless, and apparently imbecile. But eight months of good air, good food, good nursing, have changed the paralyzed child into an active girl, a capital little servant in the ward where she came a while ago as a miserable and hopeless invalid. So great is the vitality of youth, when given the least chance of throwing off disease by means of proper sanitary care, which, in such homes as these children are brought from—nay, in any working and poverty-stricken homes—is purely impossible.

Those who leave their temporary refuge are often very eager to get back to it. "At this time," said the matron, "we have a little fellow who was with us two years since. When he left I said, 'Harry, when will you come and see me?"—'Whenever I'm no weel,' answered he; and sure enough the other day his mother came and said Harry was ill, and would not let her rest till she brought him to the hospital. The next day his sister came in, also very ill. As soon as he saw her he said, 'Dinna greet, Anna; this is a grand place!' and the two soon made themselves quite happy together. There was another boy," continued the matron (from whom I have had all these true stories, as they may be gained readily by any one who visits the place—facts sadder than any fiction), "his name was Pat. He had no father, and worse than no mother. When he recovered he was very unwilling to leave us; but being cured, we could of course keep him no longer, so we gave him some warm clothing—as we generally do, for the rags the children are brought in are almost always obliged to be burnt—and then we sent him away. But for a long time afterwards poor Pat used to come and stand at the kitchen-window, when I was serving the dinners, just to get a few mouthfuls and a warm at the fire. One bitter morning in February he came begging to be taken in, but I said, 'Pat, you're not ill, and we can't have you.' Next morning he was back again, with his head all cut and bleeding. "Ye'll tak me in noo," said he, evidently quite glad of his misfortune. And, though, to his great regret, he got well in a week, still he was so eager to stay that one of our gentlemen kindly admitted him into an industrial school, and poor Pat is all right now."

Sometimes the parents are grateful, and bring little presents to the matron, or make thank-offerings of a few pence to the box at the dispensary, where, chiefly as a matter of form, it is stated that, if the applicants can afford it, the medicines are to be paid for. However, no test is possible, and thus many get gratis the medical aid they could well pay for. Still the good is done, and the charity, as a charity, reaches to the very lowest deeps of that sea of misery close by. Unhappily parents, out of ignorance or carelessness, often delay bringing their children till assistance comes too late; and yet it is hard to refuse the poor little dying creature a few hours of a quiet hospital-bed, on which to breathe its last, instead of sending it back to those pestilential holes where the slightest illness becomes almost certain doom; and death, stripped of all its peace and sacredness, breeds death on every side, by all imaginable horrors of contact with repulsive mortality.

The difficulty which some energetic adversaries of children's hospitals have upheld so strongly—that of removing a child from home and parents—has not, in the practical working of this hospital, been found to be a difficulty at all. For, among the classes for which it was chiefly intended, home is no home, and parents, instead of being the child's best guardians in health or sickness, are often, through ignorance or neglect, its very worst. Even the maternal tie—the last to survive amid the wreck of all else that is womanly—is often totally lost; witness the case of little Tommy Weir. Despite all the flimsy objections of sentimental theorists about the sanctity of the parental bond, and the danger of interfering with it, any person of common sense must see, that when parents make of themselves brute beasts, it is not only the right but the duty of national charity to step in, and say, "These are the children of the nation: give up your pretended rights and unfulfilled duties — they are no longer yours, but ours. We may not be able to save you, but these little ones *must* be saved."

A difficult question, and yet it ought to be met and looked rationally in the face, both by governments and by private schemes of benevolence.

If the high arm of righteous authority did a little more than it now does in interfering for the helpless, and breaking the bonds of the oppressed; compelling sanitary observances, laying upon ignorance as well as vice the strong hand of the law, and dragging all corruption out into the open day, it would be all the better—not for us, perhaps, but for those that shall come after us.

And for this end, hoping it will do a little atom of good to leaven this mountainous mass of misery, I tell, just at Christmas-time, when the Great Master of us all came to seek and to save that which was lost, the story of the lost lambs who are taken in and folded, either for living or for dying, into this quiet home at Meadowside House. On its arrangements I do not dilate; they are much the same as in all well-conducted hospitals, and almost identical with that of the Children's Hospital in Great Ormond Street, London, on the principle of which this one was founded. Besides, all who live within reach may go and see the place for themselves; and one hour of such a pathetic sight, either to mothers or children—and especially to childless mothers and motherless children—is worth all that ever I can write about it.

I would like, at this Christmas-time, to urge such not only to go and see, but to go and help them;—as lady-visitors, moving from crib to crib, and bestowing a kind word or a plaything or two on the little occupant; as subscribers, giving, perhaps, one small pound a year; as donors, paying a hundred pounds for the not unhappy privilege of knowing that thereby one bed, with one sick child always in it, is secured in perpetuity; as benefactors, who are willing to leave one thousand pounds of the money which they can not carry away with them—money to which no child is heir, and which, expended on the founding of a ward here, would benefit hundreds and thousands of children to all generations. Lastly, there is something which every body can do—every mother of a family who has so many worn-out and disused clothes cumbering her nursery shelves—make them up into a parcel, and send them to Meadowside House to clothe the poor little convalescents, who come there in rags, and would go out, most of them, in utter nakedness, were it not for the charitable store—never too large—which the hospital keeps, and bestows even when its professed charge of the inmates is ended.

Beyond its doors, to follow these poor children is all but impossible. Sometimes, thinking of the homes they come from, and must go back to, one is tempted to believe that the best and safest home for them is that quiet "dead-house," where so many of them are carried, and thence to a quieter spot still. And yet they do live, and He makes them live, and bids us help them to live—He in whose hands alone are living and dying. Therefore we dare not say—since He does not say it—that it were better any one of these little ones should die. We would rather hope that the life, frail as it may be, which the hospital puts into them, is put for a good end, and that the moral influence which they are subjected to under its roof, of cleanliness, order, kindliness, peace, may not be without effect on at least some of them. Small the amount of good done may be, yet have we not the highest authority for believing that "a little leaven leaveneth the whole lump?" We can but do our best and trust.

And therefore I have said my humble say, hoping that some will read it who may be able to do far more than I can ever do myself. Nor do I think that even as "a story—a true story," which children are always asking for, it would make the Christmas children less happy, if, gathered round papa's and mamma's knees at the fireside, some one would take the trouble to read to the little people, in whole or in part, what I have written about the forlorn ones so different from themselves—the sick children who are taken in and nursed well, or tended kindly till they quietly die—at Meadowside House, Edinburgh.

IN HER TEENS.

IF "the boy is father of the man," the girl is likewise mother to the woman; and the woman—oh, solemn thought, laden with awful responsibility to each tiny maiden-child that coos and crows at us from her innocent cradle!—the woman is the mother of us all. Far deeper and higher than the advocates of woman's rights are aware of, lies the truth, that women are the heart of the world. From a gynocracy, or even a self-existent, self-protecting, and self-dependent rule, heaven save us, and all other Christian communities! but the fact remains, that on the women of a nation does its virtue, strength, nobility, and even its vitality, rest. Sparta recognized this in a rough barbaric way; Judea, too, when through successive ages every daughter of Abraham was brought up to desire motherhood as her utmost honor, in the hope that of her might be born the long-expected Messiah, the promised Seed. All history, carefully examined, would, we believe, exemplify the same truth—that the rise and fall of nations is mainly dependent on the condition of their women—the mothers, sisters, daughters, wives—who, consciously or unconsciously, mould, and will mould forever, the natures, habits, and lives of the men to whom they belong. Nay, even in modern times, in looking around upon divers foreign countries—but stay, we will not judge our neighbors, we will only judge ourselves.

If things be so, if the influence of women is so great, so inevitable, either for good or for evil, does it not behoove us, who live in a generation where so many strange conflicts are waging on the surface of society, so many new elements stirring and seething underneath it—does it not behoove us, I say, to look a little more closely after our "girls?"

It is rather difficult nowadays to find a "girl" at all. They are, every one of them, "young ladies;" made up of hoop and flounce, hat and feather, plaits of magnificent (bought) hair, and heaps of artificial flowers. There is a painful uniformity, too, in them and their doings—their walking, talking, singing, dancing, seem all after the same pattern, done to order according to the same infallible rule —"What will Mrs. Grundy say?" An original natural "girl," who has grown up after her own fashion, and never heard of Mrs. Grundy, is a creature so rare, that when we find her, at any age from twelve to twenty, we are prone to fall right over head and ears in love with her, carry her off, and marry her immediately. And we hardly wonder that so many of these vapid, commonplace, well-dressed, well-mannered young ladies remain unmarried, or rush into the opposite extreme of frantic independence, and try to create an impossible Utopia, of which the chief characteristic seems to be that of the heaven of Crazy Jane in the ballad—

"With not a man to meet us there."

Which is the most harmful, this foolish aping of men's manners, habits, and costumes, or the frivolous laziness, the worse than inanity, that wastes a whole precious lifetime over the set of its hoops, the fashion of its bonnets, or the gossip of its morning callers? Between the two opposite evils, most welcome is any thing, or any body, who indicates in the smallest degree what a girl really is and ought to be; thus giving us some hope for the women that are to come, the mothers of the next generation.

Thanks, therefore, to "Lucy Fletcher"—whether that name be real or assumed—for a little unpretentious book of verses, entitled "Thoughts from a Girl's Life." Let her speak for herself, in a Preface which, for straightforward simplicity and dignified modesty, is itself almost a poem:

"These verses are the true expression of the thoughts and feelings of a girl's life, and as such they are given specially to other girls.

"I will not apologize too much for their want of poetical merit; nevertheless it is with a full consciousness of their immaturity that I send them forth. But though the deepening life of years to come may teach a fuller and a higher tone, yet I feel that the thoughts and utterances of to-day may be best fitted to reach and to help those who stand on the level from which these were written.

"I do not, of course, imply that every word in these verses is true as regards my own life; in poetry less than in any other form of expression, would that be possible; many of the incidents are idealized, and some of the feelings known more by sympathy than by personal experience.

"I send my little book with its own message to those who will care to hear it; I shall be most glad and thankful if it is able in any degree to sympathize with, to help, or to cheer those hearts to whom from my own I speak."

A girl's book—only a girl. Now, ordinarily, a youthful poetess is a very unpleasant character. The less a girl writes, the better. That is, publishes: for almost all girls write, and nothing will stop them. Nor is there any actual harm in their mild verses and elaborate love-stories—the temporary outburst of fancy or feeling that will soon settle down into its proper channel, and find a safe outlet in the realities of domestic life. But there is harm in encouraging in the smallest degree that exaggerated sentimentality which wears out emotion in expression, converting all life into a perpetual *pose plastique*, or a romantic drama of which she, the individual, is the would-be heroine. And worse still is that *cacoethes scribendi*, that frantic craving for literary reputation, which lures a girl from her natural duties, her safe shut-up home life, to join the band of writing-women—of which the very highest, noblest, and most successful feel, that to them, as women, what has been gained is at best a poor equivalent for what has been lost.

In one sense the kindest wish that a reader can wish to "Lucy Fletcher" is, that this her first book may also be her last; and yet it is a good book to have written, good and true, and valuable too—as truth always is.

A girl's life. What a mysterious thing that is! None who have reached the stand-point whence they can fairly and dispassionately look back on theirs, but must feel awed at remembering all it was, and all it promised to be—its infinite hopes, its boundless aspirations, its dauntless energies, its seemingly unlimited capacity for both joy and pain. All these things may have calmed down now: the troubled chaos has long settled into a perfect—and yet how imperfect!—world: but the mature woman, of whatever age or fortunes, can hardly look without keenest sympathy and trembling pity on those who have yet to go through it all. For, let poets talk as they will of that charming time in which a girl is

> "Standing with reluctant feet
> Where the brook and river meet—
> Womanhood and childhood sweet,"

the years between twelve and twenty are, to most, a season

any thing but pleasant; a crisis in which the whole heart and brain are full of tumult, when all life looks strange and bewildering—delicious with exquisite unrealities,—and agonized with griefs equally chimerical and unnatural. Therefore, every influence caught, and every impression given during these years, is a matter of most vital moment. Most girls' characters are stamped for life by the associations they form, and the circumstances by which they are surrounded, during their teens. They may change and grow—thank heaven all good men and women have never done growing!—but the primary mould is rarely recast; however worn or defaced, it retains the original image and superscription still.

Therefore, however long she may live to modify or expand them, Lucy Fletcher is never likely to think much different from these "Thoughts," which but echo those of hundreds of the "other girls" to whom her preface refers.

"THOUGHTS.

"My thoughts, in silence and alone,
Fronted the mystery unknown,
The meaning of our life;
The curse upon its poverty,
The wealth that brings satiety,
Dull peace, and barren strife.

"Base aims achieved, high aims that fail,
Evil that doth o'er good prevail,
Good lost that might have been;
The narrow path we dare to tread,
With all the infinite outspread,
And all that could be, seen.

"The unsolved problems that we touch
At every word, not pondered much,
Because they lie so near;
The path unknown that we must tread,
The awful mystery of the dead,
That rounds life's wondrous sphere.

"The light behind the veil unseen,
Our only clue what once hath been,—
Dark seems life's mystery;
I can not know, I dare not guess;
The greater is not in the less,
Nor God's high will in me.

"O Thou, the Infinite, Allwise,
Solve Thou for me these mysteries,
Or teach me wiser thought;
I can not see, but thou art light;
I err, but Thou canst guide aright—
By Thee I would be taught.

"Incomprehensible Thy love,
All flights of our weak thought above;
So too Thy life is high.
Make Thou our life a part of Thine,
Till in its unity divine,
To Thee we live and die.

"Content to go where Thou dost choose,
To be what Thou dost need to use,
To follow or be still,
And learn the infinite content
Of one whose yielded heart is bent,
Unto Thy loving will."

This poem, which, without striking original merit, is exceeding complete, gives a fair idea of the whole book. There we find a clear, broad, pellucid picture of a girl's life—a loving, simple, thoughtful English girl, with a keen eye for natural beauty, a strong sense of religion, a sound brain, conscience, and heart. All are as yet undeveloped; and yet there is no immaturity; the life is complete so far as it goes, and so is the book likewise. It has none of the daring originalities and imperfectnesses from which one can predict actual genius; no precocity of passion, no remarkable creative power. All is fresh and pure and still as a dewy meadow in the gray dawn of a midsummer morning. Take for instance these two pictures:

"A BUNCH OF HEATHER.

"I gathered purple heather upon the hill-side bare,
The while the bees unsettled buzzed round me in the air,
The finest on the moorlands, all that both hands could hold;
I bound it with the grasses which grow upon the wold.

"That sunny day of summer, the talk and merry speech,
The wonders we discovered, the seat beneath the beech,
Even the wood-birds singing, the light and shade which fell,
All, as I thought forgotten, I now remember well.

"For, on this very morning, I found the bunch again,
The flowers are browned and falling, scarce more than stems remain.
I cut the grass that held them, and when unloosed I found,
That all these by-gone memories were with the heather bound."

"MAY-TIME.

"It is a pleasant spot, the wind
Is hushed to silence, while behind
The screen of leaves which interlace,
In cool, sweet silence round the place,
Murmurs of far-off brook and bird
(Scarce noticed, and yet clearly heard),
Seem fitting voices to express
My spirit's dreamy happiness.

"The dusty road is far away;
Forgotten is each weary day;
The sweet leaves shade the distant view,
Yet fairer seems the tender blue
That glimmers downward, while to me
Even the future mystery,
Hid by the present, seems more dear,
And I can feel nor doubt, nor fear.

"Sometimes God sends this deepest rest;
Sometimes our spirits thus are blest
With perfect passionate content,
Wherein all love with trust is blent.
Sweet time, sweet thoughts, pass not away,
Or, if the sun forget my day,
May I remember how it shone,
And know it shaded, but not gone."

Nothing very wonderful here; nothing "to haunt, to startle, and waylay;" and yet how sweet it is! How completely it gives the portrait of the "girl"—a country girl—no town life could have produced such; with her eyes beaming thoughtfully from under her broad hat, and her busy, browned hands full of flowers. Not in the least sentimental or self-conscious, and yet in herself a perfect living poem—the best poem a man can read—a tender-hearted, high-thoughted maiden. A little dreamy, perhaps, but with dreams so innocent, pure, and true, that they strengthen rather than weaken her for the realities that are coming. Much she may have to suffer—nay, inevitably will—but we feel that she will suffer nobly, patiently, religiously, even thus:

"'AS ONE WHOM HIS MOTHER COMFORTETH.'

"I come, dear Lord, like a tired child, to creep
Unto Thy feet, and there awhile to sleep,
Weary, though not with a long, busy day,
But with the morning's sunshine and with play,

And with some tears that fell, although the while
They scarce were deep enough to drown a smile.

"There is no need of words for mine to tell
My heart to Thee; Thou needest not to spell,
As others must, my hidden thoughts and fears,
From out my broken words, my sobs, or tears;
Thou knowest all, knowest far more than I,
The inner meaning of each tear or sigh.

"Thou mayest smile, perchance, as mothers smile
On sobbing children, seeing all the while
How soon will pass away the endless grief,
How soon will come the gladness and relief;
But if Thou smilest, yet Thy sympathy
Measures my grief by what it is to me.

"And not the less Thy love doth understand,
And not the less, with tender pitying hand,
Thou wipest all my tears, and the sad face
Doth cherish to a smile in Thine embrace,
Until the pain is gone, and Thou dost say,
'Go now, my child, and work for Me to-day.'"

Hardly even dear old George Herbert could have taken a quainter, tenderer fancy, or worked it out with more delicate completeness. Indeed, one of the best qualities in our young rhymer—she would hardly wish to appropriate prematurely the high name of poet—is the care with which she finishes every thing. The chief blots upon her pages are horrible cockney rhymes, such as "born" and "dawn," and—oh, shame!—"bore" and "saw," with a few grammatical and even etymological errors, such as "thrawl" for thrall, which a more watchful press-revision of a girl's first book would easily have avoided. But her rhythm is smooth and musical; her power of expression clear; her style terse and Saxon; she neither overloads with imagery nor cumbers with unnecessary adjectives. Nor is she imitative, as are almost all young writers—the mere reflection of others whom they have read. Whatever her readings may have been—and a young girl can hardly read too much, imbibing other people's wisdom instead of prematurely forcing out her own—Miss Fletcher has fused them all in the alembic of her clear sensible brain, so that her verses come out with no perceptible flavor of Tennyson, the Brownings, or any other favorite idol who has influenced strongly the youthful minds of the age.

Another characteristic—which, among a certain set, will raise the book at once, as a gift-book, to the level of Cowper, Mrs. Hemans, and Martin Farquhar Tupper—there is not one word of love—that is, the passion of love—in it from beginning to end. Not a single outburst of rapture or despair; not a sonnet or a song which the most precise of Mrs. Ellises need hesitate at laying before the Daughters of England; who will think about such things in spite of Mrs. Ellis. But even with this peculiarity—which we name simply as a peculiarity, neither a merit nor the reverse—this book is true to itself. It comes, as it purports to come, out of a girl's life, the atmosphere of which is still cool and sweet and calm as that gray midsummer morning. Only towards its end do we catch a few arrowy rays struck upward by the unrisen sun—the sun of all human life—of which the Creator of all ordained, "Let there be light," and there was light.

Of Lucy Fletcher's career in the world of letters, we venture no prophecy whatever. Nothing in her book forbids future greatness, and nothing absolutely indicates it. On the whole, her graceful completeness rather implies that appreciative talent which observes more than it creates, and which is just under, not over, the mysterious line which marks the boundary between talent and genius. But of this, time only can decide. Whether she ever writes another book or not, this book is one which it is good for her to have written, and (stranger still) good to have published. For it is a true book—a real book, aiming at nothing higher than it achieves. It can harm and offend none; it will please and benefit very many. There is nothing morbid in it—nothing forced or factitious. Fantastic melancholy, egotistic introversion, metaphysical or melo-dramatic plumbing of the black depths of human crime and woe, are altogether foreign to this Lucy Fletcher. Hers is a healthy, happy nature, and her book is a healthy, happy book. As she says herself:

"SINGING.

"I sing my heart out for the gladness in it,
 As less a poet than a happy bird,
Singing, because I must sing, as the linnet,
 Unthinking by what ears my song is heard;
While evermore the love which doth begin it,
 To fuller gladness by the song is stirred.

"The secret of the song, the love which ever,
  Within, without, enfoldeth me in rest;
Love sings my song first, and my one endeavor
  Is but to learn the notes she chanteth best;
'Tis not my song I sing, ah! never, never,
  But love's, who lulls me gently on her breast.

"So sing I, being moved thereto unwitting
  Aught but dear love, the sun of my heart's spring,
And seeking only to find words befitting
  The music vibrating on every string;
No poet I among earth's crowned ones sitting,
  I love and I am loved, and therefore sing."

And long may she go on singing! unless her own contented heart teaches her a better song than all—silence.

CLOTHES.

MY sight not being so good as it was, my granddaughter is in the habit of reading the *Times* aloud to me daily. Possibly, this is not always a labor of love, I being a rather fidgety listener, though I trust not one of those conceited old persons who consider that to minister unto them is to the young a privilege invaluable. There have been times when, perceiving Netty's bright eye wander, and her voice drop into a monotonous absent tone, I have inly sighed over those inevitable infirmities which render each generation in its turn dependent on the succeeding one; times when it would have been easier to me to get up a peevish "There, that will do," and forfeit my own undeniable pleasure, than thus to make a martyr of my little girl. But then, few can have lived to my length of days without being taught the blessedness that lies not only in labors of love, but labors of duty; and I am glad, even at the cost of some personal pain, to see my grandchild learning this lesson; conquering her natural laziness, accommodating the frivolous tastes of youth to the prosy likings of old age, and acquiring, even in so small a thing as the reading of a newspaper, that habit of self-control and self-abnegation which we women have to practise, voluntarily or involuntarily, to the end of our lives.

So, after going steadily through the leading articles—(by the way, what a curious fact of modern intellectual advance is that page of *Times* leaders, thought out with infinite labor, compiled with surpassing skill, influencing the whole world's destinies one day, to become the next mere waste paper)—after this I said to Netty, "Now, my dear, I leave the choice to you; read any thing that you consider amusing."

"Amusing!" As if she doubted whether any thing in the *Times* could come under that head. But shortly her countenance cleared. "'An American Bridal Trousseau,' —will that do, Grannie, dear?"

I nodded, and she began to read.

"'Extraordinary Marriage Ceremony. Cuban Don—Young Lady of New York. Will no doubt amuse English Ladies.'

"Why, I declare, it's a list of her clothes! And such a quantity; only hear:

"'One blue silk, ruffled to the waist; one green and white double skirt, trimmed with black lace; one light blue silk chintz, flowers down the skirt, trimmed with deep fringe to match; one steel-colored silk, with purple velvet flowers, trimmed with wide bands of purple velvet, edged with black lace; a surplus waist trimmed to match the skirt; one Swiss dress, the skirt formed with clusters of ruffles and tucks, the waist to match; one white Swiss muslin dress, five flounces, edged with narrow Valenciennes lace; one white Swiss dress skirt, with three flounces, three ruffles on each flounce, pink ribbon underneath; one Swiss dress tucked to the waist; six dresses of poplin, merino, and Ottoman velvet;'"

"Stop, stop! let us take breath, child. Poplin, merino, Ottoman velvet; and how many more was it? Swiss muslin, silk chintz, and something with a 'surplus waist,' whatever that may be."

"Indeed, I don't know, Grandmamma," laughed the child; "though you do think me such an extravagant young lady. Not so bad as this one, any how. Just listen:

"'Eighteen street dresses, of rich, plain, and figured silks, double skirt and two flounces; also moiré antique, made in the newest and most fashionable style; twelve afternoon dresses, consisting of grenadines, organdies and tissue, all varied in styles of making; twelve evening dresses, one pink embossed velvet, trimmed with the richest point de Vénise; one white silk tunic dress, skirt embroidered and trimmed with blonde lace; one pearl-colored silk, double skirt, with bouquets of embossed velvet; three white crape dresses, ornamented with bunches of raised flowers; three white tulle dresses, with colored polka spots of floss silk, to be worn over white silk skirts; six dinner dresses, one white silk embroidered with gold; one pink moiré antique, very elegant side stripes; one blue silk, with lace flounces; one amber silk, with black lace tunic dress; one black moiré antique, trimmed with velvet and lace; one white moiré antique, with puffings of illusion, and the sleeves made in Princess Clothilde style; twelve muslin dresses, made with flounces and simple ruffles;'"

"That's a mercy, girl. I began to think the only 'simple' article the lady possessed was her husband."

"Grandmamma; how funny you are! Well, will you hear to the end?"

"Certainly. One is not often blessed with such valuable and extensive information. Besides, my dear, it may be of use to you when the Prince comes."

(This is the name by which we have always been accustomed to talk openly of Netty's possible, doubtless *she* thinks certain, lover and husband. Consequently, to no ignorant lady's-maid or silly young playfellow, but to her sage old grandmother, has my child confided her ideas and intentions on this important subject, including the imaginary portrait, physical and mental, of "the Prince," what she expects of him, and what she means to be towards him. Also, in no small degree, what they are both to be towards their revered grandmamma. Poor little Netty, she little knows how seldom is any dream fulfilled! Yet, if never any more than a dream, better a pure than a base, a high than a low, a wise than a foolish one.)

"When the Prince comes," said the little maid, drawing herself up with all the dignity of sixteen; "I hope I shall think a great deal more of him than of my wedding, and that he will think more of me than of my wedding-clothes."

"Very well, my dear, I trust the same. Now, go on reading."

She did so; and I here cut it out of the newspaper entire, lengthy as the paragraph is, to prove that I have not garbled a line; that I do "nothing extenuate, nor aught set down in malice," with regard to this young American bride, whose name is not given, and of whom I know nothing whatever:

"Three riding habits, one black Canton crape, trimmed with velvet buttons; one green merino, English style; one black cloth, trimmed with velvet; three opera cloaks, one white merino, double cape, elegantly embroidered and trimmed with rich tassels; one white cashmere, trimmed with blue and white plaid plush; one grenadine, with ribbon quilling; twenty-four pairs of varied colored satin slippers, richly embroidered; twelve pairs of white satin and kid slippers, plain; twelve pairs of white satin and kid slippers, trimmed with ribbon; six pairs of mouse-embroidered slippers, one pair of kid India mouse, embroidered; one green and gray chenille, embroidered; one purple and black silk, embroidered; two pairs of brown Morocco plain French, all made *à la Turque;* six pairs of slippers, variously embroidered in various colors for the toilette; twelve pairs of silk and satin Français, dress, habit, and walking gaiters; six pairs of walking and winter gaiters, double soles; six street bonnets, made of the most *recherché* Swiss straws, trimmed with handsome ribbon; one opera bonnet, made of white lace and long fancy marabout feathers; one black and white royal velvet bonnet, trimmed with cluster of pink roses, intermingled with black velvet leaves; six rich head-dresses, consisting of chenille, pearl and gold, and other rich materials; six sets of hair-pins, of coral, turquoise, pearl, and gold ornaments; six brettel capes of white tulle, trimmed in various styles of fancy velvet chenille and ribbon; one Bruxelles point appliqué cape, trimmed with puffings of illusion and ribbon; one dozen of French embroidered handkerchiefs, with initials richly embroidered in the corner; one dozen of real point lace handkerchiefs; one dozen of guipure lace handkerchiefs; one dozen of pine-apple handkerchiefs, embroidered and trimmed with lace: one dozen of fancy illusion sleeves for evening dresses, made flowing *à la favorite;* two dozens of glove-tops to match sleeves; one pair of glove-tops of point d'Alençon, trimmed with orange blossoms; six sets of fancy wristlets, made of velvet and laces; six French parasols, made of the most magnificent embossed velvet, with rich Chinoise carved handles; also three coquette parasols, simple and elegant; twelve pairs of open-worked and embroidered China silk hose; twenty-four pairs plain silk hose; twelve pairs Balmoral hose; twelve pairs of Paris thread hose, open-worked; twelve pairs of Paris thread hose, plain; twenty-four pairs of rich French embroidered elastics; twelve pairs of China silk under-vests; twelve dozens of French kid gloves of various colors; twelve pairs of gauntlets: buckskin and kid; twelve pairs of travelling gloves, gauntlet tops. The trousseau lace dress was the exact pattern of that used by the Princess Clothilde at the selection of the Empress Eugénie, having been reproduced in Europe expressly for this occasion. The lace is point plat, point aiguille, Chantilly, and Brussels—in fact, a combination of the most valuable lace known. Among the handkerchiefs were two of point d'Alençon lace, valued at 200 dollars each, and one Valenciennes, worth 250 dollars, the richest ever imported."

Ending, my granddaughter regarded me with a puzzled air—"Well?"

"Well, my dear?"

"Grandmamma, what do you think about it all?"

"I was thinking what a contrast all these gowns are to the one the lady must some day, may any day, put on—plain white, 'frilled,' probably, but still plain enough; since after her first dressing, or rather being dressed, in it, no one will ever care to look at it or her any more."

Netty started—"Grandmamma, you don't mean a *shroud?*"

"Why not, child?—since, with all our fine clothes, we shall all require a shroud some time."

"But it is so dreadful to think of."

"Not when one approaches as near to the time of wearing it as I do. Nor, at any age, is it half so dreadful to think of one's own body, or of any fair body one loves wrapped up in this garment,—as I wrapped your mother up, my Netty, when you were still a baby,—as to think of it decked out like that young creature whose 'trousseau' forms a feature in the public newspapers. She apparently comes to her husband so buried in 'clothes' that he must feel, poor man, as if he had married a walking linen-draper's shop instead of a flesh and blood woman, with a heart and a brain, a sweet human form, and a responsible immortal soul. Ask yourself, would you wish to be so married, Netty, my dear?"

A toss of the curls, a flash of the indignant young eyes—

"Grannie, I'd rather be married like—like—Patient Griseldis!"

Suggesting that, taken out of the region of romance into common practical life, Griseldis's costume might be, to say the least of it, rather chilly—I nevertheless cordially agreed with my little girl. And I half sighed, remembering what was said to me about forty years ago, when I came, with only three gowns, one on and two off, a moderate store of linen, and five golden guineas in my pocket, to the tender arms that would have taken me without a rag in my trunk, or a penny in my purse—ay, and been proud of it too! I did not tell Netty her grandfather's exact words;—but when she questioned, I gave her a full description of the costume in which I walked down the aisle of that village church with young Doctor Waterhouse—my dear husband who was then,—and is now, though his tablet has been in the said church aisle for twenty-two years.

When Netty was gone to her music-lesson, I sat thinking. You young folks hardly know how much we old folks enjoy thinking; the mere act of running over mentally times, places, people, and things—moralizing upon past, present, and future, and evolving out of this undisturbed quietude of meditation that wisdom which is supposed to be the peculiar quality of age. May I be allowed to take it for granted, therefore, that I am a little wiser than my neighbors, if only because I have more opportunity than they to ponder over what comes into my head during the long solitudes that any age may have, but old age must have? A solitude that ripens thought, smooths down prejudice, disposes to kindness and charity, and, I trust, gradually brings the individual nearer to that wide-eyed calm of vision with which, we believe, we shall all one day behold all things.

I could not get her out of my head—this New York

belle, with her innumerable quantity of clothes. For, disguise them as you will into "dresses," "costumes," "toilettes," they all resolve themselves into mere "clothes"—used for the covering and convenience of this perishable machine of bone, muscle, sinew, and flesh—the temporary habitation of that "ego"—the true "me" of us all. One is tempted to inquire, viewing with the mind's eye such a mountain of millinery, what had become of this infinitesimal "me"—the real woman whom the Cuban gentleman married? That is, if it were not crushed altogether out of identity by this fearful superincumbent weight—the weight—vide *Times*—of 16,400 dollars' worth of clothes?

The result of my thoughts is, if an old woman may speak her mind, rather serious: on this as well as the other side of the Atlantic. For, not to lay the whole burden on our Yankee sister—poor girl, how do I know that she may not be at heart as innocent a child as my Netty?—here is a paragraph I cut out of another paper—headed—"*Dress at Compiègne.*"

"Four toilettes a day are about the general requirement, though there are days when only three are necessary; the invitations are for eight days, and no lady is expected ever to be seen twice wearing the same gown. Count up this, and you will find an average of thirty-two toilettes to be carried to the Court. Suppose a female *invitée* to have a daughter or two with her, you come at once to ninety or ninety-six dresses! Now, the average of these gowns will be 250 francs (£10), and you reach for each person the figure of £300 or £320; if two persons, £640; if three, £960."

And all for one week's clothes!!

Far be it from me to undervalue dress. I am neither Quaker, Puritan, nor devotee. I think there is not a straw to choose between the monk of old, whose washing-days occurred about twice a lifetime, and the modern "saint," who imagines he glorifies God by means of a ragged shirt and a dirty pocket-handkerchief; they are both equal, and equal fools. Scarcely less so is the "religious" woman who makes it a matter of conscience to hide or neutralize every physical beauty with which Nature has endowed her; as if He, who "so clothes the grass of the field" that even the meanest forms of his handiwork are lovely beyond all our poor imitating, were displeased at our delighting ourselves in that wherein He must delight continually. As if "Nature" and "grace" were two opposite attributes, and there could be any beauty in this world which did not proceed direct from God.

No; beauty is a blessing; and every thing that innocently adds thereto is a blessing likewise, otherwise we should never have advanced from fig-leaves and beasts' skins to that harmony of form and color which we call good "dress," particularly as applied to women. From the peach-cheeked baby, smiling from behind her clouds of cambric, or her swansdown and Cashmere—fair as a rose-bud "with all its sweetest leaves yet folded"—to that picturesque old lady with her silver-gray or rich black silks, her delicate laces and her snowy lawns—there is nothing more charming, more satisfactory to eye and heart than a well-dressed woman. Or man either. We need not revive the satire of Sartor Resartus, to picture what a ridiculous figure some of our honorable and dignified friends would cut on solemn occasions, such as a Lord Mayor's Show, a University procession, or a royal opening of Parliament, if condemned to strut therein after the fashion of their ancestors, simply and airily attired in a wolf-skin, a blanket, or a little woad and red ochre, and a necklace of beads. We are quite convinced of the immense advantages of clothes.

No; whatever Netty may think when I check her occasional outbursts of linen-drapery splendor, I do not undervalue dress; either in theory or practice; nor, to the latest hour of conscious volition, shall she ever see her grandmother looking one whit uglier than old age compels me to look. But every virtue may be exaggerated into a vice; and I often think the ever-increasing luxury of this century is carrying to a dangerous extreme a woman's right of making herself charming by means of self-adornment.

First, it seems to me that the variety exacted by fashion is a great evil. Formerly, our ancestresses used to dress richly, handsomely; but it was in a solid, useful style of handsomeness. Gowns were not made for a month or a year; they were meant to last half a lifetime, or, perhaps, two lifetimes; for they frequently descended from mother to daughter. The stuffs which composed them were correspondingly substantial; I have a fragment of my grandmother's wedding-dress—stripes of pale satin and white velvet, with painted flowers — which might have gone through every generation from her to Netty without being worn out. This permanence of costume, both as to form and material, besides saving a world of time and trouble, must have given a certain solidity to female tastes very different from the love of flimsy change which is necessarily caused by the ever-shifting fashions and showy cheapnesses of our day. I may have an old woman's prejudice in favor of the grave rather than the gay; but Netty never takes me with her to choose her "summer dresses," that amidst all the glittering display I do not heave a sigh for the rich dark satins of my youth, that "stood alone," as dressmakers say—fell into folds, like a picture; and from month to month, and year to year, were never taken out of the drawer without seeming to dart from every inch of their glossy surface the faithful smile of an old friend—"Here I am, just as good as ever; you *can't* wear me out."

Looking the other day at the exquisite architecture, without as within, of Westminster Abbey, and thinking what infinite pains must have been bestowed upon even every square yard, I could not but contrast that century-grown grand old building, in which each builder, founder, or workman was content to execute his small fragment, add it to the slowly-advancing magnificent whole, and, unnoted, perish;—I could not, I say, help contrasting this with the Sydenham glass palace, the wonder of our modern day; but fifty years hence, where will it be? No less the difference between those queenly costumes made permanent on canvas or in illuminated missals—rich, sweeping, majestic; conveying, not the impression of a gown with a woman inside it, or a woman used as a peg whereon to hang a variety of gowns, but a woman whose gown becomes a portion of herself—a half invisible yet important adjunct of her own grace, sweetness, or dignity, though it would never strike one to criticise it as fashionable or unfashionable; certainly never to ask the address of her mantua-maker.

And this, it appears to me, is the limit at which expensive dress becomes, in every rank and degree, first a folly and then a sin—namely, when the woman is absorbed in, and secondary to, the clothes. When the planning of them, the deciding about them, and the varying them, occupy so much of her time or attention that dress assumes an importance *per se*, and she consequently, in all circumstances and societies, is taught to think less of what she is than of how she is attired. This, without distinction of station or wealth; for the maid-servant, sitting up of nights to put a flounce to her barège gown, or stick artificial flowers under her tiny bonnet, is just as culpable as the Empress Eugénie wearing, and exacting of her guests, four new *toilettes* per diem. And equally does one grieve to contemplate the American belle taking out of her youthful love-dreamings, or her solemn meditations on the state which, as *Juliet* says,

"Well thou knowest, is full of cross and sin,"

the time required merely to choose and order those fourscore dresses, which, granted that she is rich enough to afford them, she can never possibly wear out before fashion changes. Lucky will be her lady's-maid, or maids, for she must require as many "dressers" as a royal personage; and lucky the New York buyers of cast-off garments for years to come.

Then—the packing! Even should the "Cuban don" travel in the style of a hidalgo, he can not fail to be occasionally encumbered by the multiplicity of boxes which accompany his fair lady. And arrived at home—if he may hope for such a word—will it not take an entire suite of rooms in which to stow away that fearful amount of finery? "My love," we can imagine the poor gentleman saying, when fairly distracted by the goodly array, "get rid of it anywhere you like: I don't care; I married *you*, and not your clothes."

A sentiment not uncommon to the male species. If women who are supposed to dress to please this sex did but know how much valuable exertion in that line is entirely thrown away upon them—how little they care for "white tulle with colored polka spots"—"moiré antique with puffings of illusion,"—a poor illusion, indeed,—and how indifferent they are to the respective merits of "*point plat*," "*point aiguille*," Brussels and Valenciennes! Even in his most rapturous moment of admiration, a man is sure to say, generalizing, "How lovely you look!" never, "What a sweet pretty dress you have on!"—The *tout ensemble* is all he notices. Most likely, he will approve more of your neat gingham or snowy muslin—or perhaps your rich dark silk with a bright ribbon that catches his eye and pleases his sense of color, than he will for your *toilette* most "*soignée*," with all its extravagance of trimmings and ornaments. Especially if he sees upon you that ornament which all the milliners can not sell, nor all the beauties buy—"a meek and quiet spirit," which is, in the sight not only of God but man, "of great price."

"My poor New York bride," moralized I; "I wonder if, among your innumerable ornaments, you have ever dreamed of counting *that!*"

Viewed in this mood, the clothes question becomes a serious thing. It is not merely whether or no a lady is justified in spending so much money upon dress alone—or even the corresponding point, whether or no such ultra expense on costume be good for trade. It becomes less a social and political than a moral question. Even though this extravagant personal luxury be temporarily beneficial to commerce, to countenance it is most assuredly doing evil that good may come; injuring fatally the aggregate morals of a country, and lowering its standard of ideal right—the first step in its decadence and ultimate degradation. For what sort of men and women are likely to grow up from the children of a generation which has its pocket-handkerchiefs of "point d'Alençon, valued at 200 dollars each, and Valenciennes, worth 250 dollars—the richest ever imported?" Oh, my sisters over the water, these were not the sort of brides who became Cornelias, Volumnias, and mothers of the Gracchi!

Perhaps there was some foundation in the cry set up and laughed down, a while ago, that the terrible commercial crisis of 1857 was caused by the extravagance of women's dress, especially American women. Even with us here, many prudent, practical young fellows, not too deeply smitten to feel "all for love, and the world well lost," yet secretly craving for home, and its comforts and respectabilities, and acute enough to see that a bachelor is never worth half so much, either to himself, society, or the State, as a man who is married and settled, may yet often be deterred from that salutary duty by—what? A vague dread of their wives' clothes.

Not quite without reason. No wonder that when he comes home from the blaze of an evening party to his Temple chambers or the snug solitudes of his Fellow's den, the worthy gentleman shivers inwardly at the idea of converting himself into a modern Orestes, haunted by winged

Eumenides of milliners' bills—of having a large proportion of his hard-earned family income frittered away in "loves of laces," "exquisite ribbons," and all the fantasies of female dress which a man's more solid taste generally sets down at once as "rubbish." In which, not seldom, he is quite correct.

Women's modern propensities in this line might advantageously be restrained. It is frequently not the dress which costs so much as its extras; which rarely add to the effect, but often quite destroy that classic breadth and unity which, to my old-fashioned eyes, is one of the greatest charms in any costume. It is astonishing how much may be saved in the course of a year by this simple rule—never buy trimmings.

I have one more word to say, and then I have done.

A woman should always remember that her clothes should be in expense and quantity proportioned to her own circumstances, and not those of her neighbor. The mingling of classes is good—that is, the frequent association of those persons who in effect form one and the same class, being alike in tastes, sympathies, moral purpose, and mental calibre—however various be their degrees of annual income, worldly station, profession, trade, or unemployed leisure. Provided always that the one meeting-point, which likewise can alone be the fair point of rivalry, lies in themselves and not their externals. How can I, who have but £200 a year, dress like my friend Mrs. Jones, who has £2000?—but is that any reason why I, who am, I hope, as true a gentlewoman as she is, should eschew her very pleasant society, or, out of mere cowardice, ruin myself by mimicking her in the matter of clothes? Nothing is so fatal as the ever-increasing habit that I notice, of each class dressing, or attempting to dress, in a style equal to the class above it—the maid imitating her mistress, the young shop-girl the woman of fortune, and so on. Even mothers of families one sees continually falling into this error, and wearing gowns, shawls, etc., that must of necessity have pinched the family income for many a day. My dear ladies, will you not see that a good daily joint of meat on your table is far more conducive to the health and happiness of those sitting round it, than the handsomest silk gown placed at the head of it? that a good, well-paid domestic servant (and you can not expect a good one unless well paid) is of more worth to you and yours, in absolute comfort, than the very grandest of milliners or dressmakers?

I have lived long, my dears, and worn out a considerable quantity of linen-drapery in my time; but I can fearlessly assert that, at every age—as a young girl at home, a matron in her own house, and an old lady free to spend her income in her own way,—the one economy which I have always found safest to practise, as being least harmful to one's self, and least annoying to other people, was—"clothes." And I shall try, if possible, to teach it to my granddaughter. Not that mean economy which hides poor materials by a tawdry "making-up"—disguising cheap silks, coarse linen, and flimsy muslin by a quantity of false lace, sham jewelry, dirty ribbons, and *un*-natural flowers,—but that quiet independence with which, believing that the woman herself is superior to any thing she wears, we just wear fearlessly what suits our taste and our pocket; paying a due regard to colors, fashions, freshness, and cleanliness; but never vexing ourselves about immaterial items, and as happy in a dress of last year's fashion as if we had at command the whole establishment of the renowned Jane Clarke, who, they say—but for the credit of womanhood I hope it is untrue,—ordered herself to be buried in a point-lace shroud.

Ay, as I reminded my little Netty—we must all come to this last garment. To an old woman—who never will put off her black gown except for that white one,—the matter of clothes seems often a very trivial thing, hardly worth, indeed, the prosy dissertation I have been led to give upon it. Let us only so clothe ourselves, that this frail body of ours, while it does last, may not be unpleasing in the sight of those who love us; and let us so use it in this life that in the life to come it may be found worthy to be "clothed upon" with its Maker's own glorious immortality.

THE

HISTORY OF A HOSPITAL.*

"Inasmuch as ye have done it unto the least of all these little ones, ye have done it unto Me."

THOUGH this article is headed with a text, it is by no means meant as a sermon, least of all a charity sermon; being simply a record and statement of facts, which, in their sharp unvarnished outline, preach their own homily. It is intended to give, without any embellishment of fancy or glamour of sentimental emotion, the history of a hospital, of sufficiently recent date to make that chronicle possible, credible, and capable of proof, by any who will take the trouble of investigation.

Previously, however, let a word be said about hospitals in general. Many persons are in the habit of viewing them solely as charities, which is a great mistake. Charitable purposes they undoubtedly fulfill to the individual, but they are of equal importance to the community at large. Would that every wealthy sufferer, lying in as much ease as can be given him on his restless bed, knew how much he owes of relief—possibly even life—to the skill and experience learned at those forlorn hospital beds, where all the mysterious laws of disease are carefully studied, worked out into theories, and tested by incessant observation of cause and result, on a scale much wider, more complete and satisfactory, than any private practice could ever supply! Would that all of us, who at some time or other, either for ourselves or those dearer than ourselves, have known what it was to live upon every look of "the doctor"—to recognize him as the one human being who is all-important to us, on whose talent, decision, caution, tenderness, hangs every thing most precious to us

* This paper—like "Meadowside House"—was written years ago, and by no means indicates the present improved and extended condition of the hospital.

in this world—would that all could understand how much of that which makes him what he is, has been gained within those long dreary ranges of many-windowed walls, dedicated to physical suffering, and consecrated by its hopeful and merciful alleviation!

The hospital now to be written of has remarkably few of the painful characteristics of its class, as will be shortly shown. First, we have to do with its history, beginning from the very beginning.

On the 30th of January, 1850, nine gentlemen, two of whom were of the medical profession, met to consider whether it was not possible to establish in London a Hospital for Sick Children. They believed that, besides the great benefit of such an institution to a class which could with difficulty find admission to ordinary hospitals, it would supply a desideratum long wanted in London, though well provided for in foreign cities—namely, an opportunity for studying infantile diseases. These—every mother and nurse knows, or ought to know—are so sudden, so fluctuating and mysterious in their nature, so difficult of diagnosis and treatment, and often so fearfully rapid in their fatality, that they furnish a distinct branch of medical science, the importance of which can hardly be sufficiently recognized. For people forget that on the health of the growing-up generation hangs that of generations more; also that it is not merely the alternative between life and death, but between wholesome, happy, enjoyable life, and the innumerable forms of death in life, which an unhealthy or neglected childhood entails upon the innocent sufferers to the end of their days.

These nine gentlemen, deeply conscious of this fact, and anxiously desirous to remedy it, prepared an appeal, which, appendixed by letters from various eminent physicians, should, it was agreed, be disseminated as widely as possible. Afterwards, to satisfy inquiries and answer objections, a second meeting was held, and a second appeal prepared. This, signed by several well-known members of the medical profession, was forwarded to all their brethren in town or country.

For a whole year they labored silently; laying carefully the foundation-work of their plan by observation and inquiry in all directions, at home and abroad—one of their number spending some time in investigating similar hospitals in foreign cities. At length the result of all this came to light in a public meeting, which was held on March 19, 1851; Lord Shaftesbury—then Lord Ashley—being chairman.

Within a fortnight afterwards the committee found and took a large old-fashioned house in Great Ormond Street—once the residence of the notable Dr. Meade. But "festina lente" was still their wise maxim; and it was eleven months more before the Hospital for Sick Children was definitely opened, to admit—one little girl!

> "She was the first that ever burst
> Upon that unknown sea,"

across which so many frail little vessels were afterwards to be safely piloted. Poor little girl! Her name, and what became of her, history chronicleth not. Imagination might paint the forlorn wee face in its neat bed, sole occupant of the magnificent room which beauties swam through, and gallants danced through, in the old days when Bloomsbury was the fashionable part of London. But, as we said, we do not mean to deal either with the poetical or the picturesque.

After this, many influential people took up the children's cause. Charles Dickens—brilliant as large-hearted—advocated it by tongue and pen; the Bishop of London and Lord Carlisle said many a good word for it. Little money was gained thereby, but much sympathy and kind encouragement; also the best impetus that can be given to a really good cause, aware of its own value,—publicity. By-and-by the first annual report appeared, announcing as patroness of the Children's Hospital the highest mother in the realm, and then definitely stating its objects. These were: "1. The medical and surgical treatment of poor children. 2. The attainment and diffusion of knowledge regarding the diseases of children. 3. The training of nurses for children."

It is a notable report, inasmuch as it so frankly states the imperfections and difficulties of the scheme.

> "At first it seemed as if a Children's Hospital were not needed; for so few were the applicants, that during the first month only twenty-four were brought as out-patients, and only eight received as in-patients. The hospital had its character to make among the poor. Before long, greater numbers of children were brought as out-patients, but their mothers often re-

fused to let them be taken into the hospital; and only by degrees learned to place full confidence in its management, and to believe that those who asked for their suffering little ones were indeed to be trusted with so precious a deposit.

This answers an objection that has been urged against children's hospitals, infant schools, public nurseries, and the like; namely, that the mother is the only and best guardian of the child, in sickness and in health. Undoubtedly, when such care is possible. But a sick child in a rich man's well-ordered, comfortable nursery, or even in an ordinary middle-class house, is in very different circumstances from a sick child in a poor man's one room—inhabited by other children and adults—full of noise, confusion, and dirt, with perhaps a drunken father, or a mother so worn with want, and passive with misery, that, "if it please God to take it, poor lamb!" seems rather a desirable possibility than not. There can be no question that the quiet clean ward of a hospital, with a good skilled nurse, instead of a broken-down, ignorant, or careless mother, is a good exchange—under the circumstances; and in that, as in many other conjunctures of human life, we have to judge, not by possibilities, but actual circumstances—to choose, alas! not an unattainable good, but the least of two evils.

Year by year the history of the hospital progresses. Out-patients increase enormously: in-patients are still limited by the want of sufficient funds. Nevertheless, as the list of subscribers swells, and one or two legacies fall in, the number of tiny beds is added to by twos and threes. We notice another prudent peculiarity, only too rare, viz., that the official staff is kept down to the lowest limit conducive to the proper working of the charity. Reading over the items of expenditure in the yearly reports, it is plain to see that not a shilling has been spent unnecessarily.

The cause becomes gradually more known. Among the list of donors we begin to find more than one touching line, such as "A Thanksgiving," "Thank-offering for the recovery of sick children;" rich parents who have secretly poured out their full hearts in that best of gratitude to the heavenly Father—the helping of His suffering poor, whom we "have always with us." And even the poor themselves go not away thankless; for we find in the report for 1856 that a "Samaritan Fund" is started, to provide destitute children with clothing on quitting the hospital, and that this fund has been

"almost entirely supported by the spontaneous bounty of the friends of the out-patients. Boxes have been placed in the out-patients' waiting-room, and the poor frequenting it have shown their sense of the value of the hospital by their unsolicited contributions. Since the formation of the fund in May, the average weekly receipts have exceeded seventeen shillings—a large sum, when we call to mind the great distress that the present cost of provisions has inflicted upon the poorer classes."

Slowly and steadily affairs brighten. At one time, when the capital of the charity was reduced to £1000, a festival, at which Mr. Charles Dickens made one of his beautiful and touching speeches, produced the sum of £2850, out of which £500 came from an "anonymous benefactress."

Still the committee maintain their prudent carefulness. They

"beg to assure subscribers that they have no desire, even if they had the means, to erect a splendid edifice enriched with architectural adornments; for the present site would furnish, at no great expense, all that they desire for the full realization of their plan of forming a hospital with one hundred beds for sick children."

And in the following year they see their way towards purchasing the adjoining house and garden, making a communication between. This enables them to establish a convalescent-room, so that those recovering may no longer disturb the patients really sick; and a separate room for the nurses, where they can take their meals, and enjoy a little of that indispensable pause in their labors, without which the strongest and tenderest woman becomes worn out at last.

More space, also, allows the committee to carry out their third intent—the training of young women as sick nurses; to whom they offer a home within the hospital, at a charge of six shillings per week for board and lodging. And the ground-floor of the new house is converted into an infant nursery, after the pattern of the Paris "*crèches*," where the poor working mother, who is obliged to leave her child during the day, may leave it in safety and comfort, sure that it will be well fed, warmed, and tended, for the small payment of from twopence to fourpence a day according to age and diet. This also is to be a training school for young girls as nursery-maids; the committee feeling that, "to show how children should be treated in order to keep them in good health, is hardly alien to the main purpose of the institution—the restoring of them when sick."

The year 1860 records a further step in the usefulness of the hospital—the delivery, by its physician and surgeon, of gratis lectures on the diseases of children. These were attended by more than a hundred of the medical profession, and have been repeated since. And now comes the ninth and latest annual report. By it we find that the idea originated by that handful of kind-hearted gentlemen has developed itself into an established charity: not wealthy, indeed, but able to keep its head afloat among the innumerable other charities of the metropolis. Its example has been followed: similar hospitals for sick children have been started in the provinces, and in the city of Edinburgh especially. Meantime, the parent institution is able to provide fifty-two beds, which are only too constantly filled, for in-patients, and medical care for 10,000 out-patients, yearly. Out of its Samaritan Fund of £91 18*s.* 1*d.*, it has clothed within the year 127 children, besides sending others to Brighton, and to Mitcham, in Surrey, where homes are provided for the poor little convalescents, who otherwise must vanish into noisome streets and crowded alleys, where their frail spark of renewed health would soon be totally extinguished. On the whole the committee feel and acknowledge that they are a successful institution.

Now success is a curious thing. Unsuccessful people do not believe in it; they attribute it to "chance," or "luck," or "circumstances." Yet, since "there can be no effects without a cause," surely if a man, or an undertaking, fails repeatedly and hopelessly, may it not be just possible that there is some hidden cause for the same? Probably, a fault—possibly, only a misfortune; but still some tangible reason which accounts for failure. And, on the other hand, if a man or his doings are successful, is it not common sense, as well as common charity, to admit that he may deserve to succeed? There is no injustice, but inevitable necessity, in the Parable of the Talents. The solemn sentence, "From him that hath little shall be taken away even that which he seemeth to have," is paralleled by the equally solemn truth, "Unto whom much is given, of him much shall be required." This hospital, which had lived through so much difficulty into a time of comparative success, seemed worth going a good way to see—and I did so. I dislike passing out of the impersonal third person into the intrusive and egotistical "I;" but it is the simplest way of stating what I saw, and what any lady can see for herself, if she chooses, at 49 Great Ormond Street, Bloomsbury. I went there on a certain dull December day, a day that will never be forgotten by the present generation; when all business was suspended, all shops closed, and churches opened; when every body looked sad, and spoke with bated breath, often with gushes of tears, of the royal widow whose two young sons were that day standing over their dear and noble father's open grave. But this is a subject impossible to write about. From the highest to the lowest, all England felt the grief which darkened last Christmas-tide as if it had been a personal family sorrow. The bells had ceased tolling, and in the heavy gray afternoon, people stood about in groups along the shut-up streets in a Sunday-like quietness, talking mostly of the honored dead who had by this hour been buried out of sight, and of "the poor Queen," and "the children," as if she had been every body's sister, and the children every body's children. It seemed a fitting day upon which to visit a house of sorrow, as a hospital must, more or less, always be.

Only a small proportion of the well-to-do and fortunate portion of society is likely ever to have seen the interior of a hospital: once seen, it is a sight burnt into memory for life. But the room which we entered, or rather the suite of rooms—which had been the drawing-rooms of those vanished nobilities who had once inhabited Great Ormond Street—was very unlike the ward of an ordinary hospital. It was rather like a spacious night-nursery, with neat little beds scattered about; warm, cheery fires, with a couch on each side the fireplace; and a few children lying or squatting about, or sitting up in their pallets, quietly playing with toys, reading books, doing bead-work. Some, too ill for either work or play, were stretched mournfully, yet peacefully, on their pillows—solitary, it is true, but without giving any impression of dreariness or forlornness. The rooms were airy, light, and warm; there was nothing whatever of the hospital feeling and hospital atmosphere.

Yet suffering is suffering—always painful to witness. I can not even now recall the impression given by those rows of tiny beds—neat and clean, nay, pretty, as they were,—each tenanted by a poor little face and form, wasted, often distorted, always unchildlike, and marked by every gradation of diseasedness rather than mere sickness—for there is a difference—I can not, I say, call to mind this picture, without the ever-recurring question, Why should such things be? But it is not our business to puzzle ourselves over the great mystery of evil, and why it exists at all; but to lessen it as much as lies in our power—which, by an equal mystery, it is continually put into our hearts, and wills, and capabilities to do. Who could doubt this when looking on those piteous wrecks of childhood, from which every trace of the beauty, charm, and sweetness of childhood was gone, yet the nurses were taking such motherly care of them; speaking so kindly, and soothing so patiently, though the latter was hardly required?

"How exceedingly good they all seem," we noticed—as, indeed, no one could help noticing, who was at all acquainted with the difficulty of managing sick children, their extreme restlessness, fretfulness, and general "naughtiness"—poor little lambs! who have not yet learned the hard lesson of maturity, endurance without end.

"It's curious, ma'am," replied the nurse, "but they almost always are good. The amount of pain some of 'em will bear is quite wonderful. And they lie so patient-like; we hardly ever have any crossness or whimpering. Maybe, it is partly because, considering the homes they come from, they find themselves so quiet and comfortable here. But, unless they're very bad, they scarcely ever cry. Poor little dears!"

There were tears in the woman's own eyes—God bless her! She, like one or two more of the establishment, had been there from its commencement. She was evidently a great favorite, and a most important person. Her little patients, we heard, when discharged cured, continually came back to see "Nurse," and the hospital; looking upon it as a pleasant, happy home, instead of a place to be shuddered at and avoided.

Another peculiarity I noticed as much as the patience of the children that the nurses seemed to have their hearts in their work. Without a single exception every official I saw connected with the place seemed to take a personal interest in it, and to work for love as well as necessity. No doubt this arises from the strong influence exerted by the heads of the hospital over all its employées, and from the care taken that all these employées should be women of character, and capability fitted for their duties. It seemed here exactly as it is in a household, where you can usually judge not only the servants by the masters, but the masters by their servants.

The little patients were all under twelve years of age, that being the limit allowed, though no doubt it is frequently transgressed by parents eager to get their children in. Without fear of discovery, too; for the small stunted creatures looked, nearly all of them, much below that age. Few were laboring under acute illness; the complaints seemed mostly chronic, the result of "poverty, hunger, and dirt," or of constitutional congenital malady, manifesting itself in the innumerable forms of bone and joint disease, ulcerations and abscesses, brain and lung disorders, and all the long train of ills for which apparently there is no remedy but death.

This fact struck me in appalling confirmation of a state of things which physiologists have lately begun to think of sufficient moment to be written of in books, considered in social meetings, and even adverted to in *Times* leaders—the weak state of health into which, in this age, all classes seem to be sinking. In the lowest class this condition of body is often combined with disease so radically and hopelessly confirmed, that its perpetuation becomes frightful to contemplate. Looking from bed to bed of these miserable little abortions of childhood, one was tempted to believe that it might be a merciful Providence which would sweep away of a sudden half the present generation, if by that, or any means, healthy fathers and mothers might be given to the next.

But this is a subject which involves so much, that I had better leave it alone, for wiser handling. One remedy, however, lies in the power of every man, still more of every woman—to alleviate this melancholy condition of things, by acquiring, and spreading so far as each one's influence extends, sanitary knowledge, and sanitary practice. Here, beyond its medical limits, the Children's Hospital necessarily works. It is impossible but that each patient, and each parent or friend that comes to visit the patient, should carry away, consciously or not, an idea or two on the subject of cleanliness, ventilation, tidiness, and *com-*

fort—that indescribable something which the working-classes so seldom strive for, not merely because they have not the money to get it—money does not necessarily bring it—but because they literally do not know what it is. It will probably take another century to make poor people understand what in the last century even rich people were atrociously ignorant of—that a breath of fresh air is not immediately fatal; that skins were made to be washed every day: that dust and dirt and foulness of all kinds carry with them as much deadly malaria as if you took so many grains of arsenic and administered the same to your household every morning.

But I am becoming discursive. Let us proceed to the boys' ward, which is on the second floor, above the girls', and precisely similar in size and arrangement. Here, too, are the same characteristics—long-standing diseases rather than accidental sicknesses; the same patient look on the wasted faces; the same atmosphere of exceeding but not dreary quietness. One boy, whose restless eyes seemed to follow us more than the rest, I stopped and spoke to, asking if he were comfortable?

"Oh, yes, quite; but I am strange here. I only came in on Saturday."

And there was a choke in the voice, but he gulped it down, and put on a ghost of a smile, and acquiesced in the wish that he might soon get well and come out again, with a pathetic courage which doubled the hope that he would do so.

There were many convalescents, the nurse said, but they were scattered about the wards, and not in their proper room, which was being adorned with evergreens and paper roses for a grand Christmas entertainment, to which every little patient, whom it was at all safe to move, was to be brought down on a sofa, to share as much as possible in the general enjoyment.

"We don't leave any out if we can help it—it's only a little bit more trouble, and they like it so. We take them away again before they get overtired. We think it rather does them good, to get a little bit of pleasure."

As doubtless it does to the hard-worked nurses, who seemed preparing for the festival with a hearty good-will, and a surprising taste and ingenuity. They quite regretted, and we too, that we saw the preparations incomplete, and could not regale ourselves with the *tout ensemble.* It was a little bit of brightness, pleasant to contrast with the constant anxiety, labor, and suffering which must necessarily be the normal condition of a hospital.

From the convalescents' room, which is in the second house, we passed to the public nursery, to which other rooms there are devoted, pending the time when the finances of the institution will allow of converting the whole into sick-wards. There, penned in something like a sheep-fold, half a dozen infants were crawling, and a dozen more sat in tiny arm-chairs, ranged in a fixed circle, at the centre of which was a young nurse amusing them to the best of her power. A mysterious arrangement, something between a swing and a tweedle, occupied the one side of the room; on the other, several bigger children were having what appeared a very satisfactory game of play. In an inner apartment, a row of bassinets, some empty, some occupied, indicated possibilities of sleep, doubtless attainable even in that noisy room. But noise was a blessing. There was health here. Most of the children looked uncommonly fat and flourishing, and one of them, who had recognized and stretched its arms to one of the nurses, to be taken up, on being declined, set up a most unmitigated and wholly satisfactory howl, that was quite refreshing.

The fever ward, isolated at the house-top, we did not visit; but the matron took us down to the basement story, and explained all its appliances. Her numberless presses, arranged with a method, exactitude, and perfect neatness that was quite a treat to behold, and would warm the heart of all tidy housekeepers and orderly mistresses,—her culinary arrangements and statistics,—were all politely revealed. Above all, her "Samaritan" cupboard, where we saw shelf after shelf filled with children's clothes, systematically arranged, so that they could be got at a minute's notice. And, beside it, still unpacked, was a large parcel which had just come in from a Lady Somebody, containing cast-off clothing from the little great people, which would be invaluable to the little poor ones.

"We shall get several more such bundles," said the matron, cheerily; "we always do at Christmas-time, and I hope there will be inside of them plenty of little flannel petticoats and flannel night-gowns, for we want these things worse than all. Sometimes the poor little creatures are brought to us with scarcely a rag upon their backs; I wish charitable ladies only knew how much we want cast-off clothes—we can hardly get too many."

Certainly not; and it is such an easy thing to give that which costs nothing but a moment's kindly thought. Surely many a mistress of a large household, or mother of a large family, might follow the example of Lady Somebody?

And so, for it had now grown dusk, and the cook was busy sending up the extensive tea of both patients and nurses, my first visit ended.

It was out of my power to do what several lady visitors, formally appointed, are now doing; visiting the wards every week, making acquaintance with the children, bringing them toys, and picture-books; finally, when they go out of the hospital, following them to their homes, and trying to influence for good, both them and their parents. But, two months after, I contrived to pay an unpremeditated solitary little visit, to see if the second impression justified the first.

The day was one of those bright afternoons in early March, when children inaugurate the return of spring by having tea by daylight; when, if about four o'clock you take a walk through a country village, or even a London suburb, the air seems full of a distant murmur of children at play in the lengthening twilight. It makes you feel, you know not how, as if your life were like that dawning year, to begin all over again; and brings back, for a minute or two, the sensation of being a little child, going out to play before bed-time, and ignorant that there is any thing in the world except tea and play. Even when I went up into the ward of the Children's Hospital, this influence of spring seemed to be felt: a warm lilac-tinted sunset was shining into the room, penetrating to every bed, and, I doubt not, making its occupant a little more cheery, a little less weary and suffering.

It was tea-time, and each table had its cup of milk-and-water, and its plate of bread and butter, most of which I was glad to see fast disappearing. One little girl, who had a few days since undergone amputation of the foot, had craved for "a tart," and the question had been compromised with bread and jam, which she was munching with great gusto, apparently as much to the nurse's delight as her own.

Here, as in the boys' ward afterwards, I observed one cheering fact—the faces were all new. Hardly a case which I had noted two months before, and I noted some rather carefully, was now in the hospital. They could not all have died; indeed, I understood there had been few deaths lately; therefore they must have gone out cured, or at least somewhat better. It was hardly credible, remembering how severe some of the cases were; but the extraordinary vitality of nature in the young might account for it. And it was a very hopeful sign of the good the hospital was doing.

Another was the convalescent-room; where, of mornings, a certain amount of school-teaching is given to those who are able for it; but now teaching was over for the day. As soon as the door was opened, there burst forth —not, alas! that joyous "hullabaloo" which deafens and gladdens the mother of healthy children on opening her nursery door, but still a very respectable shout of play.

"You're all getting better, little people, I see."

"Oh yes!" was the response; and half a dozen white, but still merry faces, looked up beamingly.

"What were you playing at?"

"Hide-and-seek!—Puss-in-corner!"—was variously shouted, as they began jumping about—feebly, indeed, but with plenty of life in them still.

I think any mother who has watched by the bedside of her sick child for days, or weeks, or months—still more, any mother who has knelt by the coffin of her dead child, would have turned away with her heart full, and said, "Thank God!"

Doubtless, this is the sunny side of the subject. Alas! there is another side to it;—of cureless evil, or only temporary alleviation of ills which can never be removed so long as their causes remain; so long as the diseased children of diseased parents struggle into life, and struggle through it, beset by every form of physical and moral degradation.

But, sad as this condition of things is, it is capable of remedy, and every body can help to mend it a little. Men can legislate wisely concerning it, investigate the worst evils, and consider about their possibilities of cure. Women can use their influence at home, and a little way beyond it, as do the lady-visitors of this hospital. And, perhaps, even children, if they were told of a house like this, where poor little boys and girls like themselves lie all day sick, with nothing to amuse them, might be none the worse for putting aside a spare toy, or a picture-book, as mamma puts aside an old frock, or a half-worn pair of shoes, with the thought, "We'll send it to the Children's Hospital."

I meant not this to be a charity sermon—I hope I have not made it such—but confined it strictly to facts, which speak for themselves; yet I can not help ending it as I began it, with that sentence which is the Alpha and Omega of all true charity, without which benevolence, so often thanklessly and cruelly repaid, gets weary of its work, and energy sinks hopeless, and the warmest hearts grow chilled, or hardened, until they remember what the Master says:

"*Inasmuch as ye have done it to the least of all these little ones, ye have done it unto ME.*"

[P.S.—This, with several other papers of similar character written long ago, is reprinted here, because, while the insertion is not likely to hinder their sale for the use of the charity, their re-appearance in this book will act as a still wider advertisement of the objects for which they were intended.]

DEATH ON THE SEAS.

THIS New Year, which lately opened upon us, mild and sweet as spring, may, before its close, show us many sad and strange things, but it can show nothing sadder or stranger, nothing more utterly mysterious and incomprehensible—to our human eyes—than that vision of Death on the Seas, which startled all England into pity and terror; and then, as the facts of the story came out, made the nation's heart thrill with admiration of the heroic fortitude which exalts the merely terrible into the sublime, when, a few days ago, there landed at Plymouth the nineteen forlorn survivors of the Australian steamship *London.*

Every one now knows the history of that wreck; a catastrophe so sudden, so unexpected; in its causes taken (apparently) so completely out of the range of human prevision or prevention: and in its result creating so frightful a waste of human lives, destroyed in a manner which—dare we put into words the cry that must have gone up from many a desolated home?—seems so pitilessly cruel. In most calamities we have the comfort of finding some one to blame, for carelessness or neglect, frantic folly or deliberate wickedness; but here (so far as we can see) is nothing of the kind. The elements, and they alone, seem to have banded themselves together against the doomed vessel; it fell helplessly, not into the hands of man, but of Him of whom we say—and herein is the only lightening of the dark horror of the tale—"And He made the seas also." As He made death, and sickness, and physical and mental pain, and all else that came into our world with or through sin—how? and why? We must wait, if through all eternity, until He Himself sees fit to answer that question.

Even as we must wait till the sea shall give up these dead, to whom death came in such a terrible shape; and yet, after all, they may have died more easily than we shall die upon household pillows, and they sleep as safely and sweetly at the bottom of the Atlantic as we shall sleep under churchyard daisies. Oh, if we could only think so! if we could forget *how* they died, and cease to ask of Providence desperately and blindly, *why* they died—those two hundred and twenty souls, who went down in the full flush of strength, with their eyes wide open to the coming death; when—on that Thursday afternoon (just about two o'clock, while half England was sitting down cheerily to its family dinner-tables)—in the wild Bay of Biscay the good ship *London*, "settling down stern foremost, turned up her bows into the air, and sank beneath the waves."

They can not be separately recorded—that mass of human beings—men, women, and children, every one of whom will be missed and mourned by some other one, perhaps by many both in England and Australia. Most of them, probably, lived obscurely in quiet homes, outside of which they would never have had their names mentioned, but for those brief *Times* sentences which chronicled the manner of their dying. Otherwise, who would ever have heard of "Miss Marks, of Old Kent Road," who "was at first almost frantic, yet when the boat left she stood calmly on deck bare-headed, and waved an adieu to Mr. Wilson;" of "Miss Brooker, from Pimlico," who "was heard to say, as she wrung her hands, 'Well, I have done as much as I could, and can do no more,' and then became outwardly calm;" and of "Mrs. Price, Mrs. Wood (who had with her her husband and five children), Miss Brooker, and Miss Marks, who read the Bible by turns in the second cabin."

But here is what the *Western News* says of them—these hapless two hundred, just taken from warm English firesides, Christmas dinners, and New Year's gatherings, to be taught, as only the Divine Spirit teaches, and in a manner none can understand until they learn it—how to die.

"It was at 10 o'clock on the morning of that fatal Thursday that Captain Martin had the terrible task of making known to the 200 passengers that the ship was sinking, and that they must prepare for the worst. She was then as low in the water as the main chains. The whole of the passengers and crew gathered, as with one consent, in the chief saloon, and having been calmly told by Captain Martin that there was no hope left, a remarkable and unanimous spirit of resignation came over them at once. There was no screaming or shrieking by women or men, no rushing on deck or frantic cries. All calmly resorted to the saloon, where the Rev. Mr. Draper, one of the passengers, prayed aloud, and exhorted the unhappy creatures by whom he was surrounded. Dismay was present to every heart but disorder to none. Mothers were weeping sadly over the little ones about with them to be ingulfed, and the children, ignorant of their coming death, were pitifully inquiring the cause of so much woe. Friends were taking leave of friends, as if preparing for a long journey; others were crouched down with Bibles in their hands, endeavoring to snatch consolation from passages long known or long neglected. Incredible, we are told, was the composure which, under such circumstances, reigned around. Captain Martin stationed himself in the poop, going occasionally forward, or into the saloon; but to none could he offer a word of comfort by telling them that their safety was even probable. He joined now and then for a few moments in the public devotions, but his place to the last was on the deck. About two o'clock in the afternoon, the water gaining fast on the ship and no signs of the storm subsiding being apparent, a small band of men determined to trust themselves to the mercy of the waves in a boat rather than go down without a struggle. Leaving the saloon, therefore, they got out and lowered away the port cutter, into which sixteen of the crew and three of the passengers succeeded in getting and in launching her clear of the ship. These nineteen men shouted for the captain to come with them, but with that heroic courage which was his chief characteristic, he declined to go with them, saying, 'No, I will go down with the passengers; but I wish you God speed and safe to land.' The boat then pulled away, tossing about helplessly on the crests of the gigantic waves. Scarcely had they gone eighty yards, or been five minutes off the deck, when the fine steamer went down stern foremost with her crowd of human beings, from whom one confused cry of helpless terror arose, and all was silent forever."

In other versions of the story, so heroic that its horror melts into beauty—some three or four names stand out clearer than the rest. And though now far away from praise or blame, if they ever thought of either—they, living there four days in full front of death—still it is some comfort to record all we can learn of what they did and said, during the hours when they waited for that end, concerning which the only thing they knew was its inevitable certainty.

And first, the captain—J. Bohun Martin. The brave race of British commanders will never furnish a finer specimen than this man, striving with fate to the utmost; and all hope being over, "calmly walking up and down the poop" of his slowly sinking ship. Nay, when the one boat put off—leaning over the bulwarks to give the crew their course—"E. N. E. by Brest,"—which they found to be correct; adding those last words to Mr. Greenhill the engineer, which, when told among the histories of "Shipwrecks and Disasters at Sea," will yet make many a boy's heart thrill; "There is not much chance for the boat, there is none for the ship. Your duty is done—mine is to remain here. Get in and take command of the few that it will hold." Five minutes afterwards, he went down to the bottom—with his ship and all his passengers—this brave, good man, this true British sailor!

But surely, surely—

> "Although his body's under hatches,
> His soul has gone aloft."

Of the Rev. Daniel Draper, we learn only that he was a Wesleyan minister, "well known, and highly respected," in Australia, where he had resided thirty years, and whither he was returning with his wife, the daughter of one of the first missionaries to Tahiti. His devotedness must have been great. One thinks of him, the old man, for he must have been rather beyond middle age, exhorting and praying to the last. "He was heard to say repeatedly, 'O God, may those who are not converted, be converted now—hundreds of them!'" And whoever may or may not agree with the special creed of the Wesleyan minister, his faith, proved in face of a death as solemn as that of the primitive martyrs, must have been as strong and as sublime almost as theirs.

Side by side with the Christian missionary stands—in this awful picture—another figure, strangely different, and yet alike in many points—the actor. Many play-goers of ten years back may remember G. V. Brooke, whose acting, unequal as it was (and made more so by failings, upon which let there be all silence now!), possessed a certain kind of absolute genius. At one time his *Othello* put the town in a *furore;* and his *Hamlet*, so uncertainly performed that one night it would be Shakspearian, and the other mere buffoonery, is still vividly recollected by the present writer. His fine presence, his exquisite voice, made him—externally at least—the very personification of the Royal Dane. Recalling this, how touching is the "last scene of all" in the career of the poor actor, seen "in a red Crimean shirt and trowsers, bare-footed, with no hat on," working incessantly at the pumps, "more bravely than any man in the ship." And strangely touching is our final glimpse of him "four hours before the ship went down;"—"leaning with grave composure upon one of the half-doors of the companion; his chin resting upon both his hands, and his arms on the top of the door, which he gently swayed to and fro, as he calmly watched the scene." He, too, sleeps well! "Alas, poor Yorick!"

But last in the list—and greatest, if we may count greatness by the amount of loss—the blank left, which, even as to worldly work and usefulness no other man can fill (or we think so now)—comes the name of the Rev. Dr. Woolley, Principal of Sydney College. The newspapers tell his career; how, after taking a First Class at Oxford, and a Fellowship at University College, in which honors he was united with his friend Canon Stanley, Dean of Westminster, he became successively Head Master of Rossall School, in Lincolnshire; and of King Edward's School, at Norwich. Afterwards, being appointed a Professor of Sydney College, he sailed in 1852 for the "under world." Whether or not colonial life was suitable or pleasant to him, he labored there incessantly, with abundant success, until eight or ten months ago, when he came home for rest. Many friends, with many tempting offers, urged him to stay at home, and still stronger was the temptation of his own nature. One who saw him during his latest days in England, writes of him thus:

> "His tastes were those of a refined and cultivated man. He told me that his stay here, mixing in the society of men of letters, had been a delight to him beyond what I, who was always in it, could conceive. He had met Tennyson and Browning—nothing could be more to his tastes than the companionship of such men, with whom his own qualities made him a most welcome guest. He had in perfection the bright, gentle, cheery manner that characterizes the best Oxford man. In stature he was small; but his face most pleasant to look at. He was very active in all sorts of societies and institutions for the benefit of working-men, and men engaged in business. A volume of his Colonial Lectures was lately published here—but who could criticise them now? His age must have been about fifty, but he looked younger. He had a wife and six children waiting his return to Sydney, whither, as I soon perceived, he was determined to go, for he felt his work lay there and his duty. He went back to fulfill his duty, and has fulfilled it—thus."

To the same friend he wrote—what, with all its personal details excised, can scarcely be a breach of confidence to print here, seeing how clearly it demonstrates the man—almost the last letter he ever did write—dated from Plymouth. Strange it is to look at the neat handwriting, the smoothly-folded paper, still fresh and new, and to think of where that tender, delicate, generous right hand lies now.

"My dear Sir,—Will you think me very impertinent if I venture to write to you about"—a matter of business concerning a young *protégée* of his. "We are wind-bound, and I almost hope that the wind, ill to us, may prove good to her.

"My wife knew her and her family at —." And here follow minute, personal details, carefully and wisely given, showing a gentlemanly reticence in asking favors, mingled with the generous anxiety of a good heart, which even at that busy moment had time to spare for those who needed kindness, and for whom he expresses the keenest sympathy, because, as he ends by saying, "they are fighting a hard fortune brightly and bravely."

"I expect," he continues, "to sail to-day; so if you are inclined to give my young friend a trial, might I ask you to communicate with her." And then, after carefully giving the address and other particulars, he closes the letter so abruptly, that he omits the conclusion, date, and signature —probably summoned on board in haste. But the letter was posted and received, afterwards to be returned to the subject of it, and to become a permanent memorial of what another friend, writing to the *Times*, calls "the gentleness, almost feminine, of his nature: and the warmth and generosity of his heart."

And so he, also, went down with those lost in the *London*. The survivors report how, with the Rev. Mr. Draper —though, doubtless, in many points widely differing from him—Dr. Woolley conducted the religious services on the last Sunday, and, during the lingering suspense of those awful days, comforted the people with exhortation and prayer. Not much is said about him: but we know in what manner he would die, and help others to die. His public career may be told in other ways; but this one word is in remembrance of the man himself—the good man—John Woolley.

Thus they perished—these two hundred and twenty: summoned—why we know not—out of useful lives, and prosperous lives, and busy and happy lives; and the mystery of their sudden ending we dare not even attempt to understand. But we know we shall one day; that great day when "the dead that are in their graves"—sea-graves as well as land-graves—"shall hear the voice of the Son of Man, and they that hear shall live."

TO PARENTS.

GOING to and fro in the earth, and walking up and down in it (like the devil in Job), it has sometimes occurred to me, that amidst the universal preaching of the duties of children to parents, a few words might well be said on the duties of parents to children. Can these few words do any harm? I trow not. The truth never does any harm. No child, blessed with even ordinarily good parents, will love and honor them any the less for whatever may be said against bad parents. And to try and sustain the authority of the latter by false pretenses is as futile as setting up a fetish-idolatry instead of the true religion of the heart—that instinctive filial faith which is the foundation-stone of all law and order in the world. Nay, in the universe, for what would become of us in this weary existence, if we could not, from its beginning to its ending, look up and say "Our Father?"

It is a solemn and terrible truth, that there are parents who no more deserve the name than the sovereign of Dahomey deserves to be held as a "king, by the grace of God." Yet in one sense the "divine right" of both kings and parents is unalienable. "Honor thy father and thy mother" is an absolute law, given without reference to the worthiness of the individual parent; it being a duty which the child owes to himself, to honor his parents simply *as parents*, without considering whether or not they have fulfilled their duty. There is a limit beyond which human nature can not be expected to go: when actual moral turpitude renders "honor" a perfect farce; when respect becomes a mockery, and obedience an impossibility. But even then one resource remains—and remains forever—endurance and silence. The unworthy parent must be treated like the unworthy king, tacitly handed down from the position which he has proved himself unfit to occupy, neither injured nor insulted, simply deposed.

But these are exceptional cases, so exceptional that each must be decided on its separate merits; and in most instances the outside public which takes such delight in criticising, condemning, or excusing them, is quite unfit to judge them at all. But there are innumerable other instances, not the "cruel fathers" or "heartless mothers" of fiction, but every-day, well-meaning, respectable people, who are nevertheless domestic Molochs, before whom every successive child must pass through the fire; ancient Remphans, requiring living human daily sacrifices—precious indeed, for all sacrifice is lovely in the offerer—but none the less an unnecessary and cruel immolation, which lookers-on must regard with both pity and righteous wrath.

In how many ways, ignorantly or carelessly, do parents thus act as actual scourges to the children who were given them, not for their personal amusement, benefit, or pride, but for the sake of the children themselves! How entirely they seem to forget that each human soul which is sent to them through the mysteries of marriage and birth, is not their own to do as they like with, but a solemn charge, for which they will be accountable to God and man! If any weaknesses of theirs, love of power, love of ease, even love of love—often the deepest selfishness of all—lead them to ignore this charge, woe be to them and their children. "Unto the third and fourth generation" is a law, not of divine anger, but of divine inevitable necessity. One wicked father, or vicious, vile-tempered mother, often remains a family curse for a century.

It is at once the most awful responsibility, and the utmost consecration of parenthood, that of all human ties, this one requires most self-abnegation. And when we think how very few really unselfish people there are in the world—not many among women, of men almost none—we only wonder how so many decent folk do contrive somehow to bring up decent families,—or let them bring themselves up, as, strange to say, many excellent families often do. But the very fact that children left almost entirely to themselves sometimes turn out better than those who have been subjected to the sharpest parental oversight—only drives us back by implication to the truth at which we started—how few people are in the least fitted to be parents.

And perhaps no wonder. Young people falling desperately in love, marrying in haste, and repenting in leisure; other people, not young, and certainly guiltless of any youthful follies, who commit the deliberate mature sin of making marriage a mere matter of convenience; husbands wearing out their bodies and souls in the making of money, and wives frittering away their helpless, aimless lives in the extravagant spending of it—what can such as these know or feel of the duties of parenthood?

At first it is a very pretty amusement, doubtless. How delighted papa is to make after-dinner pets of his fairy girls, and encourage the obstreperousness of his fine manly boys. And mamma, with a certain natural instinct that rarely fails even in the silliest of women, is a tolerably good mother so long as her children remain in the nursery. But when they grow into youths and maidens, requiring larger wisdom, a tenderer guidance; when individual character asserts itself, as it will and must, in any creature worth becoming a man or a woman—then is the crisis—most difficult and dangerous—at which, alas, so many household histories break down.

The transition state of adolescence is a trying time. The young folks, like all half-grown animals, are awkward, unwise, self-conceited, revolutionary; while the elders find it hard to believe that "the children" are, in reality, children no more; that characters have developed and tastes matured, very likely most opposite to their own, yet not necessarily inferior characters or erring tastes. Some minds, at once strong and narrow, find it nearly impossible to comprehend this. They do not perceive when the time comes, as come it must in every family, when it is the children's right to begin to think and act for themselves, and the parents' duty to allow them to do it; when it is wisest gradually to slacken authority, to sink "I command" into "I wish," to grant large freedom of opinion, and above all in the expression of it. Likewise, and this is a most important element in family union, to give license, nay, actual sympathy, to wandering affections, friendships, or loves, which, for the time being, seem to find the home circle too narrow and too dull.

No doubt, to the parents this is rather trying. It is hard for mamma to discover that her girl not only enjoys, but craves after, a month's visit in some lively household;

that she likes the company of other girls, and forms enthusiastic friendships, which mamma (a lady of between forty and fifty) forgets that she herself ever had, and consequently thinks exceedingly silly, or idle, or wrong. Papa, too, can not see why his boys—good, affectionate lads—should find it such dull work to stay at home of an evening, or should prefer a sensation play—"so different from what the stage was in *my* time"—to the longest game of chess with himself, or the most learned conversation with his staid and sober friends. Yet all this is quite natural; the boys and girls are foolish, perhaps, but not in the least guilty. Well for the household in which this, the earliest of many impending changes, should be recognized at once, still better that the recognition should come first from the elder and wiser side of it.

But, alas, here intrudes a truth which should be touched reverently and delicately, and yet it can not be passed over, for it is a truth—that all parents are *not* wiser than their children. Sometimes a boy, quick-witted, honest, and good, finds, as he grows up, that his father is not a man to be relied on, but one of those weak souls who, without positive harm in them, are ever sinking lower and lower, and dragging their family down with them—whose authority is a mere name, whose advice is fatal to follow. Many a clever lad has come to see, even before he is out of his teens, that his only chance of getting on in the world is to rely solely on himself, and give as wide a berth as possible to his natural guardian and guide—his father. Likewise, many a girl, generous, warm-hearted, and sensitive, on passing into discriminating womanhood, feels, and can not help feeling, that if her mother had not been her mother, she would never have chosen her even as an ordinary acquaintance. These are bitter discoveries, ending in sharp daily agonies, irremediable, incommunicable. Happily the instinctive natural bond, added to the familiar habit of a lifetime, is so strong, that sometimes the sufferers themselves do not seem to feel their position quite so keenly as lookers-on, who own no softening influence of custom or affection.

These sufferings are not the less real because they sometimes take the comical aspect. Witty writers have exhausted their wit on the sad spectacle, common enough in this commercial country, of parvenus, coarse and vulgar, who are perfect terrors to their educated children. But this is a small misfortune. A man seldom raises himself very high without having something to give to society equivalent to what he has won from it. Hundreds nowadays carry with them into handsome houses, noble halls, and even palace doors, the traces of their humble origin—not pleasant, indeed, and sometimes comical—but quite bearable, from the inherent worth or talent of the individual, and never warranting the slightest complaint or disrespect from a dutiful child. Far worse to bear is that ingrained coarseness of nature, not breeding, common to all ranks, which makes many a daughter blush scarlet at things her mother says and does, which yet she can neither prevent nor notice. And what can be sorer for a young man, high-minded and chivalrous, than to live in perpetual dread lest his father, the head of the house, should disgrace it by some small meanness, some "indirect crook't ways," which force any honest observer, even his own son, to perceive, that though he may be a Crœsus of money, or a nobleman in rank, he is certainly not a gentleman!

Between these opposite poles of tragedy and comedy lies an intermediate range of miseries, small indeed, but sorely hard to bear. One is when, as is patent to every body except the parents themselves, the elder generation is, in mental and moral calibre, decidedly inferior to the younger. Not bad people, but only narrow: narrow in thought, and word, and deed; unable to recognize that what lies beyond their own limited vision has any existence whatsoever. These sort of people are very trying in all relations, the more so because, so far as they go, they are often exceedingly estimable. Only if nature has made one of their children in any way different from themselves, of larger mould and wider capacities, the extent to which that child is martyrized, even with the very best intentions, is sometimes incredible.

Yet, outside, every body says what excellent parents they are, and what a happy home their children must have! a fact of which they themselves are most thoroughly convinced. How can the young people weary of it for a moment? How can Mary, a charming, well-educated, and perhaps very clever young woman, desire any other companion than her mother? Since, of course, a mother is the best and closest companion for every girl. Most true, but not "of course," nor in virtue of the mere accident of motherhood. Sympathy comes by instinct, and confidence must be, not exacted, but won. Mary may have the strongest filial regard for that dear and good woman, to whom she owes and is ready to pay every duty that a daughter ought, and yet be inwardly conscious that nature has made the two so different in tastes, feelings, disposition, that if she were to open her heart to her, her mother would not understand her in the least. Not to speak of the difference of age, greater or less, and the not unnatural way in which elderly people who do not retain youthfulness of heart, as happily many do to the last day of life, grow out of sympathy with the young. But Providence having constituted these two mother and daughter, they must get on together somehow. And so they do. Though Mary in her secret soul may writhe sometimes, she loves mamma very dearly, and would love her better still if she would only let her alone to follow her own tastes in any lawful way. But this mamma can not do. She is like the goose with the young cygnet, always pitying herself because her child is unlike other people's children, wearing the girl's life out with endless complaints and impossible exactions, until at last Mary sinks into passive indifference, or bitter old-maidism, or plunges into a reckless marriage—any thing, anywhere, only to get away from home.

John's case is not so hard, in one sense, he being a man and Mary only a woman, but it is far more dangerous. She may be made merely wretched; he wicked, by this narrow, vexatious rule. Why should John, who is only three-and-twenty, presume to hold a different opinion on politics, religion, or aught else, from his father? Papa is the older, and of course knows best; papa has had every opportunity of forming his judgment on every subject; and he has formed it, and there it is, carefully cut and dried, easy and comfortable, without any of those doubts which are the torture and yet the life of all ardent, youthful spirits. There it is, and John must abide by it, hold his tongue, and take his obnoxious newspapers and heterodox books out of the way; which John, being a lover of peace, and trained to honorable obedience, very likely does; but he cherishes either a private contempt—we are so scornful when we are young!—or an angry rebellion against the narrow-mindedness that would compel him into his father's way of thinking, simply because it is his father's. Be the lad ever so good, a lurking sense of injustice can not fail to chafe him, and injustice is one of the most fatal elements that, at any age, can come into the sacred relation between parent and child.

Parents know not what they are doing when they rouse this feeling—the burning, stinging consciousness of being unfairly treated, disbelieved, misjudged, selfishly or wantonly punished. You find it in the maddest mob, the roughest public school, the most riotous public assembly, this rough, dogged sense of justice; dangerous to tamper with, even in the slightest degree. Far wiser is it for a parent to acknowledge to ever so young a child, "I was wrong, I made a mistake," than to go on enforcing a false authority, or compelling a blind obedience, driving the child to exclaim, or inly feel, which is worse, "You are not my ruler, but my tyrant!"

Yet many a severe parent is deeply loved. "My father was a stern man," you sometimes hear said, while the rare tear of self-restrained middle age falls unchecked over the grave's side. "He kept us in order. We were all rather afraid of him; but he was invariably just. He never broke his word, nor forgot his promise. He punished us, but not in passion: he ruled us strictly, but it was never to gratify his own love of power. If he had thrashed us twenty times, we should have submitted to it, because we knew that whatever he did was done for conscience' sake, and not out of wantonness or anger. I may bring up my children differently in some things—perhaps I do—but I'll never hear a word said against *him*. He was a just man—my father."

A just man, and an unselfish woman; these are the two first qualities which constitute true parenthood.

In this question of selfishness. Readers may start with horror at such an impossible anomaly as a selfish mother, a jealous, exacting father; and yet such there are. Especially after the children are grown up, and nature, gratitude, and the world's opinion, all agree that no devotedness can be too perfect, no sacrifices too great. Ay! but it is one thing what the child ought to offer, and another what the parent should accept. Most lovely is it to see a daughter cheerfully resigning all the external enjoyments of life, to devote herself to the higher happiness of being the sole stay and cheer of some helpless father, or solitary, sickly mother; and sweet, even amid all its daily renunciations, is the sense of duty fulfilled and comfort imparted. But to see a parent fretful, complaining, exacting, grudging the child a week's absence from home, not for love, *that* would teach self-sacrifice, but from the selfish enjoyment or ease which the accustomed companionship brings, yielding to the natural dislike of old age for any new association, and tacitly or openly keeping the young people in such bondage that they dare not ask a friend to tea, or accept an invitation—"Papa would not like it;" "Mamma might be annoyed"—this is a sight which lowers all the dignity of parenthood, and degrades filial duty into mere servitude. Yet many such cases there are, inflicted by really good parents, who are not aware that they are doing any harm, and who, in their narrow selfishness, can not perceive that the life which is to them merely "a quiet life," suited to their age and infirmities, is slowly taking all the spirit and brightness out of younger hearts, driving the boys into dissipation and folly, and dragging "the girls" (of thirty and upwards) down into premature old-maidism, dull, discontented, helpless, and forlorn. Such a life, passing gradually on into life's melancholy decline, in a round of uninteresting, compelled duties, is as different from the free, warm devotion of real filial love, as slow murder is from voluntary and glad self-sacrifice.

But here a word, lest this essay, which is especially addressed "To Parents," not being guarded, like income-tax or census papers, from any other unlawful eyes, should be taken as a loophole of excuse by readers like a certain young impertinent of my acquaintance, who, being lectured on the text, "Children, obey your parents in the Lord," immediately pointed out its correlative, "Fathers, provoke not your children to wrath."

When we speak of a parent being "deposed," we mean merely from the exercise of an authority which has become a farce, and the exaction of an obedience which a higher law, that of conscience, renders impossible. But once a parent, always a parent. It is a bond which, though in one sense a mere accident, is, in another sense, stronger than any tie of mere personal election, since it came by the ordination of Providence. It may be a great burden, even a great misfortune, but there it is: and nothing but death can end it. No shortcomings on the parental side can abrogate one atom of the plain duty of the child—submission so long as submission is possible, reverence while one fragment of respect remains; and, after that, endurance. To this generation of young England, which is apt to think so much of itself, and so little of its elders and superiors, we can not too strongly uphold the somewhat out-of-date doctrine, "Honor thy father and thy mother." Ay, though they may be very simple, common people: infirm in intellect, uneducated, unrefined: guilty of many shortcomings of temper, judgment, and even glaring errors—still, honor them, and, when honor fails, bear with them.

The question then arises, what, and for how long, a child ought to bear. And here Christianity would reply with the doctrine of "seventy times seven," pleading, also, that if to a brother so much is to be forgiven, how much more so to a parent. Ay, *forgiven.* But Christianity nowhere commands that a grown-up man or woman is to sacrifice honor, conscience, peace—in fact, the real worth of a lifetime—to either brethren or parents. Therefore, when things come to this pass, that the child, by "honoring" the parent would actually dishonor God, and defile his own soul by acting contrary to his conscience, there, so far, the duty ends. Let him or her assert, as an individual existence, the right of self-preservation—let them part. At least let the division be made firm and clear enough to secure independence of thought and action, so that the parent can no longer injure or oppress the child.

For lesser trials, the amount of patience and long-suffering shown by the child to the parent ought to be almost unlimited. At the same time, it is quite possible for young men or young women quietly to assert their individuality, and carry out, without any obnoxious rebellion, their own plan of life, even if it does differ more or less from their parents. Exceeding gentleness and yet firmness, perfect respect in word and deed, straightforwardness, honesty, and yet a courageous self-dependence, will rarely fail to win their way under ever such difficult circumstances. And one hardly knows which to despise most—the cowardice which looks like reverence, and the underhandedness which shams obedience, or that open rebellion which hastily assumes the position, more degrading to itself than to the worst of parents—that of a "thankless child."

One word more, on that prime source of misery between parents and children: marriage.

Unquestionably, if any third human being has a right to interfere in the choice which two other human beings make of one another "for better, for worse," it is a parent. No one else! neither brother, sister, aunt, uncle, cousin, nor any of the numerous relations and friends who always seem to consider a projected marriage their especial business, and not that of the lovers at all. But, happily, in our country at least, none of these, nay, not even parents, have absolute legal authority, either to make or to mar the divine institution of holy matrimony. Either John or Mary may, having arrived at years of discretion, at any time walk out of the paternal house and into the nearest church, or register office, and marry any body. And if the marriage be at all creditable, even society will wink at it; nay, perhaps smile at the "indignant parents." But a higher law than that of society enacts that such a decided step should not be taken until the last extremity.

Most natural are all the hesitations, doubts, pathetic little jealousies, and pardonable touchinesses of parents about to lose their children. It is hard to see your winsome girl, the flower of your life, plant herself, in her very sweetest bloom, in another man's garden. Hard, too, to watch your best loved son so absorbed that he has neither eyes nor ears for mother, sister, or any creature living, except "*that* young woman." Nevertheless, that a man should leave father and mother, and cleave unto his wife, is a law so immutable, so rational, that those who selfishly set their faces against it, parents though they be, are certain to reap their punishment. They may live to see sons, whom they have thwarted in a pure first love, turn to a coarse passion degrading and destroying to body and soul; daughters, denied a comparatively humble engagement with some honest penniless lover, fretfully "withering on the virgin thorn," or seeking loveless worldly marriages, which are the crushing out of all womanliness, every thing that, by making life happy, would also have made it worthy.

Sons and daughters will marry, and they ought to marry. Selfishness alone would hinder in any young man the lawful desire for a home of his own, or in any young woman the natural instinct for some one dearer than father, mother, brother, or sister, however precious these all may be. Every head, and every member of a family who loves the other members wisely and well, will not only not prevent, but encourage in every lawful way, the great necessity of life to both men and women—a prudent, constant, holy love, and a happy marriage.

One word to the parents, which of course the young people are not intended to hear.

Don't you think, my good friends, that parents as you be, with every desire for your child's happiness, it was a little unfair to give your Mary every opportunity of becoming attached to Charles, and Charles, poor fellow, all possible chance of adoring Mary? Could you expect him to see her sweet womanly ways, which make her the delight of her father's home, and not be tempted to wish her for the treasure of his own? Is it not rather hard now to turn round and object to their marrying, because, forsooth, you "never thought of such a thing," or, "Mary might have done better," or, "Charles was not the sort of person you thought she would fancy," or—last shift, and a very mean one—you "rather hoped she would not marry at all, but stay with her old father and mother?"

Hold there! We will not suppose any parents in their sober senses to be guilty of such sinful selfishness. Let us pass to the next objection, commonly urged against almost all marriages, that the parties are the last persons which each was expected to choose. Expected by whom? The world at large, or their own relations? The world knows little enough, and cares less, about these matters. And sometimes, strange to say, two people who happen really to love one another, also know one another, a little better than all their respected relations put together—even their parents. They have made (or ought to—for we are granting that the case in point is no light fancy, but a deliberate attachment—there is great meaning in that old-fashioned word) that solemn election, binding for life, and—as all true lovers hope and pray—for eternity. They have cast their own lot, and are ready to abide by it. All its misfortunes or mistakes, like its happinesses, will be their own. Give your advice honestly and fully; exact a fair trial of affection, urge every precaution that your older heads and tougher hearts may suggest, and then, O parents, leave your children free. If there is one thing more than another in which sons and daughters who are capable of being trusted at all deserve to be trusted unlimitedly, it is choice in marriage.

I have lived somewhat long in the world; have watched many a love-affair "on" and "off," gathering, rising, then breaking and vanishing like a wave of the sea; have seen many a strange union turn out well, and many a seemingly smooth and auspicious one end in much unhappiness; but I never saw any single instance in which overweening and irrational opposition to any marriage, on the part of parents or friends, did not end in misery. It either forced on to unsuitable and hasty union some fancy or passion that might otherwise have died a peaceful natural death, or it clouded, for years at least, two innocent lives; or if this were spared and the marriage accomplished, it sowed seeds of strife and bitterness between families which no after pacification could ever quite root out. Parents, whatever you do, be humble enough never to attempt to play Providence with your children!

But suppose it is not so. Suppose that Mary's father forbids Mr. Charles his house, or Charles's kindred, having taken an insurmountable prejudice against Mary, swear that if he marries her they will never have any thing more to say to him? What are the young couple to do? Are they to sacrifice the happiness of their mutual lives? Is Charles to sail for Australia, and Mary to go mourning all her days? Some strict moralists might say, "Yes. Break your hearts, both of you, but dare not to disobey your parents." Easy-going worldly-wise reasoners might agree that there would be no heart-break in the matter, that both would soon "get over it," and marry somebody else. Possibly; but the risk is considerable, involving great responsibility to the parents.

Also to the lovers themselves, who, from the instant that they have acknowledged mutual affection, have a right to one another and a duty to perform towards one another, little less sacred than that of husband and wife. Their trial is no doubt most sharp—hard in the present, sad in the future—for how bitter it must be to give to possible children the opportunity of one day saying, "You married without your parents' consent—you can not blame me if I do the same." Yet, granting its full weight to every argument, the decision arrived at in so cruel a conjuncture must, in all calmly-judging minds, surely be the same.

Unquestionably, a deliberate, patiently-delayed, well-thought-of marriage, open to no rational objection, and breaking no law either human or divine, ought to be carried out, with or without the consent of parents.

No clandestine proceedings can ever be justifiable. But when all efforts to break down prejudice and win esteem have failed, a son, or even a daughter, though that seems harder, has a perfect right to quit openly and honestly the parental roof. "Farewell," either must say—ah, how sorrowfully! yet it ought to be said—"I have tried my utmost to win you over, and it is in vain. I am not called upon to sacrifice, not only my own happiness, but another's. The just God be judge between us. I must go."

A terrible alternative, yet there can be no other; and surely if the parents never relent—never forgive—the just God will judge it tenderly, and the "curse causeless" shall not come.

But such a crisis rarely occurs in a family where the parents have themselves done their duty. No wise father would ever bring into the intimate society of his daughters a young fellow of whom, as a son-in-law, he would utterly, and with fair reasons, disapprove. And, reckless as men's passions sometimes are, very few sons of really good mothers would be likely so to have lost that ideal of womanhood which it is a mother's own fault if she does not set before her sons, that they would desire to bring into the family any girl so altogether unworthy and objectionable that her entrance therein ought to be prevented by every lawful means. The safest and only way to make children marry rightly is by setting before them such ensamples of true manhood and womanhood that they would shrink from choosing a wife or husband inferior to their own parents.

And when such is the case, when home is really home, what a haven of rest it is! How the children, married or single, will remember it, yearn over it, delight to revisit it, as the safest, sunniest nest! And as years roll on, and they have long ceased to be "the children" to any body but the old father and mother, how strong is that parental influence which has succeeded the resigned authority—how perfect the love which casts out even the shadow of fear! Duty—sacrifice—the words are a mere name, a pleasant jest, if by means of them can be given the smallest pleasure to the good parents. No self-denial seems too great if it can requite them—no, they never can be requited—but show them in some degree their children's appreciation of their innumerable self-denials, never fully understood till now, when the children have become parents themselves.

And when they really grow old—though the second generation will never quite believe it—how their weaknesses are held sacred, and their utmost infirmities dear! How the third generation are taught from babyhood to consider it the greatest honor to be of any use to grandpapa and grandmamma! How their sayings are repeated, their wisdom upheld, and their virtues canonized into a family tradition, ay, years after the beloved heads, white and reverend, have been laid tenderly " under the daisies!"

For parents, real parents, are never forgotten. Good old maids and kindly old bachelors may be remembered for many a year; but those others on whom has been conferred, with all the sorrows and cares, the great honor and happiness of parenthood, have mingled their life with the permanent life of the world. Their qualities descend, and their influence is felt, through uncounted generations. Thorny and difficult may have been their mortal path, many their anxieties and sharp their pangs, but they have done their work, and they inherit its blessing. They die, but in their posterity they enjoy a perpetual immortality.

MISERY-MONGERS.

"POOR fellow," said A. to B., looking after C. with mingled regard and regret. "He will never be happy himself, nor make any other human being happy."

It was most true. C. is an excellent man: honest, kindly, well-intentioned; prosperous in business; in his domestic relations rather fortunate than otherwise; blessed with good health, good looks, and rather more than the average brains. Altogether an enviable person—externally. Yet his friend, apparently much less lucky than himself, regarded him with the profoundest pity. "No, C. will never be happy. Nothing in this world would ever make him happy." And nothing ever did.

C. is no uncommon character. He was a misery-monger: one of those moral cuttle-fishes who carry about with them, and produce out of their own organism, the black liquid in which they swim. If they could only swim in it alone! Is it any good to show them their own likeness—these poor creatures, who, without any real woe, contrive to make themselves and every body about them thoroughly miserable. Can we shake them out of their folly by a word of common sense? Probably not; your confirmed misery-monger is the most hopeless being in creation; but there are incipient stages of the complaint, which, taken in time, are curable. To such, it may not be unadvisable to present these incurables as a wholesome "shocking example."

Misery-mongers (the word is not to be found in Johnson, yet it suits) are those who do not really suffer affliction, but make a trade of it—and often a very thriving business too. They are scattered among every class, but especially they belong to the "genus irritabile"—the second or third-rate order of people who live by their brains. Not the first order—for the highest form of intellect is rarely miserable. True genius of the completest kind is not only a mental but a moral quality. Itself creates the atmosphere it lives in: a higher and rarer air than that of common earth.

"Calm pleasures there abide;—majestic pains."

To a really great man, the petty vanities, shallow angers, and morbid crotchets of smaller natures are unknown. Above all, genius gives to its possessor a larger, clearer vision; eyes that look outward not inward. That enormous Ego—the source of so many puny woes to lesser minds—rarely grows rampant in a man who is great enough to know his own littleness. Consequently, he is saved at once from a hundred vexations which dog the heels of your giant of genius—who is always measuring himself with Tom, Dick, and Harry, and requiring, or fancying he requires, larger clothes, longer beds, and bigger hats than they. When Tom, Dick, and Harry, annoyed at these exactions, find that the supposed son of Anak is not so very much taller than themselves, and cut him up in reviews or snub him in society, great is the vexation of spirit he endures. But your real giant, who never thinks of Tom, Dick, and Harry at all, takes the matter quite calmly: whatever be his own altitude, he sees before him an ideal far higher than himself, and ten times higher than any thing they see, and this keeps him at once very humble in his own opinion, and very indifferent to theirs. The present essayist has been fortunate enough to know a good many such, and has always found them neither strutting like peacocks nor marching on stilts, but walking about as mild and tame as the elephant in the Zoological Gardens, and as apparently unconscious of their own magnitude. It is your second-rate, your merely clever man, who, apelike, is always rattling at the bars of his cage, moping and mowing to attract attention, and eagerly holding out his paw for the nuts and apples of public appreciation, which, if he does not get—why, he sits and howls!

Such people have rarely suffered any dire calamity or heart-deep blow. To have sat down with sorrow—real sorrow—frequently gives a steadiness and balance to the whole character, and leaves behind a permanent consistent cheerfulness, more touching, and oh! how infinitely more blessed, than the mirth of those who have never known grief. Also, after deep anguish comes a readiness to seize upon, make the best of, and enjoy to the uttermost, every passing pleasure: for the man who has once known famine will never waste even a crumb again. Rather will he look with compassionate wonder at the many who scatter recklessly their daily bread of comfort and peace; who turn disgusted from a simple breakfast because they are looking forward to a possible sumptuous dinner; or throw away contemptuously their wholesome crust, because they see, with envious eyes, their opposite neighbor feeding on plum-cake.

No, the miserable people whom one meets are not the really unhappy ones, or rather those who have actual misfortune to bear, there being a wide distinction between misfortune and unhappiness. How often do we see moving in society, carrying everywhere a pleasant face, and troubling no one with their secret care, those who we know are burdened with an inevitable incommunicable grief: an insane wife, a dissipated husband, tyrannical parents, or ungrateful children? Yet they say nothing about it, this skeleton in the cupboard, which their neighbors all know of or guess at, but upon which they themselves quietly turn the key, and go on their way; uncomplaining, and thankful to be spared complaining. What good will it do them to moan? It is not they, the unfortunate men, nor yet the men of genius, who contrive to make miserable their own lives and those of every body connected with them. The true misery-mongers are a very different race; you may find the key to their mystery in Milton's famous axiom,

> "Fallen cherub, to be weak is miserable,
> Doing or suffering."

There, for once, the devil spoke truth. Miserable people are invariably weak people.

> "Oh well for him whose will is strong,
> He suffers, but he will not suffer long;
> He suffers, but he can not suffer wrong."

Of course not, because his firm will must in time shake off any suffering; and because no amount of externally inflicted evil is to be compared to the evil which a man inflicts upon himself, by feebleness of purpose, by cowardly non-resistance to oppression, and by a general uncertainty of aims or acts. He who sees the right and can not follow it; who loves all things noble, yet dare not fight against things ignoble in himself or others; who is haunted by a high ideal of what he wishes to be, yet is forever falling short of it, and tortured by the consciousness that he does fall short of it, and that his friends are judging him, not unjustly, by what he is rather than by what he vainly aims at being—this man is, necessarily, one of the unhappiest creatures living. One of the most harmful too, since you can be on your guard against the downright villain, but the æsthetic evil-doer, the theoretically good and practically bad man, who has lofty aspirations without performances, virtuous impulses and no persistence—against such a one you have no weapons to use. He disarms your resentment by exciting your pity; is forever crying "Quarter, quarter!" and, though you feel that he deserves none, that his weakness has injured yourself and others as much as any wickedness, still, out of pure compassion, you sheath your righteous sword and let him escape unpunished. Up he rises, fresh as ever, and pursues his course, always sinning and always repenting, yet claiming to be judged not by the sin but the penitence; continually and obstinately miserable, yet blind to the fact that half his misery is caused by himself alone.

And this brings us to the other root of misery-mongering—selfishness. None but a thoroughly selfish person can be always unhappy. Life is so equally balanced that there is always as much to rejoice as to weep over, if we are only able—and willing—to rejoice in and for and through others.

"Time and the hour run through the roughest day"—

if we will but let it be so—if we will allow our sky to clear and our wounds to heal—believing in the wonderfully reparative powers of Nature when she is given free play. But these poor souls will not give her free play; they prefer to indulge in their griefs, refusing obstinately all remedies, till they bring on a chronic dyspepsia of the soul, which is often combined with a corresponding disease of the body.

It may seem a dreadful doctrine to poetical people, but two-thirds of a man's woes usually begin—in his stomach. Irregular feeding, walking, and sleeping, with much too regular smoking, are the cause of half the melancholy poetry and cynical prose with which we are inundated. Also of many a miserable home, hiding its miseries under the decent decorum which society has the good taste and good feeling to abstain from prying too closely into; and of not a few open scandals, bankruptcies, and divorce cases. If a modern edition of the Miseries of Human Life were to be written, the author might well trace them to that unsanitary condition, first of body and then of mind, into which civilization, or the luxurious extreme of it, has brought us, and upon which some of us rather pride ourselves, as if it were a grand thing to be "morbid;" quite forgetting the origin of the word, and that such a condition, whether mental or physical, or both combined, is, in truth, not life, but the beginning of death, to every human being.

And suppose it is so. Granted that I am a man with "nerves," or "liver," or any other permanent ailment, am I to make my ill-used and consequently ill-conducted interior a nuisance to all my family and friends? Did no man's head ever ache but mine? Is no one else blessed (or cursed) with a too sensitive organism, obliged to struggle with and control it, and at least contrive that it shall trouble others as little as possible? Why should my wife, sister, or daughter be expected to bestow unlimited sympathy upon every small suffering of mine, while she hides many an ache and pain which I never even know of, or knowing, should scarcely heed, except so far as it affected my own personal comfort, or because it is a certain annoyance to me that any body should require sympathy but myself? Have my friends no anxieties of their own, that I should be forever laying upon them the burden of mine —always exacting and requiting nothing? People like a fair balance—a cheery give and take in the usefulnesses as well as the pleasantnesses of life. Is it wonderful, then, that, after a time, they a little shrink from me, are shy of asking me to dinner?—at least, often. For they feel I may be a cloud upon the social board; my moods are so various, they never know how to take me. They are very sorry for me, very kind to me, but, in plain English, they would rather have my room than my company. I am too full of myself ever to be any pleasure or benefit to others.

For it is a curious fact that the most self-contained natures are always the least self-engrossed; and those to whom every body applies for help, most seldom ask or require it. The centre sun of every family, round which the others instinctively revolve, is sure to be a planet bright and fixed, carrying its light within itself. But a man whose soul is all darkness, or who is at best a poor wandering star, eager to kindle his puny candle at somebody else's beams, can be a light and a blessing to nobody.

And he may be—probably without intending it—quite the opposite. Who does not, in visiting a household, soon discover the one who contributes nothing to the happiness of the rest, who is a sort of eleemosynary pensioner on every body's forbearance, living, as beggars do, by the continual exhibition of his sores, and often getting sympathy—as beggars get half-pence—just to be rid of him? Who does not recognize the person whose morning step upon the stair, so far from having "music in 't," sends a premonitory shiver, and even a dead silence, round the cheerful, chattering, breakfast-table?—whose departure to business, or elsewhere, causes a sudden rise in the domestic barometer?—nay, whose very quitting a room gives a sense of relief as of a cloud lifted off? Yet he may have many good qualities, but they are all obscured and rendered useless by the incessant recurrence to and absorption in self, which is the root of all his useless woes. And, alas! while believing himself—as he wishes to be—the most important person in his circle, our miserable friend fills really the lowest place therein—that of the one whom nobody trusts, nobody leans upon; whom every body has to help, but who is never expected to help any body. How could he? for in him is lacking the very foundation of all helpfulness—the strong, brave, cheerful spirit which, under all circumstances, will throw itself out of itself sufficiently to understand and be of use to its neighbor.

Truly, as regards usefulness, one might as well attempt to labor in an unlighted coal mine as to do one's work in the world in an atmosphere of perpetual gloom. Nature herself scorns the idea. Some of her operations are carried on in tender temporary shadow—but only temporary. Nothing with her is permanently dark, except the corruption of the grave. Whenever, in any man's temperament, is incurable sadness, morbid melancholy, be sure there is something also corrupt; something which shrinks from the light because it needs to be hid; something diseased, in body or mind, which, so far from being petted and indulged and glossed over with poetical fancies, needs to be rooted out—with a hand, gentle, indeed, but strong and firm as that of the good surgeon, who deals deliberately present pain for future good.

A healthy temperament, though not insensible to sorrow, never revels in it or is subdued by it; it accepts it, endures it, and then looks round for the best mode of curing it. We can not too strongly impress on the rising generation—who, like the young bears, have all their troubles before them—that suffering is not a normal but an abnormal state; and that to believe otherwise is to believe that this world is a mere chaos of torment made for the amusement of the omnipotent—not God, but devil—who rules it. Pain must exist—for some inscrutable end—inseparable from the present economy of the world; but we ought, out of common sense and common justice, and especially religion, to regard it not as the law of our lives, but as an accident, usually resulting from our breaking that law. We can not wholly prevent suffering, but we can guard against it, in degree; and we never need wholly succumb to it till we succumb to the universal defeat, death preparatory to the immortal victory.

When one thinks of death—of how brief, at best, is our little day, and how quickly comes the end that levels all things, what folly seems the habit of misery!—for it grows into a mere habit, quite independent of causes. Why keep up this perpetual moan, and always about ourselves, because we are not rich enough, or handsome enough, or loved enough—because other people have better luck than we? Possibly they have;—and possibly not; for we all know our own private cares, but few of us know our neighbor's. And so we go on, always finding some pet grievance to nurse, and coaxing it from a trifling vexation into an incurable grief or an unpardonable wrong. Little matter what it is; to a man of this temperament any peg will do whereon to hang the gloomy pall, self-woven, of perpetual sorrow. Or else he spins it, spider-like, out of his own bowels, and when its filmy meshes grow into great bars between him and the sky, he thinks with his petty web he has blurred the whole creation.

Poor wretch! if he could only pull it down and sweep it away!—if he could accept his lot, even though a hard one,—an afflicted stomach, sensitive nerves, a naturally bad temper, or an unnaturally empty purse. Still, my friend, grin and bear it. Be sure you do not suffer alone; many another is much worse off than you. Why not try to give him a helping hand, and strengthen yourself by the giving of it? For we do not wish to make a mock of you, you miserable misery-monger, since you are much to be pitied; and there is a sad reality at the bottom of your most contemptible shams. We would rather rouse you to forget yourself, and then, be sure, you will gradually forget your sufferings. And supposing these should remain in greater or less degree, as the necessary accompaniment of your individual lot or peculiar idiosyncrasy, still, according to the common-sense argument of the sage author of "Original Poems," remonstrating with an unwashed child,

> "If the water is cold, and the comb hurts your head,
> What good will it do you to cry?"

Alack! we are all exceedingly like naughty children; we do not enjoy being made clean.

And yet, some of us who have gone through a rather severe course of lavatory education, can understand the blessing of a sunshiny face—ay, even in the midst of inevitable sorrow. Some of us feel the peace that dwells ever at the core of a contented heart, which, though it has ceased to expect much happiness for itself, is ever ready to rejoice in the happiness of others. And many of us still show in daily life the quiet dignity of endurance; of not dwelling upon or exaggerating unavoidable misfortune; of putting small annoyances in one's pocket, instead of flourishing them abroad in other people's faces, like the jilted spinster who "rushed into novel-writing, and made her private wrong a public nuisance." How much wiser is it to hide our wrongs, to smother our vexations, to bear our illnesses, whether of body or mind, as privately and silently as we can! Also, so far as it is possible, to bear them ourselves alone, thankful for sympathy, and help too, when it comes; but not going about beseeching for it, or angry when we do not get it, having strength enough to do without it, and rely solely on the Help divine.

For to that point it must always come. The man who is incurably and permanently miserable is not only an offense to his fellow-creatures, but a sinner against his God. He is perpetually saying to his Creator, "Why hast Thou made me thus? Why not have made me as I wanted to be, and have given me such and such things which I desired to have? I know they would have been good for me, and then I should have been happy. I am far wiser than Thou. Make me what *I* choose, and grant me what *I* require, or else I will be perpetually miserable."

And so he lives, holding up his melancholy face, poor fool! as an unceasing protest against the Wisdom Eternal —against the sunshiny sky, the pleasant earth, and the happy, loving hearts that are always to be found somewhere therein. Overclouded at times, doubtless, yet never quite losing their happiness while there is something left them to love—ay, though it be but a dirty, crying child in the streets, whom they can comfort with a smile or a halfpenny.

Such people may be unhappy—may have to suffer acutely for a time—but they will never become misery-mongers. There is a healthiness of nature which has the power of throwing off disease to the final hour of worn-out nature. Their souls, like their bodies, will last to the utmost limit of a green old age, giving and taking comfort, a blessedness to themselves and all about them. In their course of life many a storm may come; but it never finds them unprepared. They are sound, good ships, well rigged, well ballasted; if affliction comes, they just "make all snug," as the sailors say, and so are able to ride through seas of sorrow into a harbor of peace—finally, into that last harbor, where may Heaven bring at last every mortal soul, even misery-mongers!

AN

OLD SCOTCH LOVE-STORY.

THE MS. upon which this paper is founded came into my hands many years ago,—so many that I entirely forget through whom it came. I remember only that it was given to me with the remark, "Here, take this: it is a bit of human nature truer than any of your novels; you may use it if you like." But I never did; for only we authors know how exceedingly difficult it is to "use" nature, and how rarely it can be done without harming somebody and benefiting nobody.

Therefore I let the MS. lie by, year after year, unread. It was a dreary-looking "screed," filling the whole of an ancient copy-book, in a somewhat clerk-like hand—round, regular, formal, but decidedly illiterate, especially as to spelling. On the fly-leaf—torn, yellow, soiled, and mildewed—was a name, "George Milne, His Book;" and a date, "Auchen"—something, the rest of the word being quite illegible.

This is the only name which I mean to give *bonâ fide*; and there are so many George Milnes in Scotland, and so many places called Auchen—something or other, that it affords little or no clue to the inquisitive reader except the fact that the events recorded did take place in Scotland. Though they happened more than half a century ago, so that any one concerned therein is probably long dead, still I will take the tender precaution of falsifying every name of place or person, and of omitting all dates except the day of the month. Whether the story may "point a moral," I can not tell. Our world of to-day is much the same as the world of yesterday: women still go on breaking men's hearts and ruining their lives, and men do the same to women, though the result here is less fatal, probably because there is something purer and higher in the wrecked material, so that better things are worked out of it. Still, a "bit of human nature" is always pathetic, and not always unprofitable.

The second leaf of the old copy-book commences the history thus:

"Copy of statement of facts by William Campbell, Esquire, Writer in ——" (I leave the town blank), "written some time previous to September 29th, 18—, on which he terminated his existence."

"In drawing up an account of the facts of the connection between Miss Robina Jamieson and myself, I shall confine myself to facts alone, without making comments or drawing inferences. This most distressing task has been forced upon me by late occurrences, by which I have been much injured, and for which (I say it with sorrow) I have been determined to seek redress. I need not attempt to describe the anguish of mind which has compelled me to make the following disclosures."

These "disclosures" are terribly long-winded. They indicate plainly what sort of young man the writer was: gifted with a certain amount of talent, more appreciative than original—but enough to make him sensitive, egotistic, morbid. Not a bad fellow in his way—probably much more refined than other young men of his day and locality—we must remember he belonged to a remote country town in Scotland fifty years ago, and was then something over thirty. Not badly educated, apparently, and a man of some reading, as is obvious from his references to Shakspeare, Burns, Shenstone, and other writers. Of his external individuality, personal appearance, and so forth, I can not give the slightest information, as he never in the remotest way alludes to it.

With these premises, let Mr. William Campbell, Writer, speak for himself:

"Some years ago an intimacy and friendship commenced between Miss Jamieson and me, little known, I believe, except to ourselves. From what passed between us, I conceived myself warranted in paying my addresses to her. In this I may have been wrong, and perhaps I ought to admit that in a letter I stated to her that I had formed my attachment 'unauthorized.' This, however, was from motives of delicacy. The letter was written in August, 18— (seven years ago) and forwarded to Miss Jamieson at P——. I have no copy of it; the answer also is mislaid.

"In effect, my addresses were rejected. At the same time, I was strictly enjoined not to give up visiting at Birkenshaw (the lady's home). I felt disappointed; but from the way in which Miss Jamieson afterwards conducted herself towards me, I began to suspect she was not serious in her refusal. I, however, studied not to intrude myself, and as I felt delicate in speaking on the subject, and hearing her parents had been acquainted with my application, I wrote Mr. Jamieson, asking his forgiveness if I had done any thing wrong, and still continued visiting at Birkenshaw.

"Truth here compels me to state that Miss Jamieson now began to honor me with more attention than she had formerly done. When in town, she seldom failed to allow me the pleasure of accompanying her home; indeed she always told me when I was to be allowed that honor. My purpose in stating these facts is to show that I never at any time paid my addresses to Miss J. with the most distant view to the fortune she has lately received. Our intimacy continued and increased till the spring of 18— (the following year), when Mr. Blair left Kinnochar."

(Mr. Blair, who is never afterwards named, was probably some relative, owner of the property of Kinnochar, where the young lady was in the habit of staying, and which presently devolved to her.)

"Shortly afterwards the following note was left for me from Miss J. by one of the servants at Birkenshaw:

"'If Mr. Campbell feels inclined to extend his evening walk, a friend will have the pleasure of showing him some birds' nests in the garden of Kinnochar.—Monday morning.'

"That I willingly obeyed need not be doubted. I had afterwards other notes of similar import. These facts I mention with regret, but am determined to tell the precise truth, if I tell it at all. It has been extorted from me by cruel injustice.

"Shortly after this, Mr. Jamieson became indisposed. I frequently visited him during his illness, and at these times Miss Jamieson made appointments with me for meetings at Kinnochar. Promises were made and vows of fidelity exchanged between us, when at the approach of autumn our meetings were interrupted by masons repairing the house, and I again visited at Birkenshaw. Miss J. at this time proposed that we should meet at Plainstanes, where she was going; and that her absence should not interrupt our intercourse, it was agreed that we should write to each other.

"On the 30th August, I received the following letter:

"'Particular circumstances have occurred which prevent my going to Plainstanes this week: I therefore will not trouble Mr. Campbell to be my correspondent at present. But as I intend to make out my visit a few weeks hence, I still propose troubling him to write me. I hope Mr. Campbell will pay us a visit at Birkenshaw within these few days, and he will very much oblige ROBINA JAMIESON.

"'P.S.—Mr. Jamieson's spirits are affected by this damp weather; nothing can raise them so much as Mr. Campbell's coming to see him.'"

How clearly one sees through this mist of years the formal yet coquettish young letter-writer—the vain, self-conscious, but good-natured recipient, ready to take trouble in amusing the old man, perhaps for vanity's sake, perhaps for love's. Not a bad fellow, though, as I said before. He goes on:

"I still continued to visit at Birkenshaw. Promises were repeated over and over again. Shortly after, I received the following letter through a servant:

" 'We have received accounts of the death of my brother; he has fallen a victim to the bad climate of Jamaica. As I am afraid his loss will affect my father's spirits, could you, my dear sir, make it convenient to call on us some evening soon? You may think it strange of me to ask you to come out at present, but I trust to your good nature for excusing it, and there is not another out of my own family that I could apply to so readily; and believe me, your obliged ROBINA JAMIESON.'

"I never failed to give due attention (writes the young man, who indeed could hardly have helped succumbing to such delicate feminine flattery), and from what passed between Miss J. and myself, I conceived by this time nothing could prevent our union. She complained if I was absent, and her parents did not discountenance my frequent visits.

"The next letter I received was through the post-office, addressed 'Mr. Renton,' to my care. This was my own suggestion, lest any of my clerks should open her letters.

" 'Birkenshaw, Thursday.

" 'My father is disappointed that you do not spend any evenings with him now, and I am afraid that I am the cause of your being such a stranger here. I suppose you can not be ignorant of the report that the good people of —— have raised, and that it has prevented your coming to Birkenshaw, for fear my parents should adopt the compulsory system; but allow me to inform you they have too few daughters to force them on any man against his will. On my account they do not give young men a general invitation, for fear they should think they courted me; but those that come are none the less welcome, and none more so than you. I expected to have got word of you in —— that would have saved me from writing, but I know you have too much honor than to expose me. Will you spend an evening here this week? and you will let me know by putting a note in the post-office before two o'clock to-day, and I shall take care to take it out, or in any way you choose, for I begin to think you wish to shun me; and believe me always, your much obliged ROBINA JAMIESON.' "

One feels a sort of pity for the young woman, in having her unconscious letter copied, and kept, and republished by the lover, in spite of his "sense of honor." And yet stern feminine justice exacts the rigorous law that no woman worth the name ought to hold out the shadow of hope to a rejected swain, unless she has changed her mind, and means to marry him. Of course the poor fish leaped at the bait immediately:

"When I received this letter (writes young Campbell), I had been a week absent from Birkenshaw. I went there immediately, and found an opportunity of telling Miss J. how much she was mistaken. (It is a curious instance of the formal manners of the last generation, that these lovers never seem to dream of addressing or speaking of one another as any thing else than *Mr. Campbell* and *Miss Jamieson.*) My visits still continued, and both parents were satisfied that our union was to take place. The storm (probably some heavy snow) prevented my visiting her for a short time. I was in ill-health, and had fallen back a little in my business in consequence of having been at Aberdeen and twice in Edinburgh. Still I attended at Birkenshaw whenever I possibly could, and our intimacy continued and increased.

"Miss Jamieson now received accounts of the death of her uncle in Jamaica, that she and her mother had been left considerable sums in his will, and that she was his residuary legatee. After that I visited as formerly. From the opinion I had formed of her, I apprehended no change in her affections and behavior; and in this I was at first not mistaken. I found her the same as usual.

"On Sunday, the 5th of May, I called at Birkenshaw, as I had before intimated to her father in a letter, and found Miss Jamieson at home. Old matters were talked about, and all our old pledges and vows renewed. She declared that the fortune she had become possessed of would not alter her affections; that she was willing to become my bride. I asked if she had the consent of her parents. She most unequivocally declared she had, and the compact was solemnly sealed between us.

"It may here be necessary to state, as in her letter she gives it another meaning, that she had said to me, 'I mean to say Yes, but allow me a little time."

"I answered, 'Certainly, as much as you choose. It is nothing new; you have thought of it before, and something may intervene.'

"She replied, 'Nothing can possibly intervene. I am yours forever.'

"She then mentioned where she would wish to reside, what house she would like purchased or taken, asking how far my means would go in such a purchase, and mentioning that she would have cash of her own soon, and I candidly told her the whole state of my finances. She also made a condition about my going to church. It may here be said, in reference to what she afterwards stated as to not being allowed a few hours' consideration, that our engagement took place between ten and eleven in the forenoon, and that I did not leave Birkenshaw till about nine at night."

Brief as it is, the young man's "Statement" gives a vivid picture of that May Sunday—a grave, quiet, Scotch Sunday—yet during which was transacted this formal, prudent, but passionate Scotch courtship, full of that queer mixture of outside coldness and inside romance which is the charm of the Scotch character. We see the lover, who had been played fast and loose with so long, determined at last for the second time to try his fate—

"To put it to the touch,
And win or lose it all;"

and the lady earnest enough to say, "I am yours forever," yet practical enough to inquire his means, and to select the house she should like to live in; also, doubtless with a keen sense of respectability, making conditions about "going to church," which duty the poetical swain was probably remiss in. And we can imagine the whole of that day of courtship "till about nine at night;"—the slow saunters round the old-fashioned garden, and the parting in the gloaming—the little idyl which each generation, and each individual therein, transacts turn by turn, but on which, in its fond minute particulars, Mr. Campbell's "Statement" is silent. He goes on:

"My happy moments were soon broken in upon. On the Monday following Miss J. received accounts from her uncle's executor of the extent of the fortune she would receive in this country, as residuary legatee; likewise of that abroad, the amount of which could not as yet be ascertained. On the Friday morning Miss Jamieson, who had in the mean time written very particularly about the house, sent me the following letter:

"'Can you, will you forgive me, if I ask you to give me back the promise I gave you on Sunday last? I then asked you for a few hours' consideration; had you given me that, it would have saved me this day. I then boldly declared my mother's consent was of no consequence. This is not the case: she never will consent. I did not mention your last letter, and I hope this correspondence will be kept as quiet as possible.

"'That this will give you pain I do not doubt, but better give it now than afterwards; and, believe me, you have little to regret in the want of any nearer connection with me, unless it is my money, and that is not one-tenth part what they say it is in the neighborhood. That no one can love me better than you, I do not doubt; yet surely you might have come oftener to see me in the spring, particularly when I heard of your being at Braeside. But it is needless to say more. I shall only add that there breathes not the man in Europe I at present prefer to you, but still I consider we may be better apart. You always possess my best wishes, and I hope God will grant you every happiness. Do not absent yourself from the house: my father has little need to be deprived of any of his friends. Do answer this. Address, Jean Johnston, Post-office, ——," and a servant of ours will call for it on Thursday at noon.'

"This letter was addressed, as usual, to 'Mr. Renton,' and I received it on Thursday, May 11, at eleven in the forenoon."

It tells its own tale as to the writer's character. Many a woman may see therein her own picture—well meaning, but easily led, misled, and turned, by parents, friends, circumstances; weak, cowardly, underhand; unwilling to give pain, and yet afraid to suffer it; the sort of woman who drives men mad, all the more that she is often only too lovable—perhaps from her very weakness and malleability—a great charm to a lover so long as he fancies his influence is the only one at work. Alas! time alone teaches us that there is nothing so hopeless to guide as the sweet yieldingness which yields to every body, even as there is no person so difficult to govern as a fool.

Mr. Campbell continues:

"Far from expecting such a letter, I could hardly credit my senses. Next, I thought it must be a jest, to vex me. I was fortified in this idea by the fanciful way in which Miss J. wished to be addressed as 'Jean Johnston.' It struck me that, if she had any thing serious to communicate, she might have commanded my attendance at Birkenshaw, as she had done many times before. After consideration, however, I felt she could never surely jest upon such a subject; and while I decided thus, the answer I wrote will best show the state of my feelings. Miss J. says I wrote harshly. I am very sorry that I should have done so to her or any lady, but at the same time I could not command my feelings, and I had no leisure for reflection, and, even if I had, I was incapable of it.

"'May 8th.

"'MADAM,—I only received your letter this forenoon. The utter confusion of my mind prevented my answering it in time to send by the post-office, still I hope you will receive it safe. You know little of my feelings when you say simply that your letter will give me pain. No language could describe my feelings. I hope you will forgive if I express myself incoherently. I did not think Miss Jamieson could ever ask me any thing that I would not have granted, but I have been fatally deceived. I would sooner part with my existence than give you what you ask, come what will.

"'Two years ago, I paid my addresses to you; these were rejected. Still you gave me liberty to visit at Birkenshaw. I became resigned to my fate, and continued to do so, although some might not have thought their case hopeless. I would not for the world have intruded upon you, until you yourself began to raise my hopes. You yourself made appointments, and commanded my attendance when and where you thought proper. As far as I know myself, I am not presumptuous or sanguine, but could I receive letters from Miss Jamieson, asking me to meet her solitary in the garden and house of Kinnochar, without indulging hopes? These letters I have this day looked over with a sorrowful heart. You know you allowed many other meetings which you yourself appointed. You spoke freely of the report of our union: it is mentioned in one of your letters. I would have thought it wrong to meet you alone in the garden of Kinnochar, unless I had implicitly believed that our union was to take place. What passed between us on that and other occasions justified that. I leave it to yourself if you did not put questions which were answered by me in a way which could not admit of any other possible interpretation. I am sure you can not forget what passed on the day I called at Birkenshaw in going to the mills.

"'I will say no more of this. I looked on the promises of Sunday last as a continuation and confirmation of former pledges. Our interview was solitary, solemn, and decisive, and you pointed out the house you wished taken as a residence, and the marriage-jaunt, which was the same as you had different times before mentioned. You wrong me cruelly when you speak of your money: it never at any time entered into my calculations. I am afraid it might bring you more suitors, and on that account alone I was anxious for a renewal of our pledges. I explained to you what prevented my seeing you for some time in spring. Absence in Edinburgh had thrown me back in business, and when I was sent for to Braeside I had to go and return with all speed. I am sorry you make that an excuse for breaking faith with me, as when I came back I was received by you with as much kindness as before. I need not speak of the many and nameless endearments that passed between us; they are all forgotten now. Money has obliterated all.

" 'I leave it to your honor and conscience whether, for a year past, either you or I had any other idea than that our marriage was to take place. Sorry would I be to have sought or taken from you a rash vow, because you had come in for a fortune, which I cared nothing about. How I am to bear this sudden, unexpected calamity, God only knows. As to the keeping secret of my first letter, I now care no more for it than I do for any thing else in this world.' "

The young man goes on, repeating himself over and over again, in a feeble, dreary sort of way, harping on her accusation of his pursuit of her for her fortune, which has evidently struck him sharply. Finally, he says, referring to the excuse of her mother's non-consent:

"I was at all times aware you were capable of acting for yourself. I mean to act honestly and fairly to the last. I can not give you back your vow, or rather I should say vows. I can not give you back your letters. The use of those letters must be regulated by circumstances. I fear I can not refrain from taking steps to justify myself before your parents and the world. Unfit as I am, I must take a copy of this letter before dispatching it. Wishing you every happiness, much more than you have left me possessed of, and improvement in your health, I am, etc.,

(Signed) "WILLIAM CAMPBELL."

In the letter one traces at once the weak point of the writer—that sensitive egotism, so small in any man, but which many very good men are possessed of, though it leads them on sometimes to the meanest actions, as now. Her lover's half threat of making public his wrongs in his own self-defense, evidently frightens the young lady. She answers him at once:

"Birkenshaw, 9th May.

"I own the justice and truth of all you have written to me, and now ask your forgiveness. I had no idea of the pain my letter would have given you, but we are quits now. May God forgive you for the harshness of yours. But I will require to take care what I write, as you are a man of law, and I am not fairly matched with you. However, I hope you will answer me by the servant, and tell me whether you will or can forgive me; and, believe me, I shall endeavor not to hurt your feelings again. I own it was unguarded, and I have no excuse for myself. I have only to say one thing more: if you still wish me to become your bride, I beg that previous to my quitting my father's house all letters that have passed betwixt us may be destroyed. Write me by the bearer. You may address to my father, who is from home, and, as I know your hand, I shall open it.

"ROBINA JAMIESON."

This letter was inclosed in another, as follows:

"The inclosed was written on Friday, and I sent it into town, with orders that it should only be delivered into your own hands. You were from home. I shall now address it as formerly, and put it in the post-office; and I request you will answer it, and tell me what you intend with regard to myself. My former request will never be again made, and it would be a relief if I thought you forgave me and forgot it. Address, as before, to 'Jean Johnston, Post-office,' and I will get some one to call for it. ROBINA JAMIESON."

Poor foolish girl! timid, irresolute, deceitful; afraid to irritate the man in whose power she had put herself, wishing to temporize with him till an opportunity offered of saving herself; apt at any cajoling self-accusations, not having the strength or honesty to see that, whatever wrong she had done him, a man who could threaten to revenge himself upon a woman for a breach of promise—or, for that matter, a woman on a man; it is all one—almost justifies the infidelity.

But she gains her end. His next letter (he must have copied it, and what shall be said in defense of a man who copies his love-letters?) is as follows:

"MY DEAR MISS JAMIESON,—I am too happy not to forget and forgive. The trial was severe, but you are an angel still. God Almighty bless you! My already weakened frame, through this distress, tells me I can not live without you. You must be my bride. I have continued an evident and honorable attachment to you for years. Make of your fortune what you please, I wish neither control over it, nor the smallest benefit from it, and it will be the happiest moment of my life when I can formally renounce it. I only want Miss J., and she knows I could have begged my bread with her. My anxiety for the delivery of my last induced me to put a note in the post-office addressed to you; the meaning of it will be known to none but yourself. I am yours forever,

"WILLIAM CAMPBELL."

Evidently the man was honest, egotistically inclined, no doubt, and prone to the smallnesses which crop out in all egotists; but he loved the young woman, and had proved it pretty well.

He goes on in his "Statement:"

"I considered this a most solemn engagement, confirming former ones; and the lady herself can only account for her conduct in immediately shunning me, and setting out on a jaunt without ever letting me know, or conferring on me the honor of being her correspondent. . . . Miss J. says, in one of her letters, that I have too much honor than to expose her. In this she is correct. I only communicate this statement to her nearest relation. But has she kept her honor with me? Whatever I feel, I am determined to seek what redress may be in my power. I now say, without vanity, that for a year past, and until she received the letter from her uncle's executor, the attachment was as strong on Miss Jamieson's side as on my own, and I could not have withdrawn with honor to myself, or without her consent. This ends my statement, as sent in to Mr. Jamieson."

Therefore it seems this foolish, frantic lover took the false step of detailing all his wrongs to the lady's father! Not immediately, however, for he goes on to state how they met, and how every thing that had occurred of a disagreeable nature was buried in oblivion:

"Miss J. said she had made her request only to try me, and laughed at my having taken up the matter seriously. She also wanted a document on the subject of our engagement, but said my two letters were sufficient, and bound me irrevocably. She then, voluntarily, took a solemn oath that she would fulfill her engagements with me, and never think of retracting while she drew breath.

"She told me she wished to reside a short time at the house of Kinnochar, which she had newly come to; and that as soon as arrangements could be made our union should take place. I was happy once more, and had been so since receiving her last two letters. I could not believe that she would have entered into so many engagements, verbal and written, and then break them; that, after what had passed between her and me, she would have been so deliberately cruel again and again as to raise my hopes for the purpose of blasting them, or of amusing herself by wantonly sporting with my feelings. . . . I now know that the attendance of others, at least of one other, had become more agreeable to her than mine: circumstances so obvious that they became the subject of general conversation.

"Although she had not, for a year past, roved the smallest distance from home without acquainting me, she now went off to Edinburgh, giving me not the smallest intimation. Afterwards she said she took this jaunt for the benefit of her health. No reason for concealing it from me. Who was more interested in the state of her health than I was? My state of mind at this time admits of no description.

"It was then I wrote out the statement of facts, and sent it to her father in Edinburgh. If any thing was wrong in it, I hope I am excusable. It was useless to address *her* on the subject. I therefore sent it to Mr. Jamieson, and it was delivered into his hands by a gentleman, a friend of mine, with the following letter:

"'4th June.

"'Dear Sir,—It is with sorrow that I feel myself constrained to lay the following before you. There had already been only too much writing on the subject: but it would have been uncandid not to have put you in possession of these facts. As yet no one but Miss J. knows any thing. This, however, was not to be for long. That it will distress Miss J. and her relatives I doubt not, but they can not suffer one hundredth part of what I am suffering. When you have read the inclosed, will you return it? and lest the parcel should be opened by any one, will you address it in a fictitious name to my care? If I have done any thing wrong or strange, it must be imputed to my sufferings. I hope you are enjoying your jaunt; and with best wishes, I am, dear sir, yours, etc., William Campbell.'"

The foolish fellow! in that morbid vanity and sensitive self-consciousness which made up a considerable portion of his love, he was weaving the rope to hang himself withal. He goes on to say,

"After Mr. Jamieson returned from Edinburgh, I met him at the Bruces of Broomfield, where he tore a leaf out of his pocket-book, and wrote in pencil, 'I received your letter and statement. Robina took away the statement. After she had found it correct she *keepit* it."

This poor young lady, who did not know her own mind, was apparently growing desperate, for after her return to Kinnochar she thus addresses her persistent wooer:

"My father received your letter and statement. You have certainly proved what I never denied. I only asked you to release me from that engagement; but it seems my fortune has too many charms for you, and you are determined to prosecute me, or to have it. I contentedly will submit to any thing rather than appear in a court of law; therefore I have no alternative. But recollect that, at present, I will not leave this house. My parents allow me to decide so far for myself.

"You reproach me for going on a pleasure jaunt without informing you of it. It was for the sake of my health; and as I am offered frequent sea-excursions, I beg leave to inform you that in a few days I may be off again. That one information may serve for all. I am ordered to go to P—— shortly.

"I understood, when you were last here, you gave me up. You might at least have written to me before writing to my father; but he does not interfere. If not asking too great a favor, you will please inform me what your determinations are; and you will much oblige

"ROBINA JAMIESON."

Into whom, poor lassie, some spirit and firmness seems to have come at last. It is curious to see, by implication, how binding she considers a "promise of marriage," in the letter, at least, if not in the spirit. With all her anger and contempt, she never says decisively, "I am free; I will not marry you." Nor does it seem to enter into the deluded lover's mind how futile, how wicked, is a compulsory engagement. Yet he had some conscience, for he says,

"I must have been over-cruel and confused when I sent her the following answer:

"'11th June.

"'DEAR MADAM,—I am this day favored with yours of the 9th inst. I will not trouble you with my feelings. I wrote the statement in despair, and it was sent off in a moment. I need not say whether I have repented it or not. I am so overwhelmed; and the next instant every thing seems like a dream. You still speak of your fortune. I can not say more than

I have said already: so far from its having too many charms for me, I would most willingly die that you might be relieved of me; but that is an event over which I have no control, although I have suffered enough in mind to have broken to pieces a frame possessed of less physical strength. You accuse me of selfishness. I need not make assertions which you will now think matters of course, but if you knew my thoughts I would stand acquitted on that score. My pleasures, when I had any, were all of the simple kind, and could be gratified without a fortune. I have no right to offer better advice than I take myself; but you will find it is the fortune that makes you despise me—not me who cares for your fortune. I know you can, if you choose, take a very just view of this or any other matter. And I could mention some who worship you now that were once very ready to joke me, and not in the most delicate manner, on the report of our engagement.

" 'However, that is nothing. If I could believe I should ever enjoy a moment's peace in this world, I would grant your request, and set you free. But I can not quite extinguish hope. I know what would ensue, and perhaps can not entirely prevent this. My affections have been totally exclusive: I never could have cared for any one else under any circumstances. I have thought of no other but yourself for years. And whatever I may have written in my distress, I find it is absolutely out of my power to root out or abate my affection, even though I should be despised and spurned by its object.

" 'This being my most pitiful case, what can I do? You bid me state my determination—at the same time you hold me your own. I am ready to do every thing you wish, except giving up my interest in yourself; in mercy do not ask it again! I am obliged to act my former self to save appearances. If Captain Wilson' (apparently some supposed rival) 'were away, I might submit. I can bear you classing me with misery and contempt, for I believe you are right after all. I never had a high opinion of myself, and I can assure you it is now low enough. If a year ago you had had the same opinion of me as at present, I would have been comparatively happy now. I ask your forgiveness for all I have done amiss. I do not intentionally do wrong, and I am suffering for it all. I have been plunged all at once into such a sea of misery, and stand in need more of pity than reproach.

" 'I intend to be at Mr. Patterson's on Saturday: perhaps you are to be there, and our meeting might be disagreeable to you; if so drop a single word to me. I can safely say I am indisposed, and stop away. If you want any thing stated more explicitly I shall be happy to do it. Your letter is very acrimonious, but you shall have no more reproaches from me. I am sorry I can not consent to break our engagement. Wishing you every improvement in your health, I am, etc.,

" 'WILLIAM CAMPBELL.'

"In this letter I have neglected to notice that part of hers which states that she understood I had given her up. She must have misunderstood. I understood the very reverse. I recollect how it was. After some conversation, she asked why I looked so ill? I made no immediate answer. I confess I was a good deal affected, as she was looking very poorly herself. Miss J. then burst into tears, and said she never could forgive herself for lately acting to me as she had done. I did every thing in my power to soothe her, saying that all was now happily over: adding, 'I will vindicate you, Miss J., though I can not vindicate myself for making you suffer so much,' or words to that effect. We were both very much affected; and fearing that her father, or some other person, might enter the room and find us in this situation, we took leave of one another, Miss J. asking me to come back as soon as possible; and said we would be in higher spirits at our next meeting.

"This was the last time I visited her. In two or three days after she set out for Edinburgh with her parents without informing me, though she must have known of it at the time we met.

"Miss J. returned the following answer to my letter of 11th June:

"'It is necessary to inform you that I am not invited to Mr. Patterson's to-day. I know there are people here who think more of me than they once did, but were I as free as any one, this person whom you allude to could never be more to me than a common acquaintance. If my letter was acrimonious, recollect yours to my father was very irritating. But I beg you will address to him no more complaints of me: his health is too feeble to admit of his being agitated by scurrility. Address to myself. I before informed you I am ordered frequent change of air and sea-excursions; so in a few weeks I go to Edinburgh, and afterwards to meet my father at ——, where I trust you will not send threatening letters after me.

"'You offer to grant any request of mine save one: will you return me all the letters I have ever sent you? If so, put them in the post-office that I may get them on Monday morning, and oblige

"'ROBINA JAMIESON.

"'P.S.—I never meant to class you with misery and contempt. It was your statement to my father that made me miserable because you remembered me with contempt. But I beg you will not tease my parents with such things, for they will not interfere on your side.'"

Sad it is to see in these letters what appears in the story of many and many a life—the pale ghost, nay, worse, the ugly, decaying corpse of a dead love, once so sweet and fresh, human and fair.

William Campbell answers her brief, bitter letter by another, very long-winded (I ought to say that I have been obliged to condense a good deal, though I have interpolated nothing), in which he explains that through some delay he did not get hers till long after date. He altogether declines to return her letters. He says, "it would be like shutting the tomb upon herself." He promises never to trouble her, or appeal to her parents, but still keeps her bound to her promise of marriage. He regrets again his sending in the statement, but reproaches her for destroying it, and reminds her that he has kept an exact copy of it. He uses no actual threat, but declares that if she at any time breaks her engagement with him, he will "seek redress." Finally, he hopes her health may be benefited by her sea excursions; and ends his letter thus:

"I would fain say something more, but I shall refrain. I am unwilling to trouble you with complaints, and should wish to suffer in silence. Notwithstanding every exertion I get worse and worse. No efforts of reason to laugh away my misery have the slightest effect. My health is now suffering much, but I shall seek no remedy. Will I never be allowed to look on you again? In case any thing may happen, I shall seal and lock up your letters, and leave written instructions as to their delivery to yourself, so you need have no anxiety on that matter. If I could reveal my misery to any person it might give me some relief. I was lately one of the happiest beings in existence, and I am now the most miserable.

"WILLIAM CAMPBELL."

After copying this letter, he again reverts to old things—telling how he was constantly invited to Birkenshaw; how nothing prevented their marriage except slender means; how he used to tell her "he was saving all he could;" and she told him of her possible chance from her uncle, "which," she said, "would make all right." He also relates how, when the first account of the legacy came, all the business matters relating to it were confided to him; and it was not until it turned out to be so much larger than was at first expected, that the plighted troth was attempted to be broken. The "man of law" and the canny Scot peep curiously through the miserable lover, though not so much so as to convict him of mercenariness. Continually he repeats himself, and goes back and back upon every incident of courtship. One he especially records, referring, with true legal exactitude, to a sentence in one of his letters, reminding her of "what passed the day I called at Birkenshaw on my way to the mills."

"I found Miss J. by herself. She complained that I had been jaunting without her. I said it was not on pleasure, but business, and that the weather was very disagreeable. On my rising to go, as I had remained past their dinner-hour, Miss Jamieson went between me and the door, and said, 'We must repeat our vows.' I answered, 'There was no need, but there could be no objection.' She said, 'Every thing was understood as to our marriage; but something ought to be understood as to the time or near about it,' and proposed repeating a solemn oath. I replied, 'I could have no objection, but that it bound us whether our parents consented or not.' She said, 'They are quite agreeable. I told them of our former engagements, and it was just what they expected.'

"She then made me repeat these words: 'May I never know peace in heaven, or see God in mercy, if I marry any other but you, or if I go south again without taking you along with me as my wife!' And she took a similar oath herself."

The next phase in the story is, that the mutual friend at whose house they might have met—Mr. Patterson—

calls upon Mr. Campbell to request the return of Miss Jamieson's letters, which is point blank refused. Afterwards Campbell writes to Patterson the following letter:

"29th July.

"DEAR SIR,—After you called to-day for Miss J.'s letters, which I refused to give up, I became anxious that, in case of any misunderstanding, I should mention again what I communicated to you, and which you may communicate to Miss J.

"I have never done, or intend to do, any thing evasive, or in violation of the promise betwixt her and me. I shall be extremely sorry if she has conducted herself, or shall conduct herself, in a manner unbecoming one in her situation with regard to me. But if she does I must candidly state that, in justice to myself, I will if I live take steps for my own vindication. This I have explicitly stated to herself and to her father. I can not say more; the matter is known to herself and to her parents, and if she, with their consent, violates her engagements with me, it will be known who is to blame. I am not. No person can know the circumstances, or the extent of injury that I have sustained, except myself.

"I hope nothing can diminish the friendship between you and me.

"Yours truly, WILLIAM CAMPBELL."

It seems that, somewhat on the principle of "while there is life there is hope," the desperate lover's last scheme was to keep the girl fast bound, so that, according to the strong Scotch feeling of the sacredness of an oath, if she would not marry himself, she could not marry any other man. Nevertheless, he must have had relentings of both conscience and pity, or else he had apparently heard some news concerning her which strongly affected his already half-bewildered mind; for on the 11th of August in the same year—which has seen so much!—he thus again writes to her:

"MISS JAMIESON,—It is humiliating to me to be under the necessity of addressing you. I beg you will hear me without reference to what is past.

"No person knows the state I am in; nor do I wish it should be known. On Friday last I executed a settlement of the greater part of my small property, and from the state of my mind and health at present the settlement would only stand good in the event of my living sixty days after that date; if I die before that time Robert and my sister will be left unprovided for.

"I am now satisfied that it is your intention to break your engagements with me. I can not prevail upon myself to consent to this, but as I also can not prevent you doing what you please, it would be conferring a great favor on me if you would defer marrying another until after the lapse of the sixty days. By that time I will be no more. I now look anxiously forward to the termination of my woes. May it be the commencement of your happiness!"

This is the first indication he gives of that terrible purpose from which sane human nature involuntarily shrinks. Pitiful as it is to think of, it stamps at once the reality of the man's passion for this woman, which had now become an actual monomania. He goes on:

"In earnestly asking this favor, I do not mean to ask your pity: nor do I in consequence sanction any violation of your engagements with me. On the contrary, should I be granted strength to support existence—which I do not anticipate—I would seek every redress in my power. A single line from you—unsigned, unaddressed, and without a date—would be satisfactory; and if you wish I pledge myself to return it immediately.

"This must appear strange, and it is so. I can not help it. If I could make myself otherwise I would. I have struggled hard, but all is unavailing. I see my fate very clearly, and it can not be avoided. All my endeavor now shall be to reconcile myself to it. Oh, do not do any thing to hasten it! not for my sake, but for those who are depending on me, and who have never offended you. I never intended to offend you myself.

"Offer my best respects to your parents. I will never see any of you again, nor the garden, etc. It is better I should not. It would only make me worse; these recollections are so bitter. Will you all pray for me?"

Then, with a curious and ominous confusion of ideas, he ends, "Dear Sir, yours truly, William Campbell;" and puts as a P.S.:

"May I trouble you for this once to deliver this to Miss Jamieson? To the best of my knowledge there is nothing wrong in it, and she, I have no doubt, will communicate the contents to you if you wish it."

Whether, under all his calmness, the writer had some vague idea that the threat of suicide would be to Miss Jamieson a final compulsion to receive his addresses, one can not judge. Let us at least not judge him harshly—this poor soul, full of so many good qualities, and that best quality of all, the power of faithful love—a man, of whom a good, loving woman might have made almost any thing she pleased, and over whom a good woman of steadfast will, although unloving, might, even while rejecting him, have exercised such an influence as to save him from these deeps of misery, into which one of so frail a nature could not but go down.

Whatever was Campbell's purpose in inditing this letter, it failed. The answer comes from Miss Jamieson's old father,—short and pithy, full of capital common sense, and calmly ignoring every thing that to him, honest man, was no doubt perfectly incomprehensible.

"Kinnochar, 13th August.

"DEAR SIR,—I have perused your letter to Robina. Its contents surprise me very much indeed. This world is made for trials and disappointments. I thought you was (*sic*) one of those men that to any thing of the kind would have cried 'Buff!' on; and I am sure you have more good sense than to let any disappointment ever be known to the world, far less than to let it interfere with your happiness or peace of mind. There is as good fish in the sea as ever came out of it. Do let us see you here again as before, and believe me yours truly, DAVID JAMIESON."

This is the last letter copied. With it all correspondence and all intercourse between Mr. Campbell and the Jamieson family appear to have ceased. The rest of the MS., which consists of a good many pages, is a feeble, lengthy, and often rather incoherent statement; full of ramblings and repetitions—apparently written at different times, though headed by the sad and ominous words, "The Last."

From this—which is far too long-winded to give entire, I will merely extract sentences here and there, which seem to throw any new light on the events of the story, or on the character of the actors therein. For, as before said, I have no other possible data to go upon than this MS. in the ancient copy-book. In this final statement I shall do as I have done throughout—merely extract and excise, without adding a single line.

"A dreadful cloud has hung over me for some time past. I fear much I shall never enjoy the sunshine of this world. This paper will be laid down beside the statement of facts respecting Miss Jamieson. That lady's letters are in John Watson's little black box. I beg that special care may be taken of them and the different papers; they may perhaps be required as a qualification of my conduct, if any such be admitted, for I have suffered, and am suffering, more than I can bear. I have thought, and no doubt most people would think so too, that I was the last man in the world to be borne down by an occasion of this nature, and I might have laughed at any other person under similar circumstances. None can know, however, until they are placed in a similar position. God knows what may happen. I have no distinct views on the subject. My feelings have been wounded in a dreadful degree."

And here he wanders off into the recapitulation of his wrongs:

"I hope every person will try to think as charitably of me as possible. I will not attempt to justify my past life. I wish it had been very much better than it has been. What I most dreaded was deficiency as a practical Christian and a good man, terms of similar import; and, without taking any merit, I have had ample time for self-examination during nights when sleep has not visited me. I have found myself most lamentably deficient. All my comfort is, that I never oppressed the poor and helpless, nor did a deliberate act of cruelty to man or beast. . . . Although lately deceived where I least expected it, I was not selfish, and had no pleasure in squandering; indeed, I could not quietly do so when I had others depending on me, and I can say, as a dying man, that the accusation of Miss J., that I wished to possess myself of her fortune, is as cruel as it is unjust. . . .

"I meant to have mentioned some of my friends by name, but in the agitation of my mind I might forget some of the best of them. But may every happiness attend them through life, and may they never suffer themselves, as I have done, to place their happiness on one object. I meant to have written to my parents, but can not. I can only think of them with that dreadful degree of agony. . . . I die as I have lived—their dutiful son. It gives me some consolation at this awful juncture to think that I have not been a bad son or brother. My parents, and Robert and Isabella, can speak to that, as they are all good themselves. I feel for poor Robert; he must work away at the business. I hope some will employ him for my sake, and many for his own. A better young man, or more honorable, or more punctual, does not exist. He is well calculated to do business, much better than I was myself. I hope the brethren of the profession will be kind to him. Isabella I know will feel dreadfully. All this redoubles my agony, and urges me to a speedy termination of my woes. We will all meet in a better world; and I have one consolation—they will not be left destitute here.

"I have endeavored by every possible means to conceal the dreadful state I am in. In the course of two months I have not slept many hours. I am a complete wreck and ruin, totally unfit to do business. . . . Instead of reading my book, as I was wont, I have sought company, and even dissipation. I do not mean that I have ever taken to drinking, but I have left company with regret, knowing I had not now the power of retiring peacefully into myself. Time, which used to fly, now lags and wears me out of patience. I know myself, and know that I shall never be better, and what impels me to escape from it all is the fear of absolute insanity, when I would be deprived of the power of extricating myself from this deplorable state of existence."

Psychologists may question whether insanity had not even then begun—whether that exaggerated Ego which marks so often the thin line of demarkation between soundness and unsoundness of mind, had not for some time indicated that the poor brain was growing more or less diseased, and that the awful "escape" contemplated, however rationally and deliberately stated, was in truth only a phase of mental sickness, increased by bodily disease; though he seems never to have been actually laid aside by illness, to have gone steadily to business, and kept up a decent appearance before the world, and especially before his family—to whom he again and again tenderly refers. But the one engrossing subject is never forgotten for a moment.

"After an interval of suffering, I have taken up my pen again. But I feel no improvement, rather the contrary. . . . My chief mistake was allowing myself to get on an intimate footing with one who was great, or thought herself so. Miss J. knows what passed between us on that head; how she satisfied my scruples, and urged me on. She seemed to have convinced herself and me that our dispositions were congenial; but I should have been like the Minstrel of Donne,

"'Who prayed the great lady to be allowed
To hirple his woes to the coal-house door,
And cheer with his lays the simple and poor.'

The poor old man's feelings somewhat resemble my own. . . ."

He then refers to his threats of instituting law proceedings, but declares it was only a threat; which he never would have carried out, and once more entreats pardon for it.

"Nothing has sickened my soul so much as Miss Jamieson's accusation of my having designs on her fortune. God knows, if I had all the wealth in the world, I would give it all that I might be myself again, or even for one sound sleep. Reason and philosophy may say, 'Have you not still the objects which used to delight you—the society of friends and acquaintances, books, etc.?' But they are not the same to me; I see things through a totally different medium. My mind, which once reflected all things in such a pleasing manner to me, is now broken and ruffled, and reflects every thing distorted, hideous, and disgusting. . . . It is officious memory that puts me to the rack, and yet without it I would be a second *Edward Shore* (he here doubtless refers to Crabbe's pathetic poem of this title), and on a par with the beasts that perish. Beyond every thing I fear falling into that state. I do already find my faculties considerably impaired, and still getting worse. There is no remedy against this calamity but one, and may God forgive one of His erring creatures for presuming to have recourse to it!"

Poor unfortunate! One's heart bleeds as one copies his words, but the instance is not a rare one in this miserable, struggling, over-worked, over-sensitive world of men. It holds out a solemn warning to both men and women, to strive, from earliest childhood, after that grand quality, the balance-weight and pivot upon which our whole mental and moral machinery turns—*self-control.*

On and on, page after page, does William Campbell continue repeating himself, and going over his dreary story; referring to incidents upon which "delicacy," he says, had hitherto made him silent—how the lady, in the spring of the previous year, "in the house of Kinnochar, voluntarily and unequivocally declared her attachment;" of their many talks as to their future life, their home, and even their possible new felicities therein: "and she used to speak with pleasure of my fondness for children." He reverts sometimes to "the gentleman"—he never mentions his name—to whom apparently Miss Jamieson is shortly to be married; with whom, he says, she appeared at the theatre the day after the receipt of that last letter imploring her to defer the wedding for at least sixty days, and who is constantly seen accompanying her through the town. This gentleman, however, he allows to possess many more attractions than himself; nor does he accuse him in any way, except by suggesting that he had been a mere common acquaintance until Miss Jamieson was publicly known to have succeeded to this fortune. The poor fellow's innate kindness of heart comes out in many ways:

"In my settlement I have burdened my sister and brother with no legacies. We have poor friends of our own, and they will not forget those who have been in the habit of getting some little assistance. I have only to give the hint, and I am sure it will be obeyed. I would wish them to pay ten pounds to the Kirk Session, for the poor of our parish; ten pounds to the kirk treasurer, to be given in charity as he shall think proper: five pounds to George Black, and one pound each to John Ferguson, Alexander Graham, and Mary Lochead; and one pound to an old man, nearly blind, who often sits on the kirk-yard brae."

His great anxiety appears to have been to prove clearly that, in spite of the dreadful act he meditated, his mind was perfectly sound, so that in no way should the disposition of his property be called into question, to the injury of his family. He seems indeed to have been a man tolerably well off in the world, for he more than once reverts to his comfortable circumstances, as well as to the good health which he had invariably enjoyed until this calamity overcame him. Nor has he apparently succumbed without a struggle. He says he at one time intended to cure his despair by travelling, but was convinced of the hopelessness of this: wherever he is, or whatever he does, the one dominant idea never leaves him for a moment. But he is still capable of a good deal of curious abstracted moralizing:

"What a difference there is in the fates and fortunes of different men. I envy some whom others pity. I wish it had been my fate to die like Marshal Ney, and yet many thought him cruelly treated. What a glorious doom compared to mine, to get a few brave fellows to shower their bullets through his heart, particularly in his case, when they would only obey his own orders. I, God forgive me, am constrained to do what till now would never have had a place in my mind, and to do it myself."

This is the only clue given of the manner in which he intended to seek death, except that it is to take place in some quiet, lonely place where he wishes afterwards to be buried—possibly on that same kirk-yard "brae" where the "old man nearly blind" often sits. He also says,

"When in Edinburgh, Mr. John Graham, of that city, Mr. George Morison, of this place, and myself, agreed to attend each other's funerals, at whatever distance apart we might reside. I wish Mr. Graham accordingly invited; Mr. Morison will, of course, be there. I wish that especially, as Mr. Graham repeated this the last time I saw him, and we made promises which I should not like broken. I never did break my promises. None will be more astonished than he at my fate."

This fate seems now darkening over him, nearer and blacker. He becomes every page more vague, wandering, and incoherent in what he writes; he makes confusions of proper names, and repeats himself again and again. Whether the MS. was continued for weeks or days before he could make up his mind to the fatal end, one can not say. The last blow which unhinged him seems to have come from the fact of his discovery how Miss Jamieson, now busy about the preparations for her marriage, was "making light of and laughing at the whole matter."

"I have also from the best authority that she has spread it abroad, and mentioned circumstances which have now become public. There is no doubt she has shown and published my last letter, for Miss Allan mentioned the particulars of it to a lady in this town. Well, she has succeeded in bringing about what she wished; she is at full liberty to laugh at me. Bad as the world is, I suppose few after all would envy her her sport. It is not always the extent of the wrong, but the thought by whom it is inflicted, that plants the sting. When Cæsar saw Brutus stab at him, he offered no resistance: his heart burst, and muffling up his face in his mantle, he fell at the base of Pompey's statue.

"All is now over. I die in perfect good-will to every human being. If my feelings have led me to say any thing offensive respecting Miss Jamieson, I am very sorry for it. She has my entire forgiveness. If I have erred, I hope she will forgive me, and it will be wise in her to forget whatever may have passed between us. If I could have done this, I should have been happy."

Here the MS. abruptly ends—the story likewise; to which I can give no definite conclusion, for I find none. How, when, or in what manner the scene closed upon the unfortunate man I have no idea. The only other fact attainable concerning him is that he died.

For, in the last page of this yellow old copy-book is an inscription which purports to be "copied from the tombstone of the late William Campbell, Esq., Writer, of ——, in the church-yard of ——," the very one he indicates as belonging to the kirk of his parish. The inscription runs thus:

> "To the memory of William Campbell, Esquire, Writer, who died 29th September, 18—" (it is the year of the date of the MS.), "in the thirty-eighth year of his age. This monument is erected—"

But no: I will not give the inscription, as it might furnish some remote clue to an identification which throughout this true story I have carefully avoided. For, while the narration of so sad a tragedy of common life, hidden under the safe shelter of the anonymous, can harm no one, and may be a lesson to some, the individuality of its unhappy subject is of no moment to any human being.

Suffice it to say that this monument purports to be erected to his memory by the friends who loved and lamented him, and that, besides the record of his death—usually all that is found in Scotch church-yards—it pays a long and affectionate tribute to his worth: lingering upon his several virtues—his justice, charity, and benevolence, his firm, independent principles, and his social yet simple manners. Of his mode of death is recorded not a word—merely that "he died."

This is all. Concerning the lady whom I have called Robina Jamieson, and her after history, I can tell nothing, for nothing do I know. Most probably she too is long since dead, for her lover records of her then that "Miss J. was not so young as to be unable to judge and act for herself." It is difficult, nay impossible, to speculate as to the effect produced upon her life or character by the events of this short six months—between May and October. Perhaps they would have no effect at all. Most likely she would go on from maidenhood to wifehood, and from youth to old age, very respectable and respected: an exceedingly agreeable person, cherishing under her regular decorous church-going the sort of thing she called a conscience, and preserving safe under the matronly folds of her silken bodice that queer piece of anatomy which she supposed to be a heart.

But, God help us! hearts are living things, and even in this generation people are unfortunate enough to possess them sometimes. Let us teach our daughters to guard their own: to keep them pure and clean, unselfish, unworldly, honest, and true! so that neither their loving or not loving him can ever injure any man. For, strange as it may seem, in our own as in most other conditions of society, from barbarism upward, it is not so much the men who rule the women, as the women who guide the men. And when the life of a man, not absolutely a bad man, goes to wrack and ruin, it is not seldom some woman who, by sins of omission or commission, has been originally to blame.

A GARDEN PARTY.

WE were all tormenting Aunt Patience to tell us a Christmas Story.

Aunt Patience—every body's Aunt Patience, though she has not a relative living—is rather different from her name; being, I own, a somewhat quick-tempered little woman—that is, when you irritate her, or go against her sense of right and justice; but, these satisfied, she is a most pleasant person. Slightly deformed—not naturally, but from a weak spine neglected in childhood: and with the pathetically beautiful face that deformed people often have—a sort of mute appeal to Providence, or to the tenderness that Providence puts into good people's hearts. She has also a quantity of light-brown hair—very pretty—and unmingled with a thread of gray though she is long past forty. She possesses a small income, and a small house of her own, to which she retires, when not wanted, as continually she is, in other people's. Then she leaves it in charge of the cat and the servant; or "lets" it, as she says, though usually to poor friends who can pay no rent, or sick friends, to whom its prettiness and peace are beyond all paying for.

Miss Patience Hall was never married. Whether she was ever "attached," as the phrase is, to any body— But that is her own affair. She says she has the happiest life imaginable; and one can believe it, for she takes no trouble to make herself happy, only her neighbors.

"My dears," said Aunt Patience, crossing her little knees comfortably, and composing herself to knit away by the fire-light, "what story can I possibly tell you? You have drained me dry long ago. If I had to write a book" (here we shouted with laughter at the comicality of the idea), "I could not find any thing in the world worth saying—as is indeed the case with many voluminous authors. But" (as if she thought she had been a little too severe), "probably the reason is, that they go out of their way to invent things out of their own tired heads, or steal them second-hand from other people's; when, if they would just set down what they saw, thought, and felt—within the limitations of proper reserve—it would be far more interesting, and more original, because more natural.

"No; I'll not attempt to tell you a story. I will simply give you the history of an afternoon, spent in a family where I was visiting. It may be none the less satisfactory, on this cold, wet, wintry day, that it was a summer afternoon.

"The house was Oak Hill—Mr. Holcomb's. Possibly none of you know Mr. Holcomb; few do out of his own immediate neighborhood. But he is a remarkable man in his way. A tradesman—I am sure he would not object to the title; wealthy, and all his wealth of his own earning; a self-made, self-educated man. Whatever he owes to his antecedents—and he may owe something, for I believe in the value of race, and that when a notable man crops out in a generation, it indicates something fine in the breed—I can not tell; I never saw his father or mother. But I know what he owes to himself, and what his children will owe to him. Primarily, a worthy mother, whom he married early in life, and who, he says, has helped to make him every thing that he is,—which is easily credible when you know her.

"Once upon a time Mr. Holcomb stood behind his own counter. It is possible he may still stand there occasionally, though I should think that the guidance and management of the enormous establishment into which his 'shop' has grown, gave him much more useful work to do. But whether or no, wherever he stands, and whatever he is, you will always find him a gentleman.

"It is very pleasant staying at Oak Hill. The house is large and handsome, but its splendors are toned down by good taste, and refinement has kept pace with increasing luxury. One of the great difficulties of your self-made men, is to get accustomed to their wealth; to know how to use it levelly, and gradually and gracefully to advance with it. Otherwise the good old-fashioned hob-nailed boot is perpetually peeping out from under the purple garments, and ill-natured people who know not how difficult it is to prevent this, laugh at them for it. But nobody will ever laugh at Mr. Holcomb.

"Another pleasure in his house is its artistic treasures. He is one of the few picture-buyers who really know what a good picture is, and judge it for itself, irrespective of the reputation of the painter. Consequently, he has many in his house which are increasing in value year by year, and may pride himself—though he never does—of having been oftentimes the first discoverer of rising genius. He never buys sham 'old masters,' but he has a few good copies of known pictures. While you take your tea in his beautiful drawing-room, or drawing-rooms—there are three *en suite* —you may feast your eyes on the Madonna della Seggiola, Murillo's Virgin of the Louvre, and others:—which is rather agreeable than not.

"Though the house has been modernized to all sorts of comfort and elegance, the garden, a rarely beautiful one, has been wisely left in its primitive old-fashionedness. It has all sorts of delicious nooks, shut in and shut out by queer little hedges: a Dutch flower-garden, sheltered and sunny; two kitchen-gardens, where the vegetables grow almost as picturesquely as flowers; a fruit-garden, upon whose walls, at this time, peaches, nectarines, apricots, plums, were hanging in the most luscious plenty. Lastly, there is a huge conservatory, where the oranges and lemons of half a century's growth show their perpetual marvel of fruits and flowers at once, and the fuchsias and camellias are almost the size of trees. But the triumph of the place is an avenue of limes, the finest I ever saw.

"There is something to me strangely touching in a fine avenue of trees, formed, not by chance, but design, and in faith and unselfishness, since those whose long-dead hands planted it can never have hoped to see it full-grown. They who planted this one must have done it to be the joy of generations—as it is. In every season of the year it is beautiful. I have watched it from the dining-room window on a winter's morning, when its every branch and twig, sharply defined and white with snow, turned rose-color in the sunrise, and became like gigantic arches of coral; and looking through it this August afternoon, before a leaf had begun to fall, with its long, lofty, regular lines, perfect as those of a cathedral aisle, but lightened up with a constant rippling and flickering of light and shadow, out of the glorious irregularities and delicious varieties of nature;—it was a sight to make one's heart not only happy, but thankful.

"'How glad I am it is a fine day! The Drones will so enjoy it.'

"Until Patty Holcomb spoke, I had quite forgotten that this day there was to be a sort of garden party, mysteriously referred to in the family—which is a rather jocular and 'funny' family—as 'the Drones coming.' But who the Drones were I had never troubled myself to inquire; until, seeing that the household—the children especially—seemed a good deal to anticipate the visit, and that there were various domestic preparations afoot with regard to it, I put the direct question, 'Who were the Drones, and what was to be done with them?'

"'Didn't you know? Oh, I'll tell you all in a minute.' But ere she could do so, a sudden outcry in the nursery overhead sent Patty off like a shot.

"She is a nice good girl, Patty—Miss Holcomb, rather, as she is the eldest of the family. I have seen her grow up, and she has grown up to my mind. When she was still in short sleeves and pinafores she was 'our eldest'—a kind of little mother to all the rest. Now, though she is Miss Holcomb, fully come out, and at an age when young ladies usually think a good deal of themselves, she hardly thinks of herself at all; neither of her prettiness, which is not inconsiderable; nor of her cleverness, which is decidedly above the average. She does think about something, I presume, for she speaks little enough, being very reserved for her time of life. I hope some estimable young man will unearth her some day; dig her up out of her shyness—woo her and win her—and she will be well worth winning. Only, I warn him, it may be up-hill work, for Miss Patty is likely to be exceedingly hard to please.

"When she returned, having settled the nursery wrongs and woes, I extracted from her the mysteries of the Drones.

"They were a family bearing that odd surname—a great misnomer, they being the most industrious race possible. More than one generation of them had been in Mr. Holcomb's employ; the present one, consisting of three brothers and one or two cousins, having first come under his eye as roly-poly lads in his Sunday class, when he was himself still a young man. One by one they have entered his establishment as porters, clerks, and so on, being promoted according to their capabilities, and watched over with a sort of feudal care, which they have rewarded by an equally feudal devotedness. They have turned out, every one of them, the most faithful servants that any master could desire, and it has been an immemorial custom to invite them to an occasional holiday—they and all their belongings—at Oak Hill.

"Whatever Mr. Holcomb does, he never does by halves. This year the Drone family and their excrescences numbered about thirty souls—some of them very small souls indeed—as all the young mothers were blessed with numerous babies; and among the fathers was an invalid, whom, Patty told me, her papa had long been anxious over, and who, if he died, would leave a blank in the establishment not easily filled up. So, to get him, the mothers, and babies safely conveyed, Mr. Holcomb had chartered an omnibus, which was to call at each house successively, take up each party, and bring them in comfort through the eight miles of hot, dusty roads which lay between their town dwellings and pleasant, rural Oak Hill. That they might see it in its utmost pleasantness, on that one summer holiday—probably their only holiday in the year—had been a source of great anxiety to every body, until this morning, when Tom Holcomb, after carefully studying the barometer, declared, with the calm conviction of seventeen upon every subject on earth, that 'it was sure to be a jolly fine day.'

"Young Tom is rather an ally of mine, for I see him less as what he is now, than as what he is capable of being. Not that I think he will ever be such a man as his father; it would be foolish to expect it, he being cast in a totally different mould. He is very fond of his 'dad'—as, in strictly private life, he still affectionately calls him—but he looks down upon him from his sturdy five feet eleven, and patronizes him rather, with a tender respect that is funny, although pretty, to see. Tom is the very opposite of his father in many things: turns a decidedly cold eye upon literature and art, but loves horses and dogs with all his soul. To see him handling the 'ribbons' behind his favorite mare, or running races with his big Newfoundland, who adores him, is quite a picture. He looks so thoroughly, boyishly happy, so gloriously ignorant of all the sins and sorrows of this world. May he long continue so!

"I like Tom. He is rough and ready; a little too rough, perhaps, but he is frank and honest, and has the kindest heart in the world. About noon of this day, hours before his customary reappearance—he goes to business with his father—I found him under the lime-tree avenue, busy unpacking two huge hampers—one of apples, the other of toys—which were intently watched by his youngest sister, aged four, who always follows the big fellow about everywhere, and condescendingly addresses him as 'dear.'

"'Who are these for, Tom?' said I.

"'Don't you know? For the Drones, of course. Our apples all failed this year, so I brought a lot from the market. But don't you tell; they wouldn't care for them unless they thought they were from our trees. And look at these dolls; aren't they pretty? I went to at least a dozen shops before I could get them. Dolls for the girls, and balls for the boys—such a lot! Hollo!' (to the gardener, who was passing by) 'did you mow that bit of the paddock smooth for cricket? Some of the young men play cricket very well, Miss Patience. Will you come and score for us?'

"I promised, and then having again claimed my admiration for his dolls, Tom carefully packed the hamper up again, arranged them for distribution under a large lime-tree, shouldered his little sister, and walked away.

"Mrs. Holcomb and Patty had been invisible since breakfast, and both looked rather tired at our mid-day dinner, which was a little more hurried than usual. But afterwards, when I sat reading in the drawing-room, they reappeared, carefully dressed in demi-toilette. Miss Holcomb looked as nice as neatness and youthful bloom could make her, in a fresh muslin dress, and her mother wore a handsome silk, and a cap of the most exquisite point lace, which I could not help admiring.

"'I put it on on purpose,' said she, half-apologetically. 'I thought it would please the Drones if I dressed well to receive them.' (N.B.—I had not intended doing it, but of course I went immediately and put on my best gown for the visitors.)

"This done, I buried myself once more in my book, which was very interesting. I remember—if only for the strong contrast it made between court life and the life of these working-people, our guests—what book it was,—

that strangely touching Royal idyl, the simple, sad love-story, which this year has made England take its Queen to its heart as if she were a peasant-woman. I was near crying over it, and had forgotten all about the garden party, when I heard wheels drawing up to the front door, and one of the little ones calling out, 'Miss Patience! Miss Patience! mamma says, would you like to come and meet the Drones?'

"Of course I went. At the entrance-hall stood Mr. and Mrs. Holcomb, Patty, Tom, the governess, and all the younger children, watching the unloading of a large omnibus, full inside and out—as full as ever it could hold. Of such very respectable-looking people too; the young men dressed so well, and as for the women and children, they were all as neat as new pins. Tom made himself ubiquitous in his attentions, helping every body down, and snatching more than one bewildered infant from under the horses' feet. Patty, the governess, and I, also did our best, for there seemed not half enough mothers for the quantity of children.

"'Are you all here?' said Mr. Holcomb, after he and his wife had shaken hands with the whole party, appearing in the most miraculous manner to distinguish one from another, and to recollect which children belonged to which, who were married and who single,—facts that, to the end of the day, I altogether failed in acquiring. "Are you quite sure you have left nobody behind?'

"Here some one admitted, with a smile, that one child had actually been nearly left behind—a poor little thing, whom nobody missed, until, at the street's end, they saw a crowd gathered round it, wondering whose child it was. So they drove back and picked it up again. A very slight catastrophe, as it turned out, and the only one. The whole party, in their best clothes and highest spirits—in spite of a slight shyness on first arriving at their master's splendid home,—were evidently bent on enjoying themselves.

"And their master seemed determined to make them do so. 'We'll go through the garden first,' said he; as taking two little girls by the hands, and addressing them by their Christian names (which, I remember, were Florence and Blanche, or Ethel and Edith—something very grand), he led the way, followed by the whole party—

young men and maidens, fathers, mothers, and children, many of them babies in arms; quite a procession indeed. We fell into it; every one of us who could, carrying or leading a child, for, in truth, the young generation seemed legion. I seized upon one sweet-faced little creature, with a grave, old-fashioned look, but so very tiny that I had no idea it had passed the baby age, or was above being talked to in baby language, until, on my alluring it with a bunch of late red currants, it shook its head with a solemnity worthy Lord Burleigh, saying, in the best of English, 'No! I don't like 'em.'

"I must here notice one thing, that in all our promenades, through gardens and green-houses, pleasure-grounds and lawns, not one of the children offered to touch a fruit or a flower, or even asked for it. Some of them—the little atom in my arms especially—cast longing eyes on the posies, and, on receiving one, would clutch it eagerly, all a-smile with delight, but nothing more. Better mannered children could not be, in any rank of life—ay, even at the final test, the distribution of dolls and balls. This duty was performed by Mr. Holcomb himself, with a justice and judgment highly creditable to him, considering the difficulty of distinguishing among the small people which were boys and which were girls, and the strong illegal proclivities which some of the former seemed to have for dolls instead of balls.

"At last, the gifts being all disposed of, and supplemented by as many apples as could be stowed away, the host and hostess wisely left their guests to amuse themselves, as was not difficult in this large, lovely garden, on this exquisite August day. They subdivided; one group took to croquet, under the superintendence of the young ladies and their governess; a few strolled about in couples—of course, there were more than one pair of 'cousins' who took a special interest in one another; and several young mothers devoted themselves, singly or socially, to their endless babies. Out of the men were picked a 'jolly' set for cricket, headed by a young fellow who had brought his bat with him and with whom I had held some enthusiastic conversation on that fine old English game, where all classes meet on the noble equality of thews and sinews, skill and good-humor; where the young blacksmith may bowl out the young squire, and the farmer owe a grand series of runs to his own ploughman, with equal benefit to both.

"I have played cricket—I play no more; but thank the Fates, I still can score. So I sat in great content, and really admiring the zealous activity with which these under-sized town-bred young fellows carried on their game. It was not like a village match, certainly; but it was very respectably played. Two of the players, whenever they got in, never seemed to get out, and scored such a lot of runs, and so fast, that it needed all my attention to keep count. At length both these heroes became so exhausted, that in the intervals of business they threw themselves down on the grass to recover breath. Just then fortunately came a summons to tea, and the whole party, including Tom (I observed that Master Tom, who is a first-rate cricketer, had modestly retired into almost permanent 'long-stop'), resumed coats and waistcoats, and blossomed back into young gentlemen. For 'the gentlemen' and 'the ladies' were words most carefully made use of both by Mr. and Mrs. Holcomb and the rest of the party; and not a single member of it did discredit to the title.

"What a pretty sight it was, that tea-table! round which were gradually ranged the elders and youngsters. It was set right in the middle of the avenue, and the light and shadow of the green leaves flickered on its white damask cloth and its pretty china—the good china, no 'kitchen set'—behind which Mrs. Holcomb and I had agreed to preside, leaving to Patty's care the milk-jugs, for the children. Between the two trays, set at each end, extended a wide Debatable Land, plenteous with comestibles; and I own I dreaded the immediate forays that little hands might make into it. But no! not a finger was put forth until Mr. Holcomb had said grace; and then it was only one very small shy voice which whispered to me entreatingly, 'P'ease, me do want a tate.' (It was against the law, but—he got it).

"I despair of ever describing that tea-drinking—how my arm literally ached with holding the tea-pot, and how, 'Another cup, ma'am, please, for a lady,' became words of alarming import—for where was it to come from? since the infant battalion, which we had thought was safely consigned to Patty and milk-and-water, had much preferred tea, and came upon us in a body, draining us down to nearly *aqua pura*. And amidst our Herculean labors, we required Argus eyes to prevent china being dropped out of sticky little fingers, and to take out of mouths crammed to choking, dangerous fragments of very soppy cake. What matter? the same things happen at the most aristocratic nursery-tables. And when, his heart and lips being opened by contented satiety, my right-hand neighbor, of about seven, directed my attention to his 'new weskit,' which he said 'mother' had just made, and a friend on my left, who could not yet speak plain, was equally anxious I should admire her 'straw *rat* and ribbins,' and even her red boots, I was as much entertained as I have often been by the politest and most talented company.

"When almost nothing was left to rise from, the company rose, and being again left to amuse themselves, dispersed in various directions. Mr. Holcomb and I stood watching the sunset—which was specially grand—and the cricketers, who seemed determined to waste not a minute of daylight and fresh air. He tried to explain to me the perplexed consanguinities of the Drone family, and told me little anecdotes of them all, from their youth upward, showing me various specimens of the rising generation, who were 'the very image of their father when he first came to my class.' On their part, several of the cricketers came up lingeringly to their master's side, to tell him how the game was going on, and to remind him of various other holidays in old times—'just such a day as this, sir, if you remember.' All of them seemed to hover about him with an affectionate pleasure, as if they liked his company, and were accustomed to be talked to by him on other matters than business. Yet, unrestrained and free as they were, at any moment Mr. Holcomb's least word was instantaneously obeyed. I liked also the way they behaved to Tom and Tom to them, though he was at a difficult age and in a difficult position in the business—having, necessarily, to begin at the very beginning. Some of the men carefully addressed him as 'Mr. Thomas' and 'sir,' but others unhesitatingly called him 'Tom.' Both names the young gentleman took quite easily; indeed, throughout the day Tom Holcomb devoted himself entirely to making the visitors 'jolly,' as he called it, and never thought about himself or his dignity at all—which is a great deal to say for a lad of seventeen.

"But the sun sank lower, the grass round the cricketers began to be damp with August dews, and the little group of mothers sitting on chairs under the avenue drew their shawls closer over their babies' heads.

"'Come now,' said Mr. Holcomb, 'before we go in to supper, let us have some music—open-air music. A hymn, perhaps, to begin with?'

"The master and most of his people belonged to a Nonconformist body, and, with every respect for their theology, I own I had my doubts as to their music. These doubts, however, were soon dispelled, as they sang the Russian National Hymn, very well arranged in four parts, and then an anthem—'How Beautiful upon the Mountains'—given in a manner that would not have discredited a cathedral choir. Lastly, on Mr. Holcomb's suggesting 'something secular,' we had 'All among the Barley,' and another glee, conducted and sung with a crispness, accuracy, and firmness of tone, such as all part-singers know to be not easily attainable. As we stood in a circle, vocalists and audience, the lime-leaves overhead seemed to dance to the music, and the full moon, creeping over the shoulder of the house, broadened her round face into additional jollity as she looked at us. It was a pretty sight—a sweeter sound; but the lawn glistened like a sheet of water in the moonlight, and Mrs. Holcomb's maternal anxiety over 'all those babies' was quite irrepressible, so we hurried indoors.

"To the school-room? the servants' hall? or even the denuded and re-arranged dining-room? Not at all; but to the three splendid drawing-rooms—adorned just as they would have been for a company of Mr. Holcomb's rich neighbors, who could requite him feast for feast. How pretty the suite of rooms looked!—gleaming with lights, perfumed with flowers, bright with amber satin damask (all uncovered): every thing lovely or curious being repeated in the tall mirrors that reached from floor to ceiling, and reflected not only the pictures, but the people—these unwonted guests, who came treading softly over the rich carpets, and looking all around them with wide, admiring, wondering eyes.

"Some people might say this was a mistake: that they would have been happier in the kitchen or the servants' hall. I do not think so. I think Mr. Holcomb was quite right—that these poor working men and women were not harmed, but benefited, by being led, for one night, into such a fairy paradise; shown Canova's white nymphs and Raffaelle's Madonnas—ay, even bright mirrors and amber satin curtains. For our neighbors' splendors injure us not one bit, when we can enjoy them without envying them. And I believe these good people envied not a single luxury of the many with which their master had surrounded himself—which he has worked so hard for, and re-distributes, whenever he can, with such a liberal heart and hand.

"So, by-and-by the company settled down, ranging themselves round the room, as at an ordinary evening party, and Miss Holcomb began the entertainment by opening the piano and playing a little. Various other music followed from the visitors—'Hail, smiling Morn,' in particular, being sung so well, that it was unanimously encored. Some of the children dropped off to sleep, and were assisted away and made comfortable in quiet sofa-corners; but the greatest number kept wide awake, and sat in groups on the floor, listening intently, and altogether 'as good as gold.' One baby, of about a year old, lay on its back in the centre of the room, crowing and beating its little feet on the carpet in a perfect ecstasy of enjoyment.

"In the midst of all this youth, and life, and merry-making, was one shadow, which all felt and nobody spoke of—the invalid whom I have named. He was a young man, with a wife and two children—they sat together on the most comfortable sofa that could be found—and his face told in a moment its sad tale. White and wasted, the skin drawn tightly over the cheek-bones, the sunken eyes gleaming, and the voice having that peculiar hollowness by which one recognizes the last stage of consumption, he was a sad sight—that is, he would have been, but for his own exceeding cheerfulness. He had insisted on coming with the rest, and doing all they did, so far as he was able; and when, during the day, his little child was brought to Mrs. Holcomb's maternal doctoring with some small ailment, nothing could exceed the father's care and anxiety over her. Now, he sat with her on his lap, petting and cheering her with a self-forgetful tenderness. Would the little girl afterwards remember it? She was quite old enough to do so. For the wife, she sat beside them both, and divided her attention between them, a younger baby in her arms being luckily fast asleep.

"Was she aware, poor woman, of the fear, the almost certainty, which—as every body else could see—hung over her?—the doubt whether her husband would ever live to see another holiday at Oak Hill. Of course, nobody hinted this, but I think every body felt it; and it threw a strange solemnity over us all. In one sense, this was nothing new or remarkable. Do we, any of us, know when our time will come? Do we not continually walk on day by day in ignorance beside those whom suddenly we miss from our side?—God has lifted them from us, and made the every-day men and women whom we knew into His dead—that exceeding great army of whom we know nothing, save that they are His, and with Him. But to sit beside a person who may—nay, must—within a certain number of days and weeks, have departed from this world, have learned the great mystery, and become wiser than us all—is a different thing. Continually, in the midst of the singing, that young man's face—so death-like, yet so living in its enjoyment, and so full of peace and cheerfulness—struck me with a feeling of great awe. Did he know or guess the truth about himself? Yes, he must have known. Presently, I was convinced he did know.

"There came a pause in the singing, and Mr. Holcomb proposed that, as supper time was near, we should end our music with the Evening Hymn—'Glory to Thee, my God, this night.' Immediately the clatter of talking ceased: there fell a reverent stillness over the room; and then Mr. Holcomb gave out, two lines at a time, in Nonconformist fashion, the sweet old hymn. We sang it—not, I must confess, to the severe classic, ancient version that one hears in churches now, but to the corrupted one of mediæval and Methodist times—the lively tune of half a century ago, which has such a peculiar charm, because one learned to sing it almost as soon as one could speak. As we sang the lines—

"Teach me to live that I may dread
The grave as little as my bed,"

I stole a glance at the young man beside me. His whole expression had altered. Yes, he knew. I was sure of that. He was moving his wan lips to the words; being too weak to sing now; his eyes had a strange far-away look; and his face, bent over the curly head of his little girl, who had fallen asleep on his bosom, was grave and quiet. He held the little thing carefully and tenderly; but his mind seemed wandering far away. Was he thinking of how soon he might sleep 'another sleep than ours?' I can not tell; but whatever his thoughts were, there was no fear in them: his countenance was as peaceful as his own child's.

"The hymn over, Mr. Holcomb—in the simple and natural, yet deeply earnest habit he has of bringing his religion into daily life, without ever putting it intrusively or controversially forward, said, 'Let us read a verse or two out of the Psalms, and end with a few words of prayer.'

"Now there is a way in which the mingling of sacred and secular things may be made utterly jarring, obnoxious, and profane:—there is another way in which they can be so harmonized as to blend them into one, as it was meant they should be blended—causing us to feel that 'the earth is the Lord's, and the fullness thereof.' It did not strike me as in any sense painful or unfitting to hear through those lighted drawing-rooms the familiar words, 'The Lord is my shepherd, I shall not want,'—read on to the end of the psalm. As for the sick man, while he listened, which he did intently, his look became not merely peaceful but rapturous—as if he already walked in those 'green pastures,' and saw the *other side* of that valley of the shadow of death into which he was fast going. He may have crossed it already, or have to cross it ere long—I know not; but I believe unquestionably that the rod and the staff which David speaks of will not have failed him: he will have been 'comforted.'

"The 'few words of prayer'—only a few words, suitably and simply said by an aged minister who was present—being ended, we all rose, and stood in groups, rather silent, and wet-eyed, some of us.

"'Now,' said Mr. Holcomb, cheerfully, 'I am sure we must all be getting very hungry. Will you take a lady in to supper?'

"This remark was addressed to a gentleman, the only stranger present, who happened to be a terrible old Tory, with a keen sense of the distinctions of classes. Certainly, such a position had never occurred to him before, and I wondered a little what he would do. He was taken aback for a moment, I think, and then, being a gentleman, he did the only right and possible thing for a gentleman to do—he offered his arm to his next neighbor, and escorted her politely to the supper-table.

"What a supper-table it was! extending the whole length of the dining-room, laden not only with that 'good big piece of beef'—which I overheard Tom advising his mother to provide,—but with viands of all sorts: ham, lobsters, chicken-pie, fruit-pie, jellies, tarts, creams; the centre being adorned with a dessert fit for any dinner-party. Now I don't believe in eating and drinking as a means of festivity; I think most people eat and drink a great deal too much; but if I ever did give a feast, it should be such an one as this of Mrs. Holcomb's. When she sat down at the head of her well-filled, elegant table, and saw round it those happy-looking guests—guests who could not give her a supper back again—I think she must have felt happy too. She looked so.

"It was severe work for her though, and for us all. Tom became Briarean in his usefulness, and did the work of three waiters at once. So did the younger children; so did the active, kindly governess. Patty, who has a perfect genius for infantile government, arranged all the small fry who could be separated from their mothers, or who were not already fast asleep in different corners, on one large sofa; where she settled them down like a nest of young sparrows, and fed them by turns with any good thing that came to hand, with which they could injure neither themselves nor their neighbors. But though it was not long past eight, and they had only finished tea at six, their appetites were appalling. I thought to myself, what hard work it must be to fill those little mouths with any sort of food! Neatly dressed and comfortable looking as all these families were, life must be to them, at the best of times, a perpetual struggle.

"But no such thoughts seemed to trouble the young people—for they were all young, though most of them were married, and several were in the position of the old woman who lived in a shoe—'they had so many children they didn't know what to do!' How those frail, slender young women contrived to lug about such heavy babies—often one on each arm, or one in arms and the other toddling below—was a mystery to me. And how, upon the moderate wages of porters and such-like underlings, those young fathers ever contrived to feed and clothe their families, to say nothing of education, equivalent to their own — which I found on talking with them was above the average of working men—well, I came to the conclusion that they must be a remarkably industrious race—these Drones,—and must have a large amount of faith in Providence, or in the hands through which Providence commonly works. Ay, that was it. One small fact lay at the root of all.

"It came out quite accidentally: no toast betrayed it; no speechifying: no more than in any ordinary family meal. But once, as I was passing round the table, I felt my hand suddenly caught. It was the sick young man, who looked in my face, and held me fast, with a pathetic earnestness.

"'Ma'am, isn't this a fine sight—a great sight—isn't it, now? Just look at 'em all round the table; such a lot of young people, and all so merry; and all going the right way—the right way,' he repeated. 'And look at him,' glancing at Mr. Holcomb, who was so busy talking that he never caught a word, 'but for him we might ha' taken the wrong way. He looked after us—ever since we were little lads—he did, ma'am, he did. If we're good for any thing, it's all his doing.'

"The voice broke, the eyes filled — those poor dying eyes! They fixed themselves on his master with a mute blessing, which Mr. Holcomb never saw: but if he had, I think he would have liked it better than the loudest demonstrations.

"At nine o'clock the host took out his watch, remorselessly. 'Now, my friends, you have far to go, and lots of children with you. I must send you off. Your carriage stops the way.'

"It did 'stop the way' for twenty minutes or more, while all the active energy of us womenkind was required to find the little hats and hoods and capes, and dress the babies, or hold them while their mothers were dressing themselves. Then, every body shook hands with every one of us; and, considering their numbers were over thirty and ours not under fifteen, the quantity of hand-shakes that were performed would furnish a long arithmetical calculation. There was also some delay in apportioning seats in the omnibus; two or three young couples who had kept very close to one another during the afternoon, and who, I afterwards heard, were 'engaged'—though, with most rare and creditable delicacy, there had not been a single joke on the subject—persisting in sitting together, 'to admire the moonlight,' on the omnibus-top. A very laudable proceeding, common to young people in all ages. I only hope, in those thin muslin dresses, nobody caught cold. But that was their concern, not mine.

"The mothers and children were all, by general consent, packed inside—Tom handing them in, one after the other; and at the last minute flying off like a whirlwind to fetch his own great-coat, with which he wrapped the invalid, and settled him comfortably—his little girl still in his arms—in the omnibus-corner.—(Not a bad fellow that Tom Holcomb, as I have before remarked.)

"At last the party were all stowed away, and the large omnibus reeled with them, inside and out. Mr. Holcomb's final question—'Are you sure you haven't left a baby behind?'—awoke a shout of laughter, in the midst of which they moved slowly off, giving us as they passed the gates a hearty farewell in the form of good old English cheers.

"Dare I confess the next thing we did? It was to rush in a body to the dining-room; for, whatever our guests were, *we* were nearly starving! We said not a word till we had consoled ourselves with a hearty supper out of the remnants of the feast, and then we began to 'talk it over.' It was the candid opinion of both seniors and juniors that all had gone off well—that both entertainers and entertained had very much enjoyed themselves. Though, on comparing notes, and finding how awfully some of our legs ached with playing cricket and croquet, and how some of our poor arms were quite stiff with carrying babies, we decided that we had not spent exactly an idle afternoon.

"Finally, just as a refreshment before retiring to our most welcome beds, we, the elders of the party, emulated those young people on the omnibus-roof, and went out 'to admire the moonlight.'

"It was glorious! one of those nights, intensely clear, bright, and still, when the trees seem dead asleep, and the earth is as silent as the sky in the overpowering radiance; when the stars are almost put out, and the full moon walks, solitarily and solemnly, across those dark blue depths of space, which seem inviting us to gaze, up, up, far beyond where mortal eye can penetrate, unto the very footstool of God. A night, in which all earthly things look so small—so very small—and yet one feels they can not be quite insignificant to Him, or He would not have taken pains to give us so much innocent happiness in this world, and to make the minutest things about us so very beautiful.

"Our hearts were full, I fancy; for nobody spoke, until Mr. Holcomb said, in rather a low voice, 'I think this has been a good day.'

"'Yes,' I replied; and could not find a second word."

* * * * * * *

"Well, Aunt Patience, is that all?"

"What more did you expect? I told you you would not get a story. You have only got a bit of nature—the real history of one day, which I at least shall long remember—a 'good' day, as my friend Mr. Holcomb called it. Will any body else, of the many worthy Mr. Holcombs who have so many servants under them, give just such another? It might be the better for both men and masters."

We all agreed that this was true. And therefore we have resolved to make public Aunt Patience's history of a Garden Party.

THE TALE OF TWO WALKS,

TOLD TO SICK CHILDREN.

No. I.—MY DOG AND I.

WHEN one is ill, the last person it is advisable to think about is one's self. It does no good; for we keep on growing either better or worse all the while, and it only makes us a weariness to ourselves, and a trouble to other people. Sometimes, when pain is sharp, and sickness very heavy, it is impossible not to think about one's self; but the sooner one escapes into other thoughts the better; and our thoughts should take us out of ourselves —away from the weary body, which perhaps can not stir from bed or sofa, the dull sick-room where we are familiar with every line of the patterned paper, every angle of the furniture. The more we can shut our mind's eye upon the things around us, and open it upon those which, being invisible, we can look at whenever we please, the better will it be for us all.

Yes, my poor sick children, we sometimes keenly enjoy hearing of pleasures in which we can not actually share. When I was a little girl I used to take walks with a blind old man, not born blind, but become so gradually. He knew every inch of the country, which was a specially beautiful neighborhood; he would stop me at particular points, saying, "Now show me that view!" And I told him exactly how it looked—how this larch-wood was growing green, how the sun was shining across that angle of meadow-land, how the seven firs on the hill-top stood out sharp against the sky, and so on. How he would enjoy it! often even correcting me in my description, so vivid was his remembrance of what he once used to behold, and the pleasure of which remained to him still.

And long afterwards I knew a lady, who had not walked for many years, who then thought she would never walk again, yet every day in my rambles she used mentally to follow me; I bringing home to her in a basket a little bit of every kind of vegetation that sprang newly up —for it was April—from the first buds of yellow coltsfoot, or celandine, or anemone, on to the time of primroses and cowslips,—when we parted. She used to make quite a garden in her room, that bright little room which was, to me at least, the pleasantest in the house, arranging her mosses and lichens and bits of ground-ivy with the most exquisite taste; she said the sight of them made her so happy, that she could imagine every place in which they grew, and could follow me in my walks until it was almost as good as if she took them herself.

Now this is the kind of imaginary walk I would like to take with you. My poor little ones, try and forget your pains, and have a stroll with me, over paper and print, all among real places and people and things, for I will promise not to tell you a word that is not true.

And first, as to "My Dog and I." You would perhaps like to know who the "I" may be? Well, it is a person who likes, and is usually not disliked by, young people, whom she always finds good company, and gets for a walk whenever she can. Otherwise her chief companion is, next to a child, the best companion possible—a dog.

Now let me paint his portrait for you. He is a black, long-eared, long-tailed, and very shaggy Scotch terrier—at least, that I believe to be his breed, though whether he is valuable or not I really do not know. Nor can I say whether connoisseurs would call him handsome. From the total silence of my friends on the subject—praising him as a "good dog," an "intelligent dog," but never complimenting him on his beauty—I am afraid he has not much to boast of. But he is beautiful to me. When he comes bounding up to me, with his keen, loving, sagacious eyes, his curly black hair—all but the breast and feet, which, when he is clean, give him a most gentlemanly appearance of white stockings and white shirt-frills—I think him the handsomest dog in the world.

For he loves me, and I love him; he is faithful to me, and I am mindful of him. I make him obey me, since that is for his own good as well as mine; but I never wantonly ill-treat him, nor wound his feelings in the smallest degree. When he is hungry, he is never tantalized to beg or do tricks; if thirsty, he knows where to go for his bowl of water, which is always full. And I strictly keep my promises to him, as I would to a human being. If, on going out, I say to him, "Lie there till I come back," I always do come back, and he waits in perfect faith, assured that he will not be left forlorn. In short, I deal with him according to the law of kindness, the only safe one for either man or beast. Consequently he is so human in his affection that I sometimes call him my Black Prince, and declare that if I were to cut off his head and tail—as the king's youngest son did to the white cat in the fairy story—he would certainly change into a handsome young prince, and devote himself to me forever. Still, there might be a risk in the experiment—I might lose my dog and not find my prince—so I shall not try it just at present.

Imagine him, then, my children, as he sits watching me put on my bonnet, his head a little on one side, his eyes gleaming from under his shaggy black eyebrows, and his tail tapping the floor in a quiver of excitement, till I give the final permission, "Yes, my man, you shall go."

Then, how he leaps! with all his four feet in the air; deafens me with wild ecstatic barks, and bewilders me, as I am putting on my boots, with unavailing but desperate attempts to kiss my foot or my hand. At last I am obliged to speak to him quite sharply, and then he subsides into temporary composure, broken only by an occasional whine of delight and entreaty, until we open the door—we, for he jumps up and licks my fingers at the handle—and go out.

To describe the ecstasy with which he bounds along the road, coming back at intervals to leap after me and take my hand in his mouth in a caressing way, barking all the while furiously, is quite impossible; and probably all dogs are the same as my dog, though I am inclined to think him the one dog in the world.

He and I take our way down the solitary road—quite solitary, for we live at a sea-side place, whence, during the winter months, all the inhabitants disappear; and this is January, with a dry, black, biting January frost, which turns our usually muddy road into crisp cleanness. Not a bit of snow is to be seen, though there is a slight rime on the grass blades and the topmost twigs of the hedge; otherwise the frost is so fierce that this brilliant sunshine, coming out of a sky as blue as June, does not affect it at all.

The bare trees stand up motionless, for the air is quite still, but of the abundant animal or vegetable life that used to meet us in our walks there is hardly a trace, except the one little robin that hops about on the hedge or across the footway, scarcely a yard from my dog's nose. He is not a bit frightened, either of my dog or me—hunger has made him tame. Now he has flown back to the hedge, and sits there, ruffling up his feathers till he looks as fat and round as a ball, his bright eye fixed on me, so close that I could almost take him in my hand, or put salt on his tail, after the approved method of catching birds.

But no, my little friend, for I am well acquainted with you; you have haunted this hedge-corner for weeks past, and until this frost began you used to sing till one could almost fancy it was May; and as soon as the least mildness comes you will sing again, you pretty blithe creature, making the best of every thing, as we all ought to do.

Bless me! I thought my robin was the only bird abroad, but here is a flock of chaffinches. Probably one of the last brood of the season, which instead of separating keeps together, a troop of wandering brothers and sisters, all winter long. And what is my Black Prince barking at so furiously in that field? Rooks?—yes, there they are, rising in a body from the newly-ploughed field, wheeling round and round or hovering like a cloud above it, and finally settling on the nearest tree, which they cover entirely, hanging on its bare branches in black dots, which show sharp against the sky, like some extraordinary kind of fruit. There they will remain, making a great clatter, and cawing and clapping of wings, till we have gone safely past, then down they will drop again upon the field, marching about it after the peculiar solemn fashion of rooks. Never mind, the oats are not yet sown; they will do no harm. Perhaps good.

See!—there is another bird; sailing too high for my dog to bark at. It is not exactly a stranger, though we do not see many of them unless in stormy weather, when they are driven inland often much farther than our estuary. Some of you, my children, may have read in Mary Howitt's poems, one beginning—

"O the white sea-gull, the wild sea-gull,
A joyful bird is he."

Going on to say how—

"The ship, with her fair sails set, goes by,
And her people stand to note
How the sea-gull lies in the heaving sea,
As still as an anchor'd boat."

Well, this is the creature, and a beautiful creature he is too, if we could examine him close; but he keeps circling and circling over our heads, so that we can only see his white breast, and his great white flapping wings tipped with black, on which he goes sailing miles and miles out to sea, and beholds wonderful sights, such as we ourselves never shall behold. And probably he has built his nest, with myriads of others, on the top of a great rock in the middle of the sea, some fifty miles from hence, and only comes paying occasional winter visits to our pretty little bay.

I wish I could show you this bay. It curves in suddenly from a line of rocky coast—rocks of that picturesque sort which geologists term "conglomerate." It is shingly, not sandy, and except a few occasional masses of sea-weed, and the melancholy bits of drift-wood which imply a wreck somewhere, some time, we rarely find any very curious things; except the unfailing curiosities of every sea-shore, the ebbing and flowing of the tide, the shells clustering on bits of rock, the strange creatures—medusæ, for instance—which go floating about on the top of the waves, or lie as deep down as you can see beneath the clear water. And then there is the view—the broad blue estuary—the line of mountains beyond; but I could never paint that in pen and ink.

My dog has no eye for the picturesque, but a very sharp one to his own pleasure. He knows as well as possible the turn down to the bay, where I give him his daily swim. He stops, barks, runs forward, then turns, looks at me and barks again. He says, as plainly as a dumb beast can say, "Won't you come?"

Well, my dog, I will; though I have not your passion for sea-water in January; though I shall get my hands all wet and cold with handling that kail-stalk you are so eager to swim after; and though, after you come out, you will assuredly jump upon me, and shake yourself into a perfect watering-pot on my gown, still I'll bear it. Come, we'll go.

I pick up the kail-stalk and a piece of drift-wood which he has been eying and barking at; he plunges in after both like a hero, comes out dripping like a drowned rat,—then throws himself upon me, overwhelming me with gratitude and salt-water. "Well, that's enough! and now be a good dog and come away."

It sometimes strikes me, when I see my dog's paroxysm of grateful joy for the smallest favor—his obedient relinquishing of benefits denied, his contrition when he does wrong, and is told to "walk behind me," abject penitence depicted in his head and ears, nay, his very tail; his ecstasy when I forgive him, and speak kindly to him again—it strikes me, I say, that many of us might take a lesson from a poor brute beast.

But I promised not to preach, and shall keep my word; only sometimes you must let me have my little say in passing, as I should if we were really walking together. But for the most part we shall take these walks as country walks are best taken, with one's eyes open and one's mouth shut.

Our bay is a perpetual pleasure to me. It is calm enough now, and yet I have seen the waves come rolling in several feet high, breaking over the rocks and the little wooden pier in perfect showers of spray; to-day, however, they just come rippling in lazily, each curling over with a soft "thud" on the beach. Beyond, there hangs over the river—we call it a river, though the opposite bank is six miles off—the stillness of intense frost. Days since, the mountains disappeared in a white haze, into which the sun is just dropping, to reappear as a round red ball like molten iron, which dips slowly into the waves, dyeing them a deep blood-color.

I notice these things because, children, I want you to notice the like, walking everywhere, as I have said, "with your eyes open." Then, oh! the beautiful and wonderful things you will see every day and every hour! I leave you to find them out.

Ay, and so you would, even on a winter day like this, when people who know nothing of the country think it "dull." Dull?—why every minute we are discovering something new,—my dog and I.

He takes me along the shore-road, which is divided from the sea by a narrow belt of trees and brushwood. There he goes searching about, fancying he has found one of his old familiar rabbits; but they are safely hidden in their holes up the glen, down which the noisy burn comes tumbling, tumbling, till it joins the salt-water just here. For our seaboard is not barren nor bleak, but rich with vegetation to the water's edge. I have often seen primroses and hyacinths growing to within a yard or two of high-water mark, and mingling their woodland odor with the salt smell of dulse and carrageen.

Passing the glen, where I shall take you a walk some day, children, we come to a range of rocks gradually rising to thirty or forty feet, along the base of which the shore-road runs.

These rocks are very curious. They have evidently been the ancient sea-margin; that is to say, the estuary has been level with their tops, instead of, as it now is, many feet below. This gradual receding and advancing of the sea, leaving one shore high and dry and undermining or overwhelming another, is a very remarkable phenomenon. Scientific men might study it here with advantage; but we who are not learned, but merely simple observers of nature, can only walk under, and look up at, those great perpendicular rocks—some bare, some covered with birch-trees, whin-bushes, and heather—and wonder how many centuries it took the sea to slip away, leaving what must once have been its wonderful bottom, but which has now grown into a pretty shore, fringed with the richest vegetation, especially ivy, mosses, and ferns.

Ours is a grand country for ferns. The humidity of the climate makes them grow everywhere abundantly. You find them lurking in every cranny where it is possible for a fern to grow. Even now, in this dead season of the year, many of them are beautifully green. So are the mosses; and, mixed with brown lichens and yellow fungi, they are almost as pretty as flowers.

But we have to do at present with these rocks, which are a perpetual wonder and delight to me. I do not know what their "formation" may be, geologically; but I never look up at them in their curious jagged outlines, without thinking of the time when this great river was level with their tops, emptying itself seaward—not, as now, through two lines of busy towns, and pleasant coast villas, strung in dots, like a long white necklace, on either side the blue waters,—but flowing solitarily through primeval forests, inhabited by antediluvian or pre-Adamite beasts: creatures such as may be seen in the Sydenham Crystal Palace gardens, made in Portland cement, and set to look as if they were walking, squatting, crawling, or climbing—uncouth, grim monsters, which, we fancy, must have peopled an equally queer and monstrous world. But of that period now the most learned geologists can teach us little. We can only trace the evidence of it in these rocks, gradually worn away, some into smooth sloping surfaces, some cut down perpendicularly, as accurately as if it had been done with a hatchet.

A few masses are left standing separate from the rest. One in particular, half-covered with vegetation, looks more like a fragment of masonry, or bit of an old ruined castle, than the handiwork of Nature alone.

Nature, indeed! What strange pranks has she been playing since last week, when I came along this road! Then, every fifty yards or so, was the sound or sight of water, for ours is a watery country; from above or beneath we never have any lack of it. Now, every drop of water is turned into ice; every road-side runlet, or singing burn, or leaping waterfall—nay, nay, every little trickle that comes dripping from the roots of a heather-bush, is frozen, as if a fairy had suddenly passed by, struck it with her wand, and turned it, just as it was, into hard, clear crystal.

The shapes it takes are infinite. First, there is a part of the rocks so smooth that it holds not even a cranny where to grow a tiny fern. This has become one sheet of ice, glittering in the sun. Elsewhere there hang festoons, a yard or two deep, like glass curtains, from which depend innumerable tassels, or ear-rings, or spears—whatever you choose to liken them to—perfectly rounded, and, however thick they may be at the root, tapering uniformly to a point, slender and sharp as a needle. They are all sizes and all lengths, from an inch to two yards, and their numbers are numberless.

And now we come to the most curious sight of all. There is a place where the rock is hollowed inward, so as to form a shallow cave. This cave is completely festooned with icicles. Some are of great size, perfect sheaves of spears, united at top in a solid mass. Here and there, where the cave, which faces south-west, has been entered by the sun's light, they have slightly melted; but the drops which fell have speedily frozen again, and underneath each sheaf of downward spears a new array of upward spears has risen from the ground to meet them. Standing here, under this roof, which used to be so damp and green, or glistening with oozing water, but is now turned into a fairy palace, we can conjure up what Arctic caverns and icebergs must be. And in trying to break off one of these spears, but finding that, though it is only two inches in diameter, my hand is as weak against it as against a bar of steel, I can understand better the awfulness of that frozen sea, which has strength to lock up in its deathly bosom huge ships, and that not for weeks or months, but for whole years.

As I walk on, many a thought comes, and many a story which I should like to tell you, my boys and girls,—for girls love heroes as well as boys,—of those brave sailors who have perished in the Polar deep, or come back to tell us of their exploits, perils, and endurances. But you may read them all for yourselves in M'Clintock's "Voyage of the Fox," and in another book, interesting as a fairy tale, and simple as a story told at the fireside by word of mouth,—the Arctic adventures of the American, Dr. Kane, who volunteered to go in search of our own Franklin. The heroism of the man—he is dead now; he died not long after he came home,—his care over and fidelity to his companions, his unselfishness, patience, and self-denial—all these, not showy, but silent virtues, betrayed rather than expressed in his plain, straightforward, sailor-like narrative, compose a history, from the reading of which every man, woman, or child, with a heart and a conscience, must rise up feeling happier and better than before. For surely, if no other good has been gained by these terribly tragical adventures in search of the North-west Passage, they have taught one thing—how much for duty's sake men can do, and dare, and endure: ay, *endure*, which is not quite synonymous with *suffer*, one being active and the other passive. It touches one's inmost soul with a thrill far higher than grief or pity, to think of what these men endured, resisting to the end. What noble privations mutually borne—what brotherly clinging together of officers and crews, forgetful of all difference of rank—what heroic concealment of pain, each holding on through sickness and weakness to the last extremity, in order to help and not burden the rest! The glory of such histories can never die, nor the good influence they leave behind—no, not even though the men themselves may have long since left their bones to bleach under icebergs, or to be scattered by Arctic bears over leagues of impassable snow.

But these thoughts are growing too solemn. My dog evidently considers so. For ever so long he has been trying to catch my attention, running to and fro, barking, and looking up entreatingly to me. Ah, I see he is, like myself, very thirsty, and there is no water, only ice. Well, my man, we must just accommodate ourselves to circumstances. Come here. I break off an icicle and present him with it; he smells, and turns despondently away. He thinks I am cheating him. So, now, let us try how far his trust in me will go, and how far his reasoning powers will help his instinct in a matter upon which he has certainly never experimented before, for all his winters have been spent in a town, and I doubt much if he ever saw real ice until now. "Look here, my dog." And I break off an icicle, put it into my mouth, and show him distinctly that I am eating it and liking it, then hold it to his mouth. He regards me with a mingled expression of doubt and faith, but faith predominates. He takes a cautious bite, is astonished and charmed. It is his first experiment at eating ices, but is quite satisfactory. Between us, he and I consume two whole spears; he at last becoming so voracious, that he takes the fragments out of my hand, gnaws them, and growls over them as if they were bones. And every lump of ice which he afterwards comes to, he turns over and smells and bites at with the greatest enjoyment.

Certainly, my dog is the cleverest of all dogs, quite a reasoning animal. One thing touches me, as it always does—his unlimited trust in me. Well, my man, I think I deserve it, for you know I never restrict you wantonly in any of your harmless canine enjoyments, for I like to treat even my poor dog with that even-handed justice which is the best loving-kindness. And certainly you return it all, for you are the best companion at home and abroad that any fond brute could be.

Come, we must now bend our ways homeward for the

short afternoon is already closing. Lovely as these winter days are, they are brief enough, and we have the very shortest twilight. In summer it will be different; during June and July I have often been able to read until eleven P.M., but now the afternoon seems, after sunset, to sink suddenly into night. Nay, even before the sun has set, a white haze, slowly advancing landward, blots out both the sea and the mountains, or rather where the mountains ought to be. In this frosty weather they often vanish for days together, but when they do reappear some wondrously clear morning, with snow on their summits, which the rising sun dyes all colors, oh, how beautiful they are! But I must give a whole chapter to my mountains, or take you a special walk among them some day.

Now we turn homeward together, my dog and I; he trotting first, so close to me that, though I can only distinguish something black moving through the haze, in the dead stillness I can hear the pit-pat of his feet; as no doubt he hears the steadier tramp of mine, and is satisfied. He does not bark; probably his spirits are depressed by the fog and the chilly air, which creeps into the very marrow of one's bones.

But never mind, my dog! We have had a glorious walk, and shall have another to-morrow. Though the night looks so gloomy now, we know it will soon be morning, when we shall start off together, you and I, ay, before it is daylight. For in these northern latitudes the mornings are as dark as the evenings. At 7 30 A.M. yesterday I found the stars still shining, and saw just over that wooded hill the crescent moon lying with her horns down ward, just like a piece of silver set in the dark sky, while on either side of her, two planets gleamed like great eyes out of the deep black-blue heavens. And gradually I watched the dawn come over the mountains, changing the darkness into grayness, and then into all sorts of colors—rose, lilac, and amber—until all the sky above, and all the earth below, became clear and distinct in the brightness of perfect day.

Was not this a sight to rise early for? And we shall see it again, my dog, to-morrow, though now we go home in the mist and gloom, and shut the wicket-gate after us, thankful that we have a roof to shelter us and a good fire to creep to. And so good-bye, children! Are you glad or are you sorry to part at the walk's end with my dog and me?

THE TALE OF TWO WALKS,

TOLD TO SICK CHILDREN.

No. II.—THE FOX-HUNT.

THIS time, children, it is only I who take you the imaginary stroll. My dog lives still in peace and prosperity, but he and I are undergoing a temporary separation. I have left him behind me, some two hundred miles away, while I wander southward to a region in which climate and every thing else form the strongest contrast to that wherein you took your last stroll with my dog and me.

The poor fellow seemed to have a foreboding that he was about to lose me for a time, and time must be a rather unknown quantity in doggish calculations. The night before I left him he crept after me from room to room, watching my packing with a sad inquisitiveness, as if to say, "Oh, please tell me what is going to happen?" And not many minutes before I actually started (which I own to doing surreptitiously, during his absence in the cellar, searching eagerly for an imaginary rat) he came and laid himself on my gown-skirt, rolling over and over caressingly, pawing and licking my feet. Ah me! when I finally departed, still hearing him bark at the impossible rat, and knowing that he would soon come bounding back to the empty room, I felt not unlike a traitor.

Still it must be; and I looked forward to another happy meeting by-and-by, when I return to the familiar spot, only brightened by green leaves and unfrozen noisy waterfalls, and my Black Prince will again seek with me his natural felicities—the hunting of rabbits, birds, hedgehogs, crabs, and other amusements with which he enlivens our mutual walks.

Meantime I might, if I chose, find a substitute for my

own dog, in one that is always volunteering to accompany me here. Let me spare him a word or two, for he is a very remarkable animal. He was mentioned to me as "Our little lap-dog—a puppy only six months old," when the door opened, and in walked a gigantic deer-hound, as large as a young donkey; of the breed, now very rare, to which Sir Walter Scott's Maida belonged; the finest specimen of dog kind I ever beheld, but a little inconvenient in domestic life. For instance, his paw thrown across my lap feels as strong and solid as the arm of a big boy; his head laid on my feet—as in his extreme affectionateness of disposition he is rather fond of doing—fairly pins me to the earth, and when he jumps exuberantly upon me, he very nearly knocks me down. In a small room his large length monopolizes one half of the fireside, and when he turns round he produces an alarming disturbance both among people and furniture.

Yet he is a magnificent animal, with a head almost human in expression, and a shape of which every movement is more graceful than another. He would be a perfect study for a painter, and one here hunts him from room to room and sketches him in every possible attitude. I am always picking up stray bits of paper with portraits of this beautiful beast. He is a quiet beast too, and to see him playing with his particular friend, a Skye terrier, is quite a picture. The big dog opens his mouth wide enough to swallow the little one, who yet puts his head confidingly into it, when they roll over and over, giving caressing bites and an occasional affectionate growl, but never really quarrelling; and they hang about and whine after one another, seeming to weary for each other's company, just like friendly school-boys. And by-the-by, it sometimes strikes me, children, that if both dogs and school-boys were brought up in an atmosphere of loving-kindness, they might do with a great deal less fighting and snarling than is generally supposed necessary, since even these two dumb beasts can not live in this loving family where I now am staying, without living together in love also.

But much as I admire the deer-hound, he is not my own Black Prince, with his cheery bark, his quaint ways, and his speciality of lovingness. Nobody lies in wait for me at my room-door, and nobody scampers after me into the open air; for the splendid animal aforesaid is rather inconvenient as a companion, both in the house and out of it. He has an unlucky propensity to mistake sheep for his native deer; and even cows, bewildered by his great size, seem to think him some wild animal, and run roaring about at the sight of him; so that in this pastoral country his company in the fields is very unadvisable. And in the villages he is far too particular in his attention to the children—bends down and licks their faces in a condescending manner, while they, unable to get away, stand petrified with terror. On the whole, grand as his appearance is—so much so that every passer-by turns round to look at him—my noble friend is better left at home,—where it was unanimously decided to leave him on the day about which I am going to tell you, when I and two friends went to see a fox-hunt.

You should know first something of the sort of country where I am; far away from sea, mountains, rivers, or any of the beauties which I described last time; yet it has beauties of its own. Though inland, pastoral, and agricultural, it is not flat, but tumbled about in a charming up-and-downness which the natives politely call "hills." If they saw our hills! Still there is a wonderful beauty in these green rounded knolls, dotted with patches of brown bare woods; and in the little dales between, where usually runs, not exactly a river or a stream, but a pretty brook, whose course can be traced by its fringe of osier beds. Then the coloring of the landscape, even on this February day, is very fine; red, ploughed fields, some bare, some across which the tiny blade of springing corn throws faintest possible shade of green; pasture-fields dotted with cows, and intersected with hedges and hedge-row trees.

The trees form a great feature in this rich and luxuriant district. Even now, with not a leaf to be seen, there is no mistaking an oak for an elm, a beech for a chestnut; each keeps, down to the smallest twig, its law of individuality—its own special outline of trunk and branches, infinitely varied, and yet the same in kind; and already each is preparing to re-clothe itself for the coming year. The ash-trees are beginning to darken—

> "Black as ash-buds in the front of March."

The chestnut buds are growing "sticky;" yellow catkins

are drooping from the willow, and those soft buds which the children call "palms," and carry about with them on Palm Sunday, are already visible. Along the hedges on either side of the road, runs a reddish shade, which will by-and-by turn greenish, and then brighten into that tender color of young leaves, which six weeks or two months hence will flash out in sheltered places and gradually make all the hedgerows look as if they were blushing green.

Very pleasant is this clear, sunshiny, smooth country road, straight as one of the Roman roads, which are still to be traced in this district, as well as Roman camps on the hill-sides, and Roman villas and pavements among the valleys. This road may have been Roman for aught we know, originally planned in the days when we Britons painted ourselves with woad, and dressed ourselves in skins of bears and foxes. Which reminds me of the object of our walk, to see a "meet," or fox-hunt, this being a fox-hunting country.

Now, children, I am not going to discuss the question of fox-hunting. Some people think it a truly British sport, right and lawful and manly; others consider it exceedingly cruel and wrong. I myself have never thought much on the subject, and therefore am not competent to give any opinion. When you grow up you must judge for yourselves, and in the mean time you had better let the matter rest with older people, reading my description simply as a description of what was at least a very pretty sight. How far it is fair to turn into a "very pretty sight" the hunting of a poor beast to death, and whether, on the other hand, it is not allowable to destroy the farmer's greatest pest, are questions which I too shall leave to wiser heads than my own. We grown-up, as well as you little people, have often to learn that it is our utmost wisdom to confess humbly—"I don't know."

Well, there is the "meet." We can see it a long way off,—an upland field, with woods behind it, in the which many foxes dwell. Last night, while the creatures were prowling about in farm-yards and other places, keepers went round these woods and stopped up their "earths,"—which are great holes or burrows extending far underground. Consequently the foxes have no homes to shelter in, and will be more easily "found," as the phrase is. Good sport is evidently expected, for the road, usually so lonely, is thronged with people—fashionable people from the fashionable town a few miles off, and country people, who have come down from what the natives here call "the hills," in gigs, carts, or plough-horses, and on their own feet. They are rather a remarkable looking race, intensely Saxon, with the Saxon round, ruddy face, blue eyes, and flaxen hair; just as you might imagine the faces of Gurth the swineherd, and Wamba the jester, in Scott's "Ivanhoe," if you have read it (and if you have not, go and ask permission to do so immediately). They are mostly farmers, dressed in velveteen, with bright-colored waistcoats, breeches, and leather leggings; or farmers' laborers, wearing the usual smock-frock. All are evidently deeply interested; but in the quiet unexcitable way in which the British laborer does show his interest in things about him. They trudge soberly along, or stand in groups, staring at the grand folks in carriages, or the red-coated hunters, who every now and then gallop past, and enter the open gate of the field where the "meet" is held.

A more picturesque sight could hardly be seen than this sloping field, over which a hundred or more people, on horseback and on foot, are now moving. Sometimes a horseman darts out of the immediate circle and gives a canter round the field; and once there is great excitement. A hunter is thrown, his horse rolls over him, and there is a moment of breathless alarm, till the poor gentleman extricates himself by pulling his leg out of one of his top-boots. The horse springs up and dashes wildly about the field with the bridle dangling dangerously under its feet, a beautiful, fierce, frantic creature, whom nobody dares to catch. However, it is caught at last, and its master, with true English pluck, goes after it (limping a little, and rubbing legs and arms, but otherwise unhurt), caresses, soothes, and at last remounts it, looking very white, but still riding fearlessly and calmly, as a bold British hunter ought.

This little episode has greatly excited both us and our neighbors on either hand—a carriage full of little girls with their governess, and a couple of boys on Shetland ponies accompanying papa on his big horse,—papa who has evidently given up hunting in order to take his little sons to the "meet." We have scarcely settled down when the hounds appear, coming down the hilly road in a compact body, headed by the whipper-in, or "whip," as he is technically called. They are regular thorough-bred fox-hounds, not an attractive sort of dog to my mind, being all alike, with no individuality about them, and kept necessarily in such strict order, like a pack of wild beasts, that no special affection between dog and master can be possible. They obey the "whip," with a whip in his hand, but they take no notice of him or any body; rushing on with a savage unanimity of delight, as if they already scented the creatures they were born and reared to exterminate.

After them rides their owner (and people say they cost him £10,000 a year), the master of the hunt, a handsome, grand-looking gentleman, whose diamond ring flashes as he reins up his horse, which is a perfect picture for breed and beauty. Probably nowhere in the world could there be seen a much finer collection of splendid hunters, snorting and champing, and seeming as eager for the chase as their riders.

And now, all being assembled, the master of the hunt gives the signal to "throw off," which means letting the dogs loose to find the "scent." This is easy enough, for, even to human beings, the odor of a fox is so strong that when one has crossed the road you can know it by the scent he leaves behind him for ten minutes afterwards. The hounds rush forward into the wood, whence almost immediately rises first one yelp, then another, and finally the whole pack "give tongue." The fox is "found,"—he "breaks cover;" we can not see him, but we can hear the "view halloo" of the huntsman across the green field, and we can trace the dogs rushing forward in a compact mass, so close together that, according to the saying of the keepers, you might "cover them with a table-cloth." One after the other the huntsmen dart away, galloping so fast that their horses seem to lie level along the grass, with legs stretched out before and behind, then diminishing to mere specks of scarlet, black, or gray, and so vanishing over the top of the hill.

The hunt has begun. Poor Reynard—or "sly Reynolds," as they call him in these parts—I wonder what will become of him!

Nobody knows. In a very short time the field where the "meet" was, is totally deserted. Carriages and horsemen move lazily up and down the road, the foot people hang about, wondering what direction the hunt will take, which, seeing it all depends upon the will of the poor fox, and none of us know "sly Reynolds's" mind, is a matter of pure guess-work. We eagerly watch both the hill-side and the valley below, listen for the "view halloo," the distant yelp of the hounds, and fancy often we catch a glimpse of scarlet between the trees.

Whether fox-hunting be right or wrong, it is certainly very exciting. The little pale boys on Shetland ponies, apparently recovering from illness—for their papa has just administered a glass of wine apiece out of a flask in his pocket,—flush up with delight as they ride to and fro. Some village youths of our acquaintance, and even youths of higher class, are seen tearing up the valley, having followed the hunt on foot, ankle deep in mud, and torn with briers. As some of our companions—staid gentlemen now—own to have done when they were boys, making short cuts across country, and running for miles in order to keep up with the hunt and be "in at the death," which, with pride they avouch, they not seldom were. Bravo, lads! whether gentlemen or ploughmen. This is the good thing in hunting and all field sports,—they teach the spirit of adventure and endurance. And that it is which carries our British youth through the Indian jungle, the ice-fields of the Arctic Circle, the Australian bush, and the deathly swamps of Africa,—anywhere, everywhere, to colonize, subdue, or civilize the world.

But the hunt has evidently disappeared. Reynard, wise beast, has led them far away from his native wood and his stopped-up earth. All the company are riding or driving off, and shortly ourselves, and those two laborers in the osier-beds who have been cutting osiers the whole time without once looking up—poor men! perhaps their day's wages depend on the amount of the day's work—are alone left in the quiet valley which an hour ago was so lively and so full of people.

Suppose we take our usual walk, just as if there had been no fox-hunt,—one of those delicious field-walks in the interval between winter and early spring, when the air is so soft, the sunshine so sweet, and the whole earth full of pleasant promise. True, there is a good deal of mud, wholesome, honest, country mud; we require the strongest of boots, and clothes that will bear rough usage, for we may have to scramble over stiles, and through gaps in hedges, and amidst brushwood, and tree stumps, and brambles, and even occasionally subside to "all-fours." But we have a great delight in it; there is nothing like a regular field-walk, when we have the country all to ourselves, and can talk and sing and shout to one another, merry as crickets, and free as air.

We go right up through a gate and a lane to the wood where the fox "broke cover," for we want to find his "earth"—the nearest approach to the den of a wild animal now to be seen in England, as he himself is the only remnant of our beasts of prey; except, perhaps, the badger. We listen, by the way, to our companions' account of a wood not many miles from this, one of the very few places in England where the badger still exists: what a curious place it is, all intersected with paths and lairs, and trodden down with foot-prints of strange creatures. We think we should very much like to go and see it, though we have no particular wish for a badger-hunt. Man has, some writer observes, "a natural propensity for hunting something;" but I am not sure that woman has, and we are all women here, and our pleasures are of a different and more peaceful sort. Though we have left our childhood behind, some of us very far behind, still, my children, not one of you could enjoy more thoroughly than we all three do this day that beautiful wood which has already begun to dress itself for spring.

It is noticeable for how very short a time, even in winter, vegetation lies absolutely dormant. In reality not for a day—the young buds being formed before the old leaves drop off. Not many weeks since, before Christmas, I found in another part of the country young green thorn-leaves (what children call "bread and cheese"), daisies, dandelions, and two abortive attempts at buttercups. And here in a sheltered nook is actually a spray of honeysuckle, already green with this year's leaves. Another year!—another spring! God bless it to you all, my children, and to all good and happy people everywhere! And it must be a very hard and wicked heart indeed which will not rejoice that year after year while the world lasts God will always send us spring.

The wood is full of treasures, even so early as February, and although the trees are still black and bare; all except the juniper, which is an evergreen: the low beeches, with their rich brown leaves, which, though withered and crinkled up, persist in hanging on till spring, and the furze, which has already put out a few yellow blossoms. Then there is the ivy, very plentiful everywhere, and the queer bunches of mistletoe, which stick themselves, nobody knows how, in the topmost boughs of oak, poplar, or apple-trees. Why this odd parasite should prefer these particular trees to attach itself to, I can not say, nor how it grows there, unless from a seed left by some bird. It is a very mysterious plant altogether,—especially at Christmas-time.

Every tree-stump is a nest of curiosities—different sorts of lichens, fungi, and moss, and tiny nurseries of plants which ought to have perished long ago. We find, with great triumph, a flourishing bed of wood-sorrel, and another of wood-ruff, both quite fresh and green. And in turning up a mass of dead oak-leaves, we come upon a tiny primrose root, embedded in moss, stretching out its small leaves just like a little baby out of a cradle. If it only had a flower upon it! How one of us would delight to paint it, the little yellow darling, peering out from the green moss and dead leaves! What a pretty picture it would make under the title of—let us consider—"A Discovery!"

But we are making discoveries every minute, heedless of the brambles which tear us, and the brushwood we keep stumbling over. We have filled our baskets with moss and our hands with great heaps of the long hart's-tongue fern. Ah! February is no time for carrying nosegays, for our fingers are growing pinched and numb. In spite of the bright sunshine, and blue sky, and white fleecy clouds, we are painfully convinced that it is not spring just yet.

Still, we enjoy ourselves so much that we have almost forgotten the fox's "earth," till we come suddenly upon a hole not unlike an enormous rabbit-burrow, scooped out under the root of a nut-tree, the soil being thrown up all round it, like an embankment. Strewn about are bits of fur and hair, and a feather or two, showing that the inhabitant is not quite such an innocent animal as a rabbit. Otherwise, it is a very quiet, desolate den, and whatever murderous relics there may be at the other end of it, which is probably ever so far underground, there are none outside.

The "earth" has evidently once been stopped up, and the determined fox has burrowed his way again into his familiar hole, where, perhaps, he has long lived in peace, and brought up a large family of little Reynards; for, we are told, young foxes were often to be seen playing about in this very wood, pretty and harmless as rabbits or kittens. But we see none now. In the breeding season fox-hunters benevolently or prudently hunt no more. So it was only old habit that drew "sly Reynolds" to this hole, if, indeed, its owner be the identical fox who lately flew before the hounds.

We are almost sorry for him, in spite of our memory of lost ducklings, fowls, and geese. He is tried and punished so deliberately, and so long after the offense, that we feel for him some of the sympathy which always attends great criminals in those horrible hangings which I trust you, children, will live to talk about as things belonging entirely to the past. Poor beast! bad as his character may be for cunning and cruelty, we almost hope he has escaped, and are trying to forget all about him and the hunt in listening to a thrush, the first thrush of the year, who had just opened his mouth from a neighboring tree-top, and is pouring out his rich notes as if there was no such thing as pain or trouble in the world,—when suddenly we start, hearing close behind us a yelp and a howl.

Ah! it is the hounds. They come tumbling and tearing through the brushwood. We see no individual dog, but a mass of black and white heads, legs, and tails; and a little distance in front of them is a small brown thing. So very small it looks! How it runs, doubles, turns, and runs again; then, as if driven by a sort of desperation, it seems to spring back right in the middle of the pack. They close upon it with that horrid universal howl, and it is never seen more.

At least, we saw it no more; for we got out of the way as fast as we could, feeling sick and sorrowful, wishing we had never been to the hunt. Was that the poor fox, that tiny creature, a mere ball of brown fur worried about among the dogs? What a small thing to be the object of so much excitement, the prey which lords and gentlemen, keepers and hounds, had followed for miles and miles! Well, fox-hunting may be very good sport, but I am not quite sure, children, that if I were a man I should enjoy it with a clear conscience, and I am very sure that I should not like to be "in at the death."

We were not, though it must have happened within a few yards of us; that is, if it happened at all. We heard afterwards a report that the fox had escaped—ran into his earth; and though two or three men were "digging him out" for some time, they failed to get at him. Let us hope it was so.

But for us, our pleasure in the morning's sight—the scarlet hunters, the splendid horses, the musical-tongued dogs—was considerably damped. We felt relieved when they all vanished, which they did in a very few minutes, scouring the country in search of another fox. They left the wood, in its delicious solitude, to us and the thrush on the tree-top, who recommenced, happy bird! as soon as every thing was quiet, and sang at the top of his voice as plain as bird's notes could say—"Spring is coming! spring is coming!"

Yes, though the roads are muddy, and the fields rather damp and dreary for the young lambs—look! there are two wee, toddling creatures, showing white as daisies against the green meadow!—though for many a day our fingers will tingle and our noses get pinched; still, spring is coming! The days are lengthening and brightening, the sunshine is growing stronger; I should not wonder if before very long, under the hedge we know so well, we might find, as some of us have found every year of our lives, a little, tiny, delicate white violet, to be followed in a day or two by hundreds more, till the whole field is fragrant with them. Farther down it, hidden among the grass, we might already find those three little flat leaves of the tenderest, most delicate green, which show where, by-and-by, will rise up a flower, the very delight of our hearts—

> "Then came the cowslip, like a dancer at a fair,
> She spread her little mat of green, and on it danced she."

—as she will dance next May by thousands over this very field, and we shall drop on our knees to smell at her and admire her, just as ardently as we did—well, well, it matters not how many years ago!

Thank God, in one sense, we three shall be always children. For, I am certain, we shall never lose our delight in this beautiful world; in the day and night, summer and

18*

winter, seed-time and harvest, which He has ordained shall not cease, until He creates a new heaven and a new earth. What we shall be then, we know not; nor is it necessary for us to know; if it had been, He would have taught us. As it is, He teaches us instead—by the daily experience of life, and in many other ways, some of which you also know only too well, my poor sick children!—the two hardest things on earth for any one to learn—not seeing, to love, and not wholly understanding, to believe.

THE END.

www.ingramcontent.com/pod-product-compliance
Lightning Source LLC
LaVergne TN
LVHW020058110826
845151LV00001B/15

* 9 7 8 1 4 2 5 5 4 5 3 9 0 *